DOMESTICATED SPIRITS

ALSO BY ALICE DUNCAN

DOMESTICATED SPIRITS

A DAISY GUMM MAJESTY MYSTERY
BOOK 18

ALICE DUNCAN

ePublishingWorks!
love what you read.

February 2023
Paperback ISBN: 978-1-64457-303-7
Hardcover ISBN: 978-1-64457-304-4

ePublishing Works!
644 Shrewsbury Commons Ave
Ste 249
Shrewsbury PA 17361
United States of America

www.epublishingworks.com
Phone: 866-846-5123

ACKNOWLEDGMENTS

Mega-thanks to Peter Brandvold for giving me the aged and one-legged Lou Prophet. He's a ton of fun to write. Read Mean Pete's books if you want to know about Lou's early, feisty days.

I wouldn't be able to write at all without input from Diana Jackson, who lives in the UK! Go figure. She helps me *so* much, I'll never be able to thank her enough. Unless, of course, I become a millionaire, but that won't happen unless a whole lot more people buy my books (this is a not-very-subtle hint).

Also thanks to Nancy Arellano, who allowed me to use her maiden name (DeLoera) for my Mestizo. Love the name!

Many thanks, too, to my son-in-law, Gilbert Paull, who took a picture of the plaque in front of the altar at the Mission San Gabriel Arcángel. If he hadn't taken a photo, Daisy would never have figured out what it said because she couldn't find a Google reference to it anywhere.

Thanks to the hardworking folks at ePublishingWorks for keeping what I laughingly call my writing career staggering along. I really appreciate you.

If you enjoy this book, please tell people and leave a review somewhere online. Thank you! Authors rely on word-of-mouth. We can't survive without readers.

ONE

As I stood at the sink, having just finished washing up the breakfast dishes, I gazed with satisfaction at the backyard. My backyard. Mrs. Sam Rotondo's backyard. And his too, of course.

Sam and I had only been married for four months, but so far, I found the married state suited me just fine. We'd fallen into a comfortable rhythm almost from the first. There had been a couple of iffy moments while we were honeymooning on the east coast, but they weren't really the fault of either of us. No indeed. Sam's east-coast family didn't approve of me, and my east-coast family didn't approve of Sam.

Nertz on them. Oh, they hadn't outright *said* anything mean to either of us, but I could tell Sam's family would have preferred him to marry a nice Italian girl as he'd done the first time he'd married. His family lived in New York City. My family in Auburn, Mass-achusetts, thought I should have married another nice white Protes-tant boy, as I'd done the first time.

Both of our first spouses had died: Sam's Margaret (or Margherita, if you were Italian) of tuberculosis, and my Billy of Kaiser Bill's mustard gas and bullets. Neither Margaret nor Billy had died quick, easy deaths. They'd both lingered and been miserable for a few years before finally shuffling off this mortal coil.

This time around, I wanted Sam and me to live a long, happy life together. I wanted to show both of our families that the modern world didn't have room for stuffy prejudices. Actually, the part of my family who lived across the street from Sam and me (to wit, my mother, father, aunt and dachshund) all approved of Sam and me and our union. It was the back-east families who were the stick-in-the-muds. Or should that be sticks-in-the-mud. Well, I don't suppose it matters.

I heaved a satisfied sigh, still gazing out the window. Then something strange hove into view. I squinted, bent over the sink and got so close to the window—decorated with lovely swags and a valance made by my own talented hands—the glass fogged. Fisting my hand, I rubbed away the fog.

The strange thing remained. In fact, it sat on its disreputable orange-striped butt and licked itself in an indelicate part of its anatomy.

"Whatcha looking at?" Sam asked as he walked into the kitchen from the hallway.

"I'm not sure," I told him. "I think it's a cat, but it's about the strangest looking cat I've ever seen in my life if it is a cat."

Thinking about a cat in *my* backyard made me think about my beloved dachshund, Spike, who lived across the street with my mother, father and aunt. The only cloud occasionally marring the bliss of my personal married state was the lack of Spike. However, my father had a worsening heart condition, and I figured he needed the love and comfort of Spike more than I did at present.

Sam came to the window, stood next to me and put an arm around my waist as he, too, peered out the window. "It does look like a cat. At least I think it does."

"Huh. Wonder where it came from," I mused.

"And how it got that way," said Sam.

"Looks like it's lost part of its tail."

"And…" Sam squinted harder. "And I think it only has one eye."

"And a tattered ear. Must have hurt when it happened. Poor thing. And does it have a twisted leg? The one on its right side?"

"I can't tell. Oh. It just stood up. By George, you're right. How the devil did the thing sustain injuries like that and survive?"

"I don't know," I said. "Poor old cat."

"Thought you didn't like cats," said Sam.

"I don't dislike cats. I just like dogs better."

"Yeah, me too," said my beloved.

"That's only one of the reasons I love you, Sam."

"I'm sure," he said.

"I hope the cat vanishes before Pa brings Spike over. Spike is notorious for chasing cats. If that cat is still ailing from whatever happened to it, Spike might kill it. If it's healed and those injuries made it mean, the cat might kill Spike."

A knock came at the front door.

"Speaking of Joe and Spike," said Sam. "I'd better intercept them before Spike sees the cat."

"Good thinking. I'll help."

So Sam and I walked from the kitchen to the small entryway of our lovely bungalow on South Marengo Avenue in the beautiful city of Pasadena, California, and greeted my father and Spike. I'd left the front door unlocked for them, so their knock had been only to let us know they'd arrived.

"Morning, you two," said my father, giving me a hug and then shaking Sam's proffered hand.

"Hi, Pa." I spoke from the floor, because I'd knelt to give Spike the greeting he deserved. Well, my father deserved a hearty welcome, too, but I'd already hugged him, and Spike preferred his humans to pet him. "Glad you brought the leash with you."

"I don't like to walk him across the street without it, just in case he spies Samson and darts out in front of a car to chase him," Pa said.

"Smart thinking," said Sam.

Samson was a big orange cat belonging to my parents' neighbors to the north, the Wilsons. Spike had been chasing Samson since as long as Spike had come to live with us four years earlier, when I'd managed to finagle him from Mrs. Bissel as payment for exorcising her basement of a ghost or a spirit.

Hmm. That probably sounds odd. I'll explain later. At the moment, I was pleased to see that Pa had not only thought to bring Spike's leash with him, but he also wore his gardening gloves and had brought along a trowel, a gardening fork and some pruning shears.

"Thanks, Pa," I said. "We probably won't need the pruning shears, but we can use the trowel and fork. I only have one each of those useful items."

"I stopped by Liljenwall's on my way home from work yesterday," said Sam. "I picked up another trowel and fork. And another set of hedge clippers. I left the other ones there to be sharpened. I want to trim that boxwood down to a manageable size, and I may have to enlarge the hole I cut in it to make room for the arbor."

"Don't cut it down too far," I advised him. "Mr. Prophet likes his privacy."

All three of us grinned at the mention of Mr. Lou Prophet, who resided in the tiny house in the rear of our very large backyard. Mr. Prophet had come into our lives about a year prior and was, to put it mildly, an interesting character. A former bounty hunter in the Wild West, he'd come to Los Angeles to be an advisor for some of the hundreds of western flickers then being produced. A trip with a couple of ladies of the night and a crate of bootleg liquor in an automobile that dove off the side of a cliff in Malibu left him without a job, without one of his legs, no booze, no ladies of the night, and living at the Odd Fellows Home of Christian Charity in my fair city of Pasadena.

Sam and I had sprung him from that ghastly—and horribly misnamed—place, and he now acted as caretaker for our home. He'd kept excellent care of our property while Sam and I were on our honeymoon, and he aimed to help us in the garden today. He couldn't do a whole lot of bending or kneeling, what with having only one leg and a peg to work with, but he could help Pa supervise Sam and me while we planted the two Cecile Brunner roses sitting in pots next to the lovely arbor Sam had made for the roses to climb on. Sam was a wizard when it came to carpentry. He was also a detective with the Pasadena Police Department, but his policeman-ship wouldn't come into play on this particularly glorious January morning.

"I won't cut it down too far," Sam promised. "I just want make sure the roses have room to grow next to the hedge. The space for the arbor also needs to be big enough that the roses won't stab the people who walk through the arbor. The hedge is thick, and it's too tall. I only want to neaten it up some."

"You nearly killed yourself creating a hole in it so you could stick the arbor there. Be careful."

"I'll be careful," Sam told me. "And I didn't nearly kill myself. I wore gloves and a long-sleeved shirt, and I only got three or four scratches."

"Huh. You looked like you'd been in a knife fight when you came inside on Thursday."

"Did not," said Sam.

"Did too," said I.

Then we both laughed, and Pa joined us. Spike, who was almost always happy, wagged as he followed us through the house to the back door and out onto the porch.

"Oh, shoot, I forgot about the cat," I said, grabbing for Spike's collar. Pa had unhooked his leash.

"What cat?" asked Pa, gazing out over our backyard. Sam and I had big plans for our yard.

I peered, too. "Huh. Guess it went away. The ugliest cat I've ever seen in my life was out there a few minutes ago. Not sure where it came from or where it went, but I'm glad it's gone because I didn't want Spike to chase it."

"What color was it?" asked Pa. "Was it Samson?"

"No, it wasn't Samson. Samson's a handsome, sleek, well-cared-for cat. This cat was…Well, it was ugly. Looked as if it had run into a big dog or a car. Maybe a freight train or a combine. It was orange like Samson, but it was…Damaged, I guess is the best description I can think of."

"Good lord, was it bleeding? Maybe we should find it and take it to the Humane Society or a veterinarian or something," said Pa, whose heart was always in the right place, even if it acted up from time to time.

"No," said Sam. "It seemed to have healed from its wounds. I have no idea how, but it was relatively sprightly, considering it had a tattered ear, one eye, a shortened tail and a twisted leg."

"Lordy," said Pa. "Animals astonish me sometimes. They can go through horrors and then just get on with their lives."

"Yes," I said. "They aren't like people. If a dog or a cat gets hurt, it goes and lies down somewhere until it doesn't hurt any longer, and then it gets up and goes about its business."

"Unless it dies," said Sam.

I whacked him on the arm. "What a dismal thing to say."

"Joe! She hit me!" said Sam, sounding like a spoiled child.

"She gets like that sometimes," said my father, laughing again.

Spike had descended the porch steps and was sniffing his way around the yard, watering plants here and there and in general having a grand old time. This was a relatively new yard for him. He hadn't explored all of its intricacies yet.

"Oh, shoot, is that the cat?" asked Pa, pointing to where the naked arbor stood, stuck into the ground in the holes Sam had dug for it. The arbor would be an archway between two neatly pruned sides of the boxwood hedge separating Sam's and my house from that of Mr. Prophet. Well, Sam and I owned it, too, but Mr. Prophet lived in it. Anyhow, once we decided that's where we wanted the arbor to remain, Sam would cement it into place.

The cat had come back—that's almost the title of an old, old song, not that it matters. It sat in the center of the arbor, gazing at Spike and us as if inspecting interlopers into its domain. Stupid cat.

"Crumb. Catch Spike, will you? By his collar?" I felt panic rise in my bosom. "I really don't want a bloodbath on this glorious day."

"Good idea," said Pa, holding out the leash.

But Spike hadn't moved. He stood as still as a marvelously shiny black-and-tan statue, staring at the ugliest cat in the universe, his nose quivering as if he smelled something intriguing but wasn't sure he wanted to investigate it.

Quickly Pa clipped the leash to Spike's collar. My panic subsided.

Spike still didn't move. He tilted his head one way and then another as he stared at the orange feline catastrophe sitting calmly in the center of the arbor.

"Huh. Wonder why he's not tugging on the leash," I muttered. "He'd have chased Samson up a tree by this time."

"At least into the hydrangeas," said Sam.

"Maybe he's never seen such a cat and is interested in it. I know I've never seen anything quite like it before," said Pa.

"May I take the leash, Pa?" I asked, holding out my hand.

"Sure. Be careful," Pa said. "Don't allow Spike to pull you over or the cat to scratch you. Or Spike. That cat looks like it can take care of itself in a fight."

"I'd say you're right, if it sustained those injuries and survived," said Sam. "Want me to take Spike over to it, Daisy?"

"Naw. I'll do it." I'd taken Spike to the Pasanita Dog Obedience School three years earlier, and he was about the best-trained dog in the City of Pasadena. Mrs. Hanratty, who'd taught the class, had told me so.

Although I expected the cat to sprint—or maybe stagger—off as Spike and I approached, it didn't. It just sat there, looking at us. Kind of like a miniature tiger, actually. A miniature tiger that had been run over by a lawn mower, maybe.

When we got to about two feet of the thing, it rumbled something in its chest. It sounded almost like a purr, but I couldn't imagine a strange cat purring at my dog and me. Spike hadn't said a word. Well, you know what I mean. He hadn't barked or growled or done any of the other things dogs do when they get excited. I gazed down at him in puzzlement.

Deciding not to get any closer to the cat for fear it might lash out with its nastily sharp claws, I knelt in front of it still at a distance of about two feet. It didn't budge. Spike sat, and he didn't budge either.

What the heck was going on here?

Then something happened I wouldn't have believed, except Sam and Pa saw it too and were as flabbergasted as I.

Spike leaned his long nose forward as if to sniff the mangled cat. The cat lifted a paw—I squinted and looked for claws but saw none —and extended it. Spike's nose and the cat's paw met in the middle, and darned if the silly animals didn't seem to be introducing themselves to each other.

I don't know how many seconds ticked by as Spike and the cat made friends. Seemed like hours, perhaps because I was squatting in an uncomfortable position. But I feared to rise lest I startle the cat into hissing and scratching or the dog into barking and biting.

Because I didn't know what else to do, I said, "Hello, cat. Where did you come from and what happened to you?"

Ignoring me, the cat continued to lightly stroke Spike's muzzle. Spike finally decided to lie down on his tummy and extend a paw to the cat as if to stroke it back.

This behavior on the part of both animals directly contradicted everything I'd ever read or heard about dog and cat behavior. It also contradicted everything I'd seen of Spike's interaction with cats before that day. Granted, the only cat in Spike's world before today had been Samson, but still….

"What's going on?" Sam asked from the porch. "I don't hear any yipping or hissing."

"I'm not sure," I told him. "It sounds impossible, but it looks to me as if they've decided to become pals."

"Pals?" asked Pa, clearly incredulous. "That feisty hunting hound and that battered and bedraggled cat?"

"Yes," I said, feeling more than a trifle incredulous myself. "So far no claws, no growls, no hisses and no nips or yips. It's weird."

"Aw, hellkatoot," came the voice of Mr. Lou Prophet from behind the cat. "So that's where you got yourself off to." And darned if I didn't hear him stumping his way down the orange-tree lined path from his cottage to the arbor.

"Is this your cat?" I asked him as he came into view and stopped short. Appalled, unless I missed my guess, judging by the look on his face.

"*My* cat?" he asked in a peculiar voice. "What the hell would I be doing with a damn cat?"

From this speech, I knew he was rattled. His language was colorful, but he tried to contain the swear words when he was around regular human beings, which included my family and me. Don't have a clue what kind of language he and Sam used when they chatted.

"I don't know. That's why I asked. Oomph." That last word was the best approximation I can think of for the sound I made as I stood. My left foot had gone to sleep, and I tried to shake it without startling any of the animals—that is to say the cat, Spike or Mr. Prophet.

Sam dared to approach me slowly. He didn't want to startle anyone either. "You find a mangled cat while we were back east, Lou?"

If Mr. Prophet had possessed two legs, he'd have been digging the toe of one of his boots into the soft earth of the garden path. I'd never seen the old scoundrel appear so abashed.

"Well, hell, I guess so. The critter crawled up onto my porch while you were in New York. Don't know if he was hit by a car or got into a fight with a coyote or what, but he was a wreck. So I just kinda nursed him. He was a little kitten when I found him. I guess he's a...what are they callin' 'em in the newspapers these days? A teenager? I guess he's a teenager now."

"Oh, that's so nice of you!" I cried, making Mr. Prophet wince. "You bandaged his shredded flesh and rips and stuff?"

"Took him to the veterinarian," admitted Mr. Prophet, who had owned a horse he'd named Mean and Ugly during his bounty-hunting days. "Just down the street on Colorado. Van der Hoof. That vet."

"Oh, yes. I like him," I said. "What did you name him?"

"Name who? The vet? I just told you."

"Stop being difficult," I commanded in a sharp voice. "What did you name your cat?"

"Ain't *my* cat," said he gruffly. "He just comes around, is all."

Sam had reached Spike and me by this time. He knelt and tentatively held out a hand to the cat, which ignored the hand and began rubbing itself against Spike, who sat still and endured the action. With his tail wagging! My state of flabbergastation at the behavior of the cat, Spike and Mr. Prophet soared higher and higher.

"Very well, so he's not your cat," I said to appease the old sinner. "What do you call him? You called your horse Mean and Ugly. Do you call this animal something equally awful?"

"Mean and Ugly wasn't an awful name. Fit the animal to a T." He stopped speaking, but when I opened my mouth to repeat my question, he said, "I call the cat Yuyu."

"Yuyu?" I peered at the old man, still trying to shake my left foot into life. "What does that mean?"

"Mean? Don't expect Yuyu means anything by itself."

Becoming annoyed by his prevaricating, I demanded, "Well, what does it mean if it isn't by itself?"

"No need to get huffy," Mr. Prophet said huffily. "Yuyu's short for Yuyutsu."

I stared at the orange and white striped cat, who was now what I could only call cavorting with my ferocious hunting hound, Spike the dachshund. I'd *never* anticipated Spike would like, much less play with, a *cat*, of all creatures. "Was there somebody named Yuyutsu you knew in the bad old days?"

"They wasn't bad old days. They were *my* days, and they were grand. And yeah. Indian fellow. Yuyutsu. Mescalero Apache. Fought like hell and loved it. That's what the name means."

"Yuyutsu means he fights like…heck?" Was I embarrassingly prissy or what?

"Means he *liked* to fight like hell, yeah. He was a great damned warrior. Figured that cat was a fighter, and he might as well have a warrior's name."

Gazing again at the adolescent cat, now positively *playing* with Spike, from whom Sam had unclipped the leash, I said, "He sure looks like he's been in a fight or two. Or three or four."

"Exactly. All the Injuns got beat up, not just the Mescalero. They all did." Mr. Prophet shook his head. "We white folks beat the hell out of all the Injun tribes. The Mescalero Apaches got dumped onto a reservation in the Sacramento Mountains, and they live there now. At least it's pretty there. Most Injuns didn't get so lucky."

"The Sacramento Mountains? In California?" I asked, puzzled, never having thought of Apaches as having anything to do with California. Truth to tell, I couldn't precisely tell you what, if any, Indian tribes used to live in California. Or still did, for all I knew.

"No, not in California," said Mr. Prophet disdainfully. "They're in New Mexico. The Sacramento Mountains in New Mexico."

"I didn't know New Mexico had any mountains at all," I admitted.

"Don't surprise me none." Still disdainful.

I got the impression Mr. Lou Prophet, former Confederate soldier, bounty-hunter, womanizer, gunslinger, and all-around rough customer, was embarrassed to have been caught being kind to a bedraggled cat. The notion made me smile.

"Well, let's get you and Pa a couple of chairs, and you can supervise Sam and me while we dig holes and plant the roses." I glanced at Spike and Yuyu.

Spike now lay on his back, wriggling back and forth, and Yuyu stood on his stomach playfully boxing at Spike's paws with his. And still I saw none of his claws extended, which was a good thing. I'd heard about cats taking a dog's eyes out with sharp kitty claws. I hoped they'd continue to play and that their play—which still astounded, astonished and confounded me—didn't turn ugly.

Sam had stood by this time, and he too watched the dog and cat, who seemed to have become best friends in a matter of minutes. Maybe seconds.

"There's something you don't see every day," said my beloved.

"You sure don't," I agreed.

"Didn't expect it," said Mr. Prophet.

"Are Spike and that cat actually *playing* with each other?" asked Pa, who had wandered over from the porch to see what had enthralled the rest of us.

A trio of "Yeses" hit the air.

"Well, I'll be darned," said Pa.

Couldn't have said it better myself.

TWO

S am and I fetched two chairs each and placed them near the arbor where the two of us aimed to dig and plant rosebushes and Pa and Mr. Prophet aimed to watch us. Or maybe they'd watch Spike and Yuyu. I'd probably do the latter. I mean, watching people doing a regular old gardening chore couldn't possibly be more remarkable than watching a formerly cat-hating dog and a banged-up feline playing with each other.

"Okay, where do you want to plant these babies? Right next to each end of the arbor?" Sam asked. "I think I left enough room to plant them, but I can whack the hedge back another six or seven inches if I need to."

"Let me see." I strolled over to the north end of the arbor. Sam had painted the whole thing white, by the way, after he'd built it. It was a perfectly lovely arbor, arched and almost lacy-looking. Kneeling, I checked around. The ground was soft near where Sam had planted the end of the arbor and hard as a rock near the hedge. He'd had a heck of a time digging up the boxwood roots in order to accommodate the arbor itself. He'd left maybe a foot and a half of bare ground outside both arbor ends. I liked the idea of the roses climbing from each side of the arbor—Cecile Brunners climbed like mad—so I said, "Let's plant them right next to the ends. There's room enough, I'm pretty sure."

"Okay. Let's dig in," said Sam, attempting humor. He actually had a good sense of humor, but that comment was rather a stretch. "I'll trim the top of the hedge after we get the roses planted."

We'd both dressed both for the weather, which was nippy, and for the task at hand, which was gardening. Sam wore some old denim trousers and a flannel shirt over a long-sleeved undershirt. I wore an old faded blue day dress, two pairs of old and holey black stockings, and a long gray cardigan sweater that was probably as old as I. But the thing was warm.

Oh, and perhaps I should add another thing. I don't know the appropriate time to plant roses in other parts of the world, but in Pasadena, California, one plants roses in January. That's what Mr. Liljenwall had told us, and that's what Sam's subscription to *Sunset Magazine* had told us. I wasn't about to contradict expert advice, and neither was Sam. I'd actually planted lots of roses before, in the garden at my parents' house across the street. This would be Sam's first foray into rose planting.

"You're taking this married life thing like a champ, Sam," said my father from his chair.

"I like it," said Sam. "I've always wanted a garden. Margaret and I wanted a garden, but we never got the chance to dig one. Glad Daisy likes to garden." He gave me a happy smile, which I returned.

"Too bad she doesn't like to cook," muttered Mr. Prophet, as if he just couldn't bear anything nice about me to linger in the air longer than it had to.

"Pooh on you," I told him. "After Sam and I get the garden going, I swear I'm going to keep learning to cook. I've already begun to— Eeek!"

The notion of cooking kind of frightened me, but my exclamation wasn't about that. It came as a result of a cold dog nose pressed to my cheek as I troweled up my first clod of earth.

"Spike!" I cried, looking at my dog. "That wasn't very nice."

Spike wagged at me. Yuyu, standing beside Spike looked as if I'd offended him by my remark. He hissed softly.

"Good lord, is the cat scolding me for eeking at my dog?"

With a chuckle, Mr. Prophet said, "Probably. He's got his own ideas about things."

"I've never seen a dog and a cat make friends like that before," said Pa.

"I haven't either," said Sam. "Although I've never been around very many dogs or cats."

"Well, if Yuyu decides to scratch me, he's going to get another wound for his efforts," I warned everyone in a menacing tone. I'm sure no one, especially the battle-scarred cat, took me seriously.

So Sam and I continued to dig, I at the north end of the arbor, he at the south, and Spike and Yuyu ambled back and forth, visiting one of us and then the other, and things proceeded apace. I'd just dug a sufficiently deep hole and was about to mound some earth mixed with bone meal in the center of it, when Pa said, "What the heck does the cat have in its mouth? He just dropped it."

I looked up, not having been paying attention to the cat or the dog.

"Looks like a stick," said Sam, squinting at Yuyu, who sat in the center of the arbor's archway and nudged something with his paws. Spike had gone elsewhere for the nonce. "Never saw a cat playing with a stick before. Thought it was dogs who liked to play with sticks."

I was about to shrug and get back to mounding earth, when Mr. Prophet said, "I don't think that thing's a stick."

Looking up again, I saw he'd risen from his chair and was thumping over to the cat, which looked up at him and grinned. I swear to you, the cat grinned.

"What *is* that?" asked Sam, removing one of his gardening gloves, standing and moseying over to Mr. Prophet and Yuyu. He squatted before the cat. Then he said, "I don't believe it," and lifted his bare hand to cradle his head.

What the heck? Sticking my trowel into the ground, I rose too, and went over to see what was up with the cat and the men in my life.

"Oh, my word," I muttered as I peered down at the cat.

Then Spike bounded up to us. In his teeth he carried the jawbone of a defunct person. It looked like the lower part of a jawbone (complete with teeth) of a person who had been defunct for quite some time and buried. In *our* yard.

"Spike! Drop it!" I bellowed.

Spike, startled, nevertheless heeded his obedience training and dropped the jawbone. I walked over to him, knelt, stroked his back, said, "Good boy," and picked up the bone in a garden-gloved hand.

"Good lord," said Sam. Then he repeated, "I don't believe it."

"Holy Moses," said Pa. "Those are *bones*."

"Yeah," Sam said. "Human bones. Aw, crumb." I'm pretty sure he wanted to use a word other than crumb but didn't in deference to my father.

"What does this mean?" I asked, bewildered. Bones. In our yard. "This isn't fair!"

"Huh," said Mr. Prophet. "Fair or not, it looks like somebody buried a body in this yard." Peering down at the skeletal remains, he said, "Looks like they did it a long time ago, too."

Sam growled something I didn't catch. It was probably better that way.

Recalling my recent conversation with Mr. Prophet, I said hopefully, "Maybe they're remains of an Indian who got buried here in the olden days."

All three men turned to stare at me. Actually, Spike and Yuyu did too.

"No?" I said feebly. "You don't think so?"

"No," said Sam. "I don't think so. These bones aren't *that* old. I swear to god, Daisy, what with your record of tripping over dead bodies all the time, I'd almost think you planted these artifacts on purpose." I was about to holler a denial when he held up a hand and said, "I know you didn't. It's just...Why do dead people and you always end up in the same place?"

With a shrug, I said, "I don't know, but I wish they'd stop."

"So do I," Sam growled.

"You know," said my father, tapping his chin with a finger, "along about twenty years ago, I recall reading about a young man in this general area who disappeared. I think it happened when they were building a house near here. Golly, maybe it was this house. I wonder if these bones might be his. It was a big story at the time, and foul play seemed a possibility. The poor fellow was never found, and nobody ever knew what happened to him. We didn't even live here at the time, Daisy. We moved in a year or so later. The disappearance must have happened in 1904 or thereabouts when you were just a toddler. Hmmm. If you were a toddler, that means it happened maybe twenty-two or -three years ago."

"How do we find out if this is him? He? Whatever it is?" I asked, turning my attention to my husband since he, of all of us, probably knew the answer.

With a heavy sigh, Sam said, "We have to stop digging and call the police. I suppose it's minimally possible these are ancient remains, but if they are, it's going to cause problems because archaeologists and anthropologists from the Southwest Museum will probably have to get involved. If they're the remains of the man who disappeared twenty-some years ago, then it's a police matter, and we'll *still* have to stop digging."

"Dang," I said. "I really wanted to get the roses planted so they could start climbing the arbor."

"So did I," said Sam.

"I'd better put the leash on Spike," I muttered. "I don't want him or the cat to dislodge an entire skeleton."

"What about the cat?" asked Sam. "Do you know it well enough to pick it up, or will it scratch you?"

"Beats me," I said.

"I'll take care of the cat," grunted Mr. Prophet, stooping and scooping Yuyu from the grass. Spike made a protesting noise, but he didn't argue when I attached his leash and made him come with us.

It was a dispirited quintet—if you could call Spike part of it, and I do—that walked back to the back porch, divested ourselves of gardening gloves and tools, and went into the house. Sam called the police department.

———

I'd managed to wash my hands and face and put on a decent day dress before the police arrived. Sam put on clean trousers and another shirt, but neither of us spruced up in particular. Pa and Mr. Prophet hadn't been wearing gardening togs, so they just remained the way they'd been before the grisly discovery in the backyard. Mr. Prophet had taken Yuyu to his cottage. I guess they already had an arrangement.

Darn, darn, darn! This was *so* unfair! And I was going to get teased unmercifully about it, too, once my mother and aunt, Harold Kincaid and Flossie and Johnny Buckingham found out about it. My reputation for finding dead people was one I didn't cherish, even if I deserved it. But it wasn't my fault!

When the doorbell rang, Spike, who had been sulking on my father's lap on the sofa, jumped down and made joyful welcoming noises. I sighed heavily, said, "Spike, sit," and the poor dog stopped being joyful and sat.

Sam and I both went to the front door. When Sam opened it, two uniformed officers stood there. One of them I knew: Mr. Stephen Doan. His mother, Mrs. Rattle (first name Elvira), did housekeeping and cooking for me. I aimed to have her teach me to cook eventually.

"Come on in," said Sam, stepping aside. I did likewise, and the two uniforms entered the house.

Looking around, Stephen Doan said, "This looks like a great place, Sam. My mother loves it."

"We love having her help us out here," I said, answering for both Sam and me. I led the way into the living room where my baby grand piano, bought for me by my wonderful Sam, sat in a corner. I loved that piano. Played it every day, in fact.

"Hope you brought some shovels with you," said Sam in a

cranky-sounding voice. "Because it looks like there's a body buried somewhere in the backyard. An old body."

"Yeah, that's what the dispatcher told us," said Doan. "Two more guys are coming with the shovels and sheets and so forth. If you'll just show me where the bones were found, I'll make a note and then take statements from you and Mrs. Rotondo and…Mr. Gumm? Is that you?"

"Yes, it is," said Pa. "How-do, Stephen?"

"I'm fine, thanks." He turned to Mr. Prophet and said, "And you're…" His sentence trailed off. Guess he didn't recall having met Mr. Prophet, although he had. More than once.

"Prophet. Lou Prophet," said Mr. Prophet.

"Right. Thanks." Doan turned back to Sam and me. "Lead the way, please."

So Sam and I led the way as Doan and the other officer, whose name was Oliphant and who carried a camera, followed. Pa, Mr. Prophet and Spike brought up the rear. When we got to where what we'd decided was a rib bone and the lower jaw sat in approximately the middle of the arbor, Doan squatted down and said, "Huh. These look old."

"I thought so, too," said Sam. "According to Mr. Gumm here, a young man disappeared from this neighborhood approximately twenty to twenty-five years ago. My wife thinks they might belong to an ancient Indian. Either way, I guess we won't be able to do any gardening around this area for a while."

Standing with a grunt, Doan said, "You're right. Not sure which scenario will cause you the most grief, either."

"Yeah," said Sam glumly. "I suppose we'd better not poke around here until the men with the shovels show up. Don't want to disturb a crime scene, if it is one. I swear to god, I don't know why this had to happen in my backyard."

Doan shot me a swift glance, which I repelled with a "don't even begin to say it" frown. He only said, "I don't know either. But let's go back indoors, and I'll take statements." He turned to his uniformed cohort. "Oliphant, please take as many photos as you can without disturbing anything."

"Will do," said the obliging Oliphant, who unfolded his Kodak vest-pocket camera, knelt down, and started snapping away at the bone Yuyu had found—Mr. Prophet was the one who'd identified it as a rib bone—and the lower jaw bone Spike had found. Poor dog. I felt guilty for depriving him of a well-researched treat.

"So," said Stephen Doan, "how'd you find those bones? I only saw a couple of holes beside that wooden thing."

"That's going to be the rose arbor," said Sam.

"Sam built it," I told Doan, since Sam was being modest. "And he painted it. And we had planned to plant a Cecile Brunner climbing rosebush on each end of it and let them grow over the whole thing. It was going to be the centerpiece of our garden."

"It probably still will be," said Pa, trying to cheer me up.

"I know," I said. "I just wanted it to start being the centerpiece today. And I'm not sure what to do with those rosebushes either."

"What do you mean?" asked Mr. Prophet. "Can't they just stay where they are until you plant 'em?"

"I don't know," I admitted. "They're bare-root roses, and those *should* get planted as soon as possible. I hope this investigation doesn't take very long."

"It'll take as long as it takes," said Sam philosophically. "If it seems to be dragging on, I'll ask Mr. Liljenwall what to do with them. Maybe we'll have to stick them in dirt in buckets for a while or something."

"Nertz," I muttered.

As we climbed the back porch steps, Sam put an arm around my shoulder. "It'll be all right, sweetie. A little delay won't hurt us."

"It'll hurt *me*," I said, feeling grouchy. "So far my clients have been more or less respectful of my newly married status and haven't been hounding me to work for them for a blissful few months." Recalling my wonderful dog, I told Spike, "Sorry, Spike. It's just an expression, and it means you hounds are good at finding things."

"So's the damn cat," muttered Mr. Prophet.

"Yes," I said musingly

"Hmm," said Sam. "Maybe that's why he and Spike get along so well."

"I beg your pardon?" said Doan.

"Let's go indoors, and we'll explain everything," Sam said, opening the back door.

We all trooped inside.

THREE

P robably now would be a good time to reveal *all* about my clients, why they might be hounding me and how Mrs. Bissel paid me in Spike for ridding her basement of a ghost. Or it might have been a spirit.

It wasn't a ghost *or* a spirit, of course, because they don't exist. The entity living in her basement had been a runaway girl. The reason Mrs. Bissel, probably my favorite client because she breeds and shows dachshunds and never has hysterics, hired me to do an exorcism of her basement was because I posed as a spiritualist-medium. Made a whole lot of money doing it, too. I worked for most of the wealthy women in Pasadena.

Pasadena was, in the 1920s, a rich-man's town. The rich men came along with rich women and, as nearly everyone in the entire world had lost loved ones either in the so-called Great War or the ghastly so-called Spanish Flu pandemic immediately following it, there were more than enough bereaved people extant to keep several spiritualist-mediums (media?) busy for years.

They'd sure kept me busy. And well-paid. Until recent months, my most lucrative client, Mrs. Pinkerton, had used me for palm reading, tarot card reading, and Ouija board sessions pretty much once or twice a week. Mind you, she had plenty of reasons to be in the almost constant state of frenzy plaguing her, although none of the reasons involved dead people. She had possessed a louse of a husband, whom she eventually dumped, and she still possessed a louse of a daughter. The first husband, Mr. Eustace Kincaid, now resided in San Quentin Prison, and would probably be there for many more years. He did several bad things, including, but not limited to, trying to ruin his own bank and smuggling drugs. He'd also attempted to murder a secretary named Brenda Young and me. I resented him a lot for that last part.

Her daughter, Stacy Kincaid, currently languished in the Pasadena City Jail. She'd been a thorn in her mother's side—and mine—for years. Stacy was facing trials for several felonies, and they'd probably begin soon, so I expected Mrs. Pinkerton—she'd married Mr. Algernon Pinkerton after she'd divested herself of the evil Mr. Kincaid—to call me in a tizzy soon.

I wasn't looking forward to her call.

However, most of the other folks I worked for hired me to conduct séances and chat with dead relatives. So that's what I did. Sounds morbid, but I was good at it, having begun pretending to be a spiritualist as kind of a joke at Christmas in my tenth year. My aunt, who worked for Mrs. Pinkerton as a cook, had brought home an old Ouija board, and I was the only one who didn't claim to be afraid of using the thing. So I did. Had a lot of fun, too, and scared my sister Daphne into a shrieking fit. My mother made me put the board away then, but it didn't stay put away. As soon as Aunt Vi told Mrs. Pinkerton (then Mrs. Kincaid) about my "gift" for using the Ouija board, my career began.

When I married my childhood sweetheart at age seventeen, right out of high school, I hadn't planned to keep on spiritualist-mediuming, but life had other things in store for me. My darling Billy Majesty was shot and gassed during the war, and he'd come home in a wheelchair, unable to work. So I continued to ply my trade.

At about the same time, my father had a heart attack and was unable to continue chauffeuring wealthy Pasadenans around, so the women in my family brought home the bacon. Thank god we had Aunt Vi to cook it for us, because my mother and I were both dismal failures in the kitchen. I aimed to change this particular problem, but that's not the point right now.

At any rate, my darling aunt still worked as a cook for Mrs. Pinkerton. I was a spiritualist-medium, and my wonderful mother was the head bookkeeper at the Hotel Marengo, a darned good job for a woman. Of course, if she were a man, they'd have had to pay her more, but she still made good money.

I don't yet think I've mentioned how unfair I believe the world to be, so I'll just bring up the matter now and get it over with. If my mother were a man in the same position she held at the Hotel Marengo, she'd make twice as much money as the hotel management paid her. If my aunt were a man and did the same work she did at Mrs. Pinkerton's house, they'd call him a chef, stick a white hat on him and pay him twice as much money as she earned now.

See? *I* was the only person in the whole family who made precisely as much money as I wanted to, because I set my own prices. And I'd made up my profession out of thin air! It's insane. I mean, I couldn't talk to dead people any more than I could fly to Jupiter, but people believed I could, so I made big bucks.

Life is and always has been a mystery to me.

Then my Billy died, and I went into a tailspin of grief and melancholy. My best friend, Mrs. Pinkerton's son Harold Kincaid, took me to Egypt to cheer me up. The only thing Egypt did to me was make me sick, so we departed Egypt and went to Constantinople, where Harold and I were joined by Sam Rotondo, who'd hied after me because he didn't think I could take care of myself. His own wife had died about two years before my own Billy's demise.

A couple of years after our sojourn in Constantinople, Sam asked me to marry him, and I said yes. Then, lo and behold, he told me he didn't have to rely on his policeman's salary because he and his family owned jewelry stores in New York City, and he had mazuma by the truckload. You could have knocked me over with a spring zephyr when I found out about his relative wealth. As someone had recently knocked me over with a quite tangible automobile, I didn't faint, but I was sure surprised.

Then my father told me Sam had asked for my hand a year or two earlier and showed *him* his financial portfolio, so my father wouldn't cavil at me marrying again. Sam told *Pa*. Not me. My father.

And I was the one in the family who made the most money. See what I mean about life being unfair? It is, curse it. And even good people, like my father and Sam, just went along with it and didn't think there was anything odd about it or thought to change it or defy it or get mad about it. Sometimes, I could just stamp my feet and scream.

But I didn't because I'm an adult female person and have grown up. I still get riled when I think about the disparities in the world, though. Don't even get me started on how a nice young Negro man of my acquaintance plays the horn in a band at the Cocoanut Grove at the Ambassador Hotel in downtown Los Angeles, but they make *him* enter the hotel via the kitchen. Only *white* people are allowed to use the main entrance.

Aw, nuts. I'll quit now. But I did want to clear up the exorcism thing, in case you wondered.

Ahem. Back to the living room.

"So," Sam said to Doan, who was taking notes, "I had cut the boxwood hedge back to make a hole in it large enough for the arbor. As Daisy said, we intend to plant roses on either end of the arbor. We'd done some digging along the inside of the hedge, and I'd cut it back a good deal because it was awfully overgrown. We were just digging some holes in which to plant the roses, when Mr. Prophet's cat—"

"Ain't *my* cat!" said Mr. Prophet grumpily.

Sam continued. "When an orange cat that had been hanging around the place showed up with a bone in its mouth. At first we thought it was a stick. It was Lou who said it looked to him like a human rib bone."

"Are you an anatomist, Mr. Prophet?" asked Stephen Doan politely.

"Naw. Just seen my fair share of dead folks, some of 'em dead for a long time," said Mr. Prophet. "Skeletons, that is to say."

I squinted at him, but it didn't seem the appropriate time to ask him where he'd seen bodies so intact but skinless that he was able to identify the rib bone of a deceased person. I made a mental note to ask him later.

"I see," said Doan. "Well, I believe you, but we'd probably best wait until the guys with the sheets and shovels come and we can find the rest of the bones. You say you didn't dig them up while you were planting things?"

"Correct," said Sam. "We didn't dig up any bones. The dog and the cat brought them to us, and we haven't yet looked to see where they found them. Didn't want to disturb a scene, if there's a scene to disturb."

"Thanks, Detective," said Doan. "Wish more people did that."

With a shrug, Sam said, "They don't understand about destroying evidence and so forth."

"True," said Doan, sighing.

"What about Dr. Benjamin?" I asked suddenly. "I know it's Saturday, but he might not mind coming here to look at these bones —and any other bones your guys find—to tell us for sure if they're human and if they're just old or *really* old. I mean, like ancient."

"I hate to bother him on a Saturday," muttered Sam.

"Oh, hell, he loves sh— uh, stuff like this," observed Mr. Prophet.

"Lou's right," said Pa.

Looking at me, Sam said, "Good point. You have his number somewhere, Daisy?"

"Yes. In the telephone table drawer. In the address book I keep in there. I'll call him."

"Eager little lady, ain't she?" said Lou Prophet sardonically.

"Darn you! I just want to get my roses planted. If the police people can find the rest of the body, if the bones are nowhere near the arbor, and if Dr. Benjamin can more or less tell us if all of the skeleton's there and how old it is, maybe we can still plant those roses today!"

"She has a point," said Pa.

"True," said Sam.

"I guess," said Mr. Prophet.

Piddle on him. I'd command Spike to piddle on his wooden leg, but everyone would be horrified. Except, probably, Mr. Prophet, who was more likely to laugh than get mad. He was really something, that old rogue.

The telephone table sat in the hallway off the living room, so there I went, sat in the chair provided, opened the drawer and took out the address book. Then I pulled the switch on the table lamp so I could see what I was doing, looked up Dr. Benjamin's number, plucked the receiver from its cradle and dialed. By the way, we didn't have one of your old-fashioned wall telephones or even one of your fancier—but still old-fashioned, according to Harold Kincaid—candlestick telephones, but a desktop variety. It sat, squat and black, on its table, and it had a nice rotary dial with holes for me to stick my finger in and dial. So I did.

Harold had given us the 'phone as a wedding present, bless his heart.

Mrs. Benjamin answered the telephone on the other end of the wire. I felt guilty about bothering her on a Saturday. However, when I explained our predicament to her, she laughed.

"Oh, my word, Daisy, you know my husband! He'd love nothing more than to be involved in digging up a backyard burial, especially if the body belongs to a murdered person."

Laughing, too—with relief, truth be told—I said, "I can't guarantee a murder victim, but we've found what we think is a rib bone and the lower part of a skull."

"Hmm. Fascinating," said she, sounding almost as interested as she accused her husband of being. "Does the skull contain any teeth?"

"A few," I told her, grimacing at the dialing pad on my 'phone. "It was only the lower jawbone. With teeth attached."

"Well, that's a good thing. From everything I've heard, a person who knows his onions can tell a good deal about how a person died from the teeth in its skull."

"I didn't know that," I said, my grimace turning into a stare of revulsion.

"Oh, yes. I've picked up some interesting information over the years. Not that I could tell what I've learned at a dinner party or anything, but I know you don't mind. Let me get the doctor for you."

"Thank you," I said. Why'd she think I didn't mind learning gruesome things about murdered bodies, anyhow? When I'd had to take notes for Doc Benjamin as he'd studied a recently deceased young man's body, I hadn't found the process any fun at all. I think I'd managed to garner unto myself an unfortunate reputation, and I didn't appreciate it. I'd never tell either Dr. or Mrs. Benjamin, however, because they were both great people and wonderful friends. I swear, Doc Benjamin had kept my Billy alive for at least a year or more longer than Billy'd wanted him to.

But I didn't like to think about that.

I heard someone pick up the receiver on the Benjamins' end of the wire. "What's this Dorothy's been telling me about you digging up bodies in your yard, young woman?"

"It's not funny," I said. "And neither Sam nor I dug them up. Spike and a feline pal of his did."

"Spike has a cat as a friend?" The doctor's astonishment was appropriate. He'd witnessed Spike going after Samson a time or two.

"I'll tell you about it if you can come over here and look at the bones. Well, I'll tell you about it anyway, but I just—"

"It's all right, Daisy," said Doc, laughing. "I know what you mean. Good thing I'm in my own gardening duds this morning. You're in luck, because I just finished planting the cabbages. I'll save the leeks until this afternoon."

"Thank you very much. I'm hoping these bones won't be so ancient that the Southwest Museum demands we close off part of the yard until they get through examining them. On the other hand, I hope they're not the bones of a murdered person. Oh, bother. Pa said a young man went missing in this area around twenty years ago."

"I vaguely remember the disappearance. Don't think he was necessarily a local lad, but he was working on a house being built right— Oh, hey, I wonder if yours is the house he was working on! Nobody ever found him or heard another word from him, but I know folks looked for weeks. Maybe months."

"Oh, Lord." I whimpered. "Well, thank you very much for taking time out of your own plans to help us with ours."

"Be right there!" the good doctor said with what I considered unwarranted enthusiasm.

On the other hand, I should be grateful for his excitement. Otherwise, who knew how long we'd have to wait to plant our roses? Well, I don't suppose it mattered much. Whatever conclusions Dr. Benjamin arrived at, our plans might be blown sky-high. Hmm. I guess we could plant our two Cecil Brunners in the front yard to run along the low fence out there and buy more to swarm over the arbor later.

Bother!

I cradled the receiver, sighed heavily, and returned to the living room. "Doc Benjamin will be here shortly. He can hardly wait."

"I'll bet," said Sam.

"No, I mean it. Even Mrs. Benjamin was excited about the stupid bones. Doc says he remembers the case of the disappearing young man. Said people looked high and low for him, but nobody found anything. He also thinks that when the guy disappeared, he might have been on the crew building this very house."

Because Sam sat on one of the sofas, I joined him there, feeling despondent. He put an arm around my shoulder. "Don't worry too much, Daisy. After all, Spike and the cat found the bones. Maybe they're way off in a corner somewhere, and it won't matter if we continue to work around the arbor area."

"I hope you're right. If they're ancient, they'll probably cause us more trouble, because the archaeologists at the Southwest Museum will want to stick an oar in and block off the area while they try to find the rest of him. Her. Whoever it was."

"Don't think they're Injun bones," opined Mr. Prophet.

I glanced at him eagerly. "Really? How come?"

"They look more like bones I found in a cave on the desert once. They belonged to an outlaw I was huntin'. Got bit by a rattler, near as I could figure, and crawled into a cave to get out of the sun. Stupid thing to do. Probably more rattlers in the cave than out on the desert."

"Oh," I said, hoping I didn't appear as revolted as I felt.

"Anyhow, any Injun bones you find around here would probably be a lot darker. You drove your Injuns out of Pasadena a hundred years or more ago, didn't you?"

"I didn't drive anyone out of Pasadena!" I said, miffed.

"Not you," said Mr. Prophet with scorn. "White folks." He stopped talking and considered for a moment or two while I tried to think of something cogent to say. Couldn't, which figures. "Were there any Indians around here?" he asked after he finished pondering.

I glanced at Sam, who glanced back. We both looked at Pa, who shook his head. "Darned if I know," he said.

Looking at Mr. Prophet again, I said, "Want to go to the library with me on Monday? Regina Browning's back at work there, and I'll bet she can find us books about what, if any, Indians lived in this area."

"Sure. I'd like to go to the library with you. Anyhow, it happened everywhere," said Mr. Prophet.

"Good." I sat for a second, thinking, then added, "I mean, it's not good that we killed all the Indians, but you're probably right. If any Indians lived in this area, our forebears must have killed them or driven them away decades ago."

Nodding, Mr. Prophet said, "Injuns didn't stand a chance once we whites decided we wanted the land they'd lived on for centuries."

He was correct. I'd never even thought about how a whole race of people might have been wiped off the face of the earth so that I could live in this beautiful bungalow in the beautiful City of Pasadena, California.

I didn't want to think about it now, either.

FOUR

My musings were interrupted by a knock at the front door, so I stopped thinking glum thoughts and went to open it. As I'd suspected, it was too soon for Dr. Benjamin to have arrived. A uniformed policeman and two policemen who wore white coats over their uniforms stood on the porch. The white-coats carried shovels with them. The uniform carried a suitcase containing, I was sure, useful bone-related things.

"Come on in," I said. "Officers Doan and Oliphant are here along with my father, Detective Rotondo and Mr. Prophet." I didn't explain that Sam was my husband. They probably either already knew that, or Sam would tell them.

"Thank you," said the uniform whose name, I saw, was Blanchard.

I led the way. Sam had stood and he greeted the newcomers as they entered the room. "Come on in, Paul. Jerry and Eugene, I see you're prepared for digging. Too bad you can't help with digging holes for the roses we wanted to plant."

All three men smiled, and one of the white-coats said, "Sorry, Sam. We're here to dig up bones. Where are they?"

With a shrug, Sam said, "I don't know. A dog and a cat each

found a bone in a part of the yard we weren't working in." He glanced at me. "Did you see which way they came from?"

"No, but I can find out," I told him.

Spike, who had been a Very Good Dog and had only yipped once when the newcomers arrived, still sat on a chair with my father.

I glanced at the two of them and said, "Spike, come."

Smiling broadly—don't tell *me* dogs can't smile—Spike jumped to the living room floor and dashed to sit before me. I said, "Good boy!" His tail swished across the floor so fast that if Mrs. Rattle hadn't carpet-swept it the prior day, he'd have raised dust. "Spike, I want you to come with me. Heel."

Spike heeled.

To Sam I said, "Will you please bring that jawbone? I'm going to show it to Spike and tell him to find it."

"He already found it," said Officer Doan.

"Yes, but 'find it' is a specific command I taught Spike, and I'll bet he's smart enough to figure out what I mean. If I'm right, he'll lead us to where he and Yuyu found the first two bones."

"He and who?" asked one of the white-coats. "Your dog is Spike, right?"

"Right. Yuyu is a cat. Spike and Yuyu are friends, and they discovered or dug up the bones together."

"A dog and a cat?" said the other white-coat.

"Yes," I said, feeling snappish. "Now are you going to come with me or not? I don't know about you, but I want to get those bones out of our yard today so we can get back to work planting roses."

"Better do as she says," said Sam, grinning. "She's right about Spike. He's about the smartest dog I've ever known."

"True," said Mr. Prophet.

"Yes," said Doan. "That's what my mother tells me, too."

"Don't forget the jawbone," I told Sam.

"Already picked it up," he said, holding it aloft. It was kind of a grisly sight.

"Okay. Thanks. All right, Spike, heel."

I started walking and, with Spike at my heel, we took off for the kitchen, through the back door, down the back porch steps and into the yard. Our poor boxwood hedge and arbor looked forsaken and alone, and I wanted to hug them both. Naturally I didn't.

I did, however, kneel on the grass as soon as we'd come within a few feet of the arbor. Lifting my right hand and wiggling my fingers Samwards, I said, "Give me the bone, please."

Sam handed me the jawbone. I held it in front of Spike, who sniffed it gleefully. "Very well, Spike. Find it."

Spike took off like a rocket, aiming at the southeastern part of the backyard, toward a section we hadn't even investigated yet. We had a huge backyard and had already talked about selling off part of it so a new house or two could be built nearby.

The police contingent ran after Spike. My father, Mr. Prophet, Sam and I followed more slowly. Spike had been trained to find things and not touch them until given a signal. I reproached myself for not thinking of bringing him a bit of doggie biscuit as a reward. Ah, well. This had been a confusing day, and I don't suppose one can think of everything, can one?

"I grabbed an oatmeal cookie out of the pie safe for the dog," said Mr. Prophet, proving me wrong as soon as the last thought flittered through my tangled brain.

"Thank you! I forgot to bring him a treat."

"Yeah, I know," said Mr. Prophet.

Sam laughed. So did Pa. I wanted to throttle them all, especially Mr. Prophet, whose tone had been as dry as the blasted jawbone. What's that part of the Bible? The jawbone of an ass? Well, Mr. Prophet possessed the jawbone of an ass. I decided I'd be better off not telling him so in front of my father and Sam.

Oh, wait. I just remembered where the jawbone of an ass figured in the bible. Samson picked it up and slew a thousand people with it. Very well, forget telling Mr. Prophet anything at all about jawbones.

Anyhow, we'd arrived at the spot where three uniforms and two white-coats stood, all peering down at something. As we approached, the men parted, and we could see what they saw: Spike, standing triumphantly on a long, wide mound of dirt sprinkled here and there with weeds. This particular mound lay behind the tiny grove of orange trees on the property and up against a block-wall fence separating our property from that of the people next door. It extended eastwards all the way to the next street over, which was Garfield Avenue.

At any rate, it was a huge expanse of dirt over which Spike was displaying his talent for "finding it." Mr. Prophet strode over to him, said, "Good doggie!" and handed Spike part of the oatmeal cookie he'd snabbled from the kitchen. Spike expressed his appreciation with more wags.

"See?" I told the assemblage and pointed to the expanse of dirt to which my dog had led us.

"That's a whole lot of ground," said Doan in a frustrated-sounding voice.

"Look for doggie and kitty dig marks," I suggested. "Or wait. I have a better idea." Again, I strode to Spike and showed him the jawbone. "Find it, Spike," I said brightly. Didn't want him to think I was dissatisfied with him, just because it wasn't I who'd given him his treat.

Darned if Spike didn't turn around and scamper off a few yards before he stopped and started shoveling dirt with his two front paws as if he aimed to dig a canyon. A dachshund's front paws were built for digging into badger burrows, so they're quite effective as shovels.

"Good Spike!" I hollered at him. "Good boy. Leave it now."

Although I could tell he was terribly disappointed, Spike left it.

Again our group walked to where Spike had led. This time when we glanced down at the ground, we saw what Spike and Yuyu had discovered earlier in the day. Bones. A few scattered bones.

"Oh, brother," said one of the white coats. "Well, you've got a good dog there. He found the body, all right."

Suddenly I recalled Dr. Benjamin. "Oh, my Lord, I'd better get back to the house! Dr. Benjamin might already be here!"

"I'd best stay here," said Sam. "Go on. Maybe he can give us some information about this mess. At least maybe how old the bones are."

I scooted back to the house almost as fast as Spike, who stayed with the men. And the bones. I think he was probably more interested in the bones.

Sure enough, Dr. Benjamin had arrived at our home as we'd been in the backyard. He, being a smart man, had figured out why no one had answered the door, however. He now stood at the back gate, which led onto the back porch, waving at me as I hurried up to him.

"Oh, Doc!" I said, panting. "I'm so sorry! Spike has just led us to where the rest of the bones are. I didn't mean to forget about you. Please forgive me!"

"You're forgiven. So there *are* more bones back there?"

"Yes, there are," I said, opening the gate for him and letting him onto the porch. "Quite a few of them, and they're *way* back there. Almost to Garfield."

"Good heavens. I didn't realize your property was so large."

"Yes, it actually covers enough ground for a couple of houses. Well, three houses. It already contains two houses."

"Ah, yes. Lou Prophet lives in the mother-in-law cottage out back, doesn't he?"

"Yes." I laughed. "Can you imagine Mr. Prophet as anybody's mother-in-law? What a horror he would be!"

"Aw, he's not so bad."

"Huh," I said, reminding myself of Sam.

"Well, lead me to the bones. Don't know what I'll be able to tell you, except maybe if they belonged to a human being. I can do that for sure. It requires more education in forensic anatomy than I possess to put a skeleton together."

"I'd really like to know approximately how old they are. They might be the bones of the poor fellow who disappeared all those years ago. If they're his, I guess we should try to figure out how he died. I hope to heaven he wasn't murdered. I'd never live it down."

"You do have something of a knack, don't you, Daisy?" said Dr. Benjamin, and *he* laughed.

"Yes," I said morosely. "That's what everyone keeps telling me. But I didn't find this dead body. Spike and his cat pal did."

"You'll have to introduce me to your cat," said Dr. Benjamin.

"He's not *our* cat. He belongs to Mr. Prophet. Well, the old sinner denies it, but he rescued it when it was a kitten, and it's his cat whether he wants to admit it or not."

"Fascinating," said the good doctor. "It is kind of hard to imagine him with a tame little kitty cat, isn't it?"

"It won't be so difficult to imagine once you meet the cat," I said darkly. "If any cat and any man could be said to belong together, it's those two."

"I'm looking forward to meeting this cat."

"It's probably in hiding now, because of all the people milling around. Mind you, I don't know it for a fact, but I haven't seen it since Pa, Sam, Mr. Prophet and I took the bones into the house to call the police and you."

"How'd you find the body if your yard is so huge? I mean, did you search all over it until you found some bones?"

"We didn't. I asked Spike to do it, and he did."

Doc peered at me slantways. "He did?"

"He did."

We'd been walking as we talked, and we'd just about reached the bone site. Spike saw Dr. Benjamin and raced over, excited to see an old friend. It was nice to know my dog was having a good day, even if none of the rest of us were.

"Hey there, Spike," said Dr. Benjamin, leaning over to give him a couple of pats and a scratch or two.

Because I'd taught him not to leap upon people when he was happy to see them, Spike gamboled around our feet and made walking the last few steps toward the boneyard difficult. Sam turned and waved to us.

"We've found a few more bones here. Jerry and Eugene are laying them on the sheet they brought. They're brushing off the dirt first. Maybe you can help us put the skeleton together, Doc."

"I can probably help a little bit, depending on how much of it is left. It takes an expert to put all the bones together because there are so many of them, and so many of them look alike. How are you, Sam?"

The two men shook hands and Sam said, "I'm fine, thanks.

43

Could have done without the dog finding a pile of bones in the yard, but other than that, things are fine."

"Glad to hear it. How about you, Joe?" Doc and my father shook hands.

"Feeling pretty good, Doc. The old ticker hasn't been acting up much recently, but I keep my tablets handy."

Nodding, Doc said, "Good to hear. Keep it up."

Doc Benjamin had prescribed nitroglycerine tablets for my father to stick under his tongue if he felt his heart acting funny or he felt weak. I worried about my father. I adored him *so* much, and I wanted him to stick around for years and years.

"How-do, Lou?" Doc said to Mr. Prophet.

"Can't complain," said the old reprobate. "You?"

"Oh," said the doctor, laughing, "I can always complain. But I want to see these famous bones." He strode a few more steps until he was next to the sheet and said, "And they *are* human bones, aren't they? Hmmm. What have we here?" Kneeling, he lifted a longish bone. "Rib bone here." Squinting at the site, he said, "They managed to get scattered somehow, didn't they?"

"Yes, but not as much as I'd expect if they've been here for twenty years," said Sam. "After all, we're near the arroyo, and there are coyotes and other animals in there that might like to nibble on a nice tasty piece of person."

"Sam!" I cried, horrified.

"It's the truth," said Doc. "But if this is the fellow who disappeared all those years ago, this was a busy construction site, and I expect the critters didn't fancy running into people while they tried to get at the succulent parts."

"Ew!" I said. "Although I guess Spike might have gnawed on the blasted bone if it had been fresher, mightn't he have?"

"He certainly would have," said my laughing father. "Spike's no dummy, and free food's free food."

"The notion of we humans being food isn't an awfully appealing one," I said to no one in particular.

"Tell that to the folks on Borneo," said Mr. Prophet, who liked reading history books. "I read somewhere that people taste kind of like pork."

"Gadzooks," I said. "And here I was hoping to learn how to fix a pork roast one of these days."

"Why bother with a pig when people are easier to find?" asked Mr. Prophet, sounding innocent. I knew better.

"Nertz. You'd no more eat a person than you'd eat your silly cat!"

"Ain't my cat," said Mr. Prophet, scowling.

"Cut it out, you two," said Sam with a chuckle. "We have work to do here."

So we cut it out.

FIVE

T he two white-coated fellows, Jerry and Eugene, continued
carefully dusting off bones and placing them on the sheet. Pa,
Sam, Mr. Prophet and I watched them for a while. Dr. Benjamin
had stepped up to the sheet, kneeled beside it, and had begun
shifting bones here and there.

"Are you trying to put him back together, Doc?" I asked,
curious.

"As much as possible," he said. "As I told you, I can't really
reconstruct a skeleton. You need special pathological skills to know
precisely which bone goes where. But maybe I can tell which bones
are human. Need to get more of him before we can figure out what
happened to him. Actually, I need more of the skeleton to see if it *is*
a him. Maybe it's a her."

"Really? I didn't know that!" I said, surprised.

"Yes," Dr. Benjamin said in a distracted-sounding voice. "If we
can find the upper part of the skull, and if it has brow ridges, then
we can determine for sure this is a male skeleton. Or the pelvic bone
and a femur or two."

"Oh." I was slightly embarrassed after having heard the words "pelvic bones," but that only tells you what a prissy girl I was, I reckon.

"They're scattered all over the place," said one of the white coats. Couldn't tell which one. "Predators have dragged some of the bones away, I fear."

"Right," said Doc. "Not surprised."

Ew.

"Does he look ancient?" I asked, worried. My primary concern was that the dog and cat had found ancient Indian bones, and that the historical fellows at the Southwest Museum might step in and refuse to let us plant our roses. Does that sound trivial? Well, maybe it was.

"By ancient, what do you mean?" Doc asked, peering at me over his shoulder.

"Well, like a hundred years or more old. Could the bones have belonged to an ancient Indian?"

"Good Lord, no!" said Doc, relieving my mind, although I felt a little silly. "These bones have been here a good long time, but they're definitely not of Indian origin. I've encountered one or two bones like that in my time, and they're much darker than this. The Indians who lived around here have been gone for more than a century. They have a reservation somewhere."

"Oh. So we rousted them out and stuck them on a reservation?" I asked, feeling guilty for some reason. I mean, *I* hadn't done a solitary thing to any Indian. And probably my immediate forebears hadn't either, although I do know my relations in Massachusetts came to the U.S.A. before it was the U.S.A. They were definitely in New England a couple of hundred years before 1926, and they'd probably had something to do with wiping out some of the eastern tribes.

History can be terribly depressing sometimes, can't it?

"I suppose you might put it that way," said Doc, who was preoccupied with bones.

Turning to the men in my life, I said, "Want to go back to the house and sit some more?"

"Yeah," said Mr. Prophet. "I can't stand much longer without something to lean on."

"Likewise," said Pa.

"Think I'll stay here for a while, but I'll come in soon. Except that the bones were found on our property, I don't have to be involved," said Sam. "Thank god, I might add."

"Good," I said. "Pa, Mr. Prophet and I sure can't do much here. Anyhow, I suppose I'd better start preparing lunch."

"*You're* gonna fix lunch?" asked an incredulous Mr. Prophet.

"Yes," I said. I said it firmly, too. "I've already prepared a nice orange and grapefruit salad, and there's both ham and cheese available for sandwiches."

"You made bread for the sandwiches?" asked Mr. Prophet, his voice reeking with doubt.

"No. Aunt Vi gave me a loaf of rye bread she made."

"Huh. Didn't think you could make bread."

"Darn you, Mr. Malicious Prophet! I'm learning to cook!"

"Stop picking on my wife, Lou," said Sam, who'd decided to join us after all. "She made a great breakfast this morning."

"She did?" asked a clearly dubious Mr. Prophet.

"I did," I snarled.

"She did," said Sam.

"Huh," said Mr. Prophet.

"Stop picking on my daughter, Lou," said my father, laughing. "She's good at lots of things, and Vi has been teaching her how to cook. Says she's coming right along."

"Huh," repeated Mr. Prophet.

"Mrs. Rattle's been helping me with my cooking skills, too. You'd better start being nicer to me," I told him, "or I might just get that stupid cat of yours and skewer it over an open flame!" I have no idea where that spark of spiteful indignation came from. I'd never hurt a cat or a dog. Mr. Prophet, maybe, but he was too big to skewer.

"Ain't—"

"Your cat. Yes, we know. You just found it battered nearly to death, took it to Dr. Van der Hoof and nursed it back to life. It *is* your cat! You're just too much of a sissy to say so."

"Huh," said Mr. Prophet a third time.

By this time we'd reached the back porch. Spike, I noticed, had remained with the bones, the policemen and the doctor. Silly dog.

I washed my hands and arms up to my elbows just to make sure the dust of dead people hadn't decided to cling to them, intending then to go to the Frigidaire and remove the ham, cheese, lettuce, and onions. I knew Sam and Pa liked onions on their ham and cheese sandwiches, and I suspected Mr. Prophet did too. As I was lathering, the doorbell rang.

A note about our doorbell. The doorbell across the street at my parents' house scritched when you twisted it. Our doorbell actually rang. Or buzzed. It was loud and made me jump almost every time I heard it, but still, at least we *could* hear it, which was a bonus. Sometimes we wouldn't hear the scritch across the street.

"I'll get it," said Sam. "Lou and Joe, take a seat at the kitchen table and rest."

"I don't need to rest," said a recalcitrant Mr. Prophet.

"Well, I do," said Pa.

Both men sat at the table.

I heard Sam's surprised, "Vi! What's going on?"

My adorable aunt, walking into the house and heading toward the kitchen, said, "I saw the police cars and Dr. Benjamin's car outside your place and wanted to see what was going on. I feared Joe might have...well, you know."

"Oh," said Sam. "We should have telephoned. No, Joe's just fine."

"I'm fine, Vi!" called Pa from the kitchen table.

Sam went on, "The reason for the police contingency and Dr. Benjamin is that Spike and Lou's cat—"

"Ain't my cat!" hollered Mr. Prophet from the kitchen table.

"Oh, shush," I told him.

"Huh," he said.

"I didn't know Lou had a cat. How sweet," said Vi, as if she hadn't heard Mr. Prophet's hot denial of cat ownership.

"Anyhow," continued Sam, "Spike and Yuyu, the cat, discovered some bones in the far, far back of the yard. So we called the police and Doc Benjamin, and they're out there trying to decide if the bones are human or not. Doc Benjamin thinks at least some of them are human, although he said he can't put a skeleton together by himself. Guess that requires a different kind of doctor. All we know so far is that the bones aren't old enough to be ancient Indians."

"Hmm," said my aunt, marching into the kitchen.

She carried a wicker basket. I hoped it meant she had food in there. Not that I didn't want to show Mr. Prophet I could prepare sandwiches, but I still had trouble cutting the bread into uniform slices, and he'd surely mock my incompetence.

When my hands and arms were dry, I went up to take the basket from Aunt Vi. After setting it on the kitchen counter, I gave her a hug. "I'm sorry we didn't think to telephone, Vi. We were getting all ready to plant our roses when Spike and Mr. Prophet's cat—"

"Ain't my—"

I lifted my voice. "—found a lower jawbone and what looks like some kind of rib bone, perhaps human. As Sam told you, they discovered them in the far back of the yard, on that piece of ground that reaches Garfield."

"That's in the area you're thinking of selling, isn't it?" asked Vi, walking to the basket, opening it, and hauling out what it contained. To my pleasure and relief, it contained a good deal of food. "I decided to bring you some edibles because I didn't know what was happening here. Then I'd appear useful and not just snoopy." My aunt laughed.

"You're always welcome here," said Sam, rising and going to the counter to help her empty the basket. "Even when there aren't any police cars out front."

"And yes," I told her, "that's the area we're thinking of selling. Good thing we haven't made any definite plans about it yet, because it's going to be under police surveillance for a while yet, until they find all the bones out there."

"I brought some more bread," said Vi, hauling out a delicious-smelling loaf of newly baked bread, already sliced by my aunt and wrapped in waxed paper. "And I opened a couple of jars of chicken I put up a few months back. I know you have ham and cheese and rye bread here, but figured you might want a chicken sandwich, too. Anyhow, now you have more mouths to feed, if you count the men in the backyard."

"You're a saint, Vi," I told her. "I hadn't even begun to think about what to feed the guys in the backyard yet. In fact, I was just going to get the ham and cheese."

"I'll help," said Pa, and joined me at the Frigidaire.

"Thanks, Vi," said Mr. Prophet. "I was a little worried when Miss Daisy said she aimed to fix us lunch."

Vi actually whirled around and slammed her fists on her hips. "Lou Prophet, you take that back! Daisy's learning to cook, and she's doing a marvelous job of it."

Looking slightly chagrined, Mr. Prophet said, "Huh. Well, I'm glad to hear it."

"You owe her an apology," said my aunt relentlessly. "Daisy has always felt terrible about her cooking skills, but she's paying attention and *learning*. Her enterprise should be encouraged, not belittled."

Merciful heavens, I had *no* idea my marvelous aunt would leap so quickly and hotly to my defense. Therefore, I decided to be gracious. "It's all right, Vi," I said, perhaps slightly more self-righteously than graciously. "I'm used to him giving me grief."

"Aw, now, Miss Daisy, you know I'm only teasin' you."

"No, I don't. You're mean and cruel to me."

"I ain't!"

"Well, you say nasty things to me, and they hurt my feelings."

"I ain't never said anything nasty to you, Miss Daisy," said Mr. Prophet. Now *he* sounded self-righteous.

"Different meaning of the word," I muttered. "But I don't want to argue with you any longer. I want to fix lunch." I turned to my aunt. "Thanks so much for thinking to make chicken salad for sandwiches! Did you chop up celery and onions and mix it with mayonnaise as you taught me to do?" I wanted to stick my tongue out at Mr. Prophet, but restrained myself.

"I did indeed," said Vi. "Here, let me cut this bread. You can spread butter on the white bread and mustard on the rye when it's ready." She turned to my father. "Joe, will you help me cut some slices of rye from this loaf I brought over? Daisy's busy." Daisy couldn't cut bread for beans was what she meant, but Vi, unlike Mr. Prophet, was kind.

Because my adorable aunt had already cut the white bread, I just got the butter dish, and began spreading slices of bread with butter.

"I brought over two jars of pickles, too," said Vi. "One sour dill and one bread-and-butter."

I wasn't a fan of bread-and-butter pickles, which were too sweet for me, but I loved Vi's dill pickles. "I hope you can teach me to make dill pickles one of these days, too, Vi."

"When the cucumber crop starts coming in, we'll do that. I've already written down the instructions. We always have so many cucumbers it's hard to deal with them all."

"Oh, yes, I remember it well," I said, thinking I'd like to have a kitchen garden too.

Sam had bought our house from Mrs. Killebrew. She'd been an elderly woman and had forsaken her gardening chores for a couple of years because she'd been caring for her sick husband. So Sam and I would have to create a new kitchen garden, too. It occurred to me that it might have been better if we'd prepared the ground for vegetables before we planted roses.

But no. January was rose-planting season and by golly, I wanted to plant roses! I kept buttering.

Another ring from the doorbell sent Sam off to see who'd arrived this time.

"Peggy!" I heard his pleased cry. "We're just preparing lunch. You're right on time."

"Ma!" I set the butter knife down and raced to the front door to greet my mother. "Did you come here straight from work?" I believe

I've mentioned that my mother was the head bookkeeper for the Hotel Marengo. She worked half-days on Saturdays.

"Yes. I saw the police cars outside and got worried," said my darling mother. I really did have the world's best relatives. Well, the ones in Southern California were the best, anyway. I have to admit to having become annoyed with my eastern ones whilst on my honeymoon.

Giving her a hug and then taking her handbag and placing it on the shelf provided for things of that nature, I said, "Everyone is perfectly healthy here. Well, except for the guy in the backyard. He's a mere skeleton."

"I beg your pardon?"

I don't think I've yet revealed that my mother doesn't have much imagination or a sense of humor, in spite of being one of the sweetest, most caring and loving people on earth.

"Pay no attention to your daughter, Peggy," said Sam, setting her hat on the same shelf upon which I'd placed her handbag. "Only Spike and a…well, a new friend of his found some old bones in the backyard. Because they hadn't been buried properly, we had to call the police. Dr. Benjamin is back there, too, trying to decide which bones are human and which, if any, aren't."

"Good lord!" cried my mother. She turned to me. "Daisy, I swear to heaven—"

"It's not my fault!" I cried, feeling beleaguered. "*I* don't know why dead people and I always end up in the same places at the same times!"

"I'm sorry, dear," said my mother. "It just seems uncanny somehow. In your own backyard? I mean…Oh! I do believe I recall the disappearance of a young man in these parts several years ago. Must have been at least twenty years ago."

"That's what Pa told us," I said glumly as Sam and I escorted my mother to the kitchen, where Mr. Prophet had taken over buttering white bread and Pa had cut a lot of slices from the loaf of rye.

"Well then, it might not be a bad thing that you found his bones if they're those of the poor fellow who disappeared," said Ma.

I felt better after she said those words.

SIX

The moment my mother entered the kitchen, darned if the doorbell didn't ring *again*! What on earth was going on today? Had someone planned a party at our house and forgotten to tell me about it? But no. The police and Dr. Benjamin were only here because of the bones, and Vi and Ma had only shown up because of the police cars parked outside.

I detoured from the kitchen—truth to tell, even though I honestly *was* making a concerted effort to learn how to cook, I didn't much care for kitchens—and walked to the door. Opening it, I beheld my best friend, Harold Kincaid, holding the most spectacularly gorgeous lamp I'd ever seen in my life.

"Harold! What a magnificent lamp!"

He shoved it at me. "And a good day to you, too."

Taking the lamp and staring at it in wonder, I said, "Oh, I'm sorry, Harold. Good day to you. And this is a spectacular lamp."

"I got it for you. What the devil's going on at your place, anyhow? Don't tell me you got so mad at Sam, you knifed him!"

Still taking in the splendor of the lamp, it took me a second for Harold's words to register. Then I stiffered. "No! No, of course I didn't kill Sam, Harold Kincaid. What a horrid thing to say!" My gaze strayed back to the lamp. "Oh, but Harold, this is exquisite. Did you really intend it for *me*?"

"I *had* intended it for you, but not if you're going to call me horrid. What are all the police cars doing out there?" He pointed to the front curb.

With a sigh, I said, "When we were digging holes to plant our Cecile Brunner roses, Spike and Mr. Prophet's cat found some old bones in the back-back of the yard."

"Good god. You can't even be trusted in your own backyard?"

"It's not—"

"Your fault," said Harold, interrupting me. "I know that, but where do you want to put this spectacular lamp? It would look nice on that telephone table."

We were passing the telephone table as Harold spoke.

"It's too pretty to sit on the telephone table out of the way in the hall," I said. "We'll have to find a better place for it. But let me show it to Sam and my parents, and then you can have some lunch with us."

"The whole family's here?" asked Harold, surprised.

"You weren't the only one who noticed the police cars parked outside."

"Right," said Harold. "Makes sense." He added in amazement, "And did you say something about Mr. Prophet having a *cat*?"

"It ain't my cat!" the old rascal hollered.

We'd reached the kitchen, and I stepped inside, holding the lamp out for everyone to see. Forgetting the cat question, I said, "Look what Harold brought us, Sam!" I cried.

Everyone turned, and I heard a bunch of ooohs and aaahs. The lamp was worth every one of them and then some.

"Wow," said Sam. "That's beautiful. Thanks, Kincaid."

"I saw it and thought Daisy needed to have it," said Harold, preening. As well he might.

"Pretty lamp," Mr. Prophet said. Then he muttered under his breath, "I ain't got no cat."

The lamp was in the shape of a peacock. Bronze-colored, its spectacular peacock feathers were shaped into an oval and made up the base of the lamp. The shade, which was fashioned of thin glass in a yellow-gold color with what looked like stems and flowers on it, was held in the peacock's beak by a bronze-colored loop and connected to the lamp by a bronze flower-patterned…thing. I don't know what the parts of a lamp are called. Oh, but it was fabulous.

"Where shall we put it, Sam?" I asked, beaming at my darling husband.

"I'm not sure. We'll have to give it some thought. But we'd probably better get it out of the kitchen while all this activity is going on. If it got knocked over and broke, I'd probably kill whoever bumped it."

"And you a policeman," said Harold in a mock-scolding tone.

"And me a policeman," agreed Sam.

"Take it into the living room, and let's all look at it," suggested Vi, who'd uncovered the bowl of chicken sandwich filling she'd brought over. She quickly covered it again with the waxed paper she'd just taken off of it and washed her hands at the sink.

So I gently carried our new treasure into the living room, where everyone could see it properly. The draperies were drawn back, along with the sheers underneath them, so there was a lot of light. Everyone adored the lamp.

"I'll treasure this forever, Harold. Thank you." I gave him a kiss on the cheek.

"Yes," said Sam. "Thank you. That's about the most beautiful lamp I've ever seen." He shook Harold's hand.

"You're such a sweet boy, Harold," said Vi, and she kissed him too.

"Oh, you are!" exclaimed my mother, depositing yet another kiss on Harold's cheek.

"All right. I know I'm wonderful," said Harold. "I'm also hungry, and Daisy said something about lunch preparations. I hope she wasn't fibbing."

The teeniest bit plump, Harold did love his food. His houseboy, Roy Castillo, had been taught to cook by my very own aunt, and he fed Harold and his lover well.

Whoops. Perhaps I'd better explain that last sentence. You see,

Harold and his housemate Delray Farrington were what some people consider perverted members of society. That's because they prefer people of their own sex to those of the opposite sex. I understand there are women like that, too. That is to say, they prefer women to men. Some idiots believe the Harolds, Dels and others in the world like them to be evil and disgusting. I know such beliefs to be pure hogwash. Harold has told me, and I believe him, that he was born the way he was, and there wasn't anything he could do about it.

"Who," he'd asked me more than once, "would *want* to be cursed, vilified, demonized, criminalized, imprisoned, spat at and otherwise denigrated? If I could be other than I am, I would be!"

Made sense to me. Anyhow, I didn't call Harold and Del anything other than friends. And they were. Good ones. Harold Kincaid had even shot a man in Turkey in order to save Sam's life! How can you not love a fellow like that?

"Um," I said, getting back to the living room, "why don't I put the lamp on the piano for now. I don't think that's a good place for it to stay forever because, when we gather in the evenings to sing, somebody might bump it."

"It'll do for now," said Sam. "It looks great there, though."

"It does." I sighed, stepping back and gazing at it, glimmering in the sunshine pouring through the windows. My word, but the thing was a marvel of craftsmanship.

"Looks almost like one of those Tiffany lamps, doesn't it?" said Sam, who had an eye for beauty. Heck, he chose me, didn't he?

Just kidding. I'm not ugly, but I'm no Anna May Wong. And even though I have red hair, I'm no Clara Bow either. Darn it.

"It is danged pretty." This endorsement sprang from the lips of none other than Mr. Lou Prophet. He had an eye for beautiful women and damaged cats, but I hadn't noticed him express many opinions about artworks or furniture or anything of the like before.

"You'll have to bring Miss Li over here to see it," I told him.

He scowled at me. Oh, for pity's sake! He didn't want to admit to having a cat, and now he didn't want to admit to having a lady friend? "Fine then," I snapped. "Don't."

"Mebbe I will," he said, unbending a trifle. "She'll think it's pretty."

"You can introduce her to your cat, too," I snarled.

"Ain't my—"

"Let's have lunch!" I interrupted, perhaps a bit loudly. "I'm hungry. Somebody should go outside and ask the fellows with the bones if they'd like something to eat, too."

"They're most likely filthy by this time," Sam said. "Maybe we ought to take them a bucket to wash in and some sandwiches and lemonade on a tray or something. I expect Doc Benjamin hasn't been digging, so he can possibly come in, wash up and eat with the family."

"Why don't we set up a picnic on the back porch?" I said. "It's big enough, and then they can all just come up to the porch, wash off with the hose—I'll bring out a bar of soap and a towel—and they can sit on the steps and eat sandwiches with us."

"Sounds good to me," said Harold. "I'll prepare the tray while you and Vi get the sandwiches and whatever else we're eating with them ready."

"I made some orange and grapefruit salad, but I didn't make enough for an army," I said doubtfully.

"I'll pick some more oranges and grapefruits," said Mr. Prophet, being useful for once.

"I'll help," said Pa.

"Thanks, you two. Come on, Vi, Ma and Harold. Sam, why don't you go out and see what's going on in the back-back? You can tell them we're fixing lunch for everyone."

"Good idea, sweetheart," said Sam. He was speaking to me, in case you wondered.

He took off for the back-back. Maybe I should call it the back forty in this chronicle. So what if we weren't on a farm? The back-yard was big enough for one. Almost.

So, while Mr. Prophet and Pa foraged for citrus fruits in our little orchard, the rest of us women and Harold went back to the kitchen and finished making sandwiches. We had a huge pile of them by the time we finished, and although we'd used all the ham, there was still plenty of chicken salad and cheese left, if anyone needed more food. We put the pickles into two separate large bowls, one for the dills and another for the bread-and-butters, and I placed a pair of tiny silver tongs in each pickle bowl.

Vi had brought over two huge Ball jars of the potato salad she'd put up back in canning season. My aunt was a miracle worker. Mind you, Ma and I helped her with the canning, but we did things like peel potatoes, celery and onions and pour water into canning kettles and other things like that. Vi did the mixing and cooking because both Ma and I could ruin water. Well, Ma still could. I had actually managed to make a decent breakfast of scrambled eggs and toast for my husband that very morning.

So there, Mr. Lou, the cat-lover, Prophet.

Harold had taken me to Bullock's Department Store in downtown Los Angeles to pick out formal and informal china patterns, but I'd also made a trip to Nelson's Five and Dime to pick out some plain ordinary plates and plain unstemmed glasses for occasions like this one. Not that we normally had lunch on the back porch because of bones found in the yard. Still, I didn't want to trust men who'd been digging for the bones of a dead person to dine off either my Copeland Spode Wickerdale—the everyday china—or my special Shelley Syringa Gardenia "good" china.

Therefore Harold, who had gone with me on my mission to Nelson's and hadn't balked much at my insistence on getting plain old plates and glasses, went to the kitchen cupboard and brought out a bunch of plates. "What platters do you want to use?" he asked as he peered into the cupboard.

"Go to the china cabinet in the dining room and get one from there. But don't use the Wickerdale or the Syringa Gardenia. Get one somebody gave us as a wedding present that isn't as pretty."

"Daisy!" said my mother, who still corrected me when she thought I was being rude, even though I was a twenty-six-year-old married woman.

"I don't want my best china to get broken, Ma," I said plaintively. "There are some nice trays in there that aren't so…breakable. Or that I won't cry over if they get broken."

"She's right, Peggy," said Vi. "You know Daisy has enough china to serve all the people in Pasadena, thanks to her rich clients." To Harold she called, "Try to find a couple of sturdy ones that won't break or chip easily!"

"Will do," said Harold from the dining room.

Vi had been right about the various sets and pieces of china Sam and I had been given by my wealthy clients. I had tea sets, trays, party dishes, glass bowls, two or three punch bowls with accompanying cups, and things I never even knew existed until I was given them like, for instance, the tiny silver tongs in the pickle bowls. The china pieces wouldn't all fit in the china cabinet, so I had china stored in practically every closet in the house. I aimed to give Flossie and Johnny Buckingham, two of my best friends, a set of china someone I didn't even know had given us. Johnny was in charge of the Pasadena Salvation Army Church, and Flossie was his wife and the mother of their two adorable children, Billy and—this isn't my fault either—Daisy.

"Found a couple that will work," Harold called from the dining room. He returned bearing a pretty tray with flowers on it and another pretty tray with stripes on it. The sandwiches would cover the decorations, so it didn't matter if they matched. Not that it would matter to the diners anyway.

Mr. Prophet and Pa came back in with more oranges and a couple more grapefruit, so I went to work peeling them and cutting out nice sections, precisely as my aunt had taught me to do. "This will be a good lunch," I said happily as I sectioned the last grapefruit. Didn't even slice a finger off, by golly.

Dr. Benjamin showed up shortly after I'd finished sectioning citrus. "May I wash my hands, please? I don't want to dirty your kitchen."

"Sure, Doc," I said. "Just use the sink in the utility room." I pointed in the direction of the utility room, where resided our washing machine and an old cider press rescued from my parents' basement.

"Thanks. It's mighty fine of you to fix lunch for us. Good morning, Mrs. Gumm and Mrs. Gumm," he said to my mother and Aunt Vi. Then we all laughed.

"You know it's never any trouble for me to feed people," said Vi, telling the absolute truth. I envied her *so* much.

As Vi, Ma and I stacked sandwiches on platters, I called to the doctor, "Have you figured out whether the skeleton belongs to a man or a woman yet?"

"Found a pelvic bone, and I'm sure the bones are those of a man. Probably a young one, to judge by the remaining teeth and the sturdiness of the bones. If he were older, the bones would be more porous and brittle."

"Oh, dear," said Ma. "How sad for a young man to lose his life and not even have his family bury him."

"If we can figure out who he was," said Sam, "maybe we can find his family, if there are any family members left."

"Good idea," I said, thinking about how lonely that pile of bones must have been for the past twenty or so years, and how much a mother, father, wife or children must have grieved because they never knew what happened to the possessor of the bones.

Not that bones can be lonely, but I knew from experience how much people can grieve. And that's even when they *know* what happened to a loved one. Not knowing if a loved one is alive or dead for years and years must drive people crazy. You wouldn't know whether to cry or scream, depending on if they'd had a fatal accident or had run out on the family. I knew men did that sort of thing: run out on their families, I mean, but I couldn't fathom such behavior. That's because the men in my life were *good* ones.

Guess I was lucky. It was a crying shame more women weren't.

SEVEN

S am led the police contingent to the back porch. Jerry and Eugene no longer wore white coats, but formerly white coats now smudged with dirt and grime and little sticks, fuzzy bits of things, old peppercorns and leaves from the many pepper trees lining Marengo Avenue. Blanchard, who'd been supervising their efforts, wore a dirty uniform. Oliphant and Doan were still fairly clean. Oliphant had been photographing bones as Dr. Benjamin had placed them on a white sheet, trying to situate them where they might belong on a human body. None of the men were hot and sweaty, the day being cool. That was about the only good thing to be said as related to their jobs, I'd say.

"Thanks for the food, Mrs. Rotondo," said Doan when he and Oliphant walked onto the porch.

"You're more than welcome. My aunt, Mrs. Gumm, fixed almost everything. My mother and I only helped." I decided not to mention Harold because I doubted the policemen would appreciate him as much as I did.

I allowed him and Oliphant to use the sink on the utility porch to wash their hands. The other men had to remove their coats (formerly white and police-issued) and use the hose and bar of soap to wash themselves. I noticed almost instantly that one towel wasn't going to work for all three men, so I rushed back in and fetched another three. They thanked me once more.

And then we ate. As we did so, we all asked Dr. Benjamin what he'd discovered so far aside from the fact that the bones had belonged to a young man.

"Not much, really," said he after swallowing some of his ham-and-cheese sandwich. "I don't have a clue so far as to how he died. If we find any bones showing injuries, we might be able to figure it out, but as yet, no luck."

"It seems strange that his bones would just be lying there," I mused. I was eating a chicken sandwich, but I swallowed first.

"They weren't just lying there," said Sam. "They were under a lot of dirt and brush. "Spike and Yuyu had to dig to find the ones they discovered, and poor Jerry and Eugene are having to dig to find more of them. This whole operation is going to take more than one day."

"You're right," said Dr. Benjamin. "I suspect animals have been at the bones and scattered them. They certainly aren't buried deeply, if they were buried at all. It almost looks to me as if someone died there and managed to get some dirt dumped on top of him. Might be foul play involved, but I can't say at this point."

"How could anybody just die there?" I asked, honestly curious. "If he was young, what would he have died of? And why didn't anybody see his body?"

With a shrug, Dr. Benjamin swallowed, grimaced, and said, "I have no idea. How many homes were in this area in around 1904 or 1905, do you know, Joe?"

"1904," my father said musingly. "I can't honestly tell you. I know the house we live in had just been built at the time, and I think perhaps this one was under construction. That huge house down the way where Mrs. Mainwaring lives was here first, and this was just orange groves with two rows of pepper trees for several years. Then whoever then owned the big house sold off more land, and more houses began to spring up. We moved into the house across the street in 1908 or thereabouts, didn't we, Peggy?"

"A little earlier. 1905, I think, because we bought it from the builder."

"Must have been earlier than 1910, because I remember Christmas in that house when Vi brought home the Ouija board and my career as a spiritualist-medium was born," I said, laughing as I remembered.

"Oh, you and that board!" said Ma. Then she laughed, too.

"You're right," said Pa. "How could I forget. I thought Daphne was going to murder you, Daisy."

"So did I," I said, probably because I'd "borrowed" my older sister, Daphne's, Mexican peasant blouse for the occasion. She didn't appreciate me for that or for telling her she'd never get married or have children. As she's now happily married and has two daughters with her husband Daniel, she's forgiven me long since.

"Anyway, there were a lot of open spaces behind the pepper trees at the time. 1904, I mean. I guess some poor kid could have dropped dead—or been killed—and not been discovered. Then he'd have had to be covered up even though there seems no evidence of a grave, *per se*. That scenario seems unlikely though."

"Yes, it does," said Sam. "Unless folks were using grading equipment to prepare for building more homes. There weren't many, if any, gas-generated bulldozers back then, so I suppose they'd have to use tractors or horse-drawn machinery to grade the earth."

"Oh, yes, I remember those days well," said Dr. Benjamin. "Not necessarily here on Marengo, but I remember those gigantic draft horses hauling road-grading equipment up and down streets, and horse-drawn tractors digging and gracing earth for houses. It's possible somebody died out there and a big tractor-load of dirt was dumped on him before anybody knew he was there. Seems far-fetched, although maybe it isn't."

"How awful for the poor fellow," I said.

"Aw, hel—heck, Miss Daisy, people die all the time for all sorts of reasons in all sorts of places." Lou Prophet shook his old gray head. "I remember a feller I knew passed out drunk in Tucson once and a big pile of dry cement got dumped on him. Except the drovers didn't see him before they dumped the cement. Builders didn't find him until they got to the bottom of the pile. By then he was kind of a mess."

Silence fell upon those of us on the back porch and its steps as we contemplated Mr. Prophet's dire words.

At last Sam said, "So it's possible."

"Yes," I said. "It may be possible, however unlikely it seems. You say the newspapers reported the fellow missing, assuming that's him? He, I mean?"

"I remember hearing about the disappearance of a young man, but I don't recall whether I was told the information or read it," said Pa. "Peggy, Vi, do either of you remember any newspaper articles?"

"No," said Ma. "But I didn't read the newspapers all that well back then. Still don't, for that matter."

"Nor did I," said Vi. "I read them now, at Mrs. Pinkerton's place, when I sit down for my morning tea and toast with Mr. Featherstone."

Featherstone was Mrs. Pinkerton's butler, and the most butlerish butler I've ever seen. And I've seen lots of butlers because I work for a bunch of rich people. In 1926, butlers seemed to be going the way of the horse and carriage, but some folks clung to their traditions.

"I vaguely recall reading in the newspaper about a fellow going missing," said Pa.

"In order for people to know about his disappearance, there must have been some word printed somewhere," I said. "I can look in the library's newspaper archives when Mr. Prophet and I visit the library on Monday, but it would help to know a general date of the poor man's disappearance. Anybody remember?"

Silence greeted my question. "I can't look at every newspaper printed in 1904 and 1905, you know," I said. "I mean, I could, but it would take forever, and I want to research Indians who might have lived here way long ago."

"Why? These aren't ancient bones," said Dr. Benjamin.

"I know that, but I became curious about Indians in this area when Spike and Yuyu first found the bones. I had almost hoped they were ancient Indian bones."

"You should be glad they're not. If they were, they would have required even more fuss and bother," said Dr. Benjamin. "If, of course, you reported your find. I suppose if you found old Indian bones and just ignored them and didn't tell anyone, none of the authorities would get involved. I suspect the Southwest Museum would take a huge interest in any old Indian bones people find. In fact, I know they do, because one of my patients found an Indian skull in his yard once, and the Southwest Museum nearly had hysterics about it."

"What do you mean?" I asked, vaguely glad now that our bones weren't ancient.

"I don't know if there are any laws governing the discovery of ancient bones, but there may be," said Doc. "But when my patient called the police, the police notified the Southwest Museum, and the archaeologists and scientists from there went to his house, roped off the section of his yard where the skull had been found, and dug the place up. Made total pests of themselves, although I don't really blame them. Their job is to do research on native people from the southwest, after all."

"True," I said, nibbling some citrus salad. If anyone cares, I put a very little bit of honey—orange blossom honey, of course—in the bowl to combat some of the grapefruit's tartness. The combination of oranges, grapefruit and honey was darned good, even if I do say so myself. Vi gave me the recipe, naturally, but still....

With a sigh, Sam said, "I don't suppose we're going to solve the mystery of the bones in the backyard today, but is it all right with the Pasadena Police Department if Daisy and I plant those roses? They really need to be planted soon, according to Mr. Liljenwall."

All of the policemen present, including Sam, gazed at one another for a few seconds. Sam actually outranked the others, but he wasn't going to do anything that might be considered a violation of anything the others advised. He might not technically need his job, but he wanted to keep feelings friendly.

"Probably, the doctor is the one who's best able to advise us on that matter," Blanchard said after several seconds of contemplative silence.

With a shrug, Dr. Benjamin said, "Why not? The bones are way out there in the back forty"—he actually said those words—"and where you're planting the roses and setting up the arbor are fifty or sixty yards away from the mound with the bones in it."

"Oh, *thank* you!" I said, pleased that we'd get to plant our Cecile Brunners today after all.

"Makes sense to me," said Blanchard. The rest of the coppers nodded, including Oliphant and Doan.

"I should probably go back to the station," said Doan. "You don't need me here, and I can begin writing up a report about this. I'll look in the files to see if I can discover any information about a man who went missing twenty-some years ago, too."

"Good idea," said Sam.

"Excellent," said Dr. Benjamin. "Thanks for lunch, ladies. I want to get back out there and see if we can't find enough bones to make a complete skeleton. I'd love to know how the poor fellow died. Sure seems odd that he'd just lie down back there and allow himself to be covered in dirt and rocks and so forth."

"Very odd," I said, shuddering slightly.

"Indeed," said Pa. "Think I'll go on home and lie down for a while."

"I'll go with you," said Ma. "Daisy, you don't mind washing these dishes, do you?"

"I'll wash the dishes, Mrs. Gumm," said Harold, who had remained silent through lunch. I'm sure he was intimidated by all the policemen present, as his very being-ness (I don't think that's a word) was considered illegal. Stupid laws.

"I'll help you," said Mr. Prophet, surprising me, although I already knew he didn't care how people lived their lives as long as they didn't bother him.

"Thanks, Lou," said Harold, trying to make his voice sound deeper than it usually was.

"Excellent. Thank you both!" I said. "And thank you, Vi and Ma. I do so appreciate you bringing all this food over here. I never thought I'd be hosting a luncheon for a bunch of bone-digging policemen today. And, of course, a doctor."

"Daisy," said Ma, but she didn't sound as if she meant it. Everyone else laughed, so it was all right.

Sam stood and stretched. He was a tall man, my Sam. Six feet tall at least. Mr. Prophet was slightly taller, even though he stooped some these days, but he was leaner. Sam wasn't fat; he was well-muscled. Mr. Prophet was kind of stringy, although he too was strong as the proverbial ox. It tickled me that he'd befriended a pitiful little damaged kitten.

Which reminded me of something extremely important and which I'd totally forgotten about. "Where's Spike? Oh, lordy, you didn't leave him out there with the bones, did you?"

Talk about a series of unhappy noises and glances, I couldn't even count them all happening on our back porch just then.

"Cripes," said Sam. "Daisy, we'd better go out and see if he's scattering the bones."

"Hell, probably Yuyu's out there, too," said Mr. Prophet.

"Don't worry about Yuyu, Lou," said Sam. "Daisy and I can run faster than you can."

"True," said the old goat.

"Crumb, I hope they haven't done anything with the bones I've already laid out," said a distressed Dr. Benjamin.

"Wish I'd thought of Spike earlier," I said, feeling guilty. "I don't usually forget him."

"I know. That dog's like your kid," I heard Mr. Prophet say as Sam and I took off for the back forty at a run.

Sam got there first, startling Yuyu into a hiss and Spike into a yip. I stood there, gazing at my wonderful hound and Mr. Prophet's pathetic-looking cat with its crooked and extremely puffed-up tail, and breathed a sigh of relief.

"They haven't messed up Doc's pile of bones," I panted to Sam.

"No, they haven't. Looks like they've discovered a couple more bones, though," said Sam, kneeling and holding out a hand to Spike, who obediently hustled over and deposited some kind of bone in his hand. "Good dog." That was what Sam said to Spike.

What *I* said to Spike was, "Come along, Spike. I think you need to go across the street and help Pa take a nap." I glanced around to see where Yuyu had got himself off to, and discovered he'd climbed the block wall fence next to the mound of bone-filled dirt. He was gazing at me with his one yellow eye that gave me the creeps even in the middle of the day. "Don't you look at *me* like that, cat," I told him. "You're not supposed to be digging here."

"Cat doesn't know what you're saying," observed Sam, laughing at me.

He stood after petting Spike, who had reluctantly come at my call and now sat before me. I swear, his eyes were positively *beseeching* me to let him and his cat friend dig up more bones.

"Sorry, Spike. The police and Dr. Benjamin have to take over now. You were a good dog to find the bones you found." I turned to the scowling cat. I swear his expression could have been transferred to Mr. Prophet's face without changing a single thing about it. "And thanks to you, too, you ungrateful feline. I'll bring Spike back to play with you another day."

"Shoot," said Sam. "Your mother, father and aunt are going to have to keep a sharp eye on Spike from now on. He's likely to race across the street to see if he can find the stupid cat or more bones whenever they open the door."

"You're right," I said, distressed at the notion. Marengo wasn't a terribly busy street, but it only took one automobile to run over a dog who didn't bother to look out for cars before he darted into the road. And, for all his intelligence and training, Spike never looked both ways before crossing the street. "I should call Mrs. Bissel and see if we can get Pa a dachshund of his own. Then we can bring Spike here to live. I'd like that, and Pa would still have company."

"I'd hate to saddle your parents with a puppy, with everything that entails," mused Sam.

"Maybe Mrs. B has a retired breeding bitch or another older dog she would sell me at a discount."

"People who breed dogs retire their breeding...er, bitches?" Sam asked incredulously. "You're kidding me!"

"Am not. Mrs. Bissel doesn't allow any of her females to have more than three litters. I'll give her a call today."

"Good idea. That would probably be best, actually. Then you

can have Spike back, and Joe will still have a best friend. I know he still thinks of Spike as your dog."

Sam's words surprised me. "He does? I didn't know that!"

"Yes. He told me just the other day that he appreciates you humoring him by letting him keep Spike, but he and Spike both know Spike belongs to you."

I know it's stupid, but my eyes teared up. When I sniffled them to a stop, I said, "I'm going to telephone Mrs. Bissel right this minute."

"Don't forget the roses," Sam called after me as Spike and I headed to the house.

"I'll be back as soon as Pa, Spike, Vi and Ma leave and I call Mrs. Bissel," I told him.

"Huh," said Sam.

EIGHT

Afer I got Spike into the house and handed him off to my father, said farewell to him, Ma, Vi and Doan, I walked to the hall and sat in the chair next to the telephone table. I knew Mrs. Bissel's 'phone number by heart, so I dialed it.

"Bissel residence," said Keiji Saito, Mrs. Bissel's houseboy.

"Hi, Keiji," said I. "It's Daisy. Is Mrs. Bissel available to chat on the telephone for a minute?"

"I'm pretty sure she's out in the kennels with the dogs right now, but I'll check. If she's outside, I'll ask her to call you when she comes inside again. Once she gets out there with Mr. Palmer and her dachshunds, it takes a winch and a crane to get her away from them."

I laughed. "You're right, I know. She's got a hired man to stay with the dogs and even has heated kennels. Well, it's nice to know she treats the dogs well."

"Better than some folks treat their kids," said Keiji.

"True, unfortunately. But it's about dogs I called. I want to know if she has any adult dogs available. I want to get my father a Dachshund because I want Spike to come live with Sam and me in our house across the street. Um…did that make any sense?" How would Keiji know about my household arrangements?

"Yeah, it makes perfect sense," said Keiji, surprising me. "In fact, Mrs. Bissel was wondering out loud if your dachshund had moved into your house after you got married or stayed with your parents. She does that a lot. Talks to us servants, you know. One of the reasons I like her so well is that she treats us more like family than servants, in fact."

"Yes," I said. "She's a nice woman. She's my favorite of all my clients."

"Makes sense to me. Hold on a minute, and I'll see if she's in the house."

"Thanks, Keiji," I said. I heard the very slight noise the receiver made on his end of the wire as he gently set it on the table. Then he went for a walk. Mrs. Bissel's house was big. It wasn't a castle or anything, but it was big.

I heard some voices on the other end of the wire; probably Keiji asking one of the maids or Mrs. Cummings, Mrs. Bissel's cook-housekeeper, if they knew where the mistress was. After fully long enough for Keiji to have searched the entire house, I heard his footsteps coming back to the telephone table.

"Sorry, Daisy, she's outside with the hounds. I'll have her ring you up when she comes inside again."

"Thanks, Keiji. Feel free to tell her what I called about, too. I don't want to burden my father with a puppy, but I'd love to get him a dog of his own."

"If she doesn't have one, there's always the Pasadena Humane Society," he suggested.

"You're right. I should have thought of the Humane Society in the first place."

"Well, you like dachshunds, so it's natural you'd think of Mrs. B."

"You're right," I said, but I felt guilty. "Thanks, Keiji. Talk to you later."

"Good-bye, Daisy."

We hung up. And I still felt guilty.

All those poor dogs and cats in the Pasadena Humane Society, and I instantly thought of a purebred dachshund for my father. Ah, well. Spike was special. Guess I just had a soft spot for dachshunds. If Mrs. Bissel didn't have an appropriate one for Pa though, I'd visit the Humane Society.

When I walked to the kitchen, I noticed Harold and Mr. Prophet were both drying dishes. "Need any help here?" I asked.

"Naw," said Mr. Prophet.

"Nope," said Harold. "I got all of these dishes out in the first place, so I know where they go. The ones I don't recognize, I'll leave on the kitchen counter. They probably belong to your aunt."

"Thanks, you two," I said, truly grateful. Any time I didn't have to remain in a kitchen was a happy time for me. Even though I honestly *was* learning to cook.

"Welcome," said Mr. Prophet.

"I'll come outside and see what's going on before I leave," said Harold. "I want to see these bones of yours."

"They aren't my bones," I said. Then, feeling sassy, I added, "You might be able to meet Mr. Prophet's cat, though."

"Ain't my…Aw, hell," said Mr. Prophet, shooting me a bitter look.

"I like your cat," I told him. "He hates me, though. When I made Spike leave the boneyard, your stupid cat hissed at me."

"Huh. Knew he was a good cat."

"Right. Okay, see you fellows later," I said as I pushed open the back door and headed to…well, the boneyard. Ew. My own backyard. This wasn't fair.

But I already knew life wasn't fair, right? Right.

When I got close enough so I didn't have to bellow, I said, "How's it going out here? Find any indications of how the poor fellow died?"

"Not yet," said Doc, who was beginning to appear a trifle worn down and frazzled. "I'm going to have to leave off sorting through his bones for today, though. Not as young as I used to be."

"Who is?" asked Sam, being kind.

"But," said the doctor, ignoring Sam's question, "I want to put these bones somewhere they won't get scattered again. Want to cover them, too, because it's winter and we might actually get rain one of these days.

"Crumb," said either Jerry or Eugene, "this is no fun even when the earth's dry. I can't imagine digging out here in the mud."

Sam heaved a gigantic sigh. "I'll go to the hardware store and get some big tarpaulins. We can set aside a place on the back porch for the bones, and stake out this dirt heap so it won't get too wet if it rains. Hmm. Maybe the store will have a tent."

"It would have to be a big tent," said Dr. Benjamin.

"I was thinking of the tent for the porch, actually," said Sam. "We'll have to rig up some kind of tent-like structure to cover this dirt patch, too, but I doubt we'll be able to build a big-enough tent."

"I was a Boy Scout," said either Eugene or Jerry. "I think I can fashion a tent out of tarpaulins and some tent stakes." He glanced over the extremely large area included in the archaeological dig and added, "Maybe some of those long gardening stakes, too."

Suddenly Sam and I looked at each other. We both said, "Pudge!" at the same time.

"We'll get you another Boy Scout who'll help you," I told whoever had admitted to having been a Boy Scout.

Pudge Wilson, owner of Samson, the well-fed orange and white cat, was always doing good deeds for people. In fact, it just then occurred to me to wonder why he hadn't already come over to our house and offered his help, being a nosy sort of boy. I guess all children are nosy. Or, if not precisely nosy, they want to know what's going on when there's something of note happening in the neighborhood. I'd been the same way. Well, I still was. I guess curiosity is a human trait.

"Be back in a minute or two," I told everyone, as I began my return trudge to the house. I hoped there would be enough daylight left for Sam and me to plant those rosebushes after the men and Pudge got the bone situation taken care of.

Pudge appeared at his front door even before I knocked at it. "Miss Daisy!" he said brightly, trying to peer over my shoulder in hopes of seeing something fascinating across the street where the police cars still stood.

"Oh, Pudge, you're *just* the person I wanted to see," I told him, making his freckled face beam with joy and happiness.

"Pudge Wilson, what's going on? I told you not— Oh, Daisy!" Mrs. Wilson came into view behind her son. "I wouldn't let Pudge go over there and bother you when we saw the police cars and Dr. Benjamin's car. I wasn't sure…Well, you know."

"Yes, thank you. But my father's fine."

Pressing a hand to her heart, Mrs. Wilson said, "I'm so glad to hear it!"

"See, Ma? I told you it would be okay," said Pudge, not sounding awfully respectful toward his mother.

"I'm glad you didn't come over before, Pudge," I said, as sternly as I deemed appropriate. "We were terribly busy. You see, when Sam and I went out to plant rosebushes in the backyard, Spike and…well, a cat belonging to Mr. Prophet found some bones way far back in the unused section of the yard. That's why the police and Dr. Benjamin were there. They're trying to figure out how someone's bones got in our yard."

"Good heavens!" cried Mrs. Wilson.

"Wow! That's the berries!" cried Pudge.

"Just bones?" asked Mrs. Wilson. "Not a body?"

"Just bones. It was really annoying," I said. "But we're stuck with having to deal with them now."

"What on earth do you need Pudge for?" Mrs. Wilson sounded as if she considered her son worthless, but I don't think she meant it that way.

"Dr. Benjamin says we have to keep the bones together and dry, so we need to build a tent over the section of ground where they're buried. That is to say, they weren't actually buried."

"I beg your pardon?" Mrs. Wilson appeared confused, which made sense to me.

"Evidently, whoever belonged to the bones wasn't buried. He just ended up in that spot and got covered with dirt somehow."

"Wow," breathed Pudge.

"Good gracious," said Mrs. Wilson.

"Anyhow," I went on, "one of the policemen said he used to be a Boy Scout and could probably make a tent out of tarpaulins and tent stakes if Sam gets some at the hardware store, and I thought maybe Pudge could help him."

Swirling around to face his mother, Pudge said, "Oh, can I, Ma? Please? *Please?*"

"Well, I suppose if they need your help, you may go. But don't get in the way, and be sure you *help!*"

"I will!" Pudge promised.

Something else occurred to me. "We'll need a smaller tent on the back porch to keep the bones Dr. Benjamin has identified as those belonging to a human being dry and together. Sam thought he'd buy one at the hardware store, but do you have one? I know you go camping sometimes with your troop."

"Yeah!" said Pudge happily. "It's not very big."

"I don't think it needs to be awfully big. It just needs to sit on the back porch and keep the bones dry if it happens to rain."

"Hope we don't get any heavy winds," said Mrs. Wilson, who was prone to worrying about things. Mind you, our Santa Ana Winds were worth worrying about, but they generally happened in the autumn.

"I hope not," I said.

Pudge had already run off, I presumed to fetch his tent.

"You're doing me a huge favor, Daisy," said Mrs. Wilson. "Pudge has been driving me crazy, begging me to let him go over and see what's going on at your house across the street. I was about ready to…what does that older funny man say? Hogtie him?"

"Sounds like Mr. Prophet, all right," I said with a sigh.

"Yes, well, I was about ready to hogtie Pudge to his bed, although he'd probably just be able to pick at the knots and get out anyway."

I laughed. "He really takes his Boy Scout duties to heart, doesn't he?"

"When it suits him," Mrs. Wilson said darkly. "He had no interest in helping his father prune the roses in our backyard today. We made him do it anyway. He's only interested in doing things that will earn him merit badges."

"Sounds like a regular kid to me," I said.

"I suppose," said Mrs. Wilson.

Pudge came huffing up to us, carrying a large rolled-up piece of canvas, out of the ends of which sticks protruded. "The tent stakes are inside the tent," he said.

"Thanks, Pudge. And thank you, Mrs. Wilson. I really appreciate this."

"Well, don't let him bother you. He's going to your place to help, not interfere."

"I won't interfere," said Pudge, indignant.

"I'm sure you'll be a big help, Pudge." Over my shoulder, I grinned at Mrs. Wilson. "You're already helping by allowing us to borrow your tent."

Mrs. Wilson probably would have rolled her eyes if she did things like that. Instead, she shook her head and told me softly, "Good luck."

"Thanks."

So Pudge and I walked across the street to Sam's and my house, and Pudge took off at a gallop when I opened the back gate for him.

"Hey, Pudge," I heard Sam say. "What do you have there?"

So Pudge told Sam about the tent, Sam thanked him, and I finally got to where the police contingent was still working. Dr. Benjamin, smiling at Pudge, said, "Let's set this tent up on the porch. Then we can bring over the bones I've identified and lay them out in the tent." He turned to Sam. "You're going to try to find tenting for this huge piece of land?" He appeared skeptical. "And how will we attach the tent to the porch without making holes in the planking?"

"We can tie down the tent using the railings," Pudge said promptly. "We don't have to hammer them into the wood."

"Good idea, young man," said Dr. Benjamin.

Pudge's smile could brighten a dark day, which that day wasn't, but it was a big, big smile.

Shaking his head, Sam said, "I hope I can find enough tarpaulins to create something akin to a tent for the outdoor bones."

"I'll help fix up a tent when you come back, Detective Rotondo!" said a happy and excited Pudge, who looked as if he wanted to leap onto the dirt pile and start digging for bones. Bother. I hadn't asked Mrs. Wilson if he was wearing clothes that could be washed easily. I took in his plaid, long-sleeved shirt and dirty denim trousers and decided Mrs. Wilson wouldn't object if her son got dirtier. Getting dirty was one of the things boys were best at, from everything I'd ever heard about them.

"Thanks, Pudge," said Sam. He looked down at his own dirty clothes, shook his head and said, "Bother. Well, I don't suppose Mr. Hardin will be shocked to see a man in earth-stained trousers show up at his hardware store."

"I'm sure he won't." I got on my tiptoes and kissed Sam's cheek. "Is it all right with you if I just plant the roses? You'll have to cement the arbor into place, because I don't know how to do that."

"Sure. I'll be glad to get them planted today. I can cement the arbor into place any time. Doesn't have to be today."

"I'll help with the cement!" said an exultant Pudge. "I need to learn how to do that."

"You may help me when I'm ready to do the work," said Sam. "Don't try to do it without me."

"Aw, gee. All right."

"You've got enough to do, young man," said Dr. Benjamin, amused and trying not to sound like it. "We have a tent to erect on the back porch."

"Oh, that's right!" Pudge perked right up.

Sam and I turned and began walking back to the house. I swear, we must have put in fifty miles already that day. "You sure you want kids?" Sam asked as we walked. He took my hand and squeezed it, so I knew he was only kidding. I think.

"Maybe girls," I said.

"I'm Italian. I've got to have at least one son if I expect my family ever to talk to me again," he told me.

"Do you care if your family ever talks to you again?" I asked. I think I was kidding, too.

"No," said Sam. He *wasn't* kidding that time. I could tell.

NINE

At any rate, we got two Cecile Brunner rosebushes planted on Saturday. Sam helped plant the second one. As Spike wasn't there, I didn't have to keep the bag of bone meal on the porch railing so he wouldn't take off with it. I don't know why that dog adores bone meal so much, but he does.

After Harold and Mr. Prophet finished the dishes, Harold went home, and Mr. Prophet went to his cottage in the back of our property.

"Leg's hurtin' me. Gonna rest it for a while."

"Yuyu will probably be happy to help you rest," I said, thinking how nice pets were.

"Huh," said Mr. Prophet.

Honestly, though, now that I knew I was going to get Spike back, I positively *ached* with the missing of him. I hoped Pa wouldn't have the same problem.

But no. I'd get him a replacement for Spike.

What a dreadful thing to say! How can you replace one loved one with another? You can't. I loved my Billy with all my heart, but Sam wasn't a replacement. I loved Sam with all my heart, too. It's astonishing how much love a heart can hold, isn't it?

So why are people so mean to each other? Oh, never mind. Unanswerable question, I guess.

The telephone rang as soon as Mr. Prophet grunted another, this time inaudible, comment to my suggestion about Yuyu, so I went to answer it. "Rotondo residence," said I. Every time I said my new name, I felt a little trickle of happiness.

"Oh, Daisy, Keiji told me about your call, and I have *just* the dog for you!"

"Mrs. Bissel! How good of you to return my call. And you say you have a dog of the right age? That's astonishing!"

"Not really. My Rosebud had her third litter three months ago, so the pups are weaned, and I'd planned to find her a good home anyway. I'll have her spayed, so she can't have anymore litters. Can't over-breed these sweet ladies, because it isn't good for them to have too many litters."

"Um…I'm not familiar with that term. What does it mean to have her spayed?" I asked, feeling stupid.

"You're not the only one unfamiliar with the term and the process," said Mrs. B with great vigor and a good deal of disapproval in her voice. "People don't seem to care *how* many puppies one poor bitch is expected to bear. But we *responsible* breeders care very much." She paused to suck in air. Evidently, this was a topic close to her heart. "Of course, not very many veterinarians are equipped to do the procedure, either. What it entails is removing the female's ovaries and uterus."

"Good lord, isn't that a serious operation? I don't want to hurt the poor thing!"

"Nonsense. It's more humane than over-breeding is. For a male dog, the veterinarian will castrate him."

I grimaced. Good thing Mrs. Bissel couldn't see me. "I see," I said. My voice squeaked a little bit, so I cleared my throat. "And you say the operation isn't difficult for the dog?"

"Poor Rosebud will be sore for a couple of days, but dogs are wonderful in that they recuperate *very* quickly. She'll be right as rain a week after the operation. Probably sooner, actually."

"My goodness. I had no idea."

With a heavy and heartfelt sigh, Mrs. Bissel repeated, "Most people don't. But big-animal veterinarians have been castrating cattle for generations. It's how we get the beef we eat. From steers, which are castrated males. The intact ones are the bulls, and you usually don't want more than one bull to a herd, because they tend to gore each other."

"Oh." I squeaked again, this time getting a chuckle in reaction.

"Don't fear for the animals, Daisy. I wish we'd do the same thing to some humans I can think of."

Recalling Mrs. Pinkerton and her two children, I thought how much better the world would have been if Mrs. P had been spayed after giving birth to Harold. Anastasia "Stacy" Kincaid would never have been born to blight the earth with her evil presence.

"Yes," I said musingly, "So can I."

Then, both of us laughing, we said, "*Stacy!*" together over the telephone wires. Hope whatever operator might be listening in on our call, should one be doing so, didn't damage her eardrums.

"Oh, dear. Well, if you're sure Rosebud won't mind getting… what was it? Spayed?"

"Yes. S-p-a-y. That's what the process is called for the ladies. She won't mind at all, especially because I aim to pet her constantly as she recovers."

"This is very nice of you, Mrs. Bissel. How much do you want for Rosebud?"

"For *you?*" She sounded shocked. "Absolutely nothing! I can't think of a better home for one of my retirees."

"Oh, but I can't just take the dog," I said, feeling guilty again. It doesn't take much to make me feel guilty. "You breed spectacular dachshunds. Mrs. Hanratty told me so. They're worth more than nothing!"

"Well, of course, they are," agreed Mrs. Bissel. "But good homes —homes I *know* are good—and people I trust are priceless. So you may not give me any money, Mrs. Rotondo." She sounded firm. Sort of like granite, in fact.

Just as I was about to give in and accept her gift—although I didn't feel right about it—a brilliant idea struck me. Have I mentioned how many brilliant ideas I get on an everyday basis? A ton, is how many. Few actually turn out to be brilliant in the long run, but I had hopes for this one.

"But wait a minute! May I perform a séance for you in return for Rosebud? At least bring over the Ouija board and tarot cards and do a reading or something of that nature?"

"Are you going to continue with your job now that you've remarried? Most of us, while we were extremely happy that you and your nice detective found each other, didn't think you'd continue working."

"Really?" My day, which was already sort of bright, with a few bones thrown in, suddenly became brighter. "Actually, I had planned to retire from doing so much work as a spiritualist, but I'll be happy to accommodate my special clients, and you are at the top of the special-clients list."

"Oh, how sweet you are, Daisy," said Mrs. B.

"Nonsense. I'll be happy to work for you, Mrs. Bissel."

"Hmm. In that case, why don't I get a séance party together? Dr. Van der Hoof is equipped to do the spay operation, and I'm sure you want to get Rosebud to your father as soon as possible so you can get your precious Spike back—"

"Oh, yes!" I said, interrupting her, which was impolite, but I did *so* want my Spike back.

She didn't mind. "I understand completely. In that case, why don't I make arrangements with Dr. Van der Hoof to spay Rosebud? And can you perform the séance on, let's say…Oh, how about next Friday at eight? If he can accommodate Rosie on Monday, she'll be well enough for you to take home on Friday evening after the séance."

"She doesn't need any more time to heal than…" I had to count on my fingers. I know. Math isn't my strong suit. "…four days?"

"No. You're taking her to your father, aren't you? And he's retired, so he can keep her quiet at home, can't he?"

"Yes, he can," I said, my eyes tearing up as I considered

Rosebud and my father meeting each other. If Spike didn't kill her overnight. Séances lasted a long time, and Pa would be asleep in bed by the time I brought Rosebud home with me. But if Spike could make friends with Yuyu, he certainly wouldn't mind pretty little Rosebud. I hoped.

Oh, but wait. Rosebud would be with us and Spike would be across the street. My heart squished for a second. I wanted my dog *now*. Ah well.

"Then it's all settled," said Mrs. Bissel. "Oh, this is wonderful. Rosie's black and tan like Spike, by the way."

"I'm so glad! I like the looks of the black-and-tan dachshunds better than the solid red ones."

"So do I," said Mrs. Bissel. "Rosebud is a little over three years old, if that matters."

"Perfect," I said. "I didn't want Pa to have to fuss with a puppy, so a three-year-old will be great."

"Yes, I think you're correct."

"Thank you *so* much, Mrs. Bissel. See you Friday at a little before eight."

"Excellent. Rosebud will be waiting for you."

We said our farewells, and I hung up feeling I'd accomplished *two* worthwhile things that day. Sam and I had not only planted our roses, but I'd finagled a dog for my father.

Sam was as pleased as I was about getting Spike back. That's only partially because he liked Spike a lot. He adored my father (and me), and he knew we'd both be crushed if Spike got…well, crushed.

"I'm going to get cleaned up," said Sam after I'd given him the good news. "Is there more sandwich stuff for dinner, or do you have other plans?"

Sam was terrifically kind about my kitchen inadequacies. He knew I had a reputation as probably the worst cook in Pasadena, but he'd married me anyway and even said he'd hire a cook for us if I wanted one. I didn't. Well, Mrs. Rattle cooked for us sometimes.

Very well, that's a lie. I did want a cook. But I didn't want to admit it. So I'd declined his offer to hire a full-time cook and promised I'd learn to cook. By the time we found those stupid bones, I was able to fix a relatively decent breakfast, which was a step in the right direction.

"Nope. I can fix sandwiches. There's still cut bread in waxed paper in the bread box, and there's still chicken salad and…and… well, I don't know. I can pick more oranges, if you don't mind a sandwich and an orange."

"I don't mind at all," he said, giving me a big hug and reminding me that not only did *he* need a bath, but so did I. That's not disparaging to either one of us. We'd worked hard that day, and most of the work had been outside in the dirt.

The telephone rang just as Sam started upstairs to take his bath. He answered it and, by golly, from what I heard him say, Vi was inviting us over to the house across the street for dinner!

What a lucky day this had been. Well, except for the bones.

"Why don't you go out back and invite Lou to dinner—at Vi's request," said Sam. "I'll go up and take a bath."

"Okay," I said, not awfully enthusiastically. Mr. Prophet was always saying mean things to me, especially about my paucity of cooking skills.

With a chuckle, Sam said, "Don't let Lou get you down. He only annoys you because you show that he's annoying you."

"If you say so," I said. Then, I heaved a sigh and said, "All right. Here I go." I headed for the back door.

"And here I go." Sam headed upstairs.

By then, it had become fairly dark, so I took my trusty flashlight with me. I was careful walking across the lawn and through the arbor, because the arbor was just kind of sitting there in a couple of holes. Sam would probably cement it into place after church on the morrow.

As I approached Lou's little house, I heard voices. Turning off my flashlight, I stood behind an orange tree and listened. If he was with his lady friend from down the street, I didn't want to disturb him. The noises I heard were in the nature of loving coos and so forth, and I *really* didn't want to barge in on an indelicate scene.

I listened harder. After a few seconds, I realized what was going on.

"Who's a good kitty?"

Purr, purr, purr.

"That's right. Yuyu's a good kitty. He found them bones and just dug 'em up, didn't he?"

Purr, purr, purr.

"And you didn't let that ol' dog chase you away, neither."

Purr, purr, purr.

"Now, Spike ain't a *bad* dog, but you sure put him in his place, didn't you? Yes, you did, you good kitty, you."

Purr, purr, purr.

"You can dig more bones tomorrow if you want to."

Purr, purr, purr.

Oh, boy, did I have Mr. Lou Prophet precisely where I wanted him, or did I not?

I did, by golly!

So I turned the flashlight back on and strolled up the paved walkway to the cottage. When he saw the light, Mr. Prophet gave a start as if he'd been stung by a hornet. "What the hell?" he bellowed.

Yuyu, unaccustomed to having his peace interrupted so violently, leaped off Mr. Prophet's lap, evidently using a claw or two, because Mr. Prophet said, "Ow! God dammit, cat! What the devil are *you* doing, sneakin' up on me, Miss Daisy?" He wasn't wearing his wooden leg, and he'd propped his crutch against the rocking chair in which he'd been sitting with Yuyu.

"I didn't *sneak*. I had my flashlight with me and was walking firmly on the cement pathway. I can't help it if you're deaf in one ear and can't hear out of the other!" That's a line he'd used on me a time or two when I'd asked for clarification about one of his old-western sayings.

"You scared the cat," he said grumpily.

"What do you care? It's not *your* cat, after all. No matter that you were cooing to it like a lover not ten seconds ago."

"Was not!"

"Were too!"

"Dammit!"

"Stop swearing. Vi just called and asked us all to dinner across the street. There's still the makings for chicken sandwiches in the Frigidaire and the breadbox if you'd rather not bestir yourself, but you'll get a better meal if you walk across the street with us."

He sat in the rocking chair, glowering at me, for several seconds. I suppose Yuyu had been too badly spooked to return to the porch, because he was nowhere to be seen. At long last, Mr. Prophet said, "Aw, hell, I'll go across the street with you. I'll get a good meal that way, at least."

"Yes, you will. And I'll tell Vi that you graciously accepted her invitation."

"Don't tell nobody about me talkin' to the cat, all right?"

Mr. Prophet, former bounty hunter, western frontiersman, womanizer, expert marksman, and one-time Confederate soldier, actually sounded scared that I might tell on him. Good.

"I won't let on that underneath your leathery skin and rock-like heart, you have a soft spot for that mangy old cat," I told him.

"Ain't mangy, and he ain't old. He's just had a rough life, is all."

Recalling my conversation with Mrs. Bissel, I said musingly, "We probably should get him castrated so he won't run around impregnating all the female cats in the neighborhood."

By gracious, Mr. Lou Prophet *blushed*. I could hardly believe my eyes.

"No need for that," he said, still blushing. "When I took him to the vet, he did it then. Said he pretty much had to, the cat being in the shape he was. Poor guy. Cut off in his prime."

"Oh, brother. Unlike you, who probably have children scattered all over the United States."

"Do not."

"How do *you* know?"

My question stopped him with his mouth open. We'd had discussions before about the careless way men of his stamp wantonly scattered their seed all over the place without considering the consequences. That's because they didn't have to *face* the consequences. The poor women they were with did, and then they were labeled with vicious, demeaning names by the very men who used them so casually.

At last he said, "Aw, hell, I'll get ready to go with you and Sam."

"Thank you," I said. Then I turned and went back to the house.

I could hardly wait to tell Sam about Mr. Prophet speaking sweet words of love to his stupid cat!

TEN

L est you think I'm a terrible, awful, blabbermouth of a human being, I didn't tell anyone except Sam about the interchange I witnessed—well, heard—between Mr. Lou Prophet and his cat. Sam and I both had a good laugh, but I wasn't going to be a tattle-tale. Mr. Prophet had saved my life too many times and was old and decrepit and didn't deserve to be laughed at or about. Except by Sam and me.

We had a delicious dinner at my parents' house. Vi fixed us pork chops, potatoes, apple salad and a spice cake for dessert.

After deliberating with myself and my conscience all during dinner, I told my father about my plan to get him a young but grown-up dachshund named Rosebud and take Spike to live with Sam and me. I was about to go to great lengths in my explanation, but Pa interrupted me.

"Thanks, Daisy! I've been worried ever since we came home today about Spike getting out and haring across the street to look for more bones and his cat friend."

"We were worried about the same thing. I'm so glad you don't mind!" I said, weak with relief.

"Mind? Why should I mind? Spike's your dog. I figured I'd just

90

give Spike back to you." Pa continued, "Didn't think I'd get a dog of my own, but I'm glad. I'll miss Spike when he's gone."

"Oh heck, you need a pet. Everyone needs a pet." I tried not to glance at Mr. Prophet, but couldn't resist. He was in the process of glowering at me as he forked up a piece of spice cake. I had him at my mercy, and the old rogue was absolutely petrified I'd rat him out about the cat. "And Rosebud sounds as if she'll be perfect. She's black and tan like Spike, and she's three years old. Mrs. Bissel is retiring her as a breeding bitch."

"Daisy!" said my mother, shocked by me saying the "B" word, I suppose.

"Not my fault, Ma. That's what breeders call them. Let's just say Rosebud is retiring after successfully rearing three families."

"What with Spike being right across the street, what's to prevent her from getting more *families*?" Mr. Prophet asked in a snide-sounding voice. I'm surprised he dared, given what I'd heard from him not an hour earlier and how terrified he was that I'd spill the beans on him.

"Mrs. Bissel is taking her to get spayed on Monday. So Spike won't have any say in the matter."

A discussion ensued about the value of spaying female animals, but it didn't last long, my mother being of a sensitive nature when it came to discussing bodily functions and so forth.

"Well, thanks, Daisy. I appreciate it a lot. You'd better take Spike home with you tonight, in case he manages to sneak out when someone opens the side door or something."

My heart leaped in my chest and began dancing with joy. "Oh, *thank* you, Pa! I thought I'd have to wait until next Saturday to get him!"

"Why Saturday?" asked Vi. "I thought Ms. Bissel was going to take the new dog to the veterinarian on Monday."

"She is, but I offered to perform a séance for her in return for Rosebud. She wanted to give her to me, but I didn't want to take a valuable dog and give her nothing in return. I don't mind performing séances at her place, because she's not an idiot like—" I stopped speaking before I could disparage Mrs. Pinkerton in front of my mother.

Pa, Sam and Vi laughed. Mr. Prophet didn't, and Ma looked scoldingly at me. "It's not nice to call people names, Daisy."

"I didn't call anyone anything. I just said I don't like doing séances for idiots. I didn't say whom I considered the idiot."

"Still…"

"And if you know whose name I was going to say, you must know as well as I do that she's an idiot," I went on.

My mother's lips pruned up, but she didn't say anything else. I guess she figured she'd lost that one, which she had. I wasn't the only one in our household who had been bedeviled by Mrs. Pinkerton and her hysterics. When I'd been hit by a car and nearly killed a little over a year earlier, Pa finally had to take the receiver off the hook in the kitchen because she'd called so often and disturbed us so many times.

"Anyhow, the séance will take place on Friday night, and I won't get home until late, so that's why I figured I'd have to wait until Saturday to get Spike."

"Ah, no," said Pa. "Just take him with you tonight."

It was a happy Daisy Gumm Majesty Rotondo who snapped the leash on her dog's collar and set out to walk across the street that night. Sam collected Spike's food and water bowls. Vi packed some of the scraps she'd saved for his meals into another bowl, covered it with waxed paper, and Sam carried that, too. We always had some broken biscuit-type food we got from Dr. Van der Hoof, so I collected a sack of that from the back porch and carried it in one hand and Spike's leash in the other.

"I'll ask Mr. Larkin if he has any chopped horsemeat, too," said Vi as she saw us off at the front door of the house. "And why don't you stop by Dr. Van der Hoof's place and get some more of that broken-biscuit-type food for…what was the dog's name? Roselyn?"

"Rosebud," I said. "I'll do that. Thanks, Vi, and thanks for dinner. It was delicious."

"You're more than welcome, sweetie," said my wonderful aunt.

"Um, will Spike be able to climb the stairs at your place?" asked Pa, who'd come out onto the front porch.

I stopped in my tracks, still clutching a sack and a dog leash, and looked at Sam, who'd also stopped.

"Oh, dear," I said. "He probably shouldn't climb those stairs, should he?"

"Probably not," said Sam.

"Well..." But I guess Pa didn't know what more to say, because his words petered out.

"Hell, why don't you just set up that room downstairs as a bedroom?" asked Lou Prophet. "You're not usin' it for anything except a spare room. You can use the room upstairs as a spare."

"Brilliant suggestion!" I said. Then I wished I hadn't. Lou Prophet could be a major thorn in my side, and I think I'd just negated my hold over him by pronouncing his idea brilliant. Darn.

"We'll discuss it tomorrow," said Sam. "We'll take him outside to do his duty tonight, and I'll carry him upstairs. Then we'll figure out what to do. I might just build him a ramp to the upstairs. I like the room up there." He shook his head. "Never thought my living arrangements would be dictated by a dog."

We all laughed. I even heard Mr. Prophet's rusty chuckle.

Spike was elated to come home with us. Naturally, he wanted to go out back and dig more bones, but we'd thwarted that endeavor even before he attempted it. Not only had Sam, Pudge and the three remaining policemen placed tarpaulins over the boneyard, but they'd also hammered together a board fence around the area, so Spike couldn't get in. I'm sure Yuyu could jump onto the fence—it was only about four feet tall—but Spike's short legs couldn't make the leap.

He didn't complain, though. He dashed out the back door and rushed over to where he'd spent several happy hours with Yuyu digging up bones, but he came to a screeching halt at the fence. He sniffed it from one end to the other, found no way to breach the fortress, then figuratively shrugged his shoulders and trotted off in another direction. Dogs are so much superior to human beings in that regard. They don't fret and fuss. They just do something else if their original plans are frustrated.

Sam was as good as his word. He carried Spike upstairs when it was time for bed, and he even carried him downstairs in the middle of the night when Spike indicated he'd like to use the outdoor facilities. I absolutely adored my husband. And my dog.

The following day, Sunday, Sam and I had breakfast before church. I actually cooked it! And it didn't burn! I cut holes in three slices of bread, buttered them, laid them on the griddle on the range and broke an egg into each hole. I didn't break a single yolk. So we had what Vi calls "eggs in a nest" for breakfast that Sunday, and I only singed the outer edges of one piece of fried bread. I ate that one. Even with the singeing it tasted good. Vi'd sent home some slices of ham, so I warmed those up, too. We always had oranges for breakfast.

"Delicious, Daisy," said Sam, pleasing me greatly.

Spike, who sat at our feet, said nothing, but I know he was disappointed not to get anything to eat. So I tossed him a little bite of ham. He appreciated it.

Peering down at my wonderful dog, I asked, "What shall we do with Spike while we're at church?"

"Heck, he was at our wedding in the church, maybe he should just come with us."

"I don't think Pastor Smith would like that much," I said, wishing my words weren't true. "He was nice about Harold and Mr. Prophet sneaking him into the church for our wedding, but I don't think he'd approve if Spike started coming regularly."

"You're probably right." Sam glanced down at Spike. "Sorry, Spike. No religion for you."

Spike wagged his tail. I'm sure that's not a commentary on the state of his spiritual innards. He just liked people to talk to him.

"Vi asked us—and, of course, Mr. Prophet—to have dinner after church today, so maybe Spike can stay at the house across the street while we're at church."

"That might work," said Sam, "as long as he doesn't race across the street as soon as we come home from church."

"Hmm. That's true." Gazing at my hound, I said, "I never thought you'd be a problem child, Spike, but I fear you are."

"Maybe he's not," said Sam, being kinder than I. "You took him to the obedience place. If you tell him to s-t-a-y when we leave either house, he'll probably s-t-a-y."

It was prudent to spell things out if you were talking about Spike, because he knew a *lot* of words. "Hmm," I said again. "You may be right, although I'd hate to have to trust his memory for two hours or so."

"Aw," said Sam, leaning over to pet Spike, who appreciated it. "Your mommy doesn't trust you, Spike!"

"I do, too, trust him! Just not to remember a command for hours on end."

"Well," said Sam judiciously. "He's a pal of Yuyu's. Maybe Lou can keep him over at his place. Providing he's going to be there and doesn't go down the street to dally with Miss Li."

"Great idea! Even if Mr. Prophet leaves, there's no way Spike can get out of the backyard because it's completely fenced in."

"There you go," said Sam. "Leave some water on the back porch for him and…Crumb. What about Dr. Benjamin's bones?"

"Oh, dear. I forgot about those bones. If we tie the flap to the tent closed and tell the dog not to go in, he'll probably obey. He's a very obedient dog."

"Will he obey for two hours?" Sam asked doubtfully.

"I think he will, because it will be a specific command. It won't be just, 'Don't leave the house,' or something like that. We'll show him the tent and emphasize the fact that he's not allowed to rip it to shreds in order to pillage and plunder. He no longer chews up shoes, because he's been told specifically not to chew shoes. He's smarter than the average dog, after all."

"I guess you're right. Maybe we can block off that part of the porch, too."

"With what?"

"Good question. I don't have a supply of cement blocks to hand."

"No, but we have chairs. Maybe we can make a kind-of fence with chairs and tell him not to mess with them."

Quirking one of his black eyebrows, Sam said, "You think a fence of chairs will work?"

"I don't know," I said with a massive sigh. "But we can at least try."

So we did. First we went to Mr. Prophet's cottage and found him sitting in his rocking chair on the porch with Yuyu on his lap. Spike was ecstatic to see his feline friend, and Yuyu seemed equally pleased to see Spike. Mr. Prophet didn't appear similarly happy.

"I ain't goin' to church with you, so don't even ask," he said as a greeting.

"We aren't here to ask you to go to church with us," I barked. Which seemed appropriate under the circumstances. Yuyu had jumped down from Mr. Prophet's lap and he and Spike were chasing each other all over the small yard to Mr. Prophet's cottage. "We wanted to ask if Spike can stay here with you and Yuyu while we go to church. If you need to leave your house, just be sure Spike doesn't escape, and lock the gate behind you. We'll leave a bowl of water on our back porch. Is that too much to ask, Your Highness?"

"No need to get snippy," said the old villain. "Yeah, sure. Spike and Yuyu are pals. I'll make sure they don't get into the bones."

"Thanks, Lou. Appreciate it," said Sam. He said it quickly, before I could spill any words from my open mouth. It was probably just as well.

"Yes," I said instead of what I'd been about to say, which wasn't very nice, "thank you."

"Sure," said Mr. P. "Ain't poisoned Sam yet, I see," he added. He would.

"Daisy prepared a lovely breakfast for me this morning, Lou. Eggs, toast and ham."

"Huh. Better'n what I had."

"If you weren't so mean to me about my cooking, I might invite you for a meal once in a while," I said. Snippily, I'm sure I need not add.

"Thanks, but think I'll wait to take you up on that invite. If Sam's still alive in a month or two, I'll chance it. Maybe."

"And maybe you won't ever get an invitation to chance it!" I snarled. "You beastly old man."

Mr. Lou Prophet laughed so hard, he scared Yuyu and Spike, both of whom dashed up onto the porch to see what was the matter.

"You drive me crazy," I muttered as I turned to walk away.

Sam was laughing when he caught up with me.

It was a grumpy Daisy Gumm Majesty Rotondo who walked with her family to church that day. My grumpiness didn't prevent me from singing a lovely duet with Mrs. Albert (Lucy) Zollinger during the second verse of "Heralds of Christ," a dramatic hymn and one of my favorites.

ELEVEN

Dinner at my parents' house was, as ever, wonderful. Because it was winter and cool, Vi had put a beef roast in the oven to cook while we were at church. It was *so* good. What's more, Vi sent me home with specific instructions on how to prepare a pot roast of my own. It was worth a try, I guess. I didn't want to waste Sam's money, but that was a darned tasty roast and I might give it a go.

Lord, you'd think I was aiming to burn down the house! I really needed to get over my fear of the kitchen.

On Monday, Sam went off to work, and a couple of policemen came to the house to continue digging up bones in the back forty. Shortly after I'd let the policemen into the house, dear Mrs. Rattle showed up.

"Good morning, Daisy!" she said. She was about the jolliest woman I'd ever met. Her son, Officer Doan, didn't seem to have inherited her chipper spirit. On the other hand, his job had him chasing after criminals and locking them up all day, every day, and that probably took some of the fun out of life.

"Good morning," I said back at her. "I'm so glad we have you to clean for us."

"Nonsense. I enjoy getting out of my own house and doing this and that in other people's houses. And I do love your new home."

"Thank you. Sam and I love it, too."

"Stephen told me about the bones," she said on a more somber note. "That must have been a shock."

"It definitely was." I thought of something even more important than bones. "Oh, but Mrs. Rattle, come and see what my pal Harold brought me on Saturday. It's fragile, and I haven't quite figured out where to put it. Maybe you can think of a good place. But hang your stuff up first," I said, helping to relieve her of her coat and hat and hang them on the rack beside the front door.

She fell in love with the lamp, as was about the only thing a person *could* do with that fabulous peacock lamp.

"I've never seen anything so beautiful in my life, Daisy!" she exclaimed, her hands clasped to her bosom. "It looks wonderful there on the piano."

"It does, doesn't it?" I said, a trifle hesitant. "The only reason I don't want to leave it there is that someone might knock it over when we gather around the piano and sing. We like to do that."

"Put it in the closet when you have friends over," suggested Mrs. Rattle in a no-nonsense voice. "That's what I do with my good things when my grandchildren visit. I love them with my whole heart, but I won't have them breaking my precious keepsakes, either."

"What a great idea!" I said, wondering why I hadn't thought of something so perfect and simple. Oh well.

"Ha," said she. "I don't know how great it is. I've probably been around more ruffianly children than you have, is all."

"You're probably right."

"Well, then, I'll get to work," said the redoubtable Mrs. Rattle. "Will you be locked in your sewing room as usual, Daisy?"

I recalled wanting to visit the library to research what, if any, Indian tribes once called Pasadena home. Well, they wouldn't have called *Pasadena* home, but you know what I mean. "Actually, I do believe I'll take a trip to the library this morning," I told her.

"Oh, how nice. I know you love to read, because I find books all over the house when I clean."

"We're supposed to put them on the table beside the front door when we're finished reading them. I hope we're not leaving them in inappropriate places." What would an inappropriate place for a book be, anyway? I didn't ask.

"Good heavens, no!" said Mrs. Rattle with a laugh. "But I know both you and the good detective like to read in bed sometimes."

"True. Well, thanks, Mrs. Rattle. Just to be sure, I'll check the house for stray books before I leave."

She laughed again and headed toward the kitchen.

It was then I also recalled I'd asked Mr. Prophet if he wanted to go with me, darn it. But I wouldn't break my word, so I tramped back to his cottage. Spike had gone outside some time ago, probably to see if he could help excavate bones, but darned if I didn't find him in Mr. Prophet's yard rolling around with Yuyu! I'd never seen a dog and a cat play like that before. Mr. Prophet sat in his rocking chair, smoking one of his quirlies (cigarettes) and grinning at the cavorting pair.

"Those two are fun to watch, aren't they?" I asked as I approached the back porch. Tentatively, in case he wanted to say something mean to me.

"Yeah, they are," he said.

Encouraged by this mild response, I said, "Do you still want to visit the library with me this morning? I'm interested in finding out what Indians lived in this area, even if the bones out there aren't Indian bones."

"Yeah. I've got some books to return, so I'll get 'em. Want to leave the critters in the yard or what?"

"Good question. If I leave Spike outdoors, he might bother the men digging for bones."

"Might. Yuyu'll probably just watch 'em dig, but I ain't sure about Spike."

"Oh, I have an idea!" I said, having just had an idea. Funny how that happens, isn't it? "Why don't I take Spike to stay with Pa when

I get my family's to-be-returned books? That way Spike and Pa will each have a companion for a few hours."

"Good idea," said Mr. Prophet, who'd evidently decided to be pleasant to me for once. "I'll get my books and meet you across the street in a half-hour or so. That all right with you?"

"Absolutely," I said. Then I had to detach my dog from his playfellow, which wasn't too hard, and go inside again to get my own returnable books and clip Spike's leash to his collar.

At this point in my married life I didn't have my own personal automobile, but still drove the Chevrolet I'd bought for my parents to replace their old Model-T Ford. This worked out well for the most part, since Pa no longer cared to drive for fear he'd have a heart problem whilst behind the wheel. At one time he'd been a chauffeur to wealthy Pasadenans. He still loved to tinker with cars.

As luck would have it, Pa was sitting on the front porch chatting with Mr. Longnecker, a neighbor from down the street a house or two. They both greeted Spike and me, and I told Pa my errand on that lovely morning.

"So I came over here to take requests and pick up any books you want to return."

"Sounds like a good plan to me," said Pa.

Mr. Longnecker—don't tell anyone, but I think he was nagged a good deal by his wife—squinted at me. "Were there Indians in this part of the world? Joe was just telling me about the bones they're digging up in your yard."

I sighed heavily. "I don't know if there were Indians around here. That's one of the reasons I want to visit the library. As for the bones across the street, they aren't ancient bones. They're probably those of a young man who disappeared in this area about twenty years ago."

"Ah," said Mr. Longnecker. "I think I heard about that. Before our time in the neighborhood."

"You know where the books are, sweetheart," said Pa. "As for books, you know what I like. Any new Zane Greys or Edgar Wallaces or Burroughs. Love the *Tarzan* books, and his crazy out-of-this-world books are fun, too." He thought for a second or two.

"Actually, I wouldn't mind rereading the Sherlock Holmes stories again, come to think of it."

"I'll ask Regina," I told him. "I suspect they've been collected into a big fat volume by this time. At any rate, I'll get what they have."

"Thanks, sweetie. You know what your mother and aunt like to read."

"Same books as I like to read. Sam's much more of a fuddy-duddy. He likes historical tomes. Nonfiction historical tomes. I swear, the man knows more about history than a college professor. He's looking forward to reading about our Indians, if we ever had any."

With a chuckle, Pa said, "You've got yourself a good man there, Daisy."

"I know I do. He cemented our arbor into place yesterday afternoon so our Cecile Brunner roses will have something to climb on."

"What's that you say?" asked a suddenly interested Mr. Longnecker. "What kind of roses did you plant?"

"It's called Cecile Brunner. It's a pretty pink rose with tiny flowers that climb all over fences. I'm hoping ours will thrive and give us beautiful cascades of pink roses."

"Small buds, you say?"

"Yes. I'll be happy to pick up a book with pictures in it if you're interested. Or Mr. Liljenwall at the nursery can tell you all about them."

"Liljenwall, eh?"

"Are you the one who tends the gorgeous roses in your yard, Mr. Longnecker? I hadn't realized."

"I enjoy gardening," he said in a repressed-sounding voice. "Gets me out of the house and into the sunshine."

And away from Mrs. Longnecker. He didn't say that, but I could almost see the words in a caption over his head. Poor guy. His wife was kind of a fussy woman. Mind you, she'd had reason once or twice to be startled by goings-on in the Gumm-Majesty residence, especially when people took potshots at me, which didn't happen often. Truly.

"Ah, here comes Lou," said Pa, peering over my shoulder.

When I did likewise, I saw Mr. Prophet limping across the street with a bunch of books in his arms. "Yes. We decided to visit the library together today."

"I remember your conversation from Saturday," said my father with a grin. "What does he like to read?"

"Same kinds of books as Sam. The two of them should teach history lessons."

"That would be an exciting class," Pa said, laughing.

"Perhaps it would be," said Mr. Longnecker, who looked as if he wished he'd left before Mr. Prophet began walking his way.

For an old, wrinkled guy with one leg and a peg, Mr. Prophet could look rather savage if you didn't know him. Even if you did. Well, he'd lived a long and rough life. He'd earned his wrinkles. I'd never tell him so.

"Mornin', Joe. Mr. Longnecker," said Mr. Prophet politely as he limped up to the front porch.

"Good morning, Lou," said Pa.

"Good morning," said Mr. Longnecker, sounding scared.

"Daisy said you two are going to the library this fine morning."

"Yep. She's gonna look up Indians. Think I'll try to find a book about the Yukon. Always wanted to visit there, but never got the chance."

"Too cold for me," said Pa. "But I guess some folks found a lot of gold there in the old days."

"Yeah," said Mr. Prophet, sitting on one of the porch chairs.

Sam and I had bought my parents several chairs and a table for their enormous front porch shortly after we got home from our honeymoon. It was such a nice porch; it was a shame to have to sit on the stairs if you could sit on chairs.

"I'll be right back," I told the assembly. "I'm going to take the Chevrolet, Pa. That okay with you?"

"Of course it is. You bought it. You should be able to drive it whenever you want to," Pa said, laughing.

"Well, I never know when you'll need to go somewhere."

"I never need to go anywhere. If I need something, I'll just walk to the corner grocery."

This was true. Mr. and Mrs. Bennett ran a little dry goods and grocery store a couple of blocks away from our house. Vi generally brought food from Mrs. Pinkerton's house, where she cooked, but if we ever needed some potatoes or onions or a box of oatmeal or something, we'd get them from the Bennetts' store.

So I handed Pa Spike's leash and I went into the house, got the to-be-returned books from the table beside the front door, grabbed the keys to the car from where they hung on the coat rack on the other side of the door, and went back outside. Mr. Prophet got to his leg and his peg with a puff of air that wasn't quite a grunt.

"Need any help?" asked Mr. Longnecker. "I'll carry those books for you, Mrs. Rotondo."

"Thank you," I said, handing them over. It was quite a big pile. We all read a lot. Mr. Prophet's arms were already full with books of his own.

So he and I tootled off to the Pasadena Public Library. I *loved* our library. It was soon going to be replaced, and that made me sad. Very well, so perhaps Pasadena had grown big enough to require a larger library; still, our present library sat in a lovely park complete with a pond and a little white gazebo, and I thought it was a perfectly splendid library. I'd seen drawings of the new library being built, and it was all right. Extremely formal looking. *My* library was a cozy building. A little leaky perhaps when it rained, which I guess isn't a good thing for a library to be, but still…I'd miss it when it was gone.

"Gonna miss this place," said Mr. Lou Prophet when I pulled the Chevy up to the curb in front of the library.

I was lucky to find a parking spot so close to the entrance, because there were steps to climb. Of course, the *new* library would have even *more* steps, but…oh, never mind. It would still contain books, and I guess that was the important part about being a library.

"Yes. I will, too. I was just thinking about that. I'll bet the new library won't have a beautiful park and a pond and a gazebo."

"Expect it won't," said Mr. Prophet, shoving his door open.

"Let me help you, for Pete's sake. You don't have to be a hero any longer, you know."

"Never was no hero," he grumbled. "And I can carry my own books."

"All right then. Be stubborn. What do *I* care?"

"You care about too damned many things ain't none of your business," he snarled.

"Bother."

So I got out on the driver's side, walked around to the passenger side, and let Mr. Prophet struggle with his pile of books while I wrestled my own pile into submission. Shoot. I guess it had been a while since I'd gone to the library because we sure had a whole lot of books to return.

We didn't speak as we climbed the steps and walked along to the next set of steps leading to the library. Fortunately for both of us, somebody was leaving just as we arrived at the front door, and the kind soul held it open for us to enter.

"Thank you," I said, smiling.

"Thanks," said Mr. Prophet, not smiling.

"You're an old grouch, you know that, don't you?" I whispered to Mr. P as we walked across the library floor.

"Yeah. I like to be grouchy so you'll pick on me," he said.

"Bah."

We unburdened ourselves at the check-in table, and I shook out my arms as I peered toward the nook where Regina Browning (nee Petrie) generally sat. She wasn't there.

"Oh, nertz," I whispered.

"What's wrong?" asked Mr. Prophet.

"I don't see Regina Browning."

"She's probably helpin' somebody else. I'm going to look in the card catalogue."

"All right. I'll meet you at Regina's desk eventually."

"Right," said he. And off he clumped. He didn't make much noise, so nobody shushed him, which was a good thing. He couldn't help having a wooden leg, after all. If anyone *had* shushed him, I'd probably have told the shusher to be quiet and mind his own business and then Mr. Prophet would have become annoyed with *me*.

Golly, maybe I did care about stuff that wasn't my business, huh?

Well, never mind. I beheld Regina walking out of the stacks with a satisfied reader thanking her. We saw each other at the same time, so we waved and I didn't have to think about butting into other people's business for a little while.

TWELVE

"Indians? Native to the Pasadena region?" Regina appeared puzzled. "Why, I don't know. Let me look. There probably were Indians around here. I just don't know what the tribal name is. Or was."

"Probably was," I said. "We didn't treat any Indians too kindly when we took over their land, did we?"

"I guess not," she said. "As you know, I'm from Oklahoma, and we white Oklahomans didn't seem to treat *anybody* nicely."

"Yes. Sam told me about what I read in the newspaper as race riots were actually the bombing out of a Negro section of Tulsa."

"Yes. Shameful," said Regina.

We'd made it to the card catalogue—fortunately, the library had two or three card catalogues, so we didn't bump into Mr. Prophet—and Regina began flipping through cards. "Aha. Here we are," she said, smiling.

"We are?" I squinted at the card she'd poked into place. "What does that say?"

"Gabrielinos and Tongvas. The Tongva lived in this area."

"I've, uh, never even heard of the Gabrielino or Tongva Indians."

"That's not unusual," said Regina. "When you look at our history, you'll see that most of the Indian names remaining are those of cities, lakes, rivers, streets or whatever. The Indians themselves have all been packed off to reservations."

"That's exactly what Sam told me," I said, feeling depressed on behalf of Indians everywhere. Well, the American kind. And perhaps the Indians in India, too, since their homeland had been overrun by the British a few hundred years back.

"It's true," said Regina. "Robert loves history, and he's done a good deal of reading about various Indian groups. Their history is sad, no matter which tribes you read about."

"That's what Mr. Prophet said, too."

"I don't know if we have any books about the Tongva Indians here in the library, but Robert and I recently visited the Southwest Museum. They're sure to have relics and information about them, although I don't actually recall. But let me check. The Gabrielinos and Tongvas might be included in a general book about Indians." She riffled through a few more cards. "Ah, yes. Let's take a look at the 970s. American Indians are in 970.1."

"Oh, I can look," I offered. "You don't need to take time away from other patrons."

"What other patrons?" she asked, glancing around the almost-empty library.

I looked, too. She was right. "Good. Let's go look for Indians in the stacks, and I can tell you all about what happened on Saturday!"

Lifting a hand to her cheek, she said, "Oh, Daisy, don't tell me you found another dead body!" She whispered, mind you, as we were in the library.

I shook my head, wishing everyone I knew didn't automatically connect me with dead bodies when I told them something unusual had happened in my life. "No. Sam and I were planting roses at the time, actually. It was Spike and Mr. Prophet's cat, Yuyu, who found the bones of the dead guy. But he wasn't recently dead."

Regina stopped walking so abruptly, I strolled right past her until I realized she was no longer at my side. So I turned to find her gaping at me, aghast. I'd been aghast myself several times recently, so I recognized the symptoms.

"Um," I said. "I can explain."

Shaking her head and walking up to rejoin me, Regina said, "Please do."

By the way, Regina and I were both newlyweds, more or less. Regina and her Robert married a few months before Sam and I did. But lest you think we hadn't told each other about our respectful bliss and honeymoons, etc., we had. Often. That's why we weren't chatting about marriage but Indians today. Well…bones was another reason.

I told her the bones story, adding, "According to people who live in the neighborhood, a young man disappeared there some years back. Twenty-some years ago. We think maybe these bones belonged to him."

"Oh, dear. That's sad. What was his name?"

I shrugged. "Nobody seems to recall. I thought I'd look in the newspaper archives, but no one can give me an approximate date of his disappearance either."

"That does make it difficult, doesn't it?"

"Yes. Anyhow, when the dog and cat showed up with the bones they found, I originally wondered if they might be really ancient. That's the reason I became interested in what, if any, Indians lived in these parts before we came here and drove them out."

"I see. That makes sense. You know Oklahoma, my home state, used to be known as Indian Territory because the Federal Government set aside land for various Indian tribes. That lasted until settlers wanted the land and shoved the natives out." She shook her head. "People just don't seem to be able to get along with each other, do they? Well, unless they're alike in color, religion, customs, and so forth."

"True."

We'd made it to the 970s, so Regina ran her fingers over a row of books. "Ah. Maybe this will help you. It's *The Spanish Pioneers and the California Indians*, by Mr. Charles Lummis. He's a big contributor to the Southwest Museum and the Los Angeles Museum of History."

"Sam and I need to go see the Southwest Museum. We've been thinking about it." I didn't tell her our interest in the museum was only piqued the day before yesterday.

"Ah, here's another one. It's kind of old, and it's not bound except in paper covers, but it might help. *Indianology of California*, by Mr. Alexander Smith Taylor." She frowned as she peered at the rest of the books in the 970s. "Most of these are about Navajos, Hopis, Apaches, Comanches, Cherokees and Cheyennes. California Indians seem to be unimportant to most historians, I fear."

"Crumb," I said. "So our best bet will probably be a visit to the Southwest Museum."

"Yes, if you're really interested." Holding the two volumes she'd pulled from the stacks and handing them to me, she said, "But the bones your dog and…Did you say *Mr. Prophet* has a cat?"

"Yes. A cat named Yuyu. Named after an Apache warrior he used to know. Ugliest cat I've ever seen, but it's not his fault. He was in…an accident or something. He's got all sorts of things wrong with him, but Mr. Prophet found him in his battered condition, took him to the veterinarian and nursed him back to health."

"Mr. Prophet nursed a *cat* back to health?"

I understood her astonishment. Mr. Prophet looked as if he'd be more likely to kill something than nurse it back to health. "I know. Amazing, isn't it?"

"Well, I don't know about amazing, but certainly unexpected. At least by me."

"By me, too."

"You talkin' about me?" came a grumpy voice at my back. Both Regina and I leapt like a couple of jackrabbits—jackrabbits seeming to be more appropriate to the southwestern theme here than gazelles.

"I was just telling Mrs. Browning about Yuyu and Spike discovering those bones on our property."

"Ah. Yeah. They did that, all right," he said.

"Did you find what you were looking for?" I asked him sweetly.

"Not so much. So I figgered I'd ask Mrs. Browning for help. I'd like some books about the Yukon. Not so much the gold rush, but about the people and the Eskimos or whoever they are that live there."

"Excellent!" said Regina. I think she was attempting to be enthusiastic to disguise the fact that she found Mr. Prophet rather alarming. Most people did. "We're in the correct section for all Indians. Right here in the 970s." She poked around some more in the stacks and pulled out a skinny book called *Nanook of the North*, by someone named Robert J. Flaherty.

"Thanks!" said Mr. Prophet enthusiastically. "This looks good."

"They made a film of the family reported about in the book," said Regina. "I don't know where you can see it. It was produced in 1922. The film, I mean. I don't think he wrote the book until after the film was released."

"I didn't know that!" I said.

"No." Regina sighed. "Not many people do."

"Huh," said Mr. Prophet. "I'd like to see that flicker. Sounds more sensible than most of the so-called westerns they're showing these days."

"The westerns in the movies don't comport with Mr. Prophet's own personal memories of the Old West," I said to Regina.

Rolling his eyes, Mr. Prophet said, "They're about as far from being real as finding a bounty hunter in Pasadena."

"But you're a bounty hunter, and you're in Pasadena," I reminded him.

"I *was* a bounty hunter, and I'm only in Pasadena by accident."

"You should come with Sam and me when we visit the Southwest Museum," I told him. "You'll probably find more things of authenticity and interest to you there than in any movie palace."

"Can't find anything, much less authentic," he said.

"Is that all you want today, Daisy and Mr. Prophet?" asked Regina. "Or do you want to find some mysteries and...what kinds of books interest you, Mr. Prophet?"

"Books like this one," said he, holding out *Nanook of the North*.

"History books. Stuff like this. Real history books. About real Indians."

"I'd be willing to bet that you know more about Indians than most of the people writing about them," I said.

With a shrug, Mr. Prophet said, "Probably, but I still like to read about 'em. See what the authors get wrong."

"Any particular tribe?" Asked Regina.

"Mescalero Apaches is what I had most to do with."

"Oh," said Regina. "You mean like Geronimo?"

"He was a Chiricahua, but yeah. More or less."

"How many kinds of Apaches are there?" I asked whichever of the two other people present wanted to answer the question.

"I have no idea," admitted Regina.

Mr. Prophet squinted as if thinking hard and said, "Lemme see. There's the Mescalero, the Chiricahua, Lipan, White Mountain, Warm Springs…Aw, hell, I can't remember 'em all."

Both Regina and I gaped at the man. I said, "Wow. I've only ever heard of Apaches. I didn't know there were so many different kinds of them."

"Ain't different kinds," said Mr. Prophet. "The names just sort of identify where they live. In a way. Hel—uh, heck, I don't know. I ain't an Indian, although I knew plenty of 'em. Good folks they were, too."

"I see," said Regina faintly.

"So this is where the books about Injuns are?" asked Mr. Prophet, gesturing to the 970 stacks.

"Yes. As you can see, there are many books about many tribes, but I'm not sure if you'll find what you're interested in."

"Don't much care, really," said Mr. P. "Just kind of want to visit some old pals." He gave us both a lopsided grin. "You go and find Miss Daisy some mystery books, and I'll prowl around here for a while."

"Very well," said Regina with slightly more vigor.

"Thanks. Meet you at the check-out desk," I told my one-legged, savage-looking, wrinkled and quite old companion. He was correct in that he certainly didn't fit the mold of your average Pasadenan. Whatever that was.

Anyhow, by the time I met Mr. Prophet at the check-out desk, I not only had two books that might or might not tell me something about the Gabrielino and/or Tongva people, Regina had also given me a positive *horde* of books for my family and me to enjoy: *Poirot Investigates*, which contained several short stories about the fictional detective by Mrs. Agatha Christie; *Topper*, by a fellow named Mr. Thorne Smith; two new books by Mr. Zane Grey for Pa; *The Gatewood Caper* and *Scorch Face*, by someone named Dashiell Hammett—I have no idea how to pronounce his first name—and more. Regina gave me *The Red Lamp*, by Mrs. Mary Roberts Rinehart; *Carry On, Jeeves*, by Mr. P.G. Wodehouse; a couple of Edgar Rice Burroughs books, again for my father; and a book called *Gentlemen Prefer Blondes*, by a woman named Miss Anita Loos. She also found me several history tomes for Sam and/or Mr. Prophet.

"Thank you!" I kept telling Regina. "These will be wonderful."

"Yeah," said Mr. Prophet, who had come up to the check-out desk where Regina and I stood. "I found lots of books about my old pals." He placed five big tomes claiming to be about various American Indian tribes on the check-out desk.

"Good. I'm so glad you each found what you needed," said Regina. "I'd better get back to my post.

Mr. Prophet and I each dug out our library cards, I from my handbag, he from a pocket, and I handed mine to the check-out clerk first. He checked out my pile and then Mr. Prophet's. With a concerned frown on his face, he asked, "May I help you to your car with those?"

"Don't bother," said a familiar voice from a few feet away from where we stood.

I whirled around. "Sam!" I didn't shout. "What are you doing here?"

"Just thought I'd come here to help carry books." He winked at me. "I also have some information about our bones. Just uncovered it. So to speak."

Mr. Prophet grinned at the feeble joke. So did I.

"I'm so glad. I hope they've found them all and we can get back to using our backyard again," I said, giving Sam a peck on the cheek. Yes, I know displays of affection were taboo in public. I did it anyway. Sue me if you wish.

"Not all of them yet, but enough to more or less identify the former owner," said Sam. "They found the skull."

"More or less?" said Mr. Prophet.

"My goodness. I guess that's a good thing," I said.

"Maybe." Sam suddenly looked a trifle grim. "Maybe not."

"Is that where the more or less comes in?" I asked.

"Yeah," said Sam. He carried most of the books out to the Chevrolet and placed them in the back seat. "I'll drive home in the Hudson and meet you there. We'll have to talk about what to do next regarding the bone situation. Pick up Spike on your way, okay?"

"All right," I said. In truth, I kind of whimpered the two words.

Oh, dear. What did this mean?

THIRTEEN

Spike was happy when I picked him up and walked him across the street. Pa said he planned on napping, so that was good. He didn't need Spike to help him nap.

What I discovered upon arriving at my home—aside from Mrs. Rattle, who was cleaning the house and preparing a stew for our dinner—was a contingent of police officers, still digging. Also present was a doctor who worked with the police department, scowling over Dr. Benjamin's pile of bones on the back porch. Dr. Benjamin's pile had been added to. Someone had brought a folding table, and the skeleton was beginning to take shape, thanks to the doctor, whose name was Fabian Cuthbert, and who said his specific medical field was forensic pathology.

Whatever forensic pathology was, he seemed to be putting his knowledge of it to work in reconstructing the skeleton. The police diggers had found several new bones. Well, they were old bones, but you know what I mean.

My mouth kind of gaped when I saw the top part of the poor boney fellow's skull. It had a huge hole in it with cracks radiating from the hole in kind of a starburst pattern. I noticed one of his leg bones—I think the long bone is the femur, isn't it? Well, whatever it was, it looked as if it had been damaged, too, either when the head injury was sustained or at another time.

Holding up the skull and peering at it through thick, rimless glasses, Dr. Cuthbert said, "Of course, we can't tell at this point whether this was the cause of his death or if this injury was sustained after death. These bones were in or on the ground for at least twenty years." He bent over the bones again and started arranging them in their proper places. That is to say, they'd have been proper if they still had muscles, nerves, flesh and skin attached.

"He was a young man," the doctor muttered as he placed a rib bone where it used to belong. "You can tell the approximate age because his bones are so dense. If he'd been an old man, his bones would be more porous."

"That's sad," I said.

"It's just what happens when people age," said Dr. Cuthbert, concentrating on his work.

"I didn't mean the aging-bones thing. I meant it's sad that nobody knows who he is. Was. Can you imagine not knowing what happened to…oh, say, a son or another family member? Someone who just didn't come home one day, and you never knew what happened to him? Or her. Well, in this case, him."

"Yeah," said Mr. Prophet. "That'd be lousy."

"Your father told us this house might have been under construction at the time of the man's disappearance," said Sam. "Maybe he worked on the construction crew."

"If we had some kind of date, it would help," I said. "We could go to the library and look at the newspaper archives, but unless we have an approximate date of his disappearance, we could be looking through years' worth of newspapers."

"True, although maybe Joe will recall the time of year when the house was built," said Sam, rubbing his chin as he gazed at the bones. "That might narrow it down some."

"Some," I said doubtfully. "If it took several weeks to build the house, and Pasadena had…how many newspapers back then?"

"Haven't a clue," said Sam.

"I don't, either," I admitted. "But there might be stacks and stacks of newspapers."

"True."

Pressing a hand to his back, Dr. Cuthbert stood up. "I'm getting too old for work like this," he said "Bending over tables of bones and putting them in order makes my back ache."

"I can sympathize," said Mr. Prophet. It had never occurred to me that he might have back problems or other kinds of pain relating to age and the rheumatics or whatever. Porous bones? Maybe he had those, too. I probably should make more of an effort to be nicer to him. But only if he started being nicer to me.

"Was any kind of identification found with the bones?" I asked.

"Not so far." Dr. Cuthbert said.

"Not even...oh, say a business card or a wallet or anything like that? Even a coin might give us an approximate date."

"Anything paper would have disintegrated after being in the dirt for twenty-some years," said the doctor. "And a leather wallet or pouch would...well, it would probably have disintegrated by this time, too. Good idea about the coins, though. Maybe the men will dig some up."

"Any approximate date might help," I said, although I was beginning not to believe myself. "How the heck do you figure out who a pile of bones belong to if they've been buried for twenty years?"

"These bones don't look as though they were ever properly buried," said Dr. Cuthbert. "They appear to have lain where your... dog, was it?"

"Yes. And Mr. Prophet's cat."

No rebuttal came from Mr. Prophet. Heh. Maybe he was adjusting to people knowing he had a fondness for Yuyu.

"Well, they appear to have lain there and had dirt and rubbish dumped on top of them. If this was a construction site, it's possible nobody noticed a person lying in, say, a meadow of weeds and scrub brush and dumped loads of bulldozed dirt on top of him."

"Yes. We thought about that, too," I said, recalling Mr. Prophet's drunken friend who passed out and got dry cement poured on top of him for his sin. "I read that somewhere in Iowa—or maybe it was Idaho—some poor kid fell into a grain silo and got smothered or crushed when grain was poured in on top of him."

"Silo suffocations do happen occasionally, even here in California," said Dr. Cuthbert with a grin.

I didn't think being smothered or crushed by tons of grain was anything to grin about, but I didn't say so. "I wonder what we can do to find out who this person was."

"Stick something in the newspapers," said Mr. Prophet. "Give the general location of the bones, say he might have been working on a construction site, and maybe someone who worked with him will remember a feller who didn't show up for work one day and never came back again."

"That's a good idea," said Sam. "I'll talk to Joe and see if he can pinpoint at least the season in which the man vanished." He shrugged. "Somebody might be grieving for him still."

"Or mad as hell," said Mr. Prophet. "If he had a wife and six kids, his widow might think he got sick of all that responsibility and just took off. I knew fellers who did that sort of thing in my younger days. Didn't admire 'em much."

"No," I said. "I don't admire them one little bit."

"Knew that before you told us," said Mr. Prophet with a lopsided grin. "You're always on the wimmin's side."

Dr. Cuthbert stepped aside to receive another few bones brought to him by a policeman. I noticed the recovery party was using our outdoor water faucet and a rubber hose to rinse off the bones before handing them to the doctor. It made sense to me because some of them were *really* dirty.

Suddenly I realized something was missing from the scene being enacted in our backyard. I walked to the edge of the porch and squinted over to the back forty. "Where's Spike?" I asked anyone who might be listening. "Is he helping excavate or something?"

"If Spike is the handsome black liberty hound, yes he is," said Dr. Cuthbert with another grin, this one deserved. "He and a battered orange tabby are over there 'helping' the officers dig up bones."

"Oh, dear, are Spike and Yuyu getting in their way?"

"Don't think so," said the doctor. "Otherwise, they'd've been ousted by this time."

"I'd better go and see," I said.

"I'll go with you," said Mr. Prophet.

"I've got to get back to work," said Sam. "Be back around six, unless we get a case."

"Thanks, Sam. See you then." I stood on my toes and kissed his cheek.

"See you soon, sweetheart," he said. Then he snapped his fingers and said, "I forgot to tell you that I stopped by the Salvation Army Church this morning before I went to the library to find you."

"Why'd you go there?" I asked. Not that I thought Sam shouldn't fraternize with Flossie and Johnny Buckingham, but it seemed odd that he'd have visited them without a purpose in mind. The purpose generally involved something I'd done, said, or should have done or said, and often included saving my bacon.

"The grandfather of one of the clerks in the office died, and the clerk brought in a big carpetbag full of old cookware, clothes and miscellaneous items he didn't know what to do with. So I offered to take them to the Salvation Army. Flossie asked how you were, I told her, and she said she's doing well, and please come and visit Billy and little Daisy one of these days."

"Why did they name that poor little child Daisy?" I asked grimly.

"What's the matter with Daisy?" asked Mr. Prophet.

"I've just never much cared for my name. I mean, *Daisy*? Why not something pretty, like Victoria or Diana or Heather or Esther or something? Of course, my sister's name is Daphne, but a daphne is a prettier flower than a daisy, in my opinion. If my mother and father were so obsessed with flowers, why didn't they choose a different one? Heck, I'd have preferred *Rose*! But then my father's dog and I would have the same name, more or less. At least they didn't name me Petunia or Pansy."

Sam and Mr. Prophet laughed.

"I think Daisy suits you perfectly," said Sam. "It's perky. Like you."

"Perky? You think I'm perky?"

"Sure," said Sam. "I like your perkiness."

"I dunno," said Mr. Prophet darkly. "I think Oleander or Foxglove would have worked better. Might not be perky, but they'd've suited your personality."

"I am *not* poisonous, darn you!" As the men laughed some more, I contemplated flowers for a second longer. "Although I think Lily is a pretty name, and lilies are poisonous."

"Just be glad you're not really named Desdemona," said Sam.

"I suppose you have a good point there," I said with a sigh.

"Yeah," said Mr. Prophet. "Ain't she the lady who got killed by her husband? You wouldn't want to get Sam in trouble, would you?"

"Othello was goaded into murdering his wife Desdemona by the villainous Iago," I told him huffily. "Iago made poor Othello believe Desdemona was playing around on him, and she wasn't. She was pure as the driven snow. So Othello was duped, and he adored his wife."

"Odd way of showing it," said Mr. Prophet. "I'd'a been more apt to do in…what's his name? Igor?" He pronounced it Ee-gore.

"Iago," I said.

"Strange names those fellers had in the old days," said Mr. Prophet.

"I guess so. Shakespeare wrote those plays…what? Five hundred years ago? Things change over the centuries, including names."

"S'pose so."

"I've got to go," said Sam. "Give Flossie a call why don't you, Daisy?"

"I shall," I told him.

"Take care, Lou," said Sam.

"You too," said Mr. Prophet. "All right, Miss Daisy, let's go survey the boneyard."

So we did. Spike was delighted to see me and expressed his joy by jumping up and getting his dirty paws all over my formerly pristine day dress. I didn't mind. The dress was old and I loved my dog.

Yuyu remained in the background, eyeing Mr. Prophet and me with malevolent yellow eyes. Well, one malevolent yellow eye, as he only had the one. Boy, I'd never seen a cat and a man who went together better than Yuyu and Mr. Prophet.

"C'mon, cat," said Mr. Prophet, patting his one knee.

Oddly enough, the cat glanced at Spike, who still frolicked at my feet, hissed once, probably at me, and, making a wide circle around my sweet hound and me, sauntered over to Mr. Prophet. With a wicked wink at me, Mr. Prophet turned and limped off toward his cottage, the cat limping at his heels.

I stared after the pair of them for a second or two then asked Spike, "Want to stay here or go to the house with me?"

Sitting at my feet, Spike gazed up at me, his head tilting one way and then the other as he considered my question. Then he cast a pleading glance at the retreating form of his new best friend, hopped up onto all fours and decided to accompany me back to the house.

Just as we reached the back porch where Dr. Cuthbert was eyeing a largish bone as if contemplating where it belonged in the overall scheme of things—when I peeked, the skeleton seemed to be taking pretty good shape, considering a lot of it remained missing—Mrs. Rattle opened the back door.

"Oh, good, you're here. I was about to go looking for you," said she. "Mrs. Buckingham is on the telephone, and she said she might have some information for you."

"Thanks, Mrs. Rattle! I was just going to give her a ring."

"She's such a lovely lady," said Mrs. Rattle.

"Yes, she is. She's one of my very best friends." I headed to the telephone.

When I got there, I plunked myself on the chair—by the way, I'd embroidered a smashingly beautiful chair cushion for the otherwise plain, ladder-backed chair—and picked up the receiver Mrs. Rattle had laid on the table. "Hey, Flossie! Sam said he took you some stuff for the thrift store today."

"He did. How are you, Daisy?" I heard a baby gurgling on her lap, and my heart went all mushy.

"I'm fine. How are you and Johnny and Billy and your darling baby?"

"Oh, we're all great. Both Billy and Daisy are growing like weeds. You need to come over and see them one of these days. It's hard for me to get out and around now, what with two children to watch over. I thought one was a handful. Ha!"

"I'm hoping to find out for myself one of these days," I told her, meaning it sincerely. Sam and I both wanted children. Most of the time.

"Oh, but Daisy, Sam told us about the bones they're finding in your yard."

After heaving a sigh, I said, "Yes. What a mess. We have no earthly idea who the poor guy is. Was. I mean, they've determined he was a young man, but that's all they know so far. Oh, and one of his legs was injured, and he has a huge hole in his skull."

"Ugh. Wonder how that happened. But Daisy, I think one of our parishioners might be able to help you. A very nice fellow named Christopher Edwards has a construction company here in town. I'd say he's in his fifties now, but he's been working construction jobs all his life. Right after Sam left, Chris came to the office to talk with Johnny about an upcoming event we're planning, and I told him about your old bones!"

Wasn't altogether sure I appreciated her calling them *my* old bones, but I didn't say so. "And did he have an idea about how they got here?" I said instead.

"He did! He said he and a crew were building a house in your neighborhood approximately twenty-three years ago. I expect Chris was quite a young man then himself. Well, he told me one of the construction crew members had a terrible drinking problem. Occasionally, the boss would have to send him home when he'd show up drunk to the job."

My nose began to wrinkle as Flossie talked. So far I didn't like this story. "Really?"

"Yes. And then one day the man walked off the job, and he never came back again. The boss was really angry, but there wasn't much he could do about it. Very few had telephones in those days, you know, so he couldn't call his home."

"True."

"Chris, who is a truly good man, was trying to help the poor fellow get and remain sober. Anyhow, he went to his home to see if he was there, but his mother was frantic, because she said he'd never come home one night. I'm not sure, but I think in those days Pasadena didn't have any saloons or bars or anything. Maybe the liquor laws had lifted by then, but according to Johnny, when Pasadena was first incorporated, you'd have to go to Arcadia if you wanted to buy a drink of hard spirits."

"Yeah, I read about that in history classes at school," I told her, because it was the truth. "If I had any say in the matter, nobody'd be able to buy liquor in Pasadena now, either."

I heard Flossie heave a big sigh. "Yes, I know. But people are perverse creatures, Daisy. I have my own doubts about Prohibition."

Her words shocked me. "But Flossie! Your Johnny had so much trouble with drink! He's told me over and over that the Salvation Army saved his life!"

"Yes. It did," said Flossie, ever calm and rational. "But once you tell people they can't do something, some of them will try everything they can to do it, even if they'd never even thought about doing it before! I swear, Daisy, I think more drinking goes on these days than before Prohibition became the law of the land."

"Really? That's kind of...sad, Flossie."

"Daisy," she said in a *you of all people should know better* voice, "Piffle. You know very well what I was before you took me off the streets and flung me at Johnny."

"I didn't fling you at Johnny!" I cried, although I had. I'd kind of hoped she'd never figure it out.

"You did, too," she said, laughing so hard she could barely get the words out. "And I love you for it!"

"Well, I'm glad of that anyway," I said, feeling small and inadequate. The real, honest-to-God truth of the Flossie situation, was that when I was first more or less forced to take her under my wing, I *did*, on purpose and with...not malice, but something aforethought…make sure to put her in Johnny's way. And they'd turned out to be the perfect couple, even if my initial motives had perhaps been the least little bit less than admirable.

"However, that's not why I called," said Flossie, getting back to business. "I hope you don't mind, but I gave Chris your address, and he's going to stop by your house. He might be able to identify the property as the one he worked on, and he also said the poor man who disappeared had an injury to one of his legs, making it shorter than the other one. If the bones are his and somebody found the leg bone, a doctor can probably tell if he'd had a broken leg before he died. If the injury is like the one the fellow Chris knew had, it might help identify him."

"Oh, my word, really? Flossie! This is fantastic news! Does Mr. Edwards remember his name? We were trying to figure out how to identify the poor guy."

"Not sure about the name, but it might give you a good start in finding out who he was."

"This is amazing, Flossie. Thank you!"

"God works in mysterious ways, Daisy," Flossie said with a grin in her voice.

"He certainly does," I agreed. "And so do you."

"As do you," said Flossie.

We were both laughing when we hung up our respective receivers.

FOURTEEN

Just as Mrs. Rattle was putting on her coat and hat in order to leave for the day—she worked at our house from eight-thirty to twelve-thirty Monday through Friday—the doorbell rang. Spike and I always walked her to the door because I thought it was only polite to do so, and I also wanted her to know how very much I appreciated her. I didn't mind cleaning house, and I was learning to cook, but I *loved* having her help doing it, especially the cooking part.

As she was just then sticking a hat pin in her hat, it was I who opened the door. A cheery-looking middle-aged man stood there, He stood about medium height, had hair that was almost blue-black with streaks of silver around the edges, wore a casual suit and held a hat in his hand.

"Good day," he said, bowing a little. "I'm Chris Edwards. I think Mrs. Buckingham might have telephoned you about me?" His voice lifted on the last couple of words, making them a question.

"Yes, she did! Thank you for coming."

"Happy to help if I can."

"But please let me introduce the two of you," I said, indicating Mrs. Rattle. We had a big front door, but two women, a man and a dog made for a bit of a crowd, so I stepped back a pace, and Mrs. Rattle stepped forward. Mr. Edwards also took a step back. It looked kind of like a dance routine, actually, although Spike sat still because I'd told him to. "Mrs. Rattle, this is Mr. Christopher Edwards. Mr. Edwards, Mrs. Rattle."

Mrs. Rattle had managed to stick her pin in her hat, anchoring it to the bun on top of her head, and held out her hand. "How do you do, Mr. Edwards?"

"How-do, Mrs. Rattle? Are you by any chance related to a fellow named Mr. Gregory Rattle?"

"Why, yes! He's my husband! You two know each other?"

"Yes, we do. A fine man, your husband. We met through the Friends of the Elderly, which is associated with the Salvation Army and the Neighborhood Church. I attend services at the Salvation Army. Greg's an excellent carpenter."

Smiling with pleasure, Mrs. Rattle said, "He certainly is! Why, he's always out fixing things for old people who can no longer do things for themselves. Not that he's a youngster himself," she added with a chuckle.

"No, none of us are youngsters any longer," said Mr. Edwards, his vivid blue eyes twinkling.

"Well, I'm just on my way home, Mr. Edwards, so I'll leave you and Mrs. Rotondo to chat. It was a pleasure to meet you, and I'll give Greg your regards. I understand you're here about the old bones they're finding in the backyard."

"Yes, I'm afraid so," said Mr. Edwards, his smile fading, but leaving laugh lines around his eyes. I didn't even know the guy, but I liked him.

"Thank you, Mrs. Rattle," I said as she departed. "And thank you, Mr. Edwards," I said to him, stepping aside so he could enter the house. Spike, as previously mentioned, had sat and stayed throughout this entire passage of time because he knew it was what he was supposed to do. However, he gazed up at Mr. Edwards with excited doggy eyes, just waiting for me to give him the signal that he might meet and greet the newcomer.

"What a handsome dog!" Mr. Edwards said. He knelt before

Spike, as was Spike's due, and lifted a hand. Before using it to touch the hound, he asked, "Is it all right if I pet him?"

Add another point to the "I like Chris Edwards" checklist. "You bet it is. Okay, Spike!"

Spike leaped to his feet—to be honest, he was so short, it was difficult to tell if he was lying down or standing up unless you were well acquainted with him—and wagged and wagged at Mr. Edwards.

"What's your name, pal?" asked Mr. Edwards.

As Spike couldn't talk, I said, "We named him Spike, because he's such an energetic chaser of cats, mice, opossums and so forth. A mighty hunting hound is Spike."

Mr. Edwards, muscular but supple, got to his feet without a creak or a groan. He patted his knee. Spike was delighted to accept his invitation, and leaped up to give the man a more lively greeting. "I've only seen two or three of these dogs before. What are they called? I can't remember. I call them sausage dogs."

"Most people do," I said, grinning. "Spike is a dachshund."

"Oh, that's right. I did some work for a lady in Altadena who has some of these. Dash-hounds, did you say?"

"No. I said *dachshund*. It's a German name, Spike was born in Altadena, and I'll bet that woman was Mrs. Bissel, the woman who bred him. Well, two of her other dachshunds did!"

"It was! You two know each other?"

"We do indeed. In fact, I'm going to...go to her house this coming Friday." I had been going to mention the séance, but recalled in time that not everyone in the world knew or approved of my profession as a spiritualist-medium.

"Well, I'll be. Small world."

"It is indeed. Flossie said you don't really know what happened to the fellow to whom these bones might belong any more than the rest of us do. Is that right?"

"That's right. He just left work one day, and we never saw him again. Poor guy. Lost his way in the world as so many people do. Drank." Mr. Edwards shook his head and seemed sad about the lost people of the world.

"Yes, that's what Flossie said." I wanted to grill him about his own path in life and ask if he used to drink heavily, but I restrained myself. *Not*, I must add, an easy thing for me to do, but I can occasionally recall the manners my mother taught me.

After he finished greeting Spike, Mr. Edwards glanced around the front part of the house. "You know, I think this was the house we were building at the time the fellow went missing. I recall the front porch and the doorway. You've put in fencing since it was built. The place looks great."

"Thank you. The Killebrews put up the fencing."

"Killebrew! That name sounds *really* familiar. You know, I believe this is the very house!"

"Excellent. In that case, you might be able to help us. Come with me. Do you want to see the rest of the house to be sure or just come with me down the hall and through the kitchen? The doctor is putting the bones together on a table on the back porch."

"Think I'll skip the tour. I'll be able to tell if this is the house for sure pretty soon. I'll take a good gander at it as we go through it."

"Great. Come with me then."

So he did, peering this way and that as we walked. He admired the piano and the peacock lamp residing on it, recognized the staircase, identified the butler's pantry as the one he and his crew members worked on, and was sure this was the house he'd helped build twenty-two years prior. I felt a sense of relief when he came to this conclusion, because it might mean we were on our way to discovering who the heck had died and lain abandoned and unclaimed in our yard for so many years.

When Mr. Edwards and I got to the back door, he politely opened it for me, and we stepped out onto the porch, Spike joining us. Dr. Cuthbert stood at the table, squinting at a bone, probably trying to decide where it belonged on the table full of bones. I saw men still digging in the back forty. He laid the bone down in no particular place on the table when he heard the door open and close.

"Good afternoon, Dr. Cuthbert."

He nodded at me. "Mrs. Rotondo."

Golly, I liked being called Mrs. Rotondo.

"Dr. Cuthbert, this gentleman is Mr. Christopher Edwards, and he was working on the construction of this house when a young man disappeared twenty-two years ago. He might be able to identify something about the bones."

The doctor seemed to perk right up. "Wonderful! It would be nice to identify the poor fellow. He's been lying around in the Rotondos' backyard for at least twenty years."

"It wasn't our backyard until about seven or eight months ago," I pointed out. Not that it mattered, but I didn't want anyone to think my family had anything to do with the disappearance of the bones' original owner. "The Killebrews had the house built."

"Yes, I understand," said Dr. Cuthbert, smiling at me and probably thinking I was either nit-picky or nuts.

"The man I worked with," said Mr. Edwards, "had an old injury to one of his legs. Said he broke it when he fell out of a tree when he was a boy. I can't recall which leg it was."

"It was the right one," said Dr. Cuthbert, beginning to smile broadly. "If this is the man you knew, he'd sustained a bad break to his right leg. It had healed, but it must have hurt the poor boy a good deal, and it was definitely shorter than the left leg. Did the fellow you knew have a limp?"

Narrowing his eyes as he thought, Mr. Edwards took a few seconds to recall the young man he used to know. He walked closer to the table to observe the work Dr. Cuthbert had been doing, and his face took on a solemn mien.

"I guess we all come from dust and go back to being dust in the long run, but these bones look mighty solid. Hard to imagine them belonging to the fellow I used to know."

"We don't know that they did," I pointed out. "Not yet, anyway."

With a sigh, Mr. Edwards said, "No, we don't. Now that I think more about those days, the young man I recall did have a limp. As you said, one leg was shorter than the other, but he hated his limp and tried to hide it. In fact, he had quite a disagreeable attitude. I think he felt diminished because he limped when he walked. You know, it made him feel less of a man."

"What's that about a limp makin' somebody less of a man?" came a gruff voice at our backs.

I turned, and Mr. Edwards glanced back to see Mr. Lou Prophet, a misshapen orange cat slung over his shoulder, wooden leg in place, scowling. Dr. Cuthbert outright laughed.

"I'm absolutely sure nobody's ever said that about you, Mr. Prophet," he said.

I think he was mainly amused about the cat. Yuyu glared at each of us in turn, his lip curling. Then he spotted Spike, who'd joined us on the back porch, and made a leap. I guess he dug his claws into Mr. Prophet's shoulder as he did so because Mr. Prophet said, "Dammit, cat!"

"Mr. Christopher Edwards, please allow me to introduce you to Mr. Lou Prophet. Mr. Prophet is a friend of Sam's and mine, and he's also caretaker of our property here. That cat"—I pointed to Yuyu, who had joined Spike in a dash to the boneyard—"helped find the bones we're trying to identify. The cat's name is Yuyu."

"How-do, Mr. Prophet," said Mr. Edwards politely. I saw the twinkle in his eyes and liked him for it.

"I was doin' all right until that cat stabbed me," said Mr. Prophet. "Howdy."

"Mr. Prophet," I told Mr. Edwards in a confiding sort of voice, "used to live in the Old West. Tucson and Mexico and all sorts of other wild and woolly places."

"I see. Well, glad you made it to Pasadena, Mr. Prophet." He held out his hand.

"Not so sure I am," grumped Mr. Prophet, reaching for Mr. Edwards' hand with his. Then he looked at it, wiped it on his trousers, and said, "Sorry 'bout the blood. Cat stabbed me when he jumped off my shoulder."

Chuckling, Mr. Edwards shook Mr. Prophet's hand. "Blood doesn't bother me much. Good to meet you."

"Yeah," said Mr. Prophet, scanning Mr. Edwards from tip to toe. Mr. Prophet had been an extremely tall man, and still towered over most people even though he'd shrunk some over his many years. He was several inches taller than Mr. Edwards. "Good to meet you, too."

"Mr. Edwards was on the construction crew that built this house. He thinks he might know the fellow whose bones Spike and Yuyu found," I told the newcomer.

"Ah. And the feller had a limp, you say?"

"Yes. Fell out of a tree when he was a boy."

"Huh."

"At any rate," said Dr. Cuthbert, cutting through the chitchat. "This poor fellow had a broken right femur. It healed well, but his right leg was shorter than his left, and he must have walked with something of a limp." He glanced from the bones on the table to Mr. Edwards. "I don't suppose you recall which leg the fellow had broken, do you?"

After taking several seconds for thought, Mr. Edwards shook his head. "I'm sorry. It was a long time ago, and I just remember that he tried to hide his limp, and he had a pretty bad attitude overall. I don't know if he resented the world for something or what, but he was a surly bloke."

"I'd'a been surly too if I had to build houses fer a living," muttered Lou Prophet.

"Mr. Prophet," I said to Mr. Edwards—and to Dr. Cuthbert if he didn't already know—"used to be a bounty hunter in the wild west."

"Really? That's fascinating!" exclaimed Mr Edwards, sounding truly enthusiastic.

"It was all right," said Mr. Prophet, rather surly himself.

"As for these bones," said Dr. Cuthbert, again trying to direct the conversation in the way it should go, "I have no idea what this fellow's attitude might have been, but he had a healed right femur. He also had this huge hole in his head." He lifted the skull to show Mr. Edwards.

"Good Lord!" cried the latter. He grimaced. "He sure didn't have that hole in his head when he was working on this site. Oh, but he was missing his two front teeth." He gestured at the skull which, sure enough, was lacking its two front teeth. "Guy was always getting into fights. He'd get drunk and pick fights with people." Mr. Edwards shook his head sadly. "I tried to help him."

"Huh," said Mr. Prophet. "Do-gooder, are ya?"

I wanted to hit him. Again, I restrained myself.

But it was all right. Mr. Edwards threw his head back and roared with laughter. I glanced at Mr. Prophet and saw he was irked that his shot had missed its mark.

After hauling out a handkerchief and wiping his streaming eyes, Mr. Edwards said, "No. I'm not a do-gooder. But I felt sorry for the kid. He was young and dumb and got into trouble all the time. Just tried to be nice to him, maybe figure out what was bothering him so much he thought he had to drown his sorrows in a bottle. He was very young. I couldn't imagine him having accrued so many sorrows that he thought he had to take them out on everybody around him."

"Yeah," said Mr. Prophet, relinquishing his grump. "I knew kids like him back in the old days. Most of 'em lived hard and died young. Guess this feller did, too."

"I guess." Mr. Edwards shook his head. "Wish I could remember his name." He squinched up his eyes and thought hard for a second or two, then shook his head. "I'm almost sure he lived with his mother, and she lived on an east-west street. Can't remember the name, but I went to her place a couple of times to see if the kid had come home. He hadn't, and she was in quite a fret. I have a feeling her husband drank, too." He sighed heavily." Anyhow, I'll give it some thought. I'll bet this is him, though. Wonder if that blow to his skull killed him."

"Hard to tell," said Dr. Cuthbert. "It looks more like something hard fell on his skull while he was lying down, perhaps already dead. I can't tell if was a pre- or post-mortem wound. If he was alive when he was hit, it would have killed him. There's no doubt of that."

"Poor fellow," I said, shuddering.

Mr. Edwards had stopped gazing at the table full of bones and was now paying attention to the yard. "That concrete wall was already here when we built this house. I remember it because it seemed kind of strange."

"It goes all the way to Garfield," I said. "Sam and I are thinking of selling off the back portion of land. We don't need it, and another house could be built there."

"Yes," said Mr. Edwards meditatively. "I'm going to try my best to think of the kid's name, because he used to like to walk along the top of that wall, showing off, you know? Wouldn't surprise me if he tried to navigate it after downing a bottle of booze and fell off it."

"That's a possibility," said Dr. Cuthbert. "Because the bones have been out there so long, we have no idea of his original position, but they were found near the wall, so I expect that's about where he was when he died."

"Yeah," said Mr. Edwards. "We used to dump stuff back there. You know, dirt, rocks, gravel, all the things you need to bulldoze in order to level the land in order to erect a building." He gave a little shudder. "I hate to think of him lying there, alive, and having a ton of rocks dumped on him."

Ew.

"Knew a feller that happened to," said Mr. Prophet. "So it ain't impossible."

FIFTEEN

As Sam and I ate Mrs. Rattle's tasty chicken stew that night—almost but not quite as good as one of Vi's—we discussed the partial identification of "our" bones.

"At least we know, or think we know, he's the fellow Mr. Edwards recalls from the construction site, although we still don't have a name," I said.

"True. Did you ask him what month it was he disappeared?"

"Crumb. I forgot," I said, feeling stupid.

"It's all right. If Edwards is connected with the Salvation Army, he'll be easy to find again," said Sam lovingly, soothing my ruffled feelings. Or feelers, as I called them when a child. I tell you, I was a riot and a half when I was a kid.

"Want more stew?" I asked Sam as he scraped up the last bite of chicken, gravy, peas and carrots from his bowl. "Or another biscuit?"

I was darned proud of those biscuits. I'd made them myself. What's more, I couldn't believe how easy they'd been to make! The kitchen had terrified me for so many years, I'd even avoided learning to create the easy stuff. Silly Daisy.

"I'll take another spoonful of stew and another biscuit, thanks," said my darling husband.

He liked my biscuits! I could hardly stand it.

"There's some spice cake and ice cream for dessert," I told him. Vi had given me half of the second spice cake she'd made on Saturday, and it sat, all covered with waxed paper, in our lovely new Frigidaire, just waiting for us.

It was so nice to have hot and cold running water and refrigeration! I understood, from reading the newspapers and so forth, that we here in Pasadena were particularly lucky in the plumbing department. Most folks in the USA still depended on ice boxes, water pumps and outhouses which, according to family legend, boys liked to tip over on Halloween. Boys. I guess I wouldn't mind having one, but I had a feeling girls would be easier to rear. Or maybe not, considering some of the young females I'd met in recent years. Guess I'd find out.

"Yum," said Sam. "I'll take a piece of cake and some ice cream. Thanks, Daisy. It's nice to have a meal alone every now and then, isn't it? I love your family, and Lou's like a...well, an elderly and cranky uncle or something along those lines, but I like being alone with you sometimes."

"I feel the same way," I said, definitely feeling the same way.

"Woof," said Spike from the floor at my feet. So I gave him a little bite of chicken. He said "Thank you," afterwards. Very well, so I'm stretching a point there. He wagged at me.

Sam and I both had a piece of delicious spice cake with a dollop of ice cream on it. Then Sam retired to the living room to read one of the history books I'd got for him at the library. I washed, dried and put away the dishes. What's that old saying? A man's work ends when the day is done, but a woman's work is never done? I think that's it. It's true, too.

However, I didn't begrudge Sam his reading time. He'd earned some rest after a hard day policing Pasadena. And taking things to the Salvation Army, thereby discovering Mr. Christopher Edwards, who had known the poor lad who'd died in our backyard before it was our backyard. Wish Mr. Edwards had recalled the young man's name.

Anyhow, I joined Sam in the living room after I was through in the kitchen. Spike was curled up snoozing on Sam's lap. For some reason, this domestic scene made my heart all warm and squishy.

After looking through the stack of books I'd brought home from the library, I decided to read *Carry On, Jeeves* first. My mother and Vi would like that one, too, so I figured I'd read it quickly and take it across the street. Sam, I saw, had picked up *The Spanish Pioneers and the California Indians*, by Mr. Charles Lummis, which reminded me of a trip I wanted to take.

"Hey, Sam."

He glanced up from his book, his cheaters resting on his nose. He needed them when he had to read. "Yes?" He sounded a little nervous, unless that was my imagination.

"I'm still interested in visiting the Southwest Museum, even though we didn't find any Indian bones in the yard. Will you go with me one of these upcoming Saturdays?"

He seemed to relax. Unless, again, that was my imagination. "Sure." He lifted Mr. Lummis' book. "This is interesting. I'd like to learn more about the Indian population in California."

"Good. Thanks. I think Mr. Prophet wants to come with us. He's reading about the Yukon right now."

"Ah. Did you ever see *Nanook of the North*? I saw it in a theater in New York City before we moved to Pasadena."

"No. Regina told us about the film, though. Somebody wrote a book about the family after the film was released. I mean, the film and the book were about Nanook's family. Mr. Prophet is reading that one now. Or will be soon."

"It was a fascinating flicker," said Sam. "About real people and not make-believe ones."

"Sometimes stories about real people are more melancholy than those about make-believe ones," I muttered, clasping *Carry On, Jeeves* to my more-than-ample bosom. More than ample because the fashion designers of the day had decreed that women should have no curves. I think all fashion designers are men of

Harold's stamp. Why else would they want women to look like boys?

Oh, never mind.

"True. I read somewhere that when the people who filmed *Nanook of the North* went back to the frozen north the following year, wanting to catch up with Nanook and his family, they discovered they'd been wiped out by a blizzard."

I stared at my husband. "All of them? The whole family?"

"All of them."

"Shoot. I'm glad I live in Pasadena."

With a chuckle, Sam said, "Yeah. Me too," and he went back to his book.

We read for a while then went up to bed after allowing Spike to go outside to do his duty as a dog. Sam carried him upstairs, grumbling about building a ramp for the dog. I only smiled, knowing he'd build the ramp and be happy to do it. Sam was a *good* man.

I don't know how long we'd been snoozing peacefully when suddenly the night was split with howls and screams, the barking of a dog—Spike?—and the yowling of a cat, which must have been Yuyu. Startled awake, I groggily glanced around and didn't see my dog. I fumbled for the switch of my bedside lamp. Sure enough. No dog.

"Spike must be outside!" I said. "He climbed down the staircase! But who the heck else is out there?"

"Ugh," said Sam, heaving himself up on the other side of the bed and reaching for his bathrobe, which he always draped over a chair near the bed. I fumbled for my own robe, which I generally threw over the foot of the bed.

Both Sam and I had more or less got our slippers on and were tying the belts to our robes as we staggered down the stairs. We flipped on lights as we went and hared down the hallway, ran through the kitchen and stopped short at the back door.

There Sam said, "Stand back. Let me look first."

"Like heck," I told my beloved. I knew he wanted to protect me from whatever was out there, but I didn't want him to get hurt either.

So we both sort of slithered side-by-side through the door. Sam pulled the light cord to illuminate the back porch. We squinted into the darkness. After a moment or two, I began making out forms.

"Pudge?" I said, peering at what appeared to be a terrified, hunched-over kid with tons of freckles and what looked in the dim light like red hair. He was at present howling like a banshee. His howls weren't the only howls out there, either. "Who's there with you?"

"We-we-we saw a *ghost*!" shrieked Pudge.

Spike ran to the back porch, wagging like mad, happy to see his two humans join in the night's activities. I bent to pet him, still gazing with perplexity at Pudge.

"A ghost? What are you talking about? Why are you here?"

"A g-ghost! It w-wooed at us!" Pudge stuttered. "And shook some kind of r-rattle!"

"Wooed? I thought ghosts were supposed to boo."

Shaking his head hard, Pudge said in a high-pitched voice, "It *wooed*!"

I shook my head, too, but only because I was not quite awake. I was, however, extremely confused and irked.

"Come up here, Pudge," said Sam, taking charge. When he took charge, people didn't dither. They obeyed.

A still-tearful and clearly frightened Pudge shuffled to the back steps. Sam stepped aside to allow Pudge up onto the porch. A couple of other boys, each looking at least as frightened as Pudge, followed slowly in Pudge's wake. Along with fright, their faces, including Pudge's, had started to register chagrin.

"Sit," said Sam, pointing at several chairs on the back porch. The lads sat. So did Spike, who was accustomed to sitting on command.

One of the boys hiccupped and knuckled an eye. The other one who wasn't Pudge was gasping in huge breaths and looked as if he actually *had* seen a ghost. Or at least something pretty darned scary. Pudge sat, hunched and unhappy and hugging himself.

Pulling up two more chairs and setting them before the three boys, Sam gestured for me to sit in one as he sat in the other. "All right. Calm down, you three, and tell us precisely what you were doing. I assume you decided to take your friends on a little jaunt to where the bones are being found. Right, Pudge?"

Pudge nodded unhappily. "I-I thought it would be-be-be ex-exciting."

"To come into our backyard at night in order to see some old bones without asking for permission first?" said Sam, sounding stern.

"Well...y-yes," admitted Pudge.

"Pudge Wilson, whatever will your parents think?" I asked him sadly. "And your Boy Scout master?"

"We didn't mean any harm!" he more or less yowled, reminding me of Yuyu.

"I guess that's why Spike was barking," I said to Sam. "But I don't know how he got outside from the kitchen."

"The door wasn't quite latched," said Sam to me. "It was slightly open when we got down there."

"We should be more careful," I said into a chorus of whimpers, gasps and sobs from the three seated boys.

I expect Sam was going to agree with me, but he was interrupted.

"What the hell is going on out here?" asked a loud rusty voice from over near the arbor. "Yuyu just raced into the house with his hair standing on end and his tail about three sizes bigger'n it ought to be." Mr. Prophet appeared in the lamplight, using his crutch, as he hadn't taken time to attach his wooden leg. He too wore a bathrobe. "*You*," he said scathingly, staring at Pudge. He and Pudge hadn't got off to a good start when they'd first met, and Mr. Prophet hadn't softened his heart toward the boy yet. I'm pretty sure Pudge was terrified of the old man.

"Yes," said Sam. "Come on up, Lou. These boys have some explaining to do. Evidently, they thought it would be fun to sneak into our backyard and look at some moonlit bones, but something scared them, and they probably scared the cat."

"Hell," groused Mr. Prophet, clumping up the stairs and pulling up a chair for himself. He scowled at the three miserable boys.

"Lookin' at the bones, was ya? Stupid kids. Probably wanted a souvenir to take home." His voice held a sneer when he spoke the last sentence.

"Well, Pudge?" demanded Sam. "Tell us what you were doing in our yard at whatever ungodly hour this is. And who are these other fellows? Pudge, I know you. Who are you?" He pointed at one of the little criminals.

"R-Reggie," said one miscreant in a shaky whisper.

"Reggie what?" I asked sharply, recalling a frightening time a few months earlier when someone named Reginald had been telling tales about me to Pudge Wilson through the agency of his Boy Scout pack.

Sam swiveled his head and peered at me, surprised.

"J-Jervis," he whimpered.

The name gave me a sudden start, rather as if I'd stuck my finger into an electrical socket. Sam's head whipped back, and he stared at the Jervis boy.

"Aha!" I said in a loud, angry voice at the Jervis kid. "Don't tell me you're still trying to pull tricks on me, are you? I thought your evil sister had shot herself after she shot her friends, and you'd decided to behave yourself. If you're—"

"Wait!" roared Sam. "Are you Reginald Jervis, brother of Miss Alma Jervis?"

"Y-yes," stammered the boy, looking as if he wished he were somewhere else. Perhaps Arabia or thereabouts.

He didn't look like a villain, but I'd take a wait-and-see attitude. He'd done a villainous deed this evening if he'd sneaked into our yard in order to look at the bones.

"Cripes. Ain't we had enough trouble with your family?" said Mr. Prophet, scowling at the boy. Mr. Prophet's scowls might frighten anyone, even if he or she hadn't been caught in a misdeed. He sure frightened Reginald Jervis, who burst into tears.

"I-I'm sorry! I didn't mean anything!"

"You sneaked into our yard," said Sam. "What didn't you mean about that?"

"N-nothing!" sobbed Reggie.

"It's all my fault!" said Pudge into the uproar. "It's not Reggie and Howie's fault! It's all my fault. I thought it would be kind of fun to take a flashlight and look at where those people are digging up the bones at night. You know, s-scary, like Halloween." He seemed to swallow hard. "But then we...we...saw...something."

"A ghost," I said, not feeling especially kindly disposed towards Pudge Wilson at the moment.

"It was," said the third boy in a shaking voice. Howie, I presume. "I mean, it was a ghost. I swear it was a ghost."

"Right," said Mr. Prophet. "Gotta watch out fer them ghosts."

"It *was!*" sobbed Howie. "And it rattled something at us!"

"And then the cat hissed, and Spike started barking, and we got scared and ran," said Pudge in a small voice.

Thinking perhaps other people might have decided to take a look at "our" bones, I said, "What did this ghost of yours look like?" My voice was hard. I was annoyed with this threesome. Boy Scouts, who were supposed to do *good* deeds, for heaven's sake!

A trio of glances passed among the three criminous lads seated, hunched, on our back porch. I noticed a shrug or two, a head-shake, and maybe a few blinks and so forth. I decided to move things along.

"Pudge, you're evidently the ringleader of this band. What did your ghost look like? Tell me now."

"I'm so sorry, Miss Daisy."

"I don't care how sorry you are," I said cruelly. "What did your ghost look like?"

"It-it looked like a— I don't know." Pudge looked helplessly at his partners in crime.

"It looked like a hollow Indian," said Howie after a seconds-long pause that seemed to last a century.

Tilting my head, I repeated, "A hollow Indian?"

"Well...yeah," said Reggie. "You could see through it."

"Oh, for pity's sake!" I said, really and truly angry with these three boys. "I'm taking you home, Pudge Wilson. I don't know where you, Reggie, or you, Howie, live, but you can telephone your parents from our house. Or *I* will, and they can come and get you."

"Oh, Miss Daisy, we're sorry! Don't tell our folks! *Please!*" wailed Pudge.

"Daisy," said Sam. "Why don't you and Lou take Reggie and Howie inside and call the boys' parents. I'll take Pudge home and give him to his folks."

"No!" cried Pudge. "My pa will kill me!"

"Good," I said. Mean, I know, but I was angry.

Howie and Reggie began to protest, but when Mr. Prophet stood and loomed over them, they shut up instantly, although their sobs increased. Then they rose to their feet and followed me into the house. Mr. Prophet brought up the rear.

Three sets of parents were quite upset at their offspring that night. So were Sam, Mr. Prophet and I. Well, we weren't upset at our offspring, but we were, as Mr. Prophet so aptly said, "Mad as hell" at the three trespassers.

SIXTEEN

S am and I sat and stared groggily at each other the following
morning. I'd decided to heck with cooking anything, and we
were downing the last several pieces of spice cake with our coffee for
breakfast. Sam had come home from depositing Pudge at his
parents' house before the first set of parents of the other two boys
showed up at our house.

To say the boys' parents were displeased with their sons would
be seriously to misrepresent the case. Or cases. All four of them, Mr.
and Mrs. Jervis and Mr. and Mrs. Mason (Howie's parents) were
furious. I expected some severe punishments had been handed
down last night or would be this morning. Good. Rotten kids.

"Golly, Mrs. Jervis looked like a ghost herself when she and her
husband came to pick up Reggie," I said as Sam downed some
coffee.

"I think she and her husband are tired of their children doing
stupid, if not outright felonious, things by this time," agreed Sam.
"Small wonder the woman looks as if she's on her last legs."

"Maybe we shouldn't have kids," I mused as I forked up another
piece of cake.

"Ah, we'll have good kids," said Sam as if he believed himself.

"Our parents didn't do too badly. That might be a fair indication, although I don't suppose there's any way to tell until it's too late to do anything about it."

With a shrug, Sam said, "I expect we can drown a bad one, like they do to kittens."

"Sam! What a terrible thing to say." After thinking about his comment for another second or two, I added, "Unless one of our children starts acting like your awful nephew at a young age. Then I suppose it would be not only smart but humane to drown him before he can do anything truly ghastly."

"I didn't know Frank when he was young," said Sam. "Wonder if he was a bratty kid."

"Bet he was," I said. "I've never noticed any redeeming qualities in him. He probably didn't get that way overnight."

"Probably not," said Sam, chuckling.

Personally, I'd never seen Frank Pagano act like anything but a brute. Worse—or maybe it wasn't—he was stupid as a fallen log.

"I have a feeling Mr. and Mrs. Mason aren't accustomed to Howie acting up," said Sam musingly. "And I'm not accustomed to Pudge being a bad influence, but I'm beginning to wonder about the boy."

"He's going to be mowing our grass for the foreseeable future, right?" I said, after helping my spice cake slide into my tummy with a sip of coffee.

"Yes indeed. I got the feeling Mr. Wilson doesn't think Pudge is too big for a smack or two on the rear end, either."

"I wonder what the heck they actually saw out there. It sure as anything wasn't a ghost."

"Huh. Who knows?"

"Knock, knock," came a leathery voice from the direction of the back door.

"Come on in, Lou. Have some coffee and spice cake," said Sam looking over his shoulder at the interloper.

"Thanks. Don't mind if I do." He hobbled into the kitchen and took a seat at the table.

I waited, but he didn't say anything disparaging about me not making a hot breakfast for my poor, hardworking husband in the morning. Therefore, I cut him some cake and poured him a mug of coffee. The milk and sugar were already on the table, along with a bowl of oranges. With so many orange trees, we always had oranges.

"So what do you think those boys saw in the yard last night, Lou?" Sam said as he watched Mr. Prophet stir some sugar into his coffee cup and take a sip. Then he took a bite of spice cake and looked happier than he had when he'd entered.

"They said they saw a ghost," he said unhelpfully.

"Yes. They said they saw a see-through Indian that shook a rattle and wooed at them," I said. "I thought ghosts were supposed to say 'boo.' " Old joke recycled from last night, but it went over better today, at least with Sam, who chuckled.

"You sure there are no Indian bones out there with the other ones?" asked Mr. Prophet, sounding serious.

I turned and stared at him. "Well…yes. So far, anyway. Why? You don't really think they saw the ghost of an Indian out there, do you?"

With a shrug, he said, "Don't know, but I know me something about different Indian tribes, and I've known a good many Indians. They're far more interested in the spirit-side of life than most of us white folks are."

Sam had taken to staring at Mr. Prophet, too. "But there aren't any Indian bones out there."

"Haven't *found* any yet," said Mr. Prophet sounding rather…ta-da!…prophetic. He also sounded fairly gloomy.

"You don't think we'll find some really *ancient* bones out there, do you?" I asked. I rose and went to the kitchen range to pick up the coffee pot, which I carried to the table to refill cups.

"Don't know," said Mr. P. "But Yuyu ain't a cat that startles easy. He saw something out there, and it wasn't three damned kids. And one of those idiots mentioned a rattle, didn't he?"

Sam and I glanced at each other and then began thinking back over last night's drama. Or maybe it was this morning's drama. All I know is that neither of us got enough sleep. After thinking about the matter for a second, I said, "I think maybe two of the little vandals mentioned a rattle, or something rattling." A terrible thought occurred to me. "Good Lord, we don't have *rattlesnakes* in Pasadena, do we?"

"Ain't heard of any," said Mr. P.

"Don't think so," said Sam.

"If there are any, they might snooze in the yard. We're close to the arroyo," I said, scaring myself and vowing never to walk barefoot outside again. In fact, I might take to wearing rubber boots near where the bones were being dug up.

"Rattlers don't like commotion," said Mr. Prophet. "If there were any snakes out there, they'd have slithered off as soon as the dog and the cat started digging up bones."

"Are you sure?"

He shrugged. "Can't say for sure, but I ain't read anything in the newspapers about people around here being bit by rattlers."

"No," said Sam. "I haven't either. But what are you thinking about the boneyard, Lou? Are you serious about Indians and spirits and so forth?"

"Serious as the plague," said Mr. Prophet.

"That's serious, for sure," I said. Then I gulped. "But...but I'm a spiritualist-medium, and even *I* don't believe in ghosts!" Recalling a time or two when Rolly had escaped my control and done something outrageous—like the time he allowed the ghost of a murdered man to appear at a séance I was conducting—I backtracked a bit. "Well, not usually anyhow."

Sam pinned me with a hard look. "What do you mean, 'not usually', Daisy?"

"Um, well, I don't know if I ever precisely *told* you about this, but do you remember when I said I *knew* the younger Mr. Hastings, Edward, had been murdered and hadn't committed suicide, as everybody thought he had?"

"Yes." Sam's voice sounded as hard as his look.

"Well, that's because—I know you won't believe me—his ghost showed up during the séance I was conducting for his mother."

Sam let his head fall back and he groaned. Maybe it was more of a whimper.

Mr. Prophet snickered. "And you only *thought* you were a phony."

"I can't help it. It's the truth. And Sam," I went on, "you remember last year when Alma Jervis and those other stupid girls were following me around everywhere? Then when I conducted that séance for Mrs. Pinkerton and something stabbed me?"

"You got stabbed during a séance?" asked Mr. Prophet, staring at me as intently as Sam had been doing before he'd groaned.

"Not physically. Well, it hurt physically, but it was like being stabbed with pins and needles, and a huge pain hit me in the chest. It was…awful." I shuddered, remembering.

"Yeah," said Mr. Prophet. "That's what I'm talkin' about. I'd be willing to wager there are some Injun bones out there in the pile of dirt, and that those kids saw what they thought they saw." He shook his head. "Dammit. This ain't gonna be a good thing. I'll have to think about it fer a while."

"Are you serious?" asked Sam of Mr. Prophet, his hard stare fixed on Mr. P instead of me for a change.

"Serious as the plague," Mr. P repeated.

"Shoot," said Sam.

"Oh dear," I said.

"You two want to go to the Southwest Museum with me today?" said Sam suddenly, making me jump in my chair. "I can call into work. There's nothing going on, and they don't need me."

"Really?" I said. "You can just take off today? Oh, I'd *love* to go to the Southwest Museum with you today, Sam!"

"That the museum with all the Injun stuff in it?" asked Mr. Prophet.

"Yes," said Sam, rising and heading toward the hallway and the telephone table.

"It is," I agreed. "Want more spice cake?"

"Yeah. Don't mind if I do," said Mr. Prophet. "Thanks."

He still didn't rag me about not cooking breakfast for Sam. I guess the evening's Indian had worried him as much as it had the three miscreants.

It wasn't quite an hour later, after the bone-diggers and Dr. Cuthbert had arrived, when Mr. Prophet scooted himself and his peg into the back seat of Sam's Hudson. I got in on the front passenger's side. Spike wasn't too unhappy about being left to fend for himself because we took him across the street to keep my father company. I asked Pa if he wanted to go with us to see the Southwest Museum, but he politely declined.

So it was only the three of us who tootled through various streets to the Mt. Washington area of Los Angeles, where the Southwest Museum stood in all its glory. We had to park in a leveled-off area of ground and walk downhill to get to the entrance of the museum. Then we had to walk down a long, dark passage with recesses on both sides of it in which the museum staff had created and displayed small replicas of Southwest Indian life. Various tribes were represented, although I don't think they had a pictorial exhibit of the Gabrielino or Tongva Indians, which were the ones we were primarily interested in. Or thought we were, anyhow.

"Lotta walkin' for this old peg-legged man," groused Mr. Prophet at one point. It was true, and he had reason to gripe because it was a lot of walking for me, too, and I didn't have his leg problem.

"I'm sorry," I told him.

"Ain't your fault. These picture things are interesting, ain't they?"

"Yes," Sam and I said in a melodic duet, I in the alto range, he in the bass range.

After walking what seemed like several miles and peering at the various dioramas, we eventually got to an elevator built right into the side of the mountain, by golly. I guess the mountain was Mt. Washington, which was a pretty small mountain if you compare it to the San Gabriels or the San Bernadinos. Still, after we got on the elevator, it rose through what looked like solid rock. What a fascinating place this museum was already! Heck, even the elevator was out of the ordinary.

The elevator operator was an older man with a smile-creased face who said, "Enjoy your visit," when we exited his domain.

The lobby contained a counter behind which another elderly bloke with a friendly face sat. He also greeted us.

"Welcome to the Southwest Museum, folks. Here's a pamphlet that will help guide you through your tour of the various halls." He held up three small printed booklets.

"Thank you," Sam and I said. Sam took all three and dealt them out to Mr. Prophet and me, keeping one for himself.

"Oh, boy, where should we begin?" I asked no one in particular as I opened the pamphlet, which was folded in thirds. "Is there anything in here about the Gabrielino or Tongva Indians?"

"Gabrielinos and Tongvas?" the old man at the desk behind us repeated. "Whoo, boy, you've probably hit a snag there."

I turned and walked back to the desk. "Really? Why? I thought they were native to this precise area."

"Not precisely," he said with a grin that owed little to teeth. "But Charles Lummis wasn't especially interested in local tribes. He was more intrigued by the Pueblo and Navajo peoples."

"Arizona and New Mexico," said Mr. Prophet in his rusty voice.

"Yes," agreed the desk man.

"Bother," I said. "We need to know about Gabrielinos and Tongvas."

"You might find something in one of the display halls about them. Some of the Tongva claim to be an offshoot of the Gabrielinos, although some folks dispute that."

"Good grief, why? I mean, why don't the Gabrielinos want to claim the…what were they again?"

"Tongva. Don't ask me. I only work here." The desk man laughed.

"Oh, boy," said Sam. "Well, as long as we're here, let's look around.

"Sounds good to me," I said.

"Sounds all right to me, too," said Mr. Prophet, "although I'm gonna have to rest this leg for a bit."

"There are benches in most of the rooms," said the desk man helpfully.

"Good to know," said Mr. Prophet. "Thanks."

The three of us walked to the nearest hall containing artifacts. Sam and I walked around while Mr. Prophet sat on a bench and rested his poor leg. It probably didn't matter much. I expect he knew more about the artifacts and cultures contained in this museum than did most of the people who worked there.

SEVENTEEN

Perhaps it's because I didn't sleep enough on Monday night, or perhaps I can absorb only a little bit of intellectual stimulation in one trip; whatever my problem, I began to tire and get sick of looking at Indian artifacts before we made it to the fourth exhibit room. Not that there's anything innately boring about six thousand different kinds of woven or ceramic pots and hundreds of posted lectures above photographs and dioramas; I blame myself for starting to fade.

Mr. Lou Prophet jarred me out of my lethargy when he said, and loudly too, "That there's not right. Not right at all. Not one little bit right. It's wrong, dammit."

Snapping to attention, I glanced at where he'd affixed his venomous scowl. What I saw—well, what all visitors to the Southwest Museum saw if they made it this far—was a burial site. The caption over the mummified woman who had been buried with beaded goods—footwear, necklaces and other items a person might care to use in the afterlife—was, I thought, quite sweet. I can't recall it in its entirety, but it solemnly proclaimed the entire exhibit had been removed from where it had been originally and set up with precise accuracy in the museum. It went on to wish the deceased—deceased for a hundred or more years—a glorious life after death.

All in all, I thought it was tasteful and quite thoughtful.

"What's wrong with it?" I asked. "I think it's kind of lovely."

"Lovely, hell. No Injun wants his dead relations displayed for the whole world to see. That woman can't 'rest peacefully' after being taken away from her family and home. It's their…whattaya call it? Their culture. Their beliefs. Their religion, fer the love of god."

"Oh," I said, faintly stunned. Contemplating the nature of families, I decided I wouldn't care if, say, my great-grandfather Gumm's bones were displayed in an informational way in a museum somewhere. However, my own personal beliefs were clearly contrary to native Indian beliefs.

"Hmmm," said Sam, leaning closer in order to look at the display and read the caption. "This has upset you hasn't it, Lou?"

"*I* ain't upset," claimed the patently upset former bounty hunter. "But if anybody from that female's tribe or, god forbid, her family ever saw this display, they'd have conniptions. You can't take the body and bones away from the family group, or they'll never rest peacefully in the afterlife, whatever the hell that is. Damn. I was afraid of this."

"Wait," I said, understanding finally making a stumbling appearance in my exhausted brain. "You think the boys saw the ghost of an Indian who'd been separated from his family in the back forty last night, don't you?"

"It's what I'm afraid of," said Mr. Prophet. "If I'm right, and either the dog and cat or those police fellers have managed to disturb the bones even more, you ain't going to have very many peaceful nights until something's done about 'em."

"Them what? The bones?" I asked.

"Yeah. The bones."

"If your theory is correct," said Sam, "and I don't believe in ghosts in the first place, how in the world can we get the bones back to where they belong?"

"I dunno," said a gloomy Mr. Prophet. "But I think I need to send a cable to Arizona. Got an Injun friend there who might know what to do, if anybody can find him."

"Even if our bones were from a tribe living in California?" I asked. "I mean, if those were the bones of, say, a Danish person, and you asked, say, somebody from Argentina how to deal with them, how would the person from Argentina know what to do?"

"Ain't the same thing at all," said the stubborn old coot. "You could probably haul an Injun or a Mescin up from Mexico to do something with these bones, because the native tribes are all connected in one way or another. Ain't no Dane gonna know anything about our Injuns. The Danes have their own history and their own gods and customs and so forth. Mebbe somebody from Norway or Sweden might be able to help Danish bones, but they wouldn't do any good here."

I hate to admit it, but he almost made sense. Providing, of course, you bought the notion of a long-dead native person haunting our back-forty boneyard. Oh, dear. Recalling a couple more instances of disturbances during some séances I'd conducted, I had to sort of, kind of, almost, very nearly, in a way, believe it. Shucks, as Mr. Prophet might say if he were being polite.

"Huh," said Sam, sounding as skeptical as ever. "I don't recall any Italian customs regarding separating bones from families being a bad thing."

"In Shakespeare's *Henry V*, there's a pre-battle scene in which soldiers don't know they're talking to King Henry, and they're bemoaning the fact that when the final trumpet sounds, their bones might be scattered all over the field in France, and they'd never achieve glory."

"Yeah, I know," said Sam grumpily. "The Christian religion is as weird as any other religion, I suppose. But you can visit catacombs in Rome, where I doubt anybody's entire skeleton is buried, but I'm not sure about other cities in Italy. Of course, Italy hasn't been one united country for all that long."

"What the hell are cat— whatever you said?" asked Mr. Prophet. I'd been about to ask the same question, only more politely.

"Ancient underground tombs. I know there are some in Rome."

"And you can see people's bones in the tombs?" I asked.

"Oh, yeah," said Sam. "In fact, in one issue of the *National Geographic*, there was a photograph of a room decorated with skulls and bones. I think that catacomb was the burial place of the Capuchin monks."

"Ew," I said, thinking I'd love to see that. A room lined with skulls. Imagine it!

"Cripes," said Lou Prophet, grimacing. "I think human beings must all have crazy customs for housing their dead. Don't think I'd like to see a room lined with skulls."

"Well, there are other bones in there besides skulls. And there's a skeleton or maybe more than one dressed in monks' robes," said Sam, beginning to enjoy himself now that Mr. Prophet and I both seemed to be getting serious cases of the heebie-jeebies.

Only I wasn't. I aimed to go up to the attic and dig around in the pile of old *National Geographics* in boxes up there and see if I could find the photo of the Roman catacombs. Or…"What did you call those monks? The Cap-Cap—"

"Capuchin monks. Early Christians."

"Capuchin," I repeated, wishing I'd brought my notebook and pad with me so I could jot down the name. "Fascinating."

"Cripes," said Mr. Prophet again. "Early Christian monks aren't gonna help you get rid of that Injun in the backyard. I'm going to have to get an old pal to help, if I can find him, unless you can find one of your— What did you call 'em? Gabriels?"

"Gabrielinos," said Sam. "Or…oh, heck, what did the desk man say they were? Tong-somethings."

"I thought the tongs were Chinese," said Mr. Prophet. "I'm gettin' confused as hell."

Doing my best to enlighten him, I said, "He said the Tong-somethings might be a branch of the Gabrielino Indians, although there seems to be some dispute about that. And I don't have a clue where to find a Gabrielino or a Tong-whatever Indian."

"The San Gabriel Mission!" Sam said suddenly, startling me into a jump of surprise.

Mr. Prophet kind of jumped a little, too, and said, "Ow."

"Sorry, Lou. But the Mission San Gabriel Arcángel is supposed to hold archives relating to local Indians. San Gabriel. Gabrielino." He shrugged. "I guess it's worth a trip to San Gabriel to see if we can find out something."

"Thought you didn't believe in the ghost in your yard," said Mr. Prophet, sounding sly.

"I don't. But we might find out more about the local Indians and their customs. I mean, if you want to."

"I want to," I said stoutly. "I *do* believe Mr. Prophet about the ghost. Most of all, I believe Yuyu and Spike. Well, Spike might bark at intrusive humans, but Yuyu usually only hisses at people he doesn't like. It must take something special for him to yowl like that."

"Exactly," said Mr. Prophet, as if I'd just proved some kind of point for him.

Sam shook down his coat sleeve and glanced at his wristwatch. "It's almost noon. I'm not sure if you can just drop in at the San Gabriel Mission and look around, but it's an active Catholic Church, so you probably can. Maybe a priest or a volunteer can give us a hint about the Gabrielinos and the Tong-whatevers."

"First we'd better find out what the Tong-whatevers are actually called," I said. "And I'm hungry. Can we get some lunch somewhere first?"

"Sure," said Sam. "We can ask at the front desk if there's a café or lunch stand around here where we can grab a bite to eat."

"In that case, going to the San Gabriel Mission sounds like a great idea," I said.

"Yeah," said Mr. Prophet. "Especially if they know something about the local Injuns."

After contemplating bits and pieces of information I'd learned about the San Gabriel Mission, I said, "I think I read somewhere that when Father Junipero Serra had all the missions in California built, the priests tried to convert all the Indians. Then, of course, they used them as slaves to build their missions."

"Why 'of course'?" asked Sam.

"Because that's what people always do when they barge in on someone else's life," said Mr. Prophet. "It's why all the American Injuns live on reservations. White folks are greedy bastards."

"Probably not just white folks," I said, not feeling protective or proud of my white ancestors, but stating what I believed to be a universal truth. "Weren't some of the Negro slaves captured by other Negro tribes, who then sold them to people who stacked them in ships and brought them to the various places where slave labor was needed?"

"Criminy," said Sam. "You're as bad as Lou about describing atrocities, Daisy."

"Well, I think it stinks that people take over other people's lands and so forth, although I guess we wouldn't be living in Pasadena if our ancestors hadn't done it." I paused for a second as the three of us seemed to ponder my words. "And Mr. Prophet fought to keep slavery alive and well in the American South."

"Didn't think of it that way," said Mr. Prophet. "Just didn't want somebody from hundreds of miles away tellin' *me* how to live. My family never owned slaves."

"I believe you. But there's another example of other people telling people who are used to one way of life that they're doing it wrong. In the case of slavery, I'm all for banning it. Never thought about southern folks who didn't have slaves being affected by an edict from the north," I admitted.

"Yeah, I know," said Mr. Prophet.

"All right. No use hashing over history," said Sam. "It's history, and we can't do anything about it. We *can* have lunch and visit the San Gabriel Mission, though. Do you need to rest before we leave the museum, Lou? It's a long walk back to the car."

"Naw. I'll be fine. I'll rest up in the car. I'm hungry, too."

So we made our way back to the front desk, and Sam asked the nice man behind the desk where the nearest dining establishment was located.

"Go on up Marmion Way a bit, and you'll find a nice little café where they serve sandwiches and so forth,"

"Thanks," said Sam. "Oh, and you told us there was a band of the Gabrielino Indians that might or might not actually belong? We can't recall what you called them. Would you remind us? The word began with tong."

"The Tongva. Yes. There's some discussion about whether or not they belong to Gabrielinos or are a separate clan altogether."

"Clan," I muttered. "Another word for tribe, I guess."

"I guess," agreed Mr. Prophet. "Why not?"

"No reason I can think of," I said.

As the three of us walked to the elevator, Sam withdrew a policemanly notebook from his jacket pocket, plucked a pencil therefrom as well, and jotted down the word "Tongva." We wouldn't forget *that* one again. Or, if we did, Sam could remind us. Good detective, my Sam.

We had some soup and a sandwich at the little café the desk man told us about. Then, after using the facilities politely provided for their customers' convenience, the three of us went back out to Sam's big black Hudson and began the trek to San Gabriel. The mission was maybe fifteen miles from the Southwest Museum, which wasn't all that far. However, Sam had to take twisty roads to get there. First Arroyo Seco Drive and then onto Garfield—I don't know if it was the same Garfield we Pasadenans used—and then to Main Street and Rosemead. Finally, Sam made a turn onto a little road called Mission Drive in San Gabriel, and it took us to the museum. I don't think it took much more than an hour to get there, which I didn't consider too terrible, and Mr. Prophet got to rest his poor leg.

"We'll have to find a gasoline station in order to get home again," said Sam as he opened the front door for me and the back door for Mr. Prophet.

"If we can find people in the church, someone can probably tell us where there's a filling station," I said.

"Yeah," said Sam. "I'm sure the priests and nuns drive all over the place all the time."

"Maybe there will be other visitors who can tell us," I said.

"Shit. Priests and nuns? I don't like those folks."

"Well, this is a Roman Catholic Church," I said. "What did you expect to find here?"

"Thought we'd find an Injun or two."

"Maybe we will," I said, attempting as I spoke to take in the enormity of the old building.

"Let's look here," said Sam, indicating a historical marker with information printed on it, which was locked behind a plate of glass. "Franciscans. Evidently, Serra was a Franciscan."

"Who's Serra?" asked Mr. Prophet.

"He's the guy who started building all the missions in California. There are missions running from San Diego to…well, I don't know where. But in northern California," I said.

"Huh," said Mr. Prophet.

"Oh, my," I said. "This was the fourth mission built in California. I didn't know that."

"Dedicated on September 8, 1771," opined Mr. Prophet, also reading.

"Oh, look here. The place had a tannery and grew grapes for wine," I said. "Bet they had the Indians cultivate the ground and plant and pick the grapes."

"Probably," said Sam.

"Cripes," said Mr. Prophet, sounding shocked, which pretty much shocked me, since I'd assumed the fellow to be relatively unflappable, "There's upwards of six thousand Injuns buried here. Shoot. Wonder if there are any of 'em still alive. If they are, and if they still live around here, mebbe we can find one to talk to."

"Six thousand?" I squinted to where Mr. Prophet pointed at the informational sign. He hadn't misread it. It said there were approximately six thousand Indians buried in the cemetery at the Mission San Gabriel. "Wow. That's a lot of dead people."

"It's the oldest cemetery in the Los Angeles area," said Sam, continuing to read from the board.

"Well, I guess this is the place to go if you need to find out about the Gabrielinos and the Tong"—Mr. Prophet squinted at the board —"The Tongvas. This board don't say nothin' about Gabrielinos. It only mentions the Tongvas."

"It's still probably a good place to gather information about natives," I said doubtfully.

"I guess so," said Sam, also doubtfully. "I wonder if they have some kind of lobby or reception area for visitors."

"Guess we have to go in and look," I said.

As I glanced around, I saw huge open spaces and a lot of tiled corridors going this way and that. So we started walking down them, hoping to find a reception area of some sort.

EIGHTEEN

By golly, the mission had a reception area! It looked quite modern, in fact. Sam opened the door for Mr. Prophet and me, and I entered first, as was proper. I was only slightly taken aback to see a fellow in a brown robe and a white tonsure sitting behind what I guessed was the reception desk. He smiled kindly at us when we entered. I was glad for his smile, thinking Franciscans *should* be friendly. After all, St. Francis of Assisi loved all the animals, didn't he? And we were human animals, perhaps the least of them all, but still....

"Daisy," Sam whispered in my ear as we approached the desk, "I forgot you'll have to cover your head if we go into the church."

"Isn't my hat a good enough covering?" I asked, patting same. It wasn't fancy, but it was a nice blue cloche that went well with my checked blue day dress. Naturally I'd made them both on my mother's side-pedal White sewing machine. Which, as she never used it, I'd moved to Sam's and my house.

"Huh. Maybe so. I'm used to my female Italian relations. All the women wear black hats and scarves and look like somebody they loved just died, but I guess if you're not Italian, you can get away with wearing a blue hat."

The priest at the reception desk chuckled. "Any head covering is allowed, and the lady looks charming in her blue hat."

I know I blushed because I felt my neck and cheeks get hot. Being a redhead comes with some disadvantages, and blushing is only one of them. But were priests supposed to compliment women on their mode of dress? I thought they weren't even supposed to *notice* women. I'd have to grill Sam about the Catholic Church, since I was woefully ignorant about it.

"Thank you," Sam and I said together. We really did make a nice duet.

I heard Mr. Prophet snicker.

"Would you care to purchase one of our informational booklets?" asked the priest at the desk. Mind you, I'm only guessing he was a priest. Maybe Catholics had other people who wore brown robes and cut their hair in circles around a bald spot. I'd never understood that, either. I mean, I'd never understood the significance of that particular haircut. Maybe Sam could enlighten me later.

"Sure. Thank you," said Sam, reaching into a pocket and pulling out his change purse. "We're primarily interested in…well, I guess they're the Tongva Indians who used to live and work here."

"They still do," said the priest, taking the dime Sam held out and handing him a pamphlet in return.

Mr. Prophet had moved closer to the desk. "Any of 'em talk English? My Spanish might be a little rusty, and I never learned no Tongva. Or Gabriel-whatever."

"Gabrielino is the word you're looking for," said the priest, chuckling. "Most of our residents speak English. At least a little. What are you mainly interested in?"

Oh, dear. This might get tricky. And then I had one of my brilliant ideas and decided to butt in. "I'm doing a research project for a library presentation," I said, lying through my teeth. "I wanted to find out about Gabrielino—or Tongva, I guess—burial customs, if there were any. In particular. I mean, before they converted to Christianity and so forth." My brilliant idea started spluttering toward the end of my speech.

"Ah," said the priest. "You're interested in truly ancient history. The Tongva who live with us are Christians."

"Do you know if they still tell stories about their old religion?" asked Mr. Prophet, trying to sound friendly. "When I was in New Mexico, I knew me some Apaches who could tell stories about all sorts of stuff their ancestors did hundreds of years earlier. Before they turned Christian."

I could tell, although I hope the priest couldn't, that he nearly choked on his last sentence.

"I expect you might find an elderly man or woman sitting in the shade in our courtyard plaza," said the priest. "It's a pleasant place, and many of our elders enjoy resting out there in the afternoons. I'm sure legends about the old customs are handed down from generation to generation, even if they no longer practice them."

"Thank you," I said. "Um…where is the courtyard?"

Sam had opened his pamphlet and was perusing it. He said, "Here it is, Daisy. Right outside and down a couple of corridors."

"Indeed," said the priest. "It's a lovely place."

"The whole mission is beautiful," I said. "It amazes me that these missions were built hundreds of years ago, and they're still in use."

"Barring the occasional earthquake or fire," said the priest with a laugh in his voice.

"Yes, I suppose all of California can say that," I agreed.

The three of us turned and headed to the door. Sam said, "Thank you," to the priest as he turned the doorknob.

"Enjoy your visit," advised the priest.

Sounded like a good idea to me. I just hoped we'd learn something. I didn't fancy the notion of an unhappy Gabrielino or Tongva Indian—or any other type of unhappy ghost—haunting our backyard. The bones of the young man who'd died there were bad enough. Which made me think of something.

"Do you suppose it's not an Indian but the white guy who died out there who's haunting the boneyard?" asked my two companions.

"No," said Mr. Prophet.

"No," said Sam. "I don't think anything's haunting us, but I'll let you two figure that one out. Lou thinks it's an Indian."

"It's an Injun," said Mr. Prophet as if he was sure of himself.

Terrific.

The mission was an amazing place. Even the tiled corridors leading to the church and the plaza were gorgeous. Sure enough, when we got to the courtyard, we not only saw people sitting on benches under huge live oak trees, but somebody—I suspect Indians under priestly supervision—had built a beautiful fountain, too. And there! I tugged on Sam's coat sleeve.

"Look! It's a statue dedicated to the Tongva. So they must have lived here."

"Guess so," said he.

"Shoot," mumbled Mr. Prophet. "Probably all that's left of 'em is that statue."

"You might well be right," said Sam.

My gaze veered from the fountain and the statue and came to rest on the people in the plaza. Many sat on benches. Some of them sat on the ground. They all looked like Indians to me, too, although maybe they weren't. "Perhaps we've hit pay dirt," I whispered to my companions.

"Hope so," said Mr. Prophet. "I'm gonna see if that old guy will talk to me." He chin-pointed to an old man who looked as if he'd reached his hundredth birthday several years prior. He sat on a bench, his hands and chin propped on a stick, and he wore the kind of white trousers and shirt you see when you visit downtown Los Angeles in Mexican neighborhoods. He had a colorful striped serape over his shoulders to keep the nippy air off. The weather on that pretty Tuesday was cool enough for me to wear a sweater, but it wasn't cold-cold.

Sam and I strolled around the plaza, gazing at various plants and bushes and nodding and smiling at other people seated or standing there. Most were either Hispanic—I hesitate to say Mexican, because they were probably of Spanish descent here (then again, so were the Mexicans)—or Indian. Or a combination. Probably most were mixed. I noticed Mr. Prophet take a seat on the bench a foot or so away from the seated hundred-and-twenty-year-old.

"It will be interesting to see if he can get that fellow to talk to him," I muttered to Sam.

"I have faith in Lou," said Sam, guiding me to another bench that was unoccupied until we sat on it.

We were too far away from Mr. Prophet and his companion to hear what they said to each other, but it looked to me as if Mr. Prophet said—or probably grunted—something to the old man, who turned and grinned at him.

"He does seem to have a way about him," I said to Sam as we continued to watch, trying not to be obvious about it.

In this attempt, I pointed out to Sam, sculptures of interest every now and then, and he did likewise to me. Most of our attention, however, as much as we attempted to disguise it, was fixed on the two old men sitting on the far bench.

Sam was right. In what seemed like no time at all, Mr. Prophet and the old man—I was going to say the other old man, but that wouldn't have been fair to Mr. Prophet, who wasn't quite a hundred yet—were yakking to each other as if they'd known each other for decades. I began to relax and scooted closer to Sam so I could lean on him.

I rested and relaxed so much, I was almost asleep when Mr. Prophet finally ended his conversation and walked over to us. In actual fact, and this is embarrassing to admit, I'd have fallen off the bench if Sam hadn't caught me. As soon as I realized what was happening, I glanced at the bench where Mr. Prophet and the other man had been, only to discover it empty. Fiddlesticks. I'd missed it! Whatever "it" was.

"So what's up, Lou? Did you find out what you needed to know?"

"Think so. Want me to tell you about it?"

"Yes, please," I said.

"Well, I'm sick of sittin', so let's wander around this place some more, and I can fill you in," said Mr. Prophet.

So Sam and I got to our feet. I felt better after my little nodding nap. Peppier. We decided to head to the church next.

"I don't wanna go in there," grumped Mr. Prophet.

"You don't have to pray or anything." I told him. "Just think of it as a historical building."

"You don't even have to light a candle," said Sam with a grin.

"They got candles in there?"

"Oh yes," said Sam. "I suspect there are candles everywhere. And statues of saints. You can light a candle to any old saint you want to."

"Why do people do that?"

"Light candles to saints?" asked Sam.

"Yeah. Do they pray to saints, too?"

"Sure."

"I thought that sorta thing was called idolatry," muttered the old sinner.

"Good thing my aunt isn't here," said Sam, chuckling softly. "She'd probably smack you with her cane and give you a lecture about how every time she loses something, she lights a candle and prays to St. Anthony of Padua, who helps her find it again."

"Naw! Nobody does that."

"I thought you lived among a lot of Mexican people, Mr. Prophet. They're mostly Catholic, aren't they?" I said.

"Yeah, but they never made me go to church."

"Well, if you ever get leprosy, be sure to pray to St. Damien of Molokai. I read an article about him once. Sounded like a great guy," I told him.

"Did he cure leprosy?" Mr. Prophet asked incredulously.

"No, actually, he died from it. But he helped the people in a leper colony in Hawaii when nobody else would go near the place. He sounds like a good man."

"Shoot," muttered Mr. Prophet.

We'd come to the door of the church. Before Sam opened it for us, he said, "Okay, sober up, you two. We're entering a church a lot of people take seriously." He actually waited until both Mr. Prophet and I appeared to him to be suitably somber.

Please don't take my comments about the interior of the church amiss, but I was kind of disappointed. I'd expected something huge and with candles burning everywhere. But it wasn't all that big. There was a wide center aisle made of tiles and bench pews on either side. It didn't even have side aisles running from the ends of the pews on either side. Six saints (I guess they were saints) had been sculpted and held pride of place behind the altar, each in his or her own frame. They took up the entire back of the chancel, and the priest had to climb some lovely stairs and stand in a little wooden boxlike structure in order to deliver his homily or sermon or whatever Catholics call it. In Latin, which I'll bet nobody in the congregation understood. Huge paintings loomed at an angle over the pews with smaller paintings flat against the walls.

Whispering, I told Sam, "Where are all the candles?"

"We walked right past them," he said.

"We did?" I turned around and lo and behold, he was right. In the back (or maybe it was the front) of the church were tables with tons of little candles on them and paintings and statues of saints behind the candles. Some candles were lit, some weren't, and a little old lady with a black scarf over her head proceeded to light one even as I watched. Then she bowed her head, must have said a silent prayer, then made the sign of the cross and hobbled to a back pew. I turned around again, hoping she hadn't noticed me staring. "Yes. I see now."

"I've never been in a church this old," said Sam. "I'm used to the huge cathedrals back in New York City."

"This place is givin' me the creeps," whispered Mr. Prophet. "And is that there a gravestone in front of the altar thing there?"

"I don't know," said Sam, slowly walking up to an oblong stone plaque on the floor in front of the altar. "Yes. It's either a tombstone over the graves of several Franciscan Fathers who are buried underneath the stone, or it's a commemorative stone with their names etched on it. Maybe the fathers are buried somewhere else, say in the cemetery, along with those six thousand Indians."

"Huh. Well, I want to get out of this place. Don't like it in here. Gives me the willies."

"That's probably Satan attacking you for having the effrontery to enter a holy place," I told him.

"Wouldn't surprise me none," he said.

"We might as well go back home," said Sam. "We've seen the plaza and the church, and you've talked to someone you think might be of help to us if we actually have a ghost in our yard, right, Lou?"

"Yeah. And I'm sick of walkin'."

"I kind of am, too," I admitted. "We wandered all over the Southwest Museum this morning, and now we've walked all over the San Gabriel Mission. My feet are beginning to object. And now it looks as if it's a Tongva ghost instead of a Gabrielino ghost in our yard. I'm still confused."

"I don't like bein' so close to this kind of church," said Mr. Prophet. "Can't help thinkin' of all the Injuns they killed in order to build the place."

"They might not have killed them all," I said, my voice not carrying much conviction.

"Huh," said Mr. Prophet.

"Huh," said Sam.

Very well, then.

NINETEEN

T he nice Franciscan friar (or priest, or whatever you call those fellows) at the reception desk told us how to get to Rosemead Street in San Gabriel, where we would find a filling station.

"Then you can just take Rosemead up to Pasadena," said the priest with a smile.

"Thank you," said Sam, Mr. Prophet and I. This time, we made a not-quite lovely trio. Mr. Prophet could sing. I know he could, because I'd heard him, but his voice scratched some.

Anyhow, about an hour and a half later, Sam pulled his Hudson into my parents' driveway, because we wanted to pick up Spike. Also —and I wouldn't say this to anyone—but it was almost dinnertime. I didn't have a clue what meal I could prepare—or how to prepare it—for my darling husband, and I hoped my family would invite us to stay for dinner at their place.

I know. I'm almost as awful as Frank Pagano, except that I don't break laws or kill people.

"Oh, please stay and have dinner here," said Vi, sounding actually happy about the prospect.

A little of my guilt eased.

"I made entirely too much shepherd's pie, and since the Pinkertons plan to go to Santa Barbara tomorrow, I brought all the leftovers home with me."

"What about poor Featherstone and the Applewoods?" I asked her. I believe I've mentioned Featherstone is the Pinkertons' butler. The Applewoods are Quincy and Edie, both of whom work for either or both of the Pinkertons.

"I left some for them, of course, but Edie is quite a good cook herself, so she doesn't really need leftovers."

Crumb. Edie, an old school chum of mine, could cook well and I was barely learning. Vi kept telling me I was doing well and that I'd get better with practice. We'd just have to wait and see if she was right.

"Thanks, Vi," said Sam. "We've been walking pretty much all day, except for when we were in the automobile, and I doubt Daisy feels like cooking tonight."

"Does she ever?" asked Mr. Prophet. Snidely, I'm sure I need not add, although I did anyway.

"Stop that, Lou Prophet!" said my marvelous aunt. "Daisy is learning, and she's doing a good job of it."

"I can vouch for her," said my loyal Sam.

Mr. Prophet said, "Cripes, I can't even tease you about your cookin' any longer, can I?"

"No," I told him firmly.

"Oh, all right," he said, sounding morose.

"Come and help me set the table," Ma said to me.

So I did. As we ate Vi's wonderful shepherd's pie, which she made with lamb, claiming a pie made with beef is a cowboy pie, we told everyone what had happened in our backyard the night before.

"Pudge Wilson did that?" exclaimed my mother, sounding as surprised as I thought she should, Pudge having heretofore given no indication of criminal tendencies.

"He did. And he roped two of his scouting buddies into going on his midnight run with him," I said.

"I don't expect the Wilsons were too pleased about their son's antics," murmured Pa, grinning.

"They weren't," I said in a stern voice, thinking Pudge's misbehavior was nothing to grin about. Then again, Pa used to overturn outhouses on Halloween, so perhaps he wasn't the best judge.

"But they thought they saw a ghost, so I don't think they'll do anything like it again," said Sam.

"A *ghost*!" Pa exclaimed.

"Yup," I said, reminding myself of Mr. Prophet. "Said it wooed at them and shook a rattle."

"Was it a baby ghost?" asked my mother, automatically associating rattles with babies. "I thought the bones you found were those of a young man."

"They were," I said, deciding to give the Indian equation of the picture a miss.

"Dumb kids," muttered Mr. Prophet, who likewise seemed to want to leave native ghosts alone for the moment.

"All three of them regretted their midnight foray," said Sam, chuckling softly. "They were scared to death."

"Because they saw a ghost?" asked Pa.

"They probably saw a cat or somethin'," said Mr. Prophet. "Yuyu's eye can look pretty scary in the dark."

"I can vouch for that," said I, who recalled that yellow eye peering malevolently at me an evening or two earlier. "But the boys swore they saw a see-through ghost that wooed and rattled at them." I gave a little shrug. "Might have been a baby ghost. They were too scared to stick around and find out for sure."

"I'm sure seeing a ghost would scare me," said Pa.

Vi laughed.

"I can imagine thinking they saw a ghost would scare the boys, but why did you go to the museum and the mission? Isn't it a working day for you, Sam?" asked Ma, who knew all about abiding by the work schedules dictated to them by others.

Sam hurried to speak before either Mr. Prophet or I could. "Had the day off," he said, fibbing slightly. "Ever since Daisy started wondering if the bones in the yard were of Indian origin, even though we now know they aren't, she's been pestering me to take her to the Southwest Museum."

"I have not!"

"Have too," said Sam, grinning. "Then, after we'd stomped all over the Southwest Museum and didn't find anything relating to an Indian tribe that might have lived in this area, we decided to visit the San Gabriel Mission. We had better luck there."

"Really?" said Ma, interested.

"Yes," I answered for Sam. "Evidently the tribe that once populated this area was called the Tongva. We thought they were called the Gabrielinos, but there's a big statue at the mission dedicated to the Tongva, and we didn't see the word Gabrielino anywhere there. I don't know if the two are linked some way or another, but the only native tribe mentioned at the mission was the Tongva."

"Yup," said Mr. Prophet, reminding me of myself. "Met an old Mestizo there—"

"An old what?" I said, interrupting. How rude, huh?

"Mestizo. Mix of Spanish and Indian. Mebbe some Mexican. Anyway, he called himself a Mestizo by the name of Emilio DeLoera and claimed to be descended from the Tongva."

"Ah," said Pa. "Interesting."

"Yeah," said Mr. Prophet. "He was real interesting. Had quite a few tales to tell."

"We should visit that mission, Joe,' said Ma to Pa. "Sounds fascinating.

"It's Catholic," said Vi in a voice clearly conveying her belief that Roman Catholics weren't much better than idolaters, which reminded me of Mr. Prophet. I guess she recalled that Sam had been raised in a Catholic family, because she almost instantly added, "Not that there's anything wrong with Catholics."

Bet it almost choked her to say that.

"Place gave me the creeps," said Mr. Prophet. "Inside the church, I mean. It was dark and dismal, and I think we were walking on people's graves."

"It pretty much was," agreed Sam. "It's very old. Built in the 1700s when there wasn't a whole lot of available material, manpower or knowledge about how to build things. I guess a

Spaniard designed the building, but the friars didn't bring a lot of labor with them."

"The British built gigantic cathedrals hundreds of years earlier than the 1700s," I reminded him.

"Yes, in a country that had been civilized, more or less, for centuries. They'd built huge cathedrals in Italy and Spain, too. And France. This was an entirely new country for the Spanish."

"Not for the Injuns," said Mr. Prophet. "But the Spanish got 'em under control pretty fast, I reckon. The Spaniards had guns. The Injuns had sticks."

I cleared my throat. "I wonder if they found many bones in our yard today, and if Dr. Cuthbert managed to put more of the skeleton together." I didn't even want to *think* about Spanish atrocities committed against native populations. Not that we descendants of Great Britain could boast of a better record. The whole subjugation issue was a melancholy one for me, so I decided to change the subject.

"Spike and I wandered over to your place for a bit," said Pa. "They were still finding bones, but not as many. The doctor thinks they're nearing the end of that poor young man's remains, but he's managed to put together a nearly full skeleton."

"That's good. Maybe they'll go away soon," I said. "The bone-diggers, I mean."

"Would be nice to have our house and grounds to ourselves again," said Sam.

"Yes, it would," said Mr. Prophet with feeling.

"Oh!" I said, having had a brilliant idea. Maybe. "I think I'll visit Flossie at the Salvation Army tomorrow. She's been wanting me to go there and see Billy and Daisy." I stopped to shake my head. "And why they named that poor child Daisy, I'll never understand." Before anyone could answer or chastise me, I went on. "Maybe I can find contact information for Mr. Edwards. It's possible that he's remembered the name of the fellow who disappeared. Even if we never discover what killed him, if he has any family left, they'd probably like to know what became of him. They might even have a funeral or something."

"Good idea," said Sam.

"Yeah," said Mr. Prophet.

I almost yelled, "Hallelujah!" because he'd finally almost said something nice about me, but I didn't.

"Oh, that's so true," said Vi. "I'm sorry Paul is buried in France, but at least I know how he died and where his grave is."

We diners sobered for quite a while after Vi's remark. Her only child, Paul, was a casualty of the so-called Great War, and his bones are still over there. Guess it was a great war, if you thought of it in terms of it being huge and disastrous. There was nothing else great about it that I could think of.

Dinner ended eventually, however, and Ma and I washed up the dishes. Pa, Sam and Mr. Prophet went to the living room. On a normal evening, they might have hauled out the card table and played gin rummy. That night, though, I got a feeling both Sam and Mr. Prophet were too done in to concentrate, even on a silly card game.

Then, the three of us humans yawning and Spike leaping happily, Sam, Mr. Prophet and I waved goodbye to my folks, walked to Sam's Hudson, and he drove it across the street to our house. Short drive for once that day.

By then the shades of night had fallen. Actually, they'd fallen several hours earlier, but Pa had thoughtfully left the porch light on at our house for us. I know he'd done it because he'd told us he had. I unhooked Spike's leash from his collar as soon as Sam closed the front door, and Spike raced through the house to the back door. Guess he wanted to see what had been going on out there, too. And maybe find his new best friend, Yuyu the cat.

I still had a difficult time thinking of my fearsome hunting hound having befriended a broken-down, one-eyed yellow cat. Then again, Sam and I had befriended a broken-down, one-legged old former bounty-hunting man, so I guess odd things just happened sometimes.

I turned on the back porch light, and we all strolled outside to see the tented table where the bones of whoever he was were laid out.

"My goodness," I said, eyeing the work done that day, "he's almost back together."

"Unless you tilt the table. Then he'll just be a heap o' bones again," said Mr. Prophet, ever the voice of joy and possibility. That's a joke.

"Is Dr. Cuthbert doing anything about holding the bones together?" Sam wondered aloud as he reached for what was mostly the bones of a hand. Some of those finger bones were tiny; I don't know how anyone had figured out they were bones and not mere twigs or whatever. He gently touched a bone. It didn't move. "Ah. Looks like he's using some kind of clay substance to keep the bones where he wants them. Not sure what will happen to them eventually, but if we ever find out who he was, he'll probably have to be taken apart again."

"Unless Dr. Cuthbert wants to string him together and use him to teach students anatomy lessons," I mused.

"That's a thought," said Sam.

"Yeah. Good thought," said Mr. Prophet, which made perhaps two nice things he'd said to or about me in one whole day. I'm sure his goodwill would sink soon.

"I hope we can find out who he was," I said. "Just so we can know for ourselves. I mean, I'd like to know who he was, even if he was just a drunken lout as Mr. Edwards implied he was."

"I didn't know he'd implied that," said Sam, eyeing me thoughtfully.

"Oh. Maybe you weren't here when he came over yesterday," I said, trying to cast my mind back twenty-four or –five hours. It didn't want to be cast.

"Yeah, he did," affirmed Mr. Prophet. "And you were at work, Sam."

"Actually, he more than implied it," I said, stray comments made by Mr. Edwards peeking around corners in my brain. "Said the young man he was thinking about, the one who disappeared and never showed up again, drank too much all the time and got into fights. That's how he lost his two front teeth."

"Yeah. I remember him saying that," said Mr. Prophet. "Probably the same feller."

"Aha," said Sam. "Maybe there's a record of the work crew that built this house somewhere."

"How would we find it?" I asked.

"Beats me," said Sam.

"Dunno," agreed Mr. Prophet. "Mebbe Edwards will remember the name of the builder. Might have records written down somewhere if he's still in business."

"That's a good thought," said Sam.

"Yes," I agreed, although I did so tentatively. I wasn't sure I trusted Mr. Prophet not to verbally leap upon anything I said and rip it to tatters.

"When you see Flossie tomorrow, will you ask her for Edwards' telephone number?" said Sam. "I can give him a call tomorrow night."

"Good idea," I said.

"Yeah," said Mr. Prophet.

Spike, who had raced down the porch stairs and torn across the yard and down the arbor path, probably looking for Yuyu at Mr. Prophet's cottage, came trotting back again, tail waving in the air and looking pleased with himself. He had something in his mouth; something bumpy and brown.

"What do you have there, Spike?" Sam said, bending over to pet the hound and see if he could get Spike to release his treasure. "Let go."

Spike, who knew the command "let go" of old, let go.

"Aw, cripes," said Sam, looking unhappy.

"What is it?" I said, hurrying up to stand next to him.

"Shoot," said Mr. Prophet, also standing next to Sam. "Looks like Spike found out why the Injun's haunting your yard."

In his hand, Sam held a jawbone. An old jawbone. A dark-colored jawbone. A jawbone whose teeth seemed to have been ground down over years of chewing. A jawbone much, much, *much* older than the jawbone Spike had found on Saturday.

"Oh, no!" I wailed. Softly.

"Hellkatoot," said Mr. Prophet.

"Aw, crumb," said Sam.

Spike sat on his butt, smiling up at us and wagging his tail to beat the band.

TWENTY

O n Wednesday morning, I scrambled some eggs for Sam and me (without either burning them or leaving them too runny), fixed toast, and fried some bacon (again without burning it or leaving it raw) for breakfast. We each ate an orange to top off our breakfast.

Although I *really* hate to admit it, I did burn the coffee a little. How do you burn coffee, you might ask? Easy as pie. Easier than pie if you're me, and I am. You let it percolate until the water is almost gone and the pot begins to smoke. Sam was quite considerate about my coffee failure. Without saying a harsh word, he rinsed out the percolator, threw out the old grounds and prepared a cleaned-up percolator full of decent coffee while I finished cooking the eggs.

"Except for the coffee, it was a good breakfast though, wasn't it?" I asked my incredibly tolerant husband, feeling tentative about my question.

"Very good," said Sam, being more than benevolent, all things considered. "Don't forget that I used to have to buy a cup of coffee and a couple of sinkers for breakfast before we got married. I think you're doing very well in your cooking efforts, sweetheart."

Aww. How sweet. "Thanks, Sam."

"I have to get ready for work now. Are you still planning to visit Flossie and Johnny?"

"Yes. I'm sure I can use the Chevrolet."

"Sounds good. I'll take the Hudson."

"Excellent," I said.

Spike, who was sitting on the floor between us, listened closely to our conversation. This was primarily because he wanted to hear something about the possibility of food for him. When we didn't mention food or him, he appeared slightly downcast. I swear to heaven, that dog understands human language.

"Don't worry, Spike," I told him, leaning over to stroke his glossy head. "You can stay here with Mr. Prophet and Yuyu and the bone-diggers while your mommy and daddy are away for the day."

Shaking his head, Sam said, "If we ever have kids, that poor dog will be miserable."

"No he won't be!" I cried. "I'll love Spike forever, even if we have a hundred kids!"

"God forbid," Sam said, shuddering.

"Well, two or three," I amended.

"Better," said Sam, and he loped off to get his suit jacket and hat and brush his teeth.

"Knock, knock," came a familiar voice at the back door.

Spike dashed off to greet Mr. Prophet properly.

"Come on in, Lou," said Sam, reappearing from the hallway. "I'm just getting ready for work."

"Got any coffee left?" asked the old sinner. "I'm out."

"Sure. Have a cup," said Sam, not mentioning my coffee disaster, which I appreciated.

"Thanks," said Mr. Prophet, grabbing a cup from the cupboard, thumping to the range and pouring himself a cup of coffee. He walked back, sat across from me at the kitchen table and began spooning sugar into his cup.

"Would you like some toast or some scrambled eggs or anything else to eat?" I asked him politely, bracing myself for a nasty comment about my cooking skills.

He surprised me.

"No thanks. Had me some toast at home with Yuyu. Those guys comin' again today to dig more bones?"

"I guess so. I haven't heard anything from them. I imagine they'll show up, if only to tell us they've found all the bones there are to find." I recalled Spike's discovery of the night before, and woe darned near befell me. "Well, the bones of the young man, anyway. I don't even want to tell them about the jawbone Spike found."

"Best not to," agreed Mr. Prophet. "I've got to do some thinkin' about how to get that ghost to go away. Now we know for sure his bones were disturbed, we'll have to do something to calm him down."

"Hope they don't find any of the Indian bones while they're searching for the last of the young man."

"Cripes, I hope not, too," said Mr. Prophet gloomily.

"I'll let the two of you solve the bone problem," Sam said in a voice approximately as dry as the Mojave Desert. "I don't even believe in your ghost."

"That's okay with me," I told him, rising to accompany him to the front door, where I gave him a kiss and told him to have a good day. He reciprocated. As Sam began walking to the Hudson and I stood in the doorway in my faded old house dress, two police vehicles and Dr. Cuthbert's car drove up and parked in front of the house. "I hope they won't have to come back after today," I muttered to Sam's back.

"Me, too," he said as he made a detour and greeted the men exiting their various automobiles. He and Dr. Cuthbert spoke for a second or two. Then Sam said a few words to the four police officers, all of whom wore white jackets like the kind you see in hospitals and so forth. Guess this meant more digging.

Which again reminded me of Spike's discovery, and I almost buried my face in my hands. If these guys began finding Indian bones, I didn't have a single clue what we'd be able to do about the matter. I wanted Mr. Prophet and his Mestizo friend to deal with the ghost and its bones as quickly and quietly as possible. If the whole world found out there were Indian bones in our backyard, we'd probably never get rid of the ghost.

As you can tell, I *did* believe the ghost existed, Sam or no Sam. I'd had too many weird experiences in my career not to believe.

Nevertheless, and although I wished I didn't have to, I led the doctor and the police contingent down the hall, through the kitchen and out to the backyard. The men nodded at Mr. Prophet, who returned their nods, as they passed the kitchen table.

Hoping against hope that Dr. Cuthbert would have good news for us, I asked, "How many more days of digging do you think you'll have? The skeleton looks pretty well put together to me." I heard the wishful quality in my voice.

I think the doctor did, too, because he said, "This will be our last day. I doubt there are any more of that young man's bones yet to be found. I'm surprised so many of them were still in the yard. The bones have been there so long, I'd have expected more predation by animals, and that the animals would have carried them away."

Yick.

"You haven't yet determined the poor boy's name, have you?" Dr. Cuthbert continued.

"Not yet. However, I aim to visit my friends at the Salvation Army, where Mr. Christopher Edwards attends church. As you may have heard on Monday, Mr. Edwards thinks the bones might belong to a fellow he worked with while building this house. I want to speak with Mr. Edwards again to see if he's recalled the lad's name. Or at least the name of the contractor who built the house. Maybe there are some records somewhere. I'd like to reunite the bones with any remaining family members if at all possible."

"Good idea," said Dr. Cuthbert. "Will someone be in the house today? Or shall I give you a ring this evening to tell you the status of our dig?"

Their dig? Sounded like an archaeological project. I suppose it pretty much was. "I'm not sure if Mr. Prophet will be here, but I'll ask him."

"I'll be here," came a rusty voice at my back. I hadn't heard him walking up behind me, which was surprising. The poor fellow couldn't precisely tiptoe with a leg and a peg.

"Oh, good. Thanks, Mr. Prophet."

Looking at me slightly slanty-eyed, he said, "Not a problem, Miss Daisy."

Very well, I *know* it was silly of me always to call him Mr. Prophet instead of Lou. I just hadn't yet been able to make myself call him by his first name. Perhaps one day.

"If I'm not in this house," Mr. P continued, "I'll be in the cottage beyond the arbor and the orange trees. I'll have the dog with me, so he won't be digging with you."

"Excellent," said Dr. Cuthbert. "I don't expect we'll be here too long today."

I sure hoped they wouldn't be!

"Don't worry about Spike, Miss Daisy," said Mr. Prophet. "I'll make sure he doesn't get out of the yard."

"Thank you very much."

"You're welcome. Think I'll go back to your kitchen and read the morning newspaper now," he said.

"Good idea," I told him. "I'm going to get dressed and go visit Flossie and Billy and Daisy."

He only nodded and turned to head back to the kitchen. I stayed on the back porch for a few more minutes and watched Spike race around, greeting all the visitors to his yard. After a little while of that, I called to him, he reluctantly came, and we both went back into the house. As I walked upstairs to get ready for my trip to the Buckinghams' home, Spike stayed in the kitchen where Mr. Prophet was. More importantly to his doggy brain, food also resided in the kitchen.

"Don't give him too many treats!" I called down the stairs.

"I won't," Mr. P hollered back.

Spike didn't say a word. Then again, he never did.

Because I'd noticed the day was nippy when I'd seen my husband off to his job, I decided to wear a blue serge suit I'd made a few months back when Maxime's was having a sale on their fall and winter fabrics. On this January day, Maxime's was probably having a sale on their spring and summer fabrics. Anyway, I liked the suit. It was comfortable and had a long jacket with a rolled collar, a loose straight skirt, and the jacket had two buttons. If Flossie's house was warm, I could remove the jacket and still look stylish in the pretty white blouse I wore with it. Because I didn't expect to go anywhere else or need to look particularly professional or spiritualistic, I didn't wear a tie under the blouse's collar. I don't know how men could stand to wear ties all day every day. Every time I wore one, I felt as though somebody was strangling me.

Because I decided it would be a good idea to make sure Flossie was there before I drove to her place, I telephoned her first. Would have been a better idea to call her before I dressed for the occasion, but oh well. She was home! What's more, she claimed to be thrilled I aimed to visit her. She was probably telling the truth, as she'd been almost begging me to go see her and the children for a couple of weeks by then. Seemed to me that life was twice as complicated with two children as it was with one, to judge by Flossie and Johnny's experience. I'd keep this tidbit in mind for future use.

I wore my black shoes and hat and carried my black handbag with me as I toddled back down the stairs and went to the kitchen. Spike and Mr. Prophet were no longer there, but I noticed Mr. Prophet had washed the dishes. That was darned nice of him!

After visiting the kitchen, I went to the back porch. Dr. Cuthbert no longer leaned over the table set up for his use. He sat in a chair chatting with Mr. Prophet, who sat in a chair facing his. Spike sat alertly between the two men, but when he saw the back door open, he raced over to greet me. I love dogs. You can be out of their sight for five minutes, but they'll welcome you as if you've been gone for a year and a half when you reappear. I'd anticipated this behavior on his part so I hadn't yet put on my gloves, which I'd stuck in my jacket pocket.

"No more bones?" I asked after greeting Spike and walking to the two men.

"Not so far," said Dr. Cuthbert. "I doubt the men will find any more of them. They're raking back there now, just to see if any little bones got buried in the dirt as they dug."

"Oh. Well. It's nice of them to rake the place, although I don't suppose they're doing it to make it pretty."

With a chuckle, Dr. Cuthbert said, "No. Their primary purpose is to find any last bones, but we also don't want to leave a bunch of holes and piles of dirt for you to deal with when we leave."

"You're leaving?" I asked, trying not to sound too happy about the prospect.

"I expect we won't be here for more than an hour or so. Then we'll let the skeleton remain here for a reasonable length of time. If you can find the poor fellow's family, we can deal with the bones then. If not, I expect the city will bury the bones in the big vault at Mountain View in Altadena."

"I didn't know they had a big vault there," I said. "That's where my first husband and Sam's first wife are buried. But they both have nice headstones."

"Yes, it's a beautiful place, and many beloved family members are buried there. It's unfortunate, but we occasionally find bodies or, in this case, bones that can't be identified. The vault at Mountain View is akin to what people in the old days called potters' fields."

"Or boot hills," said Mr. Prophet. "All's you got to be is dead to get planted in Boot Hill."

"Yes. Same idea," said Dr. Cuthbert, although I sensed he was slightly taken aback by Mr. Prophet's comment. I was used to the old former bounty hunter saying things like that, so I didn't bat an eye. Or flap a lip.

"You look like you're ready to go to the Buckinghams' place," said Mr. Prophet.

"Yes. I'm still hoping to figure out some way to identify these bones."

"I've identified them," said Dr. Cuthbert, laughing at his own joke. "I just don't know whose they are."

I gave him a smile for his effort at humor. "Well, I'll try to rectify the situation."

"Good, good," said the doctor, standing up.

Mr. Prophet stood, too, and said, "C'mon, Spike. Let's you and me go visit my place and read some more about the Inuk Injuns in Canada."

"Oh, are you reading *Nanook of the North*?" I asked, thinking I wished I could see the moving picture.

"Yup. Interesting. They eat a lot of seals and walruses up there in the frozen north."

"Really? Do they eat polar bears?"

"Don't know if they eat 'em. I 'spect they do 'cause they can't afford to waste food. They sell the skins to white folks at the trading posts up there."

"Mercy sakes," I said, thinking how different some lives were from others lives. I'd freeze to death or die of starvation if I had to catch walruses and seals and figure out how to eat them. Then again, I suppose if one is born to the life in any culture, one grows to adulthood learning how to survive in it. If one didn't, one wouldn't survive for very long.

"Well, I'll see you later, Mr. Prophet and Spike. Maybe I'll see you later, too, Dr. Cuthbert." I hoped I wouldn't but was nice enough not to say so. "Good luck today."

"And good luck to you, too, Mrs. Rotondo."

"Thank you."

So, after greeting Mrs. Rattle as she arrived at the front door, I walked across the street, asked Pa if I could use the Chevrolet, got his happy permission—"It's your car, Daisy. You know that."—and drove up to Walnut Street, turned left, and arrived at the Salvation Army not too many minutes later.

TWENTY-ONE

I heard a baby wailing as I knocked on Flossie and Johnny's front door. Another thing to contemplate before having children. They cried a lot, at least at first. And poor Sam had to work every day. If a baby kept him awake all night, he'd be miserable for sure.

Well, people kept telling me children were worth it, so I'd take that into consideration too.

Then again, we had lots of rooms in our house, both upstairs and down. If a howling baby wouldn't shut up, I could carry it to another room—or another floor entirely—so Sam could sleep. Is it proper to call fictitious babies "it"? Well, who cares?

A harried-looking Flossie opened the door to me, but she broke into a huge smile and gave me a gigantic hug at the door.

"Daisy! I'm so glad you could visit today!"

"Me too," I said, hugging her back with fervor.

"Mama," said little Billy tugging at his mother's apron. "Baby's a bwat."

Letting each other go, Flossie and I both burst out laughing.

"She just has a tummy ache, Billy. She's not being bratty on purpose."

"She too loud," announced Billy disapprovingly. Glancing at me, he asked, "Mr. Pwophet?"

"Mr. Prophet couldn't visit with me today, Billy. I'm sorry."

"Huh," said Billy, reminding me of his hero, Mr. Lou Prophet. And don't ask me how that came about either. The first time Billy set eyes on Mr. Prophet, he hid his head on his mother's shoulder because Mr. P looked so frightening. But then darned if the old rogue didn't charm the socks off the little boy, and they'd been fast friends ever since their first meeting.

"I have some information for you from Chris Edwards," Flossie said as we walked into their small house. The Salvation Army couldn't afford to pay their personnel much money, but neither Flossie nor Johnny seemed to mind. They loved helping other people and were satisfied—or so it seemed to me—with what they had.

"Oh, good! I was hoping maybe he'd remember the name of the poor fellow who disappeared and whose bones we've found. Well, if they're his. A fellow named Dr. Cuthbert has pretty much put the skeleton back together again, but there are a few bones missing."

"I'm not surprised," said Flossie. "They've been there for more than twenty years, according to Chris."

"Yes, both Dr. Benjamin and Dr. Cuthbert have confirmed the approximate number of years they've been back there."

"Chris told me the name of the contractor was Bernard Bullis. I think the Bullis Construction Company is still in business. They're in the telephone directory, anyway. I wrote their number down for you. It's on a piece of paper in the kitchen."

"Thanks, Flossie! I was hoping Mr. Edwards would remember a name, either the bony guy's or the contractor's."

"The 'bony guy'?" Flossie laughed so hard, she cried. I have a feeling she was exhausted because what I'd said wasn't all that funny.

"But first let me see my namesake," I said, trying to remain cheerful, even though I disliked my name. Daisy? Phooey. Daphne was a lovely name. But Daisy? But I think I'm repeating myself. Beg pardon.

With a huge sigh, Flossie said, "She's ever so much fussier than Billy used to be. According to Dr. Benjamin, a lot of babies are colicky. Just Johnny's and my luck Daisy's one of them."

"I'm sorry. According to Sam, Daisy's a perky name. Maybe you should have named her something else," I said, hoping maybe it wasn't too late.

Flossie laughed again. "No indeed. Daisy is Daisy, and that's that. We can call her by a nickname, but we both wanted to name her after you."

"I appreciate that, but I wish I had a different name. Diana, say. I think that's a lovely name. Or Heather, if you need a flower. Or Elizabeth."

"Too late, Daisy."

"Dang."

With another laugh, Flossie, Billy and I walked to the kitchen, where little Daisy's bassinet sat, the baby bright red and screaming within it. I fear my face must have revealed my horror, because Flossie said, "You'll get used to it after a while, Daisy."

"If you say so. Is there anything you can do for a colicky baby? I should probably take notes."

Flossie lifted the screaming child—to be fair, the kid was only about a month and a half old—from the bassinet and held her to her shoulder. "Dr. Benjamin said rubbing her tummy gently might help. Also holding her like a football sometimes helps."

"How in the world do you hold a baby like a football?" I asked, curious.

"Like this." Flossie demonstrated, holding the howling infant on her tummy along her—Flossie's, I mean—forearm and holding her in place with her other hand. As if by magic, little Daisy hiccupped a couple of times and stopped shrieking.

"Wow. That's amazing," I said.

"Yes, it is. Sometimes that doesn't work. Now I'm afraid to move."

"Don't move. Well, just move enough to sit at the table. You can brace your arm better that way, too."

"Right."

"Dumb bwat," muttered Billy under his breath. I have a feeling he knew he was being naughty, because he slanted his mother a peek and ducked his head. Sure enough, Flossie gave him a "scolding-mommy" look. Billy scuffed the toe of his shoe on the kitchen linoleum and climbed onto another chair, still looking a little sulky. He was probably being as sulky as he knew he could get away with.

"Daisy," said Flossie. "Why don't you go to the cookie jar and get three or four oatmeal cookies? Then you, Billy and I can have some milk and cookies. Provided you also get some glasses and some milk out of the ice box.

"Sure will," I said, leaping to do Flossie's bidding. "Where's Johnny today?"

With a sigh, Flossie said, "Out with the band. They're marching on Colorado today. Hope people will be generous. We have so many people in need of help these days."

I poured milk. Billy, being about two and a half at this juncture, got a small glass filled halfway. I gave him a whole cookie, however, on a napkin. Flossie and I each had a whole glass of milk with our cookies. "These are delicious, Flossie. Do you have a recipe you can give me? I'm *really* trying hard to learn to cook."

"Of course, I can give you the recipe!" said Flossie. "I know you'll be a good cook one of these days, Daisy. You can do everything else. Why not cook?"

Dare I said it? Oh, heck, this was Flossie. Of course I dared. "Because I hate it?" I said.

"Aw, Daisy. Cooking can be fun and creative."

"I don't know, Flossie. I see the effort Aunt Vi puts into everything. I mean, she can slave over a hot stove for hours every day, and everybody's finished eating it in fifteen minutes. Maybe thirty if whatever she fixed is chewy. I'd rather sew. I can put as much effort into sewing a shirt or a dress that will last for years as Vi puts into a meal that's gone in minutes."

"You know," said Flossie in a musing tone, "I've never thought about cooking in that light before."

"You probably shouldn't start now," I said. "Sorry I said it."

We sat in thoughtful silence for several seconds, chewing our cookies like cows chew their cud. Then I said, "It is nice to have someone appreciate a meal, though. I know Vi truly *loves* feeding people. She's told me so a thousand times at least."

"There are meals that don't take a lot of time, but that also taste good, too, don't forget," said Flossie.

"Really?" I had a vision of my aunt cutting pastry leaves out of a crust she'd just use the main part of to cover a sirloin—or some other cut—of beef in order to make beef Wellington, and thought to myself there was no way in holy heck I'd ever do that. Maybe, if I could manage to learn how to make piecrusts, I'd bake a pie every now and then, but Sam's life would forever be bereft of beef Wellington.

Sorry, Sam. Poor guy.

"Anyway, you said it was the Bullis Company that built our house?"

"Yes. I wrote the number down for you, but I can't move right now. I put the number under the sugar bowl."

That was easy. I just pulled a scrap of paper from underneath the sugar bowl on the table.

"Feel free to use our telephone," said Flossie, tilting her head toward the telephone mounted on the kitchen wall.

"Thank you."

I went to the telephone, an old wooden number without a dialing plate, picked up the receiver, and clicked the switch-hook a couple of times to summon an operator. When one answered, I asked for the number printed on the scrap of paper, and she obligingly dialed it for me.

"Bullis Construction," came the gravelly voice of a male who picked up the receiver on the other end.

Wishing I'd started thinking about this conversation and how to start it earlier, I began clumsily. "Um, yes. My name is Mrs. Rotondo, and I live on Marengo Avenue. Our house was built by the Bullis Company in 1905 or thereabouts." I gave him the street number of our home.

"Yeah?" he said.

"Um, well, we've recently discovered some…um, bones in our backyard."

"Yeah?" he said again, a little more sharply.

"Um, and a fellow named Mr. Christopher Edwards said he worked on the construction crew when our house was being built, and that one of the workers on the project disappeared one day."

"Huh?"

Oh boy. "That is to say, he just left the job one day and never came back again. So we were wondering if these might be his bones."

After a long silence on his end of the wire, I said, "We were kind of hoping to learn the name of the fellow who disappeared. If these are his bones—and, well, I don't know how to determine that, exactly—maybe we can find any remaining family members. They might like to know what became of him."

"Yeah?"

Nertz. This guy wasn't making my task appreciably easier. "Well, I wondered if you have any records from that long ago. Perhaps with the names of the workers Mr. Bullis hired for the job. I suppose it's possible to pinpoint the name of the disappearing worker. I mean, if you had a list or something, perhaps Mr. Christopher Edwards will recognize the fellow's name."

"Huh," said the uncommunicative person at Bullis Construction.

"Do you keep records that far back?" I asked weakly.

After another moment or seven thousand of silence, the person on the Bullis end of the wire said, "Yeah. I think we do. Lemme look. Got a number where I can call you? I kind of remember a guy walking off that job and never coming back again. You say there are *bones* in your yard? Old bones?"

Hallelujah! I felt a surge of triumph for finally having caught the fellow's attention. "The forensic doctor estimates the bones have been in the yard for at least twenty years. They weren't…well, buried. It's a big yard, and nobody ever goes back there. Or they didn't until…Never mind. What Mr. Edwards thinks might have happened is that the fellow, um, drank heavily, and perhaps he, um, fell over and some construction matter might have accidentally been dumped on top of him."

"Yeah. I remember that guy. The drunk. Not Chris. Well, I remember him, too. But Chris is a good worker."

Hallelujah again!

"So you don't mind looking up old records to see if you can discover the other fellow's name?"

"Naw. I don't mind. It might take a day or two. We're pretty busy, and the old records are stored in boxes in the basement."

"That's all right," I said, my heart beginning to sink a bit. How many days constitute a "day or two," anyway?

"But give me your number, and I'll see what I can dig up."

There was a whole lot of digging up going on during that period of time, by golly. "Thank you very much. Are you Mr. Bullis?"

"Yeah. Bernard Bullis, Jr. Everybody calls me Junior. My dad started the company."

"Thank you *very* much, Mr. Bullis." I wasn't about to call a man I didn't know Junior.

"You're welcome. What did you say your name was, again?"

"Mrs. Rotondo. My husband, Sam Rotondo, is a detective with the Pasadena Police Department?"

"Yeah? Interesting. Okay, Mrs. Rotondo. I'll see what I can find out for you."

I thanked him again and replaced the receiver. Almost as soon as I removed my hand from it, the stupid telephone started ringing, Daisy resumed screeching, and Billy covered his ears with his hands. Flossie looked so distressed, I answered the telephone myself.

"Salvation Army, may I help you?"

"Who's this?" came Johnny's voice.

"It's Daisy. You just woke up the baby, Johnny Buckingham. Poor Flossie is here having a nervous collapse while you're marching up and down Colorado playing your horn. You should be ashamed of yourself!"

Johnny's laughter nearly ruptured my eardrum. When he finally spluttered to a stop, he said, "We've missed you, Daisy. Will you please tell Flossie I'm bringing dinner home with me? This baby must take after her namesake, because she's a real pain in the neck."

"I'm not a pain in the neck!" I said. Then I laughed, too. "Well, all right. As long as you're bringing dinner home to Flossie, I'll forgive you for not paying attention to your children."

"Daisy!" came Flossie's shocked voice from the kitchen table.

"Baby's a bwat," muttered little Billy.

"Please tell Flossie I love her, and that I'll be home in twenty minutes," said Johnny.

"Very well. I shall. Shirker!"

"Pain in the neck!"

"Bwat!"

I hung up the receiver and nearly collapsed onto a kitchen chair, laughing hysterically. Oh, my. I aimed to have a serious chat with Sam about the having-children dilemma.

TWENTY-TWO

O n my way home from Flossie and Johnny's house, I decided to stop in at the local corner grocery store. My father went there quite often, and I knew Mr. and Mrs. Bennett, who owned and ran the store. They were a very nice couple, and it occurred to me that Mrs. Bennett might actually be able to assist me in the preparation of easy-to-fix and hard-to-ruin meals. So I asked her.

"Oh, my word, yes! Why, you know your father comes in here and buys beans and bread and so forth all the time. He's told me more than once that your auntie does the cooking at his house, but now that you're married, you're learning to fix meals, too."

"I'll never be able to cook as well as Aunt Vi," I admitted glumly. "But I could sure use some tips on meals that are easy to prepare and difficult to ruin, although my past cooking attempts lead me to believe I can ruin pretty much anything."

With a laugh, Mrs. Bennett said, "Nonsense! What you need are a couple of these pork chops—or more of them if your husband is a big eater—and some of these russet potatoes. What you do is wash the potatoes very well, prick them a couple of times with a fork or a knife, so they don't explode in the oven, and bake them right on the oven rack for an hour or so in a hot oven. While they cook, get out your skillet, put some grease in it, heat it up—you have an iron skillet, right?"

I'd hauled my little notebook and pencil from my handbag and was writing down her instructions so desperately, I was slow to answer her question. When it registered, my head snapped up and I said, "Yes. Iron skillet. Yes, I have two or three of those in different sizes."

"Then you're all set. I see you're writing down my instructions."

"Yes. I'm really bad in the kitchen, Mrs. Bennett."

She shook her head in a gesture of commiseration. "You needn't continue to be. Chops are your friends when you need a quick, easy meal that tastes good. Do I need to go over anything again?"

I read out my notes, squinting in a couple of places where the words ran together, then glanced up at her. I'm sure hope was plain to read on my face. "Think I've got everything so far."

"Perfect. Very well, so you have your iron skillet on the top of the range, and you've put some grease in it. You can use your saved bacon grease or lard or whatever, but it's best not to use butter, because it will burn too quickly."

I made a note. "Good thing to know," I said, meaning it sincerely.

"About a half-hour after you put your potatoes in the hot oven, heat up the skillet and the grease. Just use enough grease to cover the bottom of the skillet. You don't want your chops drowning in hot grease."

I made another note.

"Put the chops in the hot skillet and fry them for about four to six minutes on each side. Don't turn them more than once, but you can lift the edge of a chop to see if it's brown enough to turn over. You can stick a fork in the edge of a chop and just lift a corner of it."

"Four to six minutes?" I asked, thinking this was too easy and I'd surely make some catastrophic mistake.

"Depending on the thickness of the chops," said Mrs. Bennett. "The thicker the chop, the longer it will take to cook. Oh, and be sure to use a goodly sprinkle of salt and pepper on each side to make them tasty."

"Sounds reasonable."

"It is. And Mr. Bennett thinks the best thing to serve with pork chops and baked potatoes is corn. And some applesauce. I have some jarred applesauce here that's pretty tasty, especially if you sprinkle some cinnamon and a little nutmeg on it. I think two cans of corn should do you. If you only use one, save the other to use later."

"Thank you *so* much, Mrs. Bennett! You may have saved my husband's life! And mine, too, come to think of it." Something important then occurred to me. "Um, what do we do with the potatoes after their hour in the oven is over?"

"Easy as pie, Daisy. Slit the tops of them open, slap a huge gob of butter on each of them, and mash them up with a fork. Mr. Bennett and I eat the skins, too, because they're tasty."

"I believe Vi has served us baked potatoes like that a few times," I said, thinking Mrs. Bennett was almost as much of a genius in the kitchen as my aunt. "In fact, I'm sure she has. They're delicious!"

"And so easy. Why, you can bake a potato and pour some sausage and gravy over it, and you have another cheap and easy meal."

"Sausage and gravy?" I asked in a small voice.

She patted me on the shoulder. "I'll give you that recipe another day. I think pork chops and baked potatoes are enough for one day."

"Oh, thank you, Mrs. Bennett! You almost give me hope."

She only laughed. Ha. If she only knew.

"Chicken is another simple, tasty meal to cook, too. If you stop by another day, I'll give you a recipe that's hard to beat in the chicken department as well as that sausage and gravy recipe."

"Thank you! You're a neighborhood treasure, Mrs. Bennett!"

"Tosh," she said. "Anyway, how many of these chops do you think you'll need for tonight? They're pretty thick, so I expect you'll have to cook them for five minutes on each side. Maybe four on the second side."

I wanted to beg her not to give me choices, because I'd surely make the wrong one, but I told myself to straighten up and behave like a grown-up married woman and didn't. I did look at the chops behind the butcher's counter and considered the possibility of Mr. Prophet daring to dine with us. If he didn't, I could save the leftover chop and make a sandwich for lunch tomorrow. Mr. Bennett did the butchering, according to Pa, who always bought bacon from the Bennetts' store because he said Mr. Bennett smoked it just right.

Assuming my most professional voice, I said, "I'll take three of the chops, please. And a jar of applesauce and two cans of corn. And some potatoes. Um…potatoes last pretty well, don't they?"

"In this cool weather, yes, they'll last well. Want a dozen of them? They're good sliced and fried for breakfast, too. With some of Mr. Bennett's bacon, which he'll slice for you."

"Sure will," said Mr. Bennett, whom I hadn't even noticed behind his butcher's counter. "A pound of bacon will last if you have a good ice box or one of them newfangled refrigerators."

"We have a Frigidaire," I said, hoping I didn't sound boastful.

"Wonderful," said Mr. Bennett, who apparently approved of Frigidaires. "Three pork chops, a pound of bacon and…anything else you need in the butcher department?"

"I don't think so," I said doubtfully. "Do you sell eggs here?"

"We sure do," said Mrs. Bennett. "Fresh from my own chickens."

"I didn't know you kept chickens!" I said, honestly surprised. "I never hear any cocks crowing."

"That's because we keep the chickens at our son's place outside the city limits," said Mrs. Bennett, chuckling. "The city decided the hoity-toity citizens of Pasadena didn't need to hear roosters crowing and waking them up at five in the morning. But most of us plain old folks couldn't care less. I grew up on a farm in Altadena before it was Altadena." She shook her head, as if bewildered by the silliness of people who wanted to eat their chickens and eggs without the bother of hearing them as they went about growing up and laying the eggs they ate.

I was on her side. Then I remembered the hog farm Billy and I had visited by accident one day before we were married and decided perhaps farms and farmers *did* fare better outside the city limits. At least the folks inside the city limits did.

Mrs. Bennett packed the bounty I'd purchased in the string bag I'd brought inside the store with me. Then I remembered Spike. How could I ever have forgotten Spike?

"Oh! Do you have any bones for the dog? I think Pa gets bones here from time to time."

"He does," said Mr. Bennett. "But what you really need the bones for is to make broth for soup."

"I do?" I asked, squeaking only a little bit.

"Don't bother Daisy with more instructions today, Mr. Bennett," advised his wife. "She's new to this housekeeping business. I'll teach her how to cook up a rich broth for soup another day."

"I ought to pay you for cooking lessons," I said, not even joking.

"Nonsense!" the two Bennetts said together. Without another word about broth, Mr. Bennett wrapped a goodly number of bones in butcher paper and handed them to me. "Free of charge," said he. "As a butcher, I have more bones than the missus can use for soups and so forth."

"That's the plain truth," said Mrs. Bennett.

"Thank you both very much."

Whew! What a productive day so far. I just hoped I wouldn't manage to ruin dinner in spite of Mrs. Bennett's instructions.

When I finally got home, it was around noonish. After I greeted Mrs. Rattle, I put the groceries away in various cupboards and the Frigidaire.

"Are there still men working outside?" I asked Mrs. Rattle.

"They left some time ago," she said, making me glad.

"Oh, good!"

"Do you need me to put on something for supper?" she asked.

I was *so* tempted, but I didn't succumb. "No, thanks. I'll fix dinner for us tonight. Thank you, though."

"You're most welcome. I do like to cook."

"You and Aunt Vi," I said, sounding sad to my own ears.

Mrs. Rattle only laughed. So I went out back to see what was going on there. What I found was a table full of bones and no people. As there was also no dog, I walked to Mr. Prophet's cottage, where I found him reading a book with Yuyu on his lap and Spike snoozing next to his peg. Spike leaped to his feet and rushed to greet me, which alerted Mr. Prophet and Yuyu to my presence.

Yuyu hissed.

Mr. Prophet said, "Welcome home."

I waited a second for him to add a cutting remark, but he didn't. Therefore, as I greeted my dog, I said, "Thank you."

"Any luck finding the name of the skeleton yet?"

"Maybe." I unbent from petting Spike and said, "Mr. Edwards, the man who visited Monday and who worked on the house, recalled it was the Bullis Construction Company that built the house. So I called Bullis, and Mr. Bullis Junior said he'll hunt up old records and see if he can find the name of the disappearing man. He remembered him, so we might yet find out whom those bones belong to."

"Good. As soon as that mess is cleared up, can you drive me back to that mission? I want to talk to the Mestizo guy, Emilio DeLoera, again so we can figure out how to get rid of the ghost. If we can reunite him with his family, that would be best. If we can't… well, I don't know, but mebbe Emilio can figure something out."

"Sure. I'll be happy to drive you to the mission again." Anything to keep the peace and rout the ghost, if there really was one. So far, three kids and one antique man who ought to know believed in the ghost, and I pretty much did too.

"Thanks."

"Glad to help. I'll be happy to have our yard back again and relieved of extraneous bones and spirits." Then, bravely daring, I said, "Want to take supper with us tonight? I stopped at Bennetts' Grocery Store, and Mrs. Bennett gave me a recipe for pork chops and potatoes she thinks even I can't ruin."

"Sure," Mr. Prophet said, sounding amazingly happy about the prospect. "Thanks for the invite."

Peering at him slanty-eyed, I said, "Really? You honestly want to eat something I aim to cook?"

With a shrug, he said, "I know I've riled you by teasing you about your cookin', Miss Daisy, but you're talking to a feller who ate beans and bacon and hard tack most of his life. Your cookin' ain't all *that* bad."

"Thank you." I think. "Want a sandwich? There's cheese in the Frigidaire and some more of Vi's bread."

"No thanks. Miss Li come over a while back and brought me some noodles for lunch."

"Noodles?"

"Them Chinese noodles are hard to beat," he said. "Mebbe I ought to get the receipt from her and you can try them."

Noodles? Well, why not? I love Chinese food. "Would you really? Thank you!"

"Ain't accustomed to lyin' about things, Miss Daisy."

"Of course not. Thank you very much. I'd love to learn how to fix some Chinese dishes. They'd better not be complicated, because I'm not ready for anything complicated yet." After a split-second's thought, I added, "I'll probably never be ready to fix anything complicated, actually."

With a shrug, Mr. P said, "Hellkatoot, millions o' Chinese people fix noodles all the time. They can't all be geniuses and great cooks. Same with Mexican chow. Now *that* I like a lot. Can't be too hard to learn Mexican cookin'. It's mostly beans and tortillas."

"I could probably manage beans, but I don't know about the tortillas. If I had to make them myself, I'd probably fail miserably."

"Eh, don't bother with the tortillas then. Boil up some pinto beans with some onions and a piece o' ham or some bacon, and you'll have a good meal. Fix some cornbread to eat with 'em. Cornbread's easy."

"It is?" I asked doubtfully.

"It is. Hell, ask your auntie. Mebbe go to the library and check out a how-to-cook book. I think everybody eats cornbread or cornpone or cornmeal mush or grits all over the country."

"What are grits?" I asked, feeling stupid as I did so.

"Same as mush, pretty much. Ground a little coarser, I think. I dunno nothin' about cookin', but even I can make mush. In fact," the old sinner said, scratching his chin as he mused about cornmeal,

"I think Sam told me the Eyetalians eat cornmeal mush, too, only they don't call it that."

"Good heavens, I think you're right. I vaguely recall him telling me about Italian cornmeal. Pol-polen...pollen? That can't be it."

"Naw. Pollen's what bees collect from flowers. But you can make lots of stuff with ground corn, whatever people call it."

"Good idea," I said, thinking I loved fried cornmeal mush. And I *knew* cornmeal mush wasn't hard to make because even my mother fixed it, and she's almost as bad as I in the kitchen. "Thanks! Think I'll stop by the store again tomorrow and get some cornmeal."

"Good idea. What time's supper?"

"Um...I don't know. Six? If Sam comes home on time, it'll be six or six-thirty. If he can't get home on time, I'll probably burn everything, so it won't matter."

With a chuckle, Mr. P said, "You're sure a confident woman, ain't you?"

"I've considered myself a failure in the kitchen for almost as many years as I've been alive, so my confidence is pretty low when it comes to cooking."

"Aw, you'll learn," said the formerly mean and cruel Mr. Lou Prophet.

Spike and I fairly danced back to the house, where I ate a cheese sandwich and an orange, and Spike ate too much cheese. Not his fault. I threw it to him.

TWENTY-THREE

B efore I get into the details of that Wednesday evening, let me announce here and now that I didn't burn a single, solitary thing and dinner was delicious! We dined at seven, because I was too nervous to put the potatoes in the hot oven until Sam came home. I prepared them thoroughly, though, scrubbing them to within an inch of their lives and poking them with holes. As soon as I heard the Hudson motor up the drive, I threw those suckers into the oven as if I actually knew what I was doing.

Then I ran to greet my husband, whose day, he said, had mainly been taken up with paperwork. Paperwork tended to accumulate while he was out detecting, so on slow days he caught up with it.

Believe me or don't, but it's the truth: Mr. Prophet wandered into the house about sixish to see how meal preparations were going. Then he astounded me by opening one of the cans of corn, dumping its contents into a little pot and gently heating the kernels. Then he emptied the pot of water (saving the kernels in the pot), added some butter, a little flour, some milk, a dash of salt and pepper and created a masterpiece. I watched this entire process with my mouth open, rapt.

"Creamed corn," he said when finished with his miracle. "You kin do that, Miss Daisy. Simple."

"I'll be darned," I said, nearly, but not quite, speechless. "That's amazing."

"It's nothin', really," said Mr. P modestly.

Sam had gone upstairs to remove his suit jacket, loosen his tie and slip on some comfy shoes. He walked into the kitchen, listened to our exchange, pulled out a chair, laughed and said, "You teaching my wife how to cook, Lou?"

"Figgered it was better'n teasing her about how she can't," said Mr. Prophet with a twinkle in his faded blue eyes.

I served the applesauce, complete with a sprinkle of cinnamon and a dash of nutmeg, in little bowls alongside dinner plates filled with pork chops, baked potatoes and creamed corn. I was terribly impressed with myself and, to be honest, Mr. Prophet. The fact that I'd entirely neglected to think about dessert didn't even matter. Much.

As we ate, I told Sam about my telephone call with Mr. Bullis. "I hope he doesn't take days and days to find the records," I said after helping myself to more creamed corn. That stuff was *good*.

"I hope it doesn't, but the poor guy is probably busy with real work. Paperwork is a pain in the rear end," said my beloved.

"Wouldn't know," said Mr. P. "Never had no paperwork to do."

"That doesn't surprise me," I said. "Although you used to use 'wanted' posters to find villains, didn't you?"

"That's not paperwork," he said. "It's just makin' a living."

"Oh, and Johnny said his and Flossie's Daisy is just like me, only he didn't say she was perky. He said she was a pain in the neck. Billy calls her a bwat."

Both men at the kitchen table laughed.

"I miss that little boy," said the generally unsentimental Mr. Lou Prophet.

"He misses you, too. He was grumpy when he realized you didn't come with me to visit."

"You'll have to invite them over for dinner one of these days," said Sam. "This is a meal fit for a king."

"You're extremely kind to me, Sam," I told him. "I nearly died of nervous prostration when I was frying those pork chops. Let's wait until I'm a little more at home in the kitchen."

The telephone rang. Sam said, "Oh, all right," as he rose and went to the telephone. That's because he saw me gnawing on a pork-chop bone and didn't want to waste time listening to the 'phone ring while I washed my hands. I know it was probably rude to gnaw on a bone, but I was in my own kitchen in my own house, I'd cooked the silly chop upon whose bone I was gnawing, and my mother wasn't there to *Daisy* me reproachfully.

I'd just laid my bone on my plate and wiped my fingers on a napkin when Sam called to me from the hallway. "Daisy, come here. It's Mr. Bullis."

"So soon?" Oh, I hoped this was a good-news telephone call!

Mr. Prophet followed me into the hallway. Sam had turned on the little lamp on the telephone table, so I switched on the hall light. I saw Sam had the receiver tucked under his chin and had picked up a pencil and a sheet of paper from the drawer. When I approached, he handed the pencil and paper to me.

"Hold on just a minute, Mr. Bullis. My wife will write the names and so forth down as I dictate. This was very nice of you. I didn't expect you to even begin to look for days yet."

I heard Mr. Bullis's voice, but couldn't make out his words.

With a grin, Sam said, "I understand. It is kind of like solving a mystery, isn't it?"

More noises from the telephone.

Sam said. "Okay now. Let me get this name right. Timothy O'Tool. Is that O'Tool with an E at the end or without an E. All right. O'Toole with an E. Thanks. Do you have an address? I don't suppose a telephone number is listed because it was so long ago."

More mumbles from the 'phone.

"Right. So it's Timothy O'Toole, and the address you had for him at the time was three-one-six East Maple Street. Did I get that right?"

'Phone noises.

"Great. Thank you. You don't know his mother's name? It's not written on the records there?"

Noises.

"Great. Thank you. I'll drive over and see if she still lives at that address. I don't relish taking her bad news, but I guess it's better than her wondering what happened to her son forever."

It sounded to me as if Mr. Bullis agreed with Sam. So did I, for what it's worth. Sam hung the receiver in the cradle and looked up at Mr. Prophet and me. "Guess that's it. Seems the bones on our back porch belong to one Mr. Timothy O'Toole, who took off from this job site on May sixteenth, 1905. Just left the job. Bullis thinks the kid—he was only about twenty-two or -three—had some serious problems, both mentally and physically. Showed up for work drunk on more than one occasion. The day he left, he had some kind of temper tantrum, threw down whatever tool he was using and marched off. Nobody was sorry to see him leave, according to Mr. Bullis. And he never showed up for work again."

"How sad," I said. "Mr. Edwards said he tried being friendly with him, but he didn't get very far."

"Nobody did, or so Mr. Bullis told me. He remembered Edwards, too. Said he was a good worker and a nice person. Anyway, I guess we can visit this Maple Street address and see if any of his family members still live there."

"Tonight?" I asked, peering at the clock on the telephone table. It was approximately 8:00 p.m. "Is it too late for a visit?"

"Don't know. What do you think, Lou?"

"Never had me no kids that I know about, but if I did and one went missin', I'd want to know if somebody found him as soon as could be. It's only eight. That ain't too late for a visit, is it?"

"It is kind of late," I said, hesitatingly. What if the entire family was comprised of dipsomaniacs? By this time of night, they'd all be drunk as skunks, wouldn't they? Prohibition or no Prohibition, people still drank if they could get their hands on liquor. If, of course, they were inclined that way.

"Oh, what the heck," said Sam after we'd all been considering our options for a minute or two. "Let's go see if there are any O'Tooles left at the Maple Street address."

"Let me clean up the kitchen first, okay?"

"We'll help," said Sam. "Won't we, Lou?"

"Yeah, why not?" said an unwilling-sounding Mr. Prophet. "Can't hurt, I reckon."

So we washed, dried and put away dinner dishes in record time, and then donned our jackets and headed out to the Hudson. Sam drove to Maple Street, which wasn't very far away. Pasadena had installed electric lights in the late 1800s, so we could see the houses on the street. Maple was a pretty little street, a little north of Walnut. 316 was east of Fair Oaks Avenue and it had a light on over the porch.

"Maybe someone's still awake," I said hopefully. "The porch light is on."

"Only one way to find out," said Sam, opening his door and coming around to open my door and Mr. Prophet's. Mr. P sat in the back seat. He could have sat next to me in front, but we'd have been squished. Anyhow, getting in to and out of cars was difficult for him because of his peg leg.

The lawn was weedy and overgrown, and I didn't see any flowerbeds as we trod the front walkway and up the porch stairs. There was no doorbell, so Sam knocked on the front door. I'm not sure how long we stood there, but we'd begun to look at one another in preparation for leaving when the front door opened to reveal a short, slender older woman wearing an old-fashioned housedress and a shawl. She'd pulled her gray hair back into a knot, and she held a ball of blue yarn with some knitting needles stuck into it.

Peering up at Sam through thick spectacles that made her eye color difficult to determine, she said, "Yes?"

Sam cleared his throat. "We're looking for the O'Toole family and were given this address. Are you an O'Toole?"

"The last one, yes. My husband died ten years ago, my daughter left home a year later and moved to Los Angeles to become a movie star, and my son just disappeared one day. That was before the others went." She shrugged as if to say she didn't know what to make of anything.

"I see," said Sam. He glanced at me, but I didn't know what to say to a woman who'd managed to lose her entire family. So he cleared his throat again. "May we come in for a moment, Mrs. O'Toole? I'm Detective Sam Rotondo from the Pasadena Police Department, this is my wife Daisy, and this is a friend, Mr. Lou Prophet. We might have some news about your son."

"Timmy? You have news about Timmy?" The old woman's eyes widened. "Lordy, he didn't kill nobody, did he? That boy was wild from the day he was born."

"No, it's nothing like that, Mrs. O'Toole," said Sam gently.

She stood in the doorway for a second or two without speaking, then sighed heavily, stepped back and opened the door wider so we could enter her shabby little house. It was clean, but it didn't look to me as if Mrs. O'Toole was rolling in wealth. The living room sofa sagged, and so did the two chairs also positioned in the living room. The antimacassars on the backs of the sofa and the chairs were clean and starched, and I got the impression Mrs. O'Toole had made them herself. Probably the yarn and knitting needles clued me in. That and the very many crocheted and knitted sofa cushions and afghans arranged here and there on the furniture.

"Take a seat," she said. "I'd offer you tea, but I don't have any so I can't. Get my pension check next Tuesday."

"It's fine, Mrs. O'Toole," I said, finally gathering a little courage. "We just had supper and don't need anything."

She nodded at me and then fixed her attention on Sam again. "He's dead, isn't he? My Timmy's dead, isn't he?"

"Yes, we believe we've found his bones, Mrs. O'Toole. I'm very sorry."

She bowed her head for a second before again peering at Sam. "His bones? You found his bones? Where'd you find his bones?" She sounded at least as dumbfounded as we'd been that first day when Spike and Yuyu had waltzed up to us with pieces of her son's skeleton in their mouths. After heaving another sigh, she bowed her head again. Her fingers dug holes in the ball of blue yarn.

After thinking about it for a second or two, Sam said, "From what we've been able to piece together, a house on Marengo Avenue was constructed in 1905. The contractor was Bernard Bullis."

"Timmy worked for Bullis. That's where he worked last." Shaking her bowed head, Mrs. O'Tocle went on, "Never came home one day, and I've never heard a word since. Except for that nice fellow who used to work with Timmy. He come around once or twice to see if I'd heard from Timmy."

"Mr. Christopher Edwards?" I asked.

Lifting her head slightly and squinting at me, Mrs. O'Toole said, "I think that might've been his name. Nice fellow. Seemed to care about Timmy."

"He did," I said firmly. I think I spoke the truth.

Mrs. O'Toole sighed. "So how'd you find Timmy's bones?"

"The house on Marengo was contracted by a family named Killebrew. My wife and I married not long back, and we bought the house when Mrs. Killebrew moved away to live with her kin."

I'm glad he didn't say Mrs. Killebrew had moved away to live with her son. I thought that might have been a little cruel on poor Mrs. O'Toole.

"Oh?" said Mrs. O'Toole, still not enlightened.

"We were working in the back garden last Saturday when we… we discovered some bones. We weren't sure at first if they were human bones, but we called the police department, and—"

"I thought you were with the police department," said Mrs. O'Toole.

"I am," said Sam. "I'm a detective with the Pasadena Police Department, but I didn't have to work last Saturday, and Daisy— Mrs. Rotondo—and I were doing some work in the backyard. That's when we found some bones and thought we'd better call the police in order to see if they might be human bones."

"And they were," said Mrs. O'Toole as if the words weighed more than she could easily bear.

"Yes, they were. The police department brought in what they call a forensic specialist. Dr. Cuthbert is able to assemble skeletons from loose bones, and he assembled these. Mr. Edwards, the man who visited you after your son disappeared, was able to help identify the body because of a healed fracture of a leg bone and the missing teeth in his upper skull."

Mrs. O'Toole heaved a gigantic sigh and reached into a pocket to pull out a large handkerchief. Her eyes leaking slowly, she nodded and said, "That's my Timmy. Took after his pa, he did. Drank and got nasty with it. Some folks can drink and be happy. Not those two. It was his pa who knocked out his two front teeth. He fell out of a tree and broke his leg when he was about five or six." She stopped speaking, wiped her eyes and dabbed at her nose. "Where are his bones now?"

"They're still at our house," said Sam. "Dr. Cuthbert put together as much of your son's skeleton as the police department personnel could find. Most of them are there. The reason we came over here tonight is that Mr. Bullis, Junior, called our home about thirty minutes ago and told us your son's name and gave us your address. We thought you'd like to know after all these years what became of Timothy."

"I can't imagine not knowing what happened to a child of mine," I said. By this time, I'd begun wiping my own leaky eyes.

"I guess," she said listlessly. "Not knowing, you can always hope they'll come home again one day. Do that with my daughter. But I guess it's best to know if they're dead. Then I'll stop wondering. Not sure what to do with the bones, though. I can't afford a funeral."

"We can find assistance for you in that department," said Sam instantly. He was talking about his own pocketbook. I adore my Sam.

"You can?" She lifted her head and blinked at Sam.

"Yes. That's not a problem. We can have him buried at the Mountain View Cemetery, if that's what you want, and provide a small headstone. Or if there's another place, let me know."

"Mountain View's the only one in this area, isn't it?" said Mrs. O'Toole.

"Yes," I said. "It is."

Shaking her head a little, she said, "Seems odd to have but one cemetery for a whole community. Back in Ohio, there are little cemeteries and churchyards all over the place. Not here."

"No," agreed Sam. "Not here."

We spoke for a few more minutes, and I agreed to pick Mrs. O'Toole up on Thursday at ten a.m. and take her to see her son's bones. Sam said he'd make burial arrangements. Mrs. O'Toole said there was no use having a big funeral because nobody'd come to it, which nearly made me cry again. Then Mrs. O'Toole saw us to the door.

"Thank you for coming by tonight. I'm sorry Timmy's gone forever, but I was afraid he'd come to no good. Guess it's better this way."

I don't think any of us knew what to say to that, so we just smiled and waved. Mrs. O'Toole watched us until we got into the Hudson and drove off.

None of us talked on the way home.

TWENTY-FOUR

Mrs. Rattle arrived at our house at 8:30 on Thursday morning, bless her. She said she'd fix us a "nice lamb stew" for supper, and I thanked her. Thursday nights were choir practice nights for me, so not having to fix a meal would mean we would not only have a decent dinner, but I almost didn't have to feel guilty about not cooking it.

"Thanks, Mrs. Rattle."

"Happy to help," she said. I think she meant it.

I told her about the bones belonging to Timothy O'Toole and about me going to fetch Mrs. O'Toole. "So it's possible Captain Buckingham, Mr. Edwards and little Billy will get here before I come back with Mrs. O'Toole."

Shaking her head, Mrs. Rattle said, "Poor woman. But I'm glad you finally discovered the name of the boy whose bones are back there. And I'll be sure to let Captain Buckingham and Mr. Edwards in. And, of course, that darling little boy."

"Thank you. I'm going to get Mr. Prophet to come over, too. Little Billy wants to see him."

"That's fine. I'll fix a batch of shortbread to keep the men entertained."

I looked at her in awe. "Shortbread? *Scotch* shortbread?"

"I think that's the only kind there is," said Mrs. Rattle with a little giggle.

Scotch shortbread might possibly be my favorite food in the whole wide world. And Mrs. Rattle said she'd make some. Just like that. Trying to hide my admiration because I thought it would be silly to admit precisely how much of a cooking failure I considered myself, I said, "Thank you. Maybe you'll teach me how to fix shortbread one of these days."

"Oh, shortbread's easy."

"Easy as pie?" I asked, not sure I wanted to hear the answer.

"*Much* easier than pie."

I let out a huge sigh. "Thank heavens."

We grinned at each other, and Mrs. Rattle bustled off to the kitchen.

After Sam left for work and before I went to fetch Mrs. O'Toole, I telephoned the Salvation Army, hoping to speak with Johnny, although Flossie would do if he was out blowing his horn again. I was in luck!

"Salvation Army. Captain Buckingham speaking," came Johnny's voice after the third ring.

"Helping Flossie today, are you, and not out gallivanting?" I said, pretending disapproval. He knew it was pretense.

"Oh, I'll get out there and exercise my lungs after a while, I expect, but I'm home right now. What's up, Daisy?"

"Mr. Edwards provided us with the name of the construction company contracted to build our house."

"Bullis Construction?" said Johnny. "Yes, he told me. Flossie said you called Mr. Bullis from our kitchen yesterday."

"I did indeed. And Mr. Bullis actually looked through his boxes of records and discovered the name of the guy who belonged to the bones on our back porch. Timothy O'Toole."

"I'll be," said Johnny, sounding surprised. "Chris tried and tried to remember the fellow's name and couldn't come up with it. The best he could remember was that it was Irish."

"He was right, I guess. O'Toole sounds Irish to me," I said.

"Yeah, me too."

"But the reason I called, Johnny, is to ask if you could perform a small graveside service for Timothy O'Toole's bones. Well, for his mother actually, but we'll be burying his bones. Sam's paying for a burial and a small headstone, but I neglected to ask Mrs. O'Toole last night if she attended a church whose minister might perform the burial service. She wanted to see her son's bones before they're laid to rest, so I'm going to pick her up at ten this morning and drive her to our house."

"That's nice of you," said Johnny. "Want me to drop by? I can at least give her some moral support. If Chris is around, I'll ask him to come with me. He knew the O'Toole boy."

"That would be perfect," I told him. "Thank you, Johnny. You're not such a shirker after all."

"Ha! Your namesake is still a pain in the neck," he told me.

"It's probably her parents' fault," I said.

"I won't tell Flossie you said that. She'll probably take it seriously."

"Good heavens, I didn't mean it!" I blurted out.

"I know. Anyway, guess I'll see you in a while. Is Lou there? If he is, maybe I'll bring Billy, if Lou won't hate it too much."

"Are you kidding? He said he actually *misses* Billy. Especially after I told him Billy called his sister a bwat."

Laughing again, Johnny said, "Okay. See you soon."

"Thanks, Johnny."

We both hung up, and I glanced down at the dog at my feet.

"All righty, Spike. Want to walk out back and tell Mr. Prophet he's going to have a visitor soon?"

Spike said he'd be delighted to do that, so we walked to Mr. Prophet's cottage. There he sat, same as yesterday, cat on his lap and book in his hands. He had gnarly fingers, I presume from the rheumatics and arthritis. Something to look forward to in my own old age, I reckon. I could hardly wait. He glanced up as we approached.

Today, Yuyu didn't hiss. He jumped from Mr. Prophet's lap and sauntered down the porch steps to greet Spike, who obligingly rolled over onto his back and batted the cat's paws.

Shaking his head as he observed this phenomenon, Mr. Prophet said what I was thinking. "Never seen a cat and a dog play like that before in my life."

"I haven't either. But Mr. Prophet, I'm going to pick up Mrs. O'Toole and bring her down here to look at her son's bones before the undertaker comes to get them. So I called Johnny Buckingham, and he's coming over to give Mrs. O'Toole any spiritual comfort she might require. He's hoping to find Mr. Edwards, since he at least tried to be friendly with Timothy O'Toole, and he's bringing little Billy with him because Billy wants to see you."

"Hellkatoot. Well, it'll be good to see the kid again, too, I suppose. Gotta see if I can find an Injun arrowhead or somethin' to give him."

"You probably shouldn't give him things every time you see him, or he'll grow to expect it."

"Who cares?"

He had me there. "I don't know. Just make sure the arrowhead you give him isn't one you found in our yard. I don't want exorcizing our ghost to be any more complicated than it already will be."

"Good idea. Ain't seen no artifacts out there anyhow. All the arrowheads I have are Apache or Comanche."

"My goodness. You've lived an adventurous life, Mr. Lou Prophet."

"Yeah. It was pretty fun until I ended up in Pasadena."

"Oh, bother you! I'm going to get Mrs. O'Toole. After you hunt for arrowheads, will you go to our house to let Johnny and Mr. Edwards in if they get here before I do? Mrs. Rattle's in the kitchen making shortbread, so you can be on door duty."

"Can do," he said and heaved himself to his leg and his peg.

"Thanks," I said. Spike wanted to remain with Yuyu so, feeling deserted by my best pal, I went back to the house, changed out of my faded gray day dress—it used to be blue—and into a nice brown skirt and white blouse. Then I donned some sensible walking shoes, my brown cloche hat, my brown gloves and picked up my brown handbag. I also put on the beige sweater Aunt Vi had knitted for me at Christmas.

After doing all that, it was almost ten o'clock. Therefore, I bade farewell to Mrs. Rattle, walked across the street, said hi to my father and borrowed the Chevrolet. Technically, I guess it actually *was* my car, as I'd paid for it and Pa and I were the only ones who could drive it. Still, I left it in my parents' drive because I didn't want my father to think he had no escape if he ever decided he wanted to go farther afield than up or down the block, if you know what I mean.

Mrs. O'Toole was waiting for me in a rocking chair on her front porch when I pulled up in front of her house on Maple Street. When she saw me get out of the Chevrolet, she rose and began making her slow way down the porch steps, holding the railing with one hand and a cane with the other. I didn't know the woman, but I felt sorry for what appeared to be her loneliness.

I met her halfway up the walk and offered her my arm as a substitute for the stair railing. She accepted gladly and thanked me for taking her to see the remains of her son.

"I'm only sorry it's necessary," I said. "Very sorry for your loss. Well, all of your losses." I kind of wanted to ask about her daughter, but she hadn't sounded as though the topic of her daughter was one about which she was especially pleased, so I didn't.

With a sigh, she said, "I was a fool to marry Mr. O'Toole. My folks told me he was no good, but you know what girls are like. Think they know everything. I didn't realize my folks were right about him until we'd moved from Ohio to California, and then it was too late."

"I'm sorry," I said again.

"Did I recall right that your husband said the two of you are recently married? You weren't stupid when you were a girl, it looks like."

"Oh, yes I was," I said with a sigh of my own. "I got married right out of high school to my lifelong sweetheart. Seventeen years old and as stupid as any other seventeen-year-old. But almost as soon as our wedding was over, my Billy went off to war and came home after he was shot and gassed. He died three years ago."

Shaking her head, Mrs. O'Toole said, "That's almost harder than marrying a skunk, maybe."

"Oh, I don't think so. My Billy was a good man, but the Kaiser and their guns and gas did him in eventually. We had a few really rough years. Sam Rotondo, the man you met last night, was widowed about two years before Billy died. We only married last September."

"Well, at least you're both old enough to know what to expect," said Mrs. O'Toole.

"I hope so," I said, telling her the truth.

By that time we'd made it to the Chevrolet, so I opened the front passenger's side door, and Mrs. O'Toole creaked into the seat.

When I got behind the wheel and started the car, I said, "I meant to ask you, Mrs. O'Toole. Do you have a church you attend regularly and a minister whom you'd like to conduct a graveside service for your son?"

"A church?" She sounded a little startled. "Well, I don't know. I used to go to St. Andrews there on Raymond, but it's hard for me to walk, and no one else in my neighborhood goes there."

"I see. I have a friend who attends St. Andrews, but he doesn't live nearby either." In actual fact, the friend was Delray Farrington, Harold's mate. Del was a fervent church-goer. Harold called St. Andrews "Our Lady of Perpetual Malice," but not in front of Del. I didn't tell Mrs. O'Toole any of that.

Silence prevailed in the car until I got to Marengo and turned south. Then Mrs. O'Toole surprised me. "I don't want a Catholic ceremony anyhow. The church never did anything for me, and I'd as soon have nothing to do with it."

I wasn't sure what to say, so I didn't speak.

"I suppose that's sinful," said Mrs. O'Toole as if she wished she hadn't spoken.

"Not to me, it isn't," I said. "My husband and I go to the Methodist-Episcopal Church on Marengo and Colorado, and so does the rest of my family. My Sam was reared a Catholic, but he left the Catholic Church to attend the little Unitarian-Universalist Church in Pasadena."

"I don't even know what that kind of church is," said Mrs. O'Toole.

"I think they're non-denominational. Anybody can go who wants to, kind of like the Salvation Army. One of my best friends is the wife of a captain in the Salvation Army. In fact, Captain Buckingham said he'll come to our house this morning. If you need any comfort, I can't think of a better person to get it from than Johnny Buckingham. He's a truly good man. Actually, it was through the Salvation Army that we discovered who the bones in our yard belonged to. Mr. Chris Edwards tried to be friends with your son, and he attends the Salvation Army Church."

"My goodness." Mrs. O'Toole sounded perkier than I'd heard her sound yet. "The Salvation Army, you say?"

"Yes. I consider it a great organization because they try to help people without judging them. I know from my own experience that not judging people is a hard thing to do, but Johnny and his wife, Flossie, are experts at it."

"My goodness," said Mrs. O'Toole again.

"I wouldn't be at all surprised if the Salvation Army offers transportation to their services on Sunday mornings. They're just on Walnut and Fair Oaks, so it's not far away, although it's certainly too far for you to walk."

"Maybe that would be nice," said Mrs. O'Toole doubtfully. "I can't walk much at all any longer because my feet and my back are both bad."

"Well, you don't have to decide today if you want to attend services there, but Captain Buckingham has offered to conduct a graveside service for your son, if you'd like him to. At Mountain View."

"And it won't cost anything?"

"Not a thing," I said, speaking for Johnny, although I wasn't worried about the money for Tim O'Toole's burial. If Sam was going to pay for the burial and the headstone, I'm sure he wouldn't mind slipping Johnny some money for the Salvation Army's coffers.

"That's...that's k-kind of him." Mrs. O'Toole sniffled and had to grab for a hankie.

"Captain Buckingham is one of the kindest people I've ever met," I told her with absolute honesty.

What's more, he, little Billy and Chris Edwards were already at Sam's and my house when I pulled up in front of it. Mr. Edwards was the one who unlatched the front porch gate and hurried to the Chevrolet to assist Mrs. O'Toole from the car. I managed to get out of it on my own.

"Mrs. O'Toole," said Mr. Edwards. "I'm so sorry to meet you again for this reason. I'm Chris Edwards. Don't know if you recall, but I went to visit you a couple of times after Tim went missing."

"Thank you," said Mrs. O'Toole. "I do remember you." She leaned on Mr. Edwards as she slowly exited the automobile. "It was kind of you to come here today."

"I'm only glad Mr. and Mrs. Rotondo and the police folks were able to identify your son's bones. At least now you know what happened to him."

More or less. We didn't actually have a notion in the world what had happened to him, but I didn't say so. All we knew for sure was that he somehow ended up in our yard.

I really hate unsolved mysteries.

TWENTY-FIVE

Mrs. O'Toole broke down and sobbed when she gazed at what was left of her only son. Johnny was on the spot with an arm to put around her shoulder and a handkerchief to lend. I just stood there, not knowing what to do and thanking whatever imp of common sense had led me to telephone Johnny that morning. After a moment or two of indecision, Mr. Edwards and I stepped back several paces. Again, it was almost as if our moves had been choreographed.

Little Billy and Mr. Prophet had taken seats at the other end of the porch on a couple of chairs there, and Mr. Prophet was regaling a rapt and happy Billy with tales of arrowhead-hunting and so forth. Mrs. Rattle peeked out the service porch door and gestured for Mr. Edwards to join her in the kitchen. He obeyed. Shortly thereafter, he rejoined us on the porch carrying a tray laden with tea things and a big platter of Scotch shortbread. I'd only ever had Vi's shortbread, but when I sampled Mrs. Rattle's, I had to admit that it tasted pretty much the same as Vi's. Maybe shortbread really *was* easy to make.

As soon as the food appeared, so did Spike. He raced up the

porch steps as if he'd never heard of a cat named Yuyu, but he knew when cookies arrived on any given scene. Yuyu remained elsewhere. Guess the cat didn't care for shortbread.

The back porch was big, and there was lots of room on it. Sam and I had placed a couple of tables and several chairs there, so Mr. Edwards set the tray on a table, and he and I each took a seat and a piece of shortbread. I poured each of us a cup of tea and took one to Mr. Prophet.

He scowled up at me. "Any coffee?"

"Sorry. Only tea."

"Huh."

Mrs. Rattle appeared as if by magic to hand Billy a glass half filled with milk. I thanked her and let out a big sigh of relief. Figuring Johnny and Mr. Prophet were taking care of the two most burdensome tasks to be undertaken, I placed several pieces of shortbread on a napkin and took the napkin and cookies to Mr. Prophet and Billy, both of whom seemed pleased. Little Billy even said, "Tank you, Mrs. Wotundo."

He was so cute. "You're welcome, Billy."

Mr. Prophet only said, "Huh," again, although there was a lift to the syllable that made it sound as if he was glad.

By the way, there had been a time when Mr. Prophet had been absolutely terrified of Mrs. Rattle. He denied it then—a year or so back—and he denies it now, but he thought the woman was sweet on him. He did everything he could to hide whenever she came around. That wasn't often back then because she was only helping out as I recovered from having been hit by a car. Still and all, he had been scared of her. When he discovered she was married, I could feel his relief from across the room, which was where I stood when she first talked about her Gregory.

Johnny and Mrs. O'Toole still stood huddled over Tim O'Toole's bones, and it looked to me as if Johnny might actually be helping Mrs. O'Toole as she came to grips with this, her latest loss. Perhaps not the latest, but the latest known to her.

I found myself hoping her daughter would come to her senses

and at least visit her mother soon. Becoming a star on the silver screen was just every young girl's dream in those days. Thousands of them came to Los Angeles to attempt the task, but few actually made it big. The newspapers were filled with stories about those who fell (or leaped) by the wayside as their dreams died.

I'm not sure how long Mrs. O'Toole stayed on our back porch. Eventually, she and Johnny came over to join Mr. Edwards and me, and they each took a cup of tea and a piece of shortbread.

"If you'd like me to, Mrs. O'Toole, I'll make arrangements with the cemetery and the funeral home," said Johnny. "I'm used to doing that sort of thing."

After wiping her eyes for perhaps the hundredth time, Mrs. O'Toole sniffled and said, "That would be kind of you, Captain Buckingham." She turned to me. "Are you certain about a little graveside service at Mountain View, Mrs. Rotondo? My pension is tiny, and I can't afford much."

"Everything will be taken care of," I assured her. "You won't be billed for a single thing."

She peered at me closely, then shook her head. "Well, I don't understand how, but I'm grateful. Thank you." She switched her attention back to Johnny. "And I can't thank you enough for helping me today and for performing a service for Timmy." She barely got her son's name out before she broke down again. I felt *so* sorry for the poor woman, and I wished like anything we could tell her precisely what had happened to her son.

Ah well.

Not long after we'd sipped tea and eaten shortbread, Johnny and Mr. Edwards offered to drive Mrs. O'Toole home.

"You don't mind taking care of Billy for a few minutes, do you, Daisy?"

"Heavens, no. Happy to help," I said.

In truth, I wasn't accustomed to boy children. My sister Daphne and her husband had two little girls. I told myself this would be practice, in case Sam and I had a son one day. Anyhow, Mr. Prophet and Mrs. Rattle were at the house, too, so I wouldn't be stranded and alone if little Billy decided to have a fit of temper or fell down and broke his neck or whatever.

"Thanks, Daisy," said Johnny, grinning at me as if he knew precisely what I was thinking. I expect he did.

Mrs. O'Toole left with the two men, and I joined Mr. Prophet and Billy at their table after taking the tray laden with used cups, saucers and the teapot back to the kitchen.

"Look!" Little Billy cried when I sat across from him at his table. "Mr. Pwophet gave a Ca-ca-moooch—"

"Comanche," prompted Mr. P.

"A Comanche awwowhead!" He held up his prize as if he'd chipped it himself from a piece of flint or bone or antler or whatever they used.

"How fascinating, Billy!" I exclaimed.

Mr. Prophet's gaze paid a visit to the porch awning, but I pretended not to notice. "Did he tell you how the Comanches made their arrowheads?"

"Yes," said Billy confidently. "They stwuck pieces of stone with other pieces of stone until flakes fell off, an' they kept doing that until they made a point at the end of a twiangle. It's called flint nap-nap…" He peered at Mr. Prophet.

"Flint-knapping," he prompted.

"Yeah. Flint-knapping."

"Very good," I said, amazed. I glanced at Mr. Prophet. "You're an excellent teacher."

"Yeah. Spent lots of years learnin'," he said drily.

We dawdled at the table for maybe forty-five minutes before Johnny and Mr. Edwards returned. I hope I didn't look as relieved as I felt when the two men walked out onto the back porch. Evidently I failed miserably.

"Thought we were going to abandon my son into your care forever, did you, Daisy?"

"Such a thing never crossed my mind," I fibbed nobly.

"It sure did mine," grumbled Mr. Prophet.

"Look, Daddy!" said little Billy, climbing down from his chair and running to his father. "Mr. Pwophet gave me a Co-man-chee awwowhead!"

"Wow, that's a real treasure," said Johnny. "You thanked him properly, I hope."

"He did," said Mr. P, rising from his chair. "You got a good kid there, Buckingham."

"Thanks," said Johnny. "Flossie and I try. So far we're having better luck with the boy than the girl." He gave me a slanty-eyed look and grinned.

"Never shoulda given the baby that name," said Mr. Prophet.

"Flossie insisted," said Johnny.

"Hey!" I said, pretending indignation.

"Baby's a bwat," said little Billy.

Mr. Edwards just laughed, and the two men and little Billy took their leave, Billy holding his arrowhead, flat-handed so as not to get stabbed, to his chest. He waved madly with his other hand as his father carried him back into the house. Mr. Prophet and I waved back.

"Gawd," said Mr. Prophet. "You and Sam really want kids?"

After hesitating for far too long, I told the truth. "I think so."

"Cripes. Better you than me," said the old sinner as he took off for his cottage.

Spike and I retreated into the house, and then we both retired to the sewing room as Mrs. Rattle continued her good works around the house. She knocked on the sewing room door while I was busy gathering threads in order to make a ruffled curtain trimming. "Come on in!" I called.

"I'm leaving now, Daisy," said Mrs. Rattle. "Just want you to know I left the pot of stew on the warming plate. It should be a meal all by itself, because it has meat and vegetables already in it. I don't think you'll need anything else, unless you want to make biscuits or some cornbread to go with it."

"Cornbread," I said, recalling that I'd meant to visit the Bennetts that day to buy cornmeal. "I meant to get some cornmeal today. Piffle."

"Cornbread's almost as easy to make as shortbread," said Mrs.

Rattle with a laugh. "Just follow the directions on the box, if you get a box, which is probably all you'll need."

"Oh. Thank you for letting me know." I rose from the White side-pedal sewing machine and walked with Mrs. Rattle to the front door, Spike at my side. "And thank you for all your hard work. *And* your shortbread. I love shortbread."

"There's plenty left for dessert tonight if you want to have it twice in one day," she told me.

"I could have shortbread for breakfast, lunch and dinner every day. I love the stuff!"

She laughed, but I meant it. I waved her away at the door, and she walked off jauntily. Nice woman, Mrs. Rattle. I appreciated her more every day.

As soon as the door shut behind her, I glanced down at my dog. "Hey, Spike. Want to go for a walk to the corner grocery?"

Spike leaped up and wagged his approval, so I got his leash, clipped it to his collar and, after putting my sweater back on, the two of us walked across the street to see if Pa wanted to join us.

"Walk to the store with you?" said Pa. "Sure. Let me get my hat and coat."

So the three of us walked to the grocery store, where I told Mrs. Bennett about my plans to make cornbread. She rattled off a recipe as she lifted down a box of cornmeal from a shelf behind her.

"Wait a minute," I said, panic in my voice. "I need to write this down."

"No, you don't," she told me. "The recipe's right here, printed on the back of the box."

She turned the box of Quaker Cornmeal around and, sure enough, there was a recipe, all printed and ready to use. "How clever!" I said. "And I didn't know Quaker made cornmeal as well as oatmeal."

"There are many brands of cornmeal," said Mrs. Bennett. "This one was just handy, and it's small. I don't expect you'll be making cornbread every day, although some folks pretty much live on it. Just follow the recipe. Use one of your small iron skillets. Be sure to butter the skillet real good before you pour in the batter."

"I will, thanks," I said. I don't know what Mrs. Bennett thought of me. I mean, I heard the awe in my own voice and nearly winced. I'm sure she and her husband—and maybe even Pa—were thinking it was silly to be enamored of so simple a thing as a recipe for cornbread. Ha. They just didn't *know*. Well, Pa did, but he was kind enough not to tell on me.

Spike sat before the butcher's case, gazing at the meat therein, also in awe. I acquitted him of being a bad cook. He just liked meat, and he'd never seen so much of it in one place before.

At any rate, Pa, Spike and I left the Bennetts' store, I with a box of cornmeal, some baking powder and a pound of butter, because I couldn't remember how much we had left in the Frigidaire. I almost bought some milk, too, but recalled the bottle from which Mrs. Rattle had poured Billy's milk that afternoon and didn't. Pa bought some navy beans with the intention of making Boston baked beans on Saturday night.

By golly, I made cornbread! Without burning it or leaving it raw in the middle—I tested it with a broom straw, just as Vi had told me to do several thousand times when she'd tried and failed to teach me to cook. It went really well with Mrs. Rattle's lamb stew.

Sam walked me to choir practice that evening. Mr. Floy Hostetter, our choir director, had selected "O, For a Thousand Tongues to Sing" as Sunday's anthem. We Methodist-Episcopals were pretty much born knowing that hymn, because it was the first hymn in any Methodist hymnal. Even better, he had Lucy Zollinger and me sing a duet on the second and fourth verses. I guess I was a natural show-off, because I loved singing duets with Lucy. Of course, being an alto, I got to sing harmony, but I didn't mind.

"You sounded really good in your duet," Sam told me as he walked me home again. The night was chilly, and he had an arm around me. I appreciated him a lot for that.

"Thank you. Oh!" I exclaimed, having just thought of something. "Tomorrow I get Rosebud for Pa."

"The dachshund?"

"Indeed. Rosebud, the dachshund. After the séance I'm conducting for Mrs. Bissel. Hope Rosebud and Pa get along well."

"I'm sure they will. I hope Spike doesn't decide to kill her," said Sam.

"I don't think he will," I said, a trifle doubtfully. "If Spike can get along with Yuyu, he can surely get along with a pretty little girl dog."

"You hope," said Sam.

"I hope," I admitted.

And then came Friday.

TWENTY-SIX

Friday was a pretty quiet day at the old homestead. Johnny telephoned to say the Lamb Funeral Home aimed to pick up Tim O'Toole's bones at about eleven in the morning, so I told Mrs. Rattle to expect a ring at the door at that approximate time. Then Spike and I went across the street to take a walk with Pa.

When we returned home, the telephone was ringing, so I called out to Mrs. Rattle that I'd answer it and did.

"*Daisy!*" came a well-remembered voice I'd kind of hoped I wouldn't hear for another several weeks. Or months. Or years. I'd become so accustomed to *not* hearing it, I'd neglected to hold the receiver away from my ear and nearly lost an eardrum.

Shutting my eyes and wishing I'd stayed outside longer, I said in my soft, soothing spiritualist's voice, "Good morning, Mrs. Pinkerton. I haven't heard from you for quite a while."

"I know," she said, sobbing pitifully. "Harold told me to leave you alone because you just got married and are settling in and so forth, but oh, *Daisy*! I *need* you! It's *Stacy!*"

As far as I knew, Anastasia "Stacy" Kincaid still resided at the Pasadena City Jail, a suitable place for her. Maybe she got shanked like her old gangster pal, Jinx Jenkins. One could always hope, although I didn't hope awfully hard. "What's the matter with Stacy?" I asked, trying to sound concerned.

"Another inmate tried to *kill* her!"

Mercy sakes! Just as Stacy'd tried to do to me, by golly. I didn't say so to Mrs. Pinkerton. "Oh dear. How? And the inmate didn't succeed?" I think I kept the fervent wistfulness out of my voice.

"No, but Stacy's in the prison ward at the Castleton Hospital."

"Hmm. I didn't know they had a prison ward there."

Sniffle. "There is. And Stacy's there. Oh, Daisy! I know you'll be at Griselda's tonight for a séance. I'll be there, too. Do you think you can read some tealeaves for me or something? I'm so *worried* about Stacy!"

Good lord. "You know, Mrs. Pinkerton, the only person for whom I can read leaves or the Ouija board or the tarot cards or the crystal ball is the person asking for help. Neither the leaves nor Rolly can tell *you* anything about *Stacy*. I know you know that."

Her voice a mere whisper, Mrs. Pinkerton said, "I know. I know. You've told me so over and over, and so has Harold. I just keep hoping, I guess."

Very well, I know I'm a soft touch. And I know Mrs. Pinkerton had been a thorn in my side for decades. But she'd also been my most lucrative client, and I couldn't help but feel a bit sorry for the woman. Not, mind you, as sorry as I was for Mrs. O'Toole—but there was always a chance that the next time an inmate knifed Stacy, Stacy would succumb, which would be nice for the rest of the world but hard on Mrs. P. Terrible thing to write, isn't it? That's only because you don't know Stacy. Trust me on this.

At any rate, I found myself saying, "Well, you never know. Perhaps Rolly will be able to give you a hint or two regarding Stacy. However," I said in order to prevent any true expectations on Mrs. Pinkerton's part, "the séance is being conducted for a specific purpose." In truth, I didn't know that. Mrs. Bissel hadn't told me she wanted me to get in touch with any particular dead relations or late dachshund breeders, but then again, I hadn't asked. I probably should do so in order to prepare.

"I know it," said Mrs. Pinkerton, sounding happier than she had when I picked up the receiver. "But Rolly knows how terribly worried I am about Stacy."

"He does."

"Perhaps he might have a word or two of encouragement for me?" She lifted the end of her sentence to make it sound like a question.

"Perhaps he might," I said, attempting to quell any joyful anticipation on Mrs. P's part. After all, Mrs. Bissel was paying me in Rosebud for the upcoming séance, and I aimed to direct my attention to her needs, not Mrs. Pinkerton's.

"Harold will be joining me at Griselda's tonight," said Mrs. Pinkerton, making my day bright and cheerful all of a sudden.

"Oh, I'm so glad! I haven't seen Harold since Monday, when he brought us the most *beautiful* lamp I've ever seen in my life. I miss Harold!"

"He's a good boy," said Mrs. P, as if Harold were little Billy's age instead of in his early thirties. Ah well. As Mrs. O'Toole had demonstrated the day prior, one's child is always one's child.

"Well, good luck to Stacy," I said. "But I need to hang up now, Mrs. Pinkerton. I have things to attend to before tonight's séance." I tried to make my voice sound sepulchral, although I was out of practice. Still, I guess it worked.

Mrs. P hurried to say, "Of course. Of course. I know how much work you put into your séances, Daisy. Thank you *so* much."

"You're welcome," I said, not having a clue what she was thanking me for. "Have a lovely day."

"Yes, thank you. I feel better after talking to you, my dear. You're always *such* a comfort to me."

How nice. As soon as she hung up on her end of the wire, I clicked the hook a couple of times and dialed Mrs. Bissel's number. Keiji Saito, Mrs. Bissel's houseboy, answered on Mrs. Bissel's end.

"Hi, Keiji. It's Daisy. I wanted to ask Mrs. Bissel if there's anyone she's interested in speaking to at this evening's séance. Is she around the house somewhere?"

"She is indeed. I'll get her. Be right back."

I heard him softly place the receiver on the hall table. He walked so quietly, I didn't hear his steps. I did, however, hear him and Mrs. Bissel chatting as she came to the telephone.

"Daisy!" she said, sounding delighted, which was a nice change from Mrs. Pinkerton.

"Good morning, Mrs. Bissel. I just wanted to know if there's anyone in particular you want me to get in touch with at tonight's séance."

"Oh, dear, I hadn't actually thought much about it," she admitted.

Her words cheered me. If she'd wanted me to chat with a dead person I'd never heard of, I might have had a hard time of it. This proved how out of practice I was at my business. Usually I found out instantly to whom I'd be speaking when I booked a séance. That way, if I'd never heard of the person, I could go to the library and look him or her up in whatever records were necessary to the purpose. "We can just let Rolly carry the evening, if you don't have any special plans," I said, hoping she'd like my idea.

"Brilliant, Daisy!" she said, warming my heart. "Of course, Madeline is in a state over that horrible daughter of hers."

"Yes, she just called me. I can't seem to make her understand that Rolly can't answer questions about Stacy because Stacy isn't the one asking, if you know what I mean."

"I know precisely what you mean, dear. Madeline's heart is in the right place, but I think she parked her brain someplace and forgot where."

Attempting not to laugh out loud, I said, "I fear you may be right."

"Oh, I know!" said Mrs. Bissel as if she'd just had one of my own personal brilliant ideas. "Why don't you find out how those bones got in your backyard? That might even be useful."

"It might," I said, thinking this was just like Mrs. Bissel, who had a thought to spare for other people's problems, unlike Mrs. P, who only cared about her own. "Thanks. We found out to whom the bones belonged in life by doing a little research and having some really good luck."

"Oh, my," she said, surprised. "Then maybe you don't need to find out anything about them."

"In point of fact, while we know who he was, we don't know how he died, so that's a good idea." I didn't mention the bones in the backyard of true concern to me, as evidently, the spirit belonging to them seemed to be haunting the yard. I feared the notion would sound too ridiculous if spoken aloud to anyone other than Sam and Mr. Prophet.

On the other hand, I was talking to a woman who'd had me speak to a deceased dachshund breeder twice. *And* exorcise a ghost from her basement. Unless it had been a spirit.

Naw. I didn't want to complicate my life, which seemed plenty complicated already.

"Well, then, perhaps Rolly can get in touch with the late person's—who was he, by the way?" said Mrs. Bissel.

"A young man named Timothy O'Toole. He worked for the contracting company that built this house. According to the Bullis Company and a fellow who worked with him, he walked off the job one day and never came back. Nobody knows how his bones got in our backyard. The only thing we know for sure is that he was never properly buried. As odd as it sounds, it seems most likely that he died back there and nobody noticed while they dumped construction debris on top of him. But he was only in his early twenties, so I don't know how he could have just up and died."

"Well, you never know about these things. My friend Judith's boy died of ptomaine poisoning about five years ago. I guess ptomaine can happen to anyone, although it seems less common these days, as we have good refrigeration and so forth. Of course, when your house was built, ptomaine was probably much more prevalent."

"True. I never even considered ptomaine poisoning." Just goes to show. I figured Timmy O'Toole had drunk himself to death and hadn't given a thought to other possible causes. Bad Daisy!

"Well, just have Rolly talk to anyone he wants to," said Mrs. B with a laugh. "I'm sure there are millions of dead folks on the other side. Some of them might have exciting stories to tell to those of us still here on earth."

What a horrifying notion!

I didn't say so.

"Of course. Rolly's friendly. I'm sure he'll find someone to chat with," I said, trying to summon a laugh of my own. Didn't work very well.

Then the doorbell rang, and I had to say goodbye to Mrs. Bissel. The ring belonged to the people from Lamb's Funeral Home, so I told them where the bones were, said I'd open the back gate for them, did so, and they hauled off Timothy O'Toole's bones. They were relatively blasé about the task. Guess they were accustomed to handling dead people and their bones.

The rest of the day passed peacefully enough. Vi telephoned to ask Sam, Mr. Prophet and me to dinner that evening, so neither Mrs. Rattle nor I had to deal with meal preparations. I don't know about Mrs. Rattle, but I was overjoyed.

Mr. Prophet moseyed into the house around about noon, and Mrs. Rattle fixed each of us a cheese-and-tomato sandwich. Actually, she fixed Mr. P two of them, and he ate them both. Nothing wrong with the old ruffian's appetite. We both thanked Mrs. Rattle for a delicious lunch.

"Come into the living room with me for a minute or two, okay, Miss Daisy?" Mr. P said after finishing his cup of coffee. I'd had milk with my sandwich.

"Sure. What's up?"

"Tell you when we get there," he said, frowning at me and pointing his stubbly chin at Mrs. Rattle, who was busily washing up the few lunch dishes at the kitchen sink.

"You need a shave," I told him.

"Hellkatoot," he told me back.

So we walked into the living room and each took a chair near the piano. The peacock lamp Harold had given Sam and me looked absolutely spectacular on our baby grand. I'd almost decided it could stay there except when we had company that might possibly bump into the piano as, for instance, when my sister's two daughters visited. Then I'd hide the lamp away where nobody could possibly, even by accident, knock it over.

"All right, what's the big secret?" I asked Mr. P after we were both seated.

"Ain't no secret, but you're havin' that big hoodoo thing tonight, aren't you? Gettin' your pa's dog for him?"

"Yes. Why? You want me to get in touch with the spirit of our Indian ghost or something?"

"Naw." His bushy gray eyebrows formed a V over his nose on his wrinkled forehead. "I want you to take me to the mission tomorrow, so I can get the DeLoera feller out here to get rid of the ghost. I don't like havin' that thing anywhere near me. Scares Yuyu."

I'll just bet the ghost of the dead Indian scared Yuyu. Mr. Prophet had lived among Indians long enough to dislike having an Indian haunting ground near his cottage. Probably feared the ghost would scare his lady friend away. I didn't tell him my thoughts on the matter.

"I guess that would be all right. Séances usually last a long time, so I won't get home until late. I'll also have Pa's dog, Rosebud, with me. I don't know how complicated that's going to be because I don't know how Spike will react to an intruder into what he considers his own territory."

"With any luck, he'll roll over on his back and play with the new dog like he did with Yuyu," said Mr. Prophet.

"With any luck, he will. But then I'll have to take the dog across the street in the morning. I can't just hand Rosebud over to Pa and go away again without being there while he and Rosebud get to know each other. I guess we can go after lunch tomorrow, if that's all right with you. But do you expect Mr. DeLoera to spend the night here? I have to sing in the choir on Sunday mornings. How late will we be up Saturday night if he does the exorcism or whatever it is?"

"Aw, hell, *I* don't know. Take me to the mission and I'll talk to the guy. He can tell me about the process then. Mebbe it doesn't have to be Saturday night. Mebbe he can do it on *Sunday* night. That any better?"

After thinking about it for a second or three, I said, "Yes. That *would* be better. The only person who truly has to get up early on Monday morning is Sam. Poor Sam."

"Aw, hell, Sam don't even have to be there when DeLoera does his...whatever it is he does. Sam don't believe there's a ghost back there anyhow."

I tilted my head to help myself think better—doesn't always work—and decided Mr. P was right. "You're right," I told him.

"And if DeLoera has to spend the night, he can do it at my place. It has two bedrooms."

"I forgot about that. A mighty nice 'cottage' you have there, Mr. Prophet."

"Yeah, it is, and I appreciate it, even if it is in Pasadena."

I laughed. Couldn't help it. "You're so welcome." Then I thought about the coming...whatever you'd call it. I guess ridding the yard of our ghost would truly be an exorcism, only the spirit Mr. DeLoera would be getting rid of wasn't precisely evil; it just seemed lost and unhappy. "I hope nothing awful will happen when he gets the ghost to go away."

"Probably won't. Might involve some incantations and dancing and shaking rattles. Mebbe some singing. Might have to take that skull somewhere. Most Injuns don't like being separated from their families, and that includes after they die. I expect that's why the Injun in the backyard is so miserable. Not only got separated from his kin, but ended up amongst a herd of white people." He shook his grizzled head. "Can't think of any Apache I ever knew who wouldn't think of that as some kind of hell, and I expect this Tongva feller ain't any different."

"Oh dear. That exhibit at the Southwest Museum really upset you, didn't it?"

"With the dead lady in it? Yeah. It did. It was wrong. Everything about it was wrong. No Injun I ever knew would allow that. Having someone stare at a dead relation is just wrong. Bad wrong."

"Yes, I got that impression from you at the museum."

"They should remove the exhibit and return it to the Injuns they stole it from."

"But how would any of the rest of us know about their burial customs if they did that?" I asked, thinking I'd learned a lot from that exhibit.

"You can read, can't you?"

"Right. You're right. Very well. Tomorrow after lunch, *if* I'm not still exhausted from the séance and if Pa and Rosebud get along all right, we can go to the Mission San Gabriel and try to find your friend Mr. DeLoera."

"Ain't my friend. But he knows how to get the ghost to go away. He told me he sits in the courtyard every afternoon, so he'll probably be there. The priests make all the Injuns go to Mass on Sundays, so he keeps all his Injun stuff at another location. The priests don't know about it. If they did, they'd take it all away from him."

Dismayed, I said, "Would they really take his mementoes and treasures away?"

"Ain't you learned *nothin'* about how we treated the Injuns? Didn't they teach that at your fancy school?"

"My school wasn't fancy!" I said, slightly stung. "We learned about the Navajos and Hopis and made some sheep out of papier-mâché. We made some bowls out of rolls of clay stacked on top of each other. Then we smoothed them out and painted them, but that's about all we learned," I admitted.

"What's *papermatchee*? And you made sheep out of it?"

"It's paper—we collected newspapers—torn up and mixed together with water and flour to make a paste. You can build things out of it. They don't last. But we made some sheep. We built a hogan too."

"A hogan. So you learned about the Navajos, who mostly live in Arizona and New Mexico. But you never heard of a Tongva."

"Nope. Never heard of a Tongva. Tongvas would have been more pertinent to where we live, wouldn't they?"

"Probably." Sarcastic. Mr. Prophet was being quite sarcastic. "So they didn't teach you that the whites took Injun kids from their families and sent 'em to schools miles away, where they forced 'em forget their native customs and languages and made 'em learn how to live white?"

I stared at him, aghast. There I went, being aghast again. But I was. "I can't think of anything more awful than someone taking my child away to learn how not to be like the people in my family."

"You just hit the nail on its big, fat head," said Mr. Prophet. "Injuns don't like it either. Pisses 'em off. Nothin' they could do about it."

"Oh, lord. We *have* to get that poor ghost out of our yard and back with its people!"

"Just what I was tellin' ya."

"Okay. Saturday, for *certain*, I'll take you to the San Gabriel Mission."

"Thanks, Miss Daisy. 'preciate it."

"I'll appreciate getting that poor ghost out of our yard and back with its family."

"If it can be done," he said soberly. I have a feeling sobriety hadn't been a huge part of his life until he moved to Pasadena.

"If it can be done," I repeated, fervently hoping it could be. Heck, I'd even pray about it. Johnny Buckingham would have been pleased that I'd eventually thought about prayer.

TWENTY-SEVEN

The evening meal was delicious, as were all of Vi's meals. She fixed us braised short ribs, whatever they were, and made gravy with onions and pan drippings (I think pan drippings mean the fat from the ribs). She served the ribs and gravy with mashed potatoes and served green beans and corn cakes along with everything. I made a mental note to ask Vi how to cook everything she served that night.

However, since I had to get to Mrs. Bissel's house in order to conduct a séance, I only had time to don an apron and help Ma with the dishes. Then I went across the street to dress for the séance, all the while hoping my mental note about short ribs and corn cakes would stay in my brain and not bolt. Because I aimed to use the Chevrolet, I returned to my parents' house, where Sam, Mr. Prophet and Spike had remained while I went home to change.

The weather remained nippy, so I wore my cobalt blue dress with long bishop sleeves and a rounded neck. I'd embroidered the neck and the gored hem of the dress, and it had a sash belt. If I'd followed the pattern, which I'd copied from an issue of *Vogue* I'd found at the library, the belt would have had a big bow at the front. I didn't care for big bows, however, so it didn't. It had more embroidery on the sash. It was a plain but pretty gown, and I had a perfectly gorgeous black velvet cape lined with soft black flannel that didn't look like flannel. That cape was *warm*. I accessorized my outfit with black double-strapped shoes, a black bag and black gloves. As I didn't want to wear a hat all evening, I threaded an embroidered blue bandeau (same fabric as the dress) through my thick reddish bob, then toddled to the bathroom to fix my face.

After I'd brushed my teeth, I used some light powder to cover my freckles. Then I squinted into the mirror for a few seconds in order to decide what to do with my baby-blues. Decision made, I lined my lower eyelids with a little black eyeliner, used Maybelline mascara on my eyelashes, blinked a few times, wiped mascara off my upper cheeks, peered into the mirror again and decided I was ready. The evening wasn't a big gala event or anything, so there was no need to look extremely ghostly or spiritualistic. Just normally "pale and interesting" would do.

According to my relatives and Mr. Prophet, I'd actually exceeded my expectations when I loped back across the street to get the Chevrolet. Everyone had gone to the living room to chat for a while.

"You look perfectly glorious this evening!" Aunt Vi exclaimed when I walked through the front door.

"Beautiful," said Pa.

"You do look very nice, dear," said Ma, who didn't want me to get conceited.

"That's my darling wife," said Sam, gazing at me with appreciation.

"Lookin' good, Miss Daisy," said Mr. Prophet. From him, this was high praise indeed.

Spike, who never cared how I looked, merely wagged and appreciated my enthusiastic greeting of him.

"Thanks, everyone," I said. Then I spoke seriously to my hound, who resided on Sam's lap. "Spike, I'm going to be bringing home another dog tonight, but I don't want you to be jealous."

Spike gazed at me from Sam's lap and wagged some more.

"This will be a young lady dog, about a year younger than you

237

are. She's not going to take your place in anyone's heart. You're still the best-trained dachshund in Pasadena, and you're my special boy."

More wags and a few chuckles from bystanders.

"I don't expect you to love and adore Rosebud. All I ask is that you not try to murder her when I bring her home with me. Do you think you can do that, Spike?"

Spike told me he'd be happy to do that, bless the dog.

So I bade farewell to everyone and drove up to Mrs. Bissel's house, which resided on the corner of Foothill Boulevard and Maiden Lane in Altadena. I parked the Chevrolet in the circular drive in her backyard. Inside the circular drive grew a *huge* monkey puzzle tree. That tree had more than once dropped a spiky leaf on me and snagged my hosiery, so I parked as far away from it as I could, then made my way to the back door without incident.

"You're looking lovely tonight, Daisy. As usual," said Keiji as he opened the door for me.

"Thanks, Keiji. Everyone is gathering in the living room, I see." The living room was right off the sunroom, which was right off the patio, which was right off the circular drive. That's the reason I knew folks were gathered in the living room: I could see them.

"Yep. Mrs. Bissel's in there with Mrs. Pinkerton and Mr. Kincaid. A couple of others are expected to join the party. Can't remember who."

"I'm glad Harold's here, anyway. Is Mrs. Pinkerton crying yet?"

"I'm afraid so," Keiji said with a small laugh as he took my cloak and handbag and hung them both on the rack in the sunroom.

Because I hadn't brought any of my spiritualistic accoutrements with me—well, except for Rolly, who resided in my head along with my mental note about short ribs—I felt nearly naked as I walked into the living room from the sunroom.

"Good evening, everyone," I said, attempting to smile mysteriously for Mrs. Pinkerton's sake. Neither Harold nor Mrs. Bissel cared how I smiled.

"Oh, *Daisy!*" shrieked Mrs. P, heaving herself up from a sofa and lumbering at me.

Bless Harold for a saint, he bounced up from the same sofa and grabbed his mother's arm to slow her down. I swear, one of these days, Mrs. P was going to plow into me, and we'd both tumble over. She'd probably squash me to death, what's more.

"Hold on, Mother," said Harold sharply. "Daisy will join us. You needn't fetch her for us. She's walking fine on her own."

"Thank you, Harold. Thank you, Mrs. Pinkerton. Yes, I'm fine to walk on my own."

Mrs. Bissel remained seated, laughing at the three of us. "Madeline, come back here. Daisy's here for my sake tonight, don't forget." She was easygoing and her words weren't meant to scold, but they kind of did anyway.

Mrs. P stopped trying to tug her arm away from Harold and looked abashed. "I'm so sorry, Griselda. I'm sorry, Daisy. I'm just so *happy* to see you! It's been so long, and I've missed you so."

"Thank you, Mrs. Pinkerton," I said in my most soothing voice. It was actually slightly raspy from lack of use. I'd have to brush up on my sympathetic tones and my wafting if I aimed to continue spiritualist-mediuming now that I was a married woman. "Let's sit on the sofa and chat for a while."

"Oh, *thank* you, dear."

Harold's gaze paid a visit to the chandelier on the ceiling and he eased up on the hold he had on his mother. "Good evening, Daisy," he said formally.

"Good evening, Harold. I'm happy you decided to come tonight."

"Didn't dare stay away," he said, slipping a sideways glance at his mother.

Behind us, Mrs. Bissel laughed again. "Come over here, Daisy. I had Mrs. Cummings fix some tea for us. I think Madeline has plans for the leaves in her cup." She winked at me.

"Oh, dear," said Mrs. P, sounding as if she felt guilty. "I didn't mean to take over your evening, Griselda."

"You won't, Madeline. I won't let you. But let Daisy have a cup of tea at least before you start in on her."

"Of course. Of course." A chastened Mrs. Pinkerton walked

with Harold and me back to the sofa. I decided to sit on one of the artistically placed chairs near the sofa, since both Mrs. B and Mrs. P were quite large and I didn't want to be crowded.

"How have you been, Daisy?" asked Harold. "Did you figure out who those bones used to be?"

"Yes, oddly enough, we did," I told him. Then I regaled everyone who didn't already know with the story of Timothy O'Toole. "We still don't know how he ended up in our yard, though," I ended.

"Perhaps you can ask Rolly to find him and ask," suggested Mrs. Bissel. "Depending on how he landed in your yard, knowing how he died might ease his poor mother's heart."

I doubted that, given what I'd already learned about the late Timothy O'Toole, but I said, "Maybe so," trying to sound as if I meant my words.

"Um…" said Mrs. Pinkerton tentatively, from which I gathered she'd drunk her tea and wanted me to peek at the leaves remaining in the bottom of her cup. "Daisy…um…"

"I'll be happy to look at your tealeaves, Mrs. Pinkerton," I said in my smoothest, most soothing voice. Sometimes I wasn't sure why I bothered being soothing with Mrs. P, as she never got the hint and calmed down.

"Oh, *thank* you, dear."

I saw Harold and Mrs. Bissel exchange a sly glance but pretended I didn't. They knew, as did I, that Mrs. P pretty much always got her way. Except when it came to her horrible daughter.

Delicately taking Mrs. P's nearly empty teacup, I peered within. I saw a little liquid and some random leaves glopped together in the bottom of the cup. "Hmmm," I said mysteriously.

"Oh, do you see something?" asked an eager Mrs. Pinkerton.

"Hmmm," I repeated even more mysteriously.

Mrs. P said something that sounded like, "Ooooooooh!"

Harold said, "Hush, Mother! If you keep making a commotion, Daisy will never receive whatever message the leaves are trying to tell her." You can see why I consider Harold such a good friend.

"Oh," she whimpered. "I'm sorry."

I allowed another few seconds to pass before I said, still sooth-ingly darn it, "The message is unclear. The leaves seem to be obscuring it...oh, wait. Things are becoming clearer. The leaves say...they say..." I shook my head hard as if attempting to bring something into focus. In truth, I could still see the gloppy tealeaves in the bottom of the moist teacup. Mrs. P sucked in approximately six gallons of air and, before she could expel them and blow us all out of the room, I said, "They're saying your road will have many hills and valleys, but you must continue to seek serenity and not depend on others to help you achieve peace of mind."

There. Was that a solid message, or was it not?

"Ha!" said Harold. "Told you so. If you expect Stacy to clean up her act and behave like an adult human being with solid values and an iota of decency, you're going to be waiting a long time, Mother. Why don't you make an appointment with the Swami Vivekananda? Maybe he can help you achieve inner peace."

The Swami Vivekananda had been in the newspapers recently. He reportedly assisted people out of their money by teaching them how to meditate and relax. "That sounds like a good idea, Mrs. Pinkerton. Do you know anyone who's been to the Swami Vivekananda?"

"Oh," said she, "I believe Hazel Peterson has been to him. She spoke highly of his teaching, too. I didn't think I'd get much help out of a fellow from India, but perhaps she was correct."

"Wouldn't hurt to try," said Mrs. P's loyal son.

"Oh, look!" said Mrs. Bissel. "I think Dennis and Patsy are here."

Thank god for that! The Swami Vivekananda was welcome to Ms. P's patronage. The longer I remained in her company, the more I realized I didn't *want* to remain in her company. That probably sounds mean of me, as Mrs. Pinkerton had been my most loyal and profitable client for my entire career, but I wanted to do other things now. Like be a wife. Maybe a mother, although that part of my future remained hazy. Hazy Daisy. If I called myself that, nobody would *ever* call on me to do anything at all.

The last guests to show up were Dennis and Patsy Bissel, Mrs.

Bissel's son and daughter-in-law. I knew and liked both of them, so I rose and went to greet them. Was that officious? I didn't mean it to be.

"It's good to see you two." I said, happily shaking Dennis's hand and giving Patsy a little hug. "Did you hire a babysitter for the evening?" They'd had a baby girl about a year or two prior.

"We have a nanny," said Patsy happily. "She doesn't mind if Dennis and I have an evening out every now and then."

"That's nice," I said, wondering how much nannies cost in the overall scheme of things. Not that I wanted one. I'd take care of my own child. How brave and modern of me, huh?

"I told them to bring Gracie over here along with Mrs. Phipps, but they said they didn't want to ruin her nightly schedule," said Mrs. Bissel with what sounded like mock disapproval.

"You wouldn't like to have a baby start screaming while you were in the middle of the séance, would you?" asked Patsy playfully.

"I guess not," said Mrs. B, pouting for fun.

If a baby started screaming in the middle of one of my séances, I'd be absolutely furious. I didn't say so but only chuckled pleasantly.

"You did the right thing," said Harold, joining me in greeting the younger Bissels. "I sure don't want to listen to a baby squawk and squeal."

"I think you're mistaking human babies for bird babies," I told him.

"Pooh. Good to see you, Dennis! Did you hear the Shakespeare Society plans to put on another Gilbert and Sullivan operetta one of these days?"

Harold, Dennis, Patsy and I had all been involved in *The Mikado* a couple of years prior. It had been scary—I'd had a pretty big part in the play—but a lot of fun.

"No!" said Dennis. "Which one are they going to stage? And where? At Daisy's church again?"

"I'm not sure Pastor Smith will allow our church to be used for another operetta," I said, my mind roaming to play rehearsals of yore. They'd been fun though. Well, except for when people began killing each other, but I didn't like to recall those parts.

"They're trying to decide among *H.M.S. Pinafore*, *Pirates of Penzance* and *Ruddigore*," Harold said. "I think they're leaning towards *Ruddigore*."

"Isn't that the one in which the people step out of picture frames and sing?" I asked. I had a piano bench full of music, including a lot of Gilbert and Sullivan's operettas. "I love the patter song they sing in that one."

"They have patter songs in all their shows," said Harold.

"But that one's especially funny," I said.

"If you say so, my dear," said Harold. "I want them to stage *Pirates*, so I can be the pirate king. Or maybe Frederic."

The pirate king was a tall, well-built, heroic villain. I think that's a contradiction in terms, but it'll have to do. Frederic, the hero of the piece, was a young, slender sailor boy. I squinted slightly at Harold, who was rather soft and round, and opened my mouth but didn't get the chance to say anything.

"And don't you *dare* say I'm too old and fat to play either of those parts!" he told me.

"Wouldn't dream of it," I said.

"I don't even know what you two are talking about," said Dennis, laughing. "You know a lot more about music than I do."

"Me too," said Patsy, shaking her head. "It was fun to sing in the play, but I don't know if I'd want to do it again, what with little Gracie and all."

"Children *do* get in the way of a good time, don't they?" said Harold.

"I think I'd better go set up the séance room," I told everyone, and scrammed out of the living room before a fight could commence.

TWENTY-EIGHT

The séance was to take place in Mrs. Bissel's breakfast room, which was directly off the kitchen. Mrs. Cummings, Mrs. B's cook-housekeeper, lived in the suite of rooms off the breakfast room, but her door remained closed during séances. The breakfast room itself was fully as large as my parents' dining room. Mrs. B's place also contained a formal dining room on the other side of the house, which could seat I don't know how many people, but a whole lot of them.

Preparations for the séance were easy. I placed one cranberry-glass candle holder in the middle of the table, and I was through. Keiji would shut off the lights when I gave him the signal, and turn them on again when I deemed the séance to be over. I sat at the head of the oval table.

Thinking again that I probably should have practiced my spiritualist act a little at home before coming here, I finally decided it was too late now and got on with it. "Okay, Keiji, I guess you can tell everyone to come on in. I haven't done this for a long time. Hope I remember my act."

Laughing, Keiji said, "I'm sure you will. It's probably like riding a bike. Once you learn, you have the skill for life."

"I hope you're right."

I heaved a huge sigh as Keiji left to round up the séance partici-pants. I expected he was correct about my séance skills. If he wasn't, we'd both find out soon.

The group walking into the breakfast room that evening seemed a jolly one. Mrs. Bissel sat beside me on my right and leaned over. "I want you to meet Rosebud after the séance, Daisy. She's healed from her surgery, and she's the sweetest baby girl you can imagine."

"I can hardly wait," I said, telling the truth. I'd rather visit with Rosebud and the rest of Mrs. B's hounds than conduct this stupid séance, but I'd brought it on myself so I'd carry it through.

Harold sat next to me on my left side, which made me happy. There were only five participants, which also made me happy. Large groups were harder to control than small ones.

"Let us take hands," I said after everyone was seated. I waited a few moments before issuing my command in order to make people nervous. Worked every time.

So we took hands.

"Keiji? The lights, please," I said next.

The lights went out, and only the faint glow of the candle in the cranberry lamp shone in the room. The effect was rather eerie, and hope rose in my chest. I said, "Please remain quiet while I attempt to get in touch with Rolly on the Other Side."

Silence more or less resulted from my command. Not a single séance I'd ever conducted had achieved perfect silence. I think you have to be dead to accomplish that degree of silence. Or maybe a spy.

Then I went into my act. I shut my eyes and pretended to send out tendrils of magical thought in order to locate Rolly, my spirit control. When the natives began to get restless in the breakfast room, I let out a soft sigh, slumped slightly in my chair and said, in my best Scottish accent an octave lower than my normal speaking voice, "Och, my dear, what can I do for you this fine evening?"

"Rolly," I said to myself in my normal voice, "we're here this evening to attempt to find out how Timothy O'Toole, a young man, died approximately twenty years ago. Have you seen Mr. O'Toole on the Other Side? His bones were discovered in my own backyard and, while we finally determined his name, we know nothing about how he died or why."

"A puzzling circumstance, to be sure," Rolly said to me. "Let me see what I can discover."

Again silence more or less ensued. I had a mental image of good old Rolly shuffling through a file drawer crammed full of death records. After a few seconds of that, I opened my mouth to utter some platitude about either Rolly not being able to find Mr. O'Toole or Mr. O'Toole saying he'd fallen off the wall in our back-yard and knocked himself unconscious. And that's precisely what happened.

"Oh, my dear. The poor lad doesn't know how he got here. He tells me he did a stupid thing by bringing a bottle to the back wall. There he drank it. He doesn't know what happened next, but he thinks he fell off the wall. The next thing he remembers was being on the Other Side."

"Ah," I said, pleased with Rolly. "We thought that's what might have happened to the poor boy. Does he have a message for his mother? She has missed him." Again I opened my mouth, prepared for a heartrending message from Timothy O'Toole to his poor mother.

Rolly, blast him, had other ideas. I swear to goodness, I made him up when I was ten. It really bothered me when he got out of hand, which he did from time to time.

"Ah," said Rolly from my mouth, "I...can't...No, 'tis dark. Another soul has emerged. 'Tis through a fog I see him. Smoke. A weird chanting noise. He holds a rattle the likes of which I've never seen. He's...he's..."

And then, dad-blast it, a low humming chant arose in that simple, everyday—if rather expensive—breakfast room, and we heard the faint clack of beads or sticks or something. The quiet beating of drums arose. An odd singing sound emerged from the atmosphere, which I swear to heaven, smelled of smoke. Accompanying the drums, songs and smoke, I heard a strange rattling sound.

Good heavens! Was *this* what Pudge and his sneaky friends

encountered in our backyard last week? No wonder they'd been scared out of their wits.

After several suspenseful seconds—maybe a minute—of this, a scratchy male voice scarcely made itself heard over the other sounds. The voice seemed to swirl through the smoke. "*Patria*," it said. "*El sacerdote me disparó. Llévame a casa. Casa patria. Patria. Por favor.*" A soft brushy "plop" sound on the table right in front of me made me jump slightly in my seat.

Then, as if nothing else had happened since Keiji turned off the lights, the room cleared of fog, smoke and sounds with a loud "swoosh!" and we sat around the table, dumbstruck. Well, I was dumbstruck. Not sure what anyone else was feeling.

"Let me get the lights," said Harold, who was closest to the light switch.

"Th-thank you," I said, my voice shaking a bit.

As soon as the lights were on, we all unclasped our hands. Every single one of us also looked at what had been plopped in front of me through the smoke. We beheld the tiniest woven basket I'd ever seen in my life. Lifting my right hand, I held it out over the basket, unsure whether or not to touch it. Was it magic? Was it on fire? What the flaming heck *was* it?

"Oh my, Daisy!" said Mrs. Bissel. "I don't think that was Mr. O'Toole, but I think you got some kind of message, and I'm pretty sure it was meant for you and none of the rest of us."

"I'll be damned," said Harold, staring at the tiny woven bowl. "Did you find Indian bones in your backyard as well as that O'Toole character's?"

I cleared my throat, which felt clogged, probably due to the smoke. Perhaps terror. "Um, yes. Yes, we did. We haven't mentioned them to anyone because we weren't sure what to do about them."

"Take 'em back to wherever they came from would be my advice," said Harold in a giving-orders voice. "That's what the fellow told you to do. He wants you to take him back to his home-land. That's what he said in Spanish."

"But...but where *is* his homeland?" I asked pitifully.

247

"How the devil should I know? Not only that, but he said a holy man killed him."

"*What?*" I squeaked, shocked.

"That's what he said," claimed Harold. "He said, '*el sacerdote me disparó*', and that means 'the holy man killed me'. Bet it was a priest with a gun. When the Spaniards were building all those missions in the seventeen hundreds, they murdered thousands of Indians."

"Good Lord," I whispered. Lou Prophet had been right. "But I'm not sure where his homeland is," I said, although I thought I might have at least an inkling.

Harold, as levelheaded as always, said, "Ask that bounty-hunter friend of yours. And pick up that basket. I want to see it, but I'm afraid to touch it until you do. The Indian fellow clearly meant it for you. It's probably a clue."

"Thanks heaps, Harold," I said. But, moving slowly and gingerly, I allowed my fingertips to touch the basket. When my hand didn't catch fire and the rest of me didn't instantly disintegrate, I dared pick it up with my thumb and forefinger. Honestly, it was too small for any other fingers to fit. Placing it on the palm of my left hand, I held it up so Harold and Mrs. Bissel could see it. I swear, I've never seen a smaller piece of workmanship, but it even had an itty-bitty design on it. The design consisted merely of a black wavy line, but it was a design and not an accident; you could tell by looking.

"Oh, my goodness!" said somebody, probably Patsy. "May we see it, too? I had no idea a séance could be so exciting!"

It had been exciting, all right. "Sure. Please don't touch it. I'm not altogether sure about it. I don't think it holds any evil. I think the poor Indian fellow only wants to get home, wherever that is. I hope to heaven we can figure it out."

Everyone got up and crowded around me, staring intently at the minute woven basket in my left palm.

"My goodness," said Mrs. Pinkerton, for once not worried on her own account. "I've never seen anything like that happen in one of your séances, Daisy."

"No," I said, "I haven't, either." And thank god for it!

"It was darned entertaining," said Dennis Bissel.

"Dennis," said Mrs. B austerely. "It might have been enter-taining for you, but I think Daisy needs a soothing cup of cocoa or tea or something."

"Oh, right," said Dennis. "Sorry, Daisy."

"It's all right. But I'd love a cup of cocoa, Mrs. Bissel. And Rose-bud. I want to meet Rosebud."

"Absolutely! Come along Dennis, Patsy and Madeline. We're going to retrieve a hound for Daisy to take to her father." And bless Mrs. Bissel's heart, she rose from the table and shooed everyone except Harold and me out of the breakfast room. They headed through the side door into the big entry hall, so I suspected Rosebud might be upstairs in Mrs. B's sitting room.

Mrs. Cummings opened the door to the kitchen and said, "Cocoa in the living room in ten minutes, Mrs. Rotondo and Mr. Harold. I have some little cherry tarts to eat with them, too."

"Thank you so much, Mrs. Cummings." I suspect she'd been listening at the kitchen door, which was fine by me.

I let out a huge sigh as soon as Harold and I were alone together.

"All right, Daisy Gumm Majesty Rotondo, what the hell is going on with that Indian ghost fellow? Did you really find Indian bones in your backyard along with that other guy's?"

"Yes. Spike found a skull we think belongs to an old Indian. Well, I mean the skull was really old. Like before Pasadena was settled. It was dark brown, and I think it must have been in the ground for decades."

"I guess so," I said, shaking my head and staring at the tiny woven bowl.

"I don't even know what tribe or tribes lived here before the Spanish came," said Harold in a thoughtful voice. "They didn't teach us that in school."

"No. We only learned about the Navajo and Hopi, and I think they're in Arizona. But we went to the San Gabriel Mission, and evidently this neck of the woods was once occupied by a tribe called the Tongva."

"Never heard of them," said Harold.

"I hadn't either. But Mr. Prophet met a fellow at the mission who claimed to be descended from the ancient Tongva. Mr. Prophet thinks he'll be able to tell us how to get this poor Indian back to his family, if not his precise, technical homeland."

"So you had this all figured out ahead of the séance, did you?" asked Harold disapprovingly.

"No! No, I hadn't planned anything at all for this séance. In fact, I'm totally out of practice in conducting séances. I had planned to have Rolly say that Timothy O'Toole got drunk, fell off the back wall in the yard, and they dumped a bunch of construction detritus on him while he was sleeping it off."

"Good god, you weren't going to have him phrase it precisely like that, were you?"

"Of course not. But I don't think the skull Spike found came from the San Gabriel Mission area. I think it might be even older than that. I read somewhere that Indian artifacts were discovered in the Arroyo Seco area when they were building the Devil's Gate Dam."

"Oh, yeah, I vaguely recall that, too. What did they do with the stuff they found?"

"I don't have a single clue," I said, feeling hopeless and miserable. "They sure didn't give it to the Southwest Museum, which doesn't have any information at all about the Tongva." I *really* wanted to get that ghost out of our yard and with his family if at all possible. If that wasn't possible, I at least wanted him to go away.

"I have faith in you," said Harold drily. "Although I have more faith in Mr. Prophet. I have a feeling he'll be able to get his new Tonka—"

"Tongva," I said, interrupting.

"Whatever. Tongva friend, then. I have a feeling he and his Tongva friend will figure out a way to rid your yard of the Indian bones."

"I hope to heck you're right," I said fervently. Something occurred to me.

"Say, Harold, would you mind following me home tonight? If

Mr. Prophet is still awake, I want you to tell him what happened here. He'll believe it if you tell what you saw and heard. Not sure about Sam."

"Sam's too practical," said Harold.

"Maybe," I said. "But he's a good man, and I love him. Even if he won't believe the ghost of a long-dead Indian is haunting our backyard."

I was busy leaning over and picking up my handbag. When Harold didn't speak, I sat up, handbag in hand and glanced at him, wondering why he wasn't talking. "What?" I asked. "Why are you looking at me that way?"

"The ghost who appeared here tonight is haunting your *backyard*? You didn't tell me that, Daisy Gumm Majesty Rotondo!"

I drooped as I sighed. "I know. I don't know whether to say I'm sorry or not. It's such an incredible, unbelievable thing to happen, I guess I didn't think anyone with half a brain would believe me."

"I have an entire brain, and it's functioning quite well, thank you. Unless you've added a lot of special effects to your act, I believe that apparition was the ghost of an Indian."

"I haven't, and it was."

"Very well. I'll follow you home. But let's get some cocoa and cherry tarts first."

"And Rosebud."

Harold gave me the stink-eye. "And Rosebud," he snapped.

So, after I tucked the tiny woven bowl in my handbag, we departed to the living room.

TWENTY-NINE

Rosebud was sitting upright on Mrs. Bissel's lap on the sofa across the room when Harold and I entered the living room through the sun porch. She looked up and barked at Harold and me, too, what's more. Her tail wagged, though, so I don't think she was displeased. Her bark wasn't as deep as Spike's. She was a lady after all.

Instantly I fell in love. "Oh, Mrs. Bissel, she's *gorgeous*!"

"Looks like Spike to me," said Harold in a soft voice beside me.

"She does not," I protested. "She's black and tan, like Spike, but she's beautiful. Spike's handsome."

"If you say so." I didn't look at him, as I had aimed myself for Mrs. B and Rosebud as soon as I saw them, but it wouldn't have surprised me if Harold had rolled his eyes when he uttered his comment.

Because I knew better than to rush up to a strange-to-me dog and immediately begin petting her, I slowed my steps as I approached Rosebud and held out my hand, palm up, in a gesture of friendly greeting. Rosebud backed up and snarled at me. Oh dear. What did this mean?

"Rosebud! Don't you growl at Daisy! She's going to be your new

252

mommy. Well, your new auntie, anyway." Mrs. Bissel glanced up at me. "Sit beside me, dear. It might take her a few minutes to warm up to you. She's gone through a lot this week, what with her operation and all."

"Of course she has," I said, thinking how silly I was not to understand the dog might be touchy after having been hauled off to the doggie hospital and had some of her innards taken out. "Rosebud, you're a beautiful girl," I said in the silly voice most of us use for our pets.

"She's the beautifullest girl in the whole wide world," cooed Mrs. Bissel in approximately the voice I'd used. I think it's universal. People turn into idiots when introduced to adorable animals.

"Yes, she is," I agreed. Really, she was. Shiny seal-black with tan dots above her eyes, around her muzzle, on her chest and on the lower parts of her little legs and feet, she was absolutely stunning! I mean, really. Dachshunds are such great dogs. Harold keeps telling me they're an acquired taste, but I don't agree. I fell in love with Spike upon first meeting him, and I already loved Rosebud.

Oh, all right. I know not everyone likes small dogs. Some people (I'm thinking about Mr. Prophet here) even want cats. Cats are fine and dandy, but for a pet, I'll take a dog, thank you very much. And as far as I was concerned, dachshunds were the cream of the doggie crop. Not the least bit biased, am I?

"Here you go, Daisy," said Patsy, bringing me a plate with a couple of cherry tarts on it and a cup of hot cocoa. She placed the plate and the cup and saucer on the little table at the end of the sofa.

Rosebud leaped from Mrs. Bissel's lap, jumped on mine and made a bee-line to the plate.

Mrs. Bissel cried, "Rosebud, no!"

I, having been trained in how to train dogs by Mrs. Pansy Hanratty, dog-trainer extraordinaire, grabbed Rosebud by the middle and hauled her back. Rosebud turned her head and glared at me, but she didn't growl or snap. I considered both of these actions on her part encouraging. Holding her on my own lap and petting her, I spoke gently. "Rosebud, you can't just snatch other people's cherry tarts, you know. You need to ask politely." To Mrs. Bissel I said, "Dachshunds are such pigs, aren't they?"

"They are indeed," she said, shaking her head sadly. "But you already know about them. I think you'll get along just fine with Rosebud. And your father will, too."

"Hope he doesn't succumb to those big, begging eyes too often," I said, thinking I'd have to give Pa a stern lecture on how not to allow his dachshund to get fat because fattitude—I think I just made up another word—was so hard on their backs.

Rosebud, who knew to whom I spoke, looked not the least bit guilty. Rather, she tilted her head sideways and turned her pleading gaze on me.

"Oh, my goodness, how can you resist that face?" asked Mrs. Pinkerton. When I turned to see her, I saw she'd clasped her hands to her bosom and got the feeling she'd fallen in love with Rosebud too. I hope to heaven Mrs. Bissel wouldn't let Mrs. P have one of her dogs. Mrs. Pinkerton only thought of herself. She'd have everyone on her household staff pampering any dog she ever got, and it would become spoiled rotten. Worse, the entire staff would end up hating the dog, and that wouldn't be fair to the poor dog.

"Resistance gets easier with practice," I told Mrs. Pinkerton. To Rosebud I said, "We'll have to get you a pretty pink collar and leash, won't we?"

I'm pretty sure Rosebud nodded at me.

"I've got a handler's lead for you so you can get her home, Daisy," said Mrs. Bissel.

"Thank you! I didn't think to bring one of Spike's, which was stupid of me."

"Not at all. I'm also giving you a little bit of the broken-biscuit food I get from Dr. Van der Hoof. Mix it with a little meat, and she'll be fine. Try to keep rich meats and gravies away from her, because she'll only get fat or they might make her sick."

"Right. That's what we feed Spike, too."

"I know you do. You're so good to that dog."

"He's been good for me," I said, recalling when I took the puppy Spike home with me and set him on Billy's lap as he sat in his wheelchair. Giving Spike to Billy was probably the most inspired thing I'd ever done in my life. It hadn't prohibited Billy from killing himself in the long run, but Spike made Billy's last days on earth a little brighter. Silly me, I teared up, thinking about Billy and Spike. "And for Billy," I said in a wobbly voice.

"Cut it out, Daisy," said Harold. "We have to get you and that dog home. Remember?"

Oh yeah, that was right. I heaved another sigh. "Yes, I know, Harold. But let me drink my cocoa and have at least one of these beautiful tarts, all right?"

"All right, but only one. I'll save you the temptation and eat the other one for you."

"You're a true pal, Harold."

"You bet I am!"

Everyone—they'd all gathered around to see how Rosebud and I would get along—laughed. And Harold ate one of the cherry tarts. So I picked up the other one, broke a tiny piece of the crust off, and said, "Rosebud? Here's your treat."

The stupid dog almost ripped my hand off taking the bite of crust. Everyone laughed about that, too.

"Okay, we're going to have to work on your table manners, young lady," I told Rosebud as I finished the tart before she could snatch it from me.

Laughing, Mrs. Bissel said, "Oh dear, you might have a handful in Rosebud, Daisy, but I'm sure you'll train her properly eventually."

It was the "eventually" part that troubled me. Not, however, enough to leave Rosebud at Mrs. Bissel's house.

Keiji brought the handler's lead to me, and I slipped it over Rosebud's head and snugged it around her neck. Placing her on the floor, I stood beside her. Darned if she didn't sit like a good girl and stare up at me, as if she knew she was going home with me!

"Progress already, by heaven!" exclaimed Mrs. Bissel.

"I hope so," I said, hardly able to believe it.

The entire group of us walked to the sun porch. There, Mrs. Bissel held Rosebud's leash while Harold helped me with my cloak and gave me my handbag. Then we all cheek-kissed each other and bade each other farewell.

Rosebud jumped right into the Chevrolet, by golly! She wanted to sit on my lap on the way home, but I finally convinced her to sit on the passenger seat. I hoped I hadn't picked out a replacement for Spike that would be too much for my father to handle. Probably not. He was easygoing and looking forward to receiving Rosebud. They'd probably become accustomed to each other soon.

I parked in our drive rather than that of my parents, and Harold parked in front of our house when we got home. Sam heard the car in the drive and had opened the front door for me by the time I got there. Because I wasn't sure what would happen when Rosebud and Spike met, I carried Rosebud into the house.

"Boy," said Sam, taking my shawl and hanging it on the rack. "She looks a lot like Spike, doesn't she? This is Rosebud?"

"This is Rosebud," I confirmed.

Mad barking came from the living room. I quirked an eyebrow at Sam.

"Lou's in there with Spike," he said. "Figured we'd better hold both dogs while they meet."

"Good idea. I'm so glad it isn't too late. I feared the séance would go on forever, but it was really pretty short."

"How'd that happen?" he asked. Then he peered out the front door. "Oh, Kincaid's coming in?"

"Yes. We need to speak with Mr. Prophet."

"Why?"

"I'll tell you after we introduce the dogs. Lordy, I hope they get along all right."

"Me too."

"Me three," said Harold, entering the house and hanging his hat and coat on the coat tree. "Good evening, Sam."

"Evening, Harold," said Sam, as friendly as you please.

When they'd first met, Sam hadn't liked Harold because of Harold's being what he was. He eventually got over it. Harold had always had a fondness for Sam, because he found his attitude funny. Harold is a lot more happy-go-lucky than I'd ever be. Mr. Prophet didn't give a hoot what anyone else did on this earth as long as they left him alone. He'd never had a problem accepting Harold.

"Spike, quiet!" I called from the hallway. Then, taking in a deep breath and still carrying Rosebud, I walked into the living room.

Spike, who'd been lounging on a chair with Mr. Prophet, sat up straight and stared at Rosebud in my arms. Perhaps I was mistaken, but I thought I saw indignation in his doggie expression.

"It's all right, Spike," I told him soothingly. "Rosebud here isn't going to take your place. She's going to live across the street with my mother and father and Aunt Vi."

"Bring her over here," said Mr. Prophet. "See if he decides to kill her or not. I'll set him on the floor. You kin sit here." He patted the chair next to his. I noticed the men had set up a card table and had been playing cards. Didn't look like gin rummy, but I didn't know many card games.

I did as he suggested and sat, still holding Rosebud, on the chair next to his. Spike, interested, lifted a paw to my knee. Tilting his head, he scrutinized Rosebud, who scrutinized him back.

Harold, Sam and Mr. Prophet, who had risen from his seat, gathered around to watch introductions. "Spike," I said, knowing I was being impolite as I did so, "please allow me to introduce you to Rosebud. Rosebud? This is Spike. This is his house, so you need to be nice to him." I know you're supposed to introduce the girls to the boys and not the other way around, but that doesn't count with dogs. Bravely daring, I stood, lifted Rosebud and set her gently on the floor, making sure there were a couple feet of space between the two dogs.

For a few seconds, they squared off at each other, reminding me of a couple of kids trying to decide if they were going to play ball or knock each other senseless. Then Rosebud, taking the lead, sort of bowed to Spike. Spike lifted his head for a second or two, and then he more or less bowed at Rosebud.

After that, it was butt-sniffing time. As soon as I knew they weren't going to try to murder each other, I sat on the piano bench and let out a deep and grateful sigh. "I think they'll be all right together," I said tentatively.

"Looks like it so far," said Sam, also tentative.

"If anybody starts a fight, it'll be that gal," said Mr. Prophet.

Harold only laughed.

"All right, so tell me why tonight's séance was cut short," said Sam, sounding as if he wasn't going to like my answer.

"It wasn't precisely cut short," I said. "It just ended shortly after it began."

"Stop equivocating, Daisy," said Harold sternly. "The séance ended early because that blasted Tonka—"

"Tongva," I said, interrupting again. "It's Tongva, Harold."

"Whatever the hell it is, the spirit of whatever Indian's bones got into your yard showed up, complete with smoke, rattling, singing and dancing. Even dropped a pot on the table in front of Daisy."

"What?" said Sam, staring at Harold in a disbelieving sort of way.

"Aw, hell," said Mr. Prophet. "Let's see the pot. Is it clay, stone or straw?"

I dug the pot out of my handbag. It was so small, it had slipped to the bottom of the bag, but by being extremely careful, I managed to get it out without squishing it. As I felt it some more, I realized it might be difficult to squish, it was so firmly woven together. It also felt as though it had been coated in…something. I have no idea what.

"Woven," said Mr. Prophet, squinting at the basket residing in my palm. "Don't know many Injuns who made woven pots. Gotta be from around here somewhere. Probably Emilio DeLoera can tell us."

"Who's Emilio whatever you said?" asked Harold.

"Tongva feller I met at the mission in San Gabriel. He said he might be able to help get the poor ghost back with his family. Or at least back to where he came from. And if that's impossible, he might be able to get him to go away."

"I hope we can reunite him with his family," I said. "That's what he asked us to do during the séance."

Holding up a big, square hand, Sam said, "Hold on a second.

You mean he actually *talked* to you during the séance? You didn't have Rolly make him talk?"

I slumped on the piano bench. "Neither Rolly nor I had a single thing to do with what happened tonight," I told Sam. "I think I'm going to give up spiritualist-mediuming. It's beginning to scare me. It's almost as if the spirits themselves have decided I'm no longer a phony and are using me."

"Didn't know you was a medicine woman, eh?" asked Mr. Prophet, positively chortling with glee.

"Is that what I am? Maybe I should consult with Mrs. Jackson." Mrs. Jackson, mother of Mrs. Pinkerton's gatekeeper, was a real, honest-to-god Voodoo Mambo from New Orleans. She'd given both Sam and Me Voodoo jujus. I wore mine everywhere. I think Sam wore his all the time, too.

"Wouldn't hurt," said Mr. Prophet, who had much more faith in the otherworldly aspects of spiritualism than I'd ever possessed. Then again, his life had been infinitely more exciting and wide-ranging than mine. "So you're going to take me to the mission tomorrow, and we'll fetch that Tongva feller?"

"We are?" asked Sam, looking from Mr. Prophet to me and back again.

"I think we'd better, Sam."

"Definitely. If you want that ghost out of your life, it's probably a good idea," said Harold.

"But what about the dog?" said Sam. "Rosebud, I mean."

"We can take Rosebud over to Pa in the morning, and then we can drive to the mission if you don't mind too much, Sam," I said.

"What the hell," said Sam. "Worth a shot, I expect."

"That's how the poor Indian fellow died," said Harold. "A priest shot him."

"He didn't actually say a priest shot him," I protested weakly.

"What he said was, and I quote almost exactly, *"El sacerdote me disparó. Llévame a patria."*"

"Hellkatoot," said Mr. Prophet. "That means the priest killed him. Probably with a gun. Wouldn't surprise me none. So he was murdered."

"Murdered?" I asked.

"What would you call it?" he said grimly.

"Yes. You're right. If the priest killed him, it must have been murder. The poor fellow didn't sound as if he'd been putting up a fight or anything."

"Probably wanted to do one of his people's dances or a blessing ceremony or something. Because the Catholics wouldn't want none of that shi-stuff going on in their holy place, one of the priests probably shot him to death. Y'know, that skull might have belonged to one of the Injuns' holy men. The priests would have wanted to get rid of their holy men and medicine women more than the everyday folks. Now the poor guy wants to get back to his homeland."

"Wherever that was," I said.

"Probably close by."

Then something Mr. Prophet had said jolted me into sitting upright on the piano bench. "Good lord," I said. "Do you mean they might have shot *me* if I'd been there at the time?"

"Wouldn't surprise me," said Mr. Prophet with a crooked grin. "I've wanted to shoot you a time or two myself."

"Don't shoot my wife, Lou," said Sam, laughing, the rat. "Now that she's learning to cook, I need her."

"Oh, all right," said the old scoundrel.

Laughing, Harold said, "Call me when you perform this exorcism. After the séance tonight, I can't wait to see how you get rid of that poor, lonely ghost."

"If Mr. Prophet's friend is willing, I'm hoping it will be tomorrow night," I said.

"Yeah," said Mr. Prophet. "The sooner, the better."

"I guess so," said Sam upon what sounded like a deep and heartfelt sigh.

"I'll bring dinner," offered Harold. "The Chop Suey Palace packs up food for people to take home and eat these days."

"Chinese? Sounds great," said Mr. Prophet.

"Thanks, Harold," said Sam.

"Yes. Thanks, Harold," I said in my turn.

"Well, good," said Harold. "I'll get going now. This should be fun."

"I hope it's no more than merely fun," I said, feeling a little darkish around the edges.

So Harold tooled off in his beautiful red Hispano Suiza, Mr. Prophet left for his cottage and Yuyu, and Sam and I again sat in the living room, this time on the sofa together. For the record, the two dogs were now snoozing on the hearthrug, back-to-back, as if they were happy as little canine chums who'd known each other forever. I love dogs.

Sam and I had to disturb them in order to carry them upstairs with us, but they didn't seem to mind.

THIRTY

O n Saturday morning, after a breakfast of bacon and toast
with cheese melted on top of it—it's really good that way—
Sam and I walked Spike and Rosebud across the street to meet my
father. Spike and Rosebud still seemed to get along well. I appreciated their companionable attitudes as I had plenty of other things to
worry about. Didn't need peevish dogs added to the burden.

"Well, will you look at them!" Pa exclaimed when he saw Spike
and Rosebud saunter into the house together. "They look like twins!"

"Aren't they darling together?" I said, beaming upon the pair of
black-and-tan hounds as if they were my own children.

"Yes, they are," agreed Pa. He got down on a knee and held out
a hand to the dogs, who were sticking together until Spike wagged
and jumped on his knee, nearly knocking him over backwards.

"Whoa, Spike!" said Sam, reaching down to steady man and
dog. "Don't get too rambunctious. Your grandpa wants to meet your
pal Rosebud now."

"Wonder if she's as strong as Spike," said Pa, steady on one knee
again and still holding out his hand. This time it was Rosebud who
leaped on his knee. What's more, she began licking his chin as if she

knew this was her father, and why had it taken everyone so long to reunite them?

"Aw, jeez," said Sam, again leaning over to straighten Pa out.

My father only laughed. "Hey, Vi!" he called. "Come in here and meet Rosebud." My mother had already left for her job at the Hotel Marengo. She only had to work half-days on Saturdays, but she still had to work.

Wiping her hands on her apron, Vi appeared at the door to the kitchen. Smiling broadly, she walked through the dining room and into the living room. "Well, my goodness, you look just like Spike! Only you're a little more feminine."

"Feminine?" I asked, laughing. "She nearly knocked Pa over onto his back."

"Well, you'd better teacher her better manners, Daisy," said Vi as she bent to pet Rosebud.

Spike, who knew and adored Vi because she was the keeper of the foodstuffs, shoved Rosebud out of the way and made Vi pet him. Rosebud gave a soft growl, and I went on instant alert. But it was a false alarm. After she realized Vi had two hands, she forgave Spike for being rude.

We didn't remain at my parents' house for very long. Sam and I wanted to fetch Mr. Prophet and take him to the San Gabriel Mission. I hoped really hard that Mr. DeLoera would be sitting in the courtyard again.

***

He was! Sam, Mr. Prophet and I gave the mission office a miss that lovely late Saturday morning and walked directly to the plaza area, which was again full of people. Some sat, some walked, some stood in groups chatting, many folks looked as if they'd come just to visit the mission on a day trip.

"Right where I left him," muttered Mr. Prophet, leaving Sam and me at the fountain in the center of the plaza and limping to where Mr. DeLoera sat on a bench, alone, staring into space. Or maybe he was recalling days gone by. If the latter case prevailed, I hoped his memories were good ones.

When Mr. Prophet approached, Mr. DeLoera lifted his head, covered this day in a large straw sombrero, and gave Mr. P a huge smile. Compared to Mr. Prophet, who was and looked old, Mr. DeLoera looked as though he'd lived approximately 125 years or thereabouts. Weathered. The man was weathered. So was Mr. Prophet, but Mr. DeLoera's whiskery face looked like a spider's web of wrinkles.

"Interesting looking fellow," Sam murmured to me as the two men met and shook hands. Mr. DeLoera gestured for Mr. Prophet to sit next to him on his bench, and Mr. P took him up on his offer.

"I hope he's willing to come to Pasadena with us," I said, taking a seat on another bench.

Sitting next to me, Sam said, "I guess I hope so, too. Wish I'd been at your séance. I don't think either you or Kincaid are fibbing, but if what you both say what happened actually happened, I'd like to know how it did."

"Unless Mrs. Bissel possesses supernatural powers of her own— and she's never mentioned them to me—what happened happened."

"Must have," Sam said, shaking his head as if he still considered such carryings-on beyond his ken. As they were also beyond mine, I didn't scold him.

The two bent old men across the plaza from us chatted for several minutes, and then they both rose to their feet. Mr. DeLoera, I saw, used a craggy, polished piece of wood as a cane. It was almost as tall as he, which wasn't very. Mr. Prophet, who'd stood, by his own reckoning, six feet and four inches in his young manhood, still topped Mr. DeLoera by seven or eight inches.

I had a moment of panic when Mr. D hobbled off in one direction and Mr. P hobbled to Sam and me.

"What's wrong?" I asked when he was close enough for me to whisper my question.

"Nothin'," he said. "Emilio's gone to get his sack of tricks. Just like yours, Miss Daisy."

"Not precisely like mine," I said, although it was true I carried my Ouija board and tarot cards in special pouches I'd sewn for them.

"Close enough," said Mr. P.

"And he's willing to come to Pasadena with us?" Sam said, sounding surprised.

"When I told him about what happened last night, he paid attention. When I told him Chinese food was involved, he couldn't accept my invite fast enough. Of course, we'll have to get him back here tomorrow morning."

"Oh, dear," I said. "I have to sing in the choir tomorrow."

"Skip it," said Mr. P, who didn't have many good things to say about churches of any sort.

"Lucy and I are supposed to sing a duet during the anthem," I told him, fretting. Oh dear. I hoped to heaven—which was almost appropriate—this wouldn't be a deal-breaker. "I guess I could call Mr. Hostetter and tell him I'm sick, but I don't like lying."

"Hellkatoot, let me call him. I got no scruples about lyin'," said Mr. Lou Prophet, not telling me anything I didn't already know.

"Don't worry about it, either of you," said Sam. "You go to church with your folks, Daisy, and I'll drive Lou and Mr. DeLoera back to the mission."

"You don't mind?" I asked my darling husband.

He peered down at me with the same expression Mr. Prophet had on his face, only Sam's wasn't marred by wrinkles. My Sam didn't give a rap about churches of any type any more than Mr. Prophet did. He'd gone to the Unitarian-Universalist Church with his late wife, but he'd been born and reared in the Roman Catholic Church. I knew by this time that he'd rather be out detecting something than wasting every Sunday morning at church. He'd consider it time wasted. I...enjoyed singing in the choir.

Oh dear. Maybe I should visit Johnny and Flossie again soon. Seemed I might need a boost in the religious department.

But none of that mattered now. "Thanks, Sam."

"You're welcome," said Sam, grinning. "Ah, here he comes. That sack he's carrying might be heavy."

"I'll help him. He don't know you yet, so you'd best wait here." So saying, Mr. Prophet limped over to greet Mr. DeLoera. The two men met on the pathway, and it looked to me as if Mr. P asked Mr. D if he needed help carrying his load. Mr. D. shook his head and then shook his sack, which I think was made of burlap. The sack didn't appear awfully heavy.

Sam and I rose to meet Mr. P and the newcomer, who removed his sombrero with the hand holding his sack and nodded his head at me and then at Sam. Polite fellow.

"Thank you for helping us," I said, hoping it was the correct thing to say.

"Lou, he says you got a *fantasmo cautivo* you gotta get rid of. Lou, he say the poor man is Tongva. He say the *fantasmo* gave you a pot? You got it with you?"

"Yes. Here, I'll show it to you." I dug in my handbag and withdrew the pot, which I'd carefully wrapped in one of my pretty embroidered handkerchiefs. When I unfolded the hankie around the pot, Mr. DeLoera drew in an audible breath. Quickly I lifted my head to look at him, only to find him nodding sadly.

"*Sí*," he said. "Your *cautivo* is one of the old ones. He needs to go home again."

"Do we know where his home is? Was, I mean?" I asked.

"I find out," said Mr. D in a firm tone.

"Thank you," said Sam.

"Oh, yeah, I 'spect I ought to introduce you," said Mr. Prophet. "Emilio, this here is Sam Rotondo, a pal of mine. This is his wife, Daisy, who's also a pal of mine." He didn't choke on the last sentence, so I guess he really had decided not to harass me any longer. I hoped it would last.

"Pleased to meet you," I said, holding out my hand to him, only to realize he couldn't shake hands with anyone, what with his staff in one hand and his sack in the other. Idiot Daisy!

But Mr. D solved the problem handily—so to speak—by moving his sack to his staff hand and shaking my hand with his old, dry wrinkly one. His hand felt rather like crushed cardboard, if that makes any sense.

Then Sam and he shook hands.

"Okay," said Mr. Prophet after introductions were over, "let's get this show on the road."

So we did. Sam and I sat in the front seat, not speaking much on the way home. I was pretty nervous. Sam seemed calm and collected, but then, he almost always seemed calm and collected. As for the two elderly gents, they sat in the back seat of Sam's big Hudson, speaking to each other softly in Spanish. I knew Lou Prophet had spent a good many of his early years in or near Mexico, but I hadn't realized until then how well he could speak Spanish. Learn something every day, by golly.

We reached home about an hour after we'd picked up Mr. DeLoera, and when he slowly and creakily got out of the car, he glanced around with interest. With a gesture to our pepper-tree-lined street, Marengo Avenue, he smiled and said, "You got *árboles de pimientos. Muy bonito.*"

"Yeah," said Mr. Prophet. "The whole street's lined with them trees on both sides. Nice and shady. *Naranjas* in the backyard. Along with the *fantasmo.*"

"Ah," said Mr. DeLoera. "*Bien, bien.*"

"But let me take you out to my place. You probably need to rest up after that drive," said Mr. Prophet.

"Thank you, my friend. I will look at where the *fantasmo cautivo* lives, too, *por favor.* This might take some deep thinking."

"Would you like to come inside for a glass of orange juice first? Or a cup of coffee? Or tea?" I asked, thinking Mr. Prophet was being rather precipitate.

"*Gracias, señora* Rotondo. A glass of juice sounds good."

"Great. I squeezed a lot of oranges yesterday, so we have plenty of juice in the Frigidaire."

Mr. DeLoera looked at Mr. P and winked. "Modern *aparatos* in there, eh?"

"Lots of 'em," said Mr. Prophet.

I wondered what an *aparato* was when it was at home, but I didn't ask.

"He means you got modern kitchen stuff, Miss Daisy," said Mr. P, reading my mind, blast him.

"Oh. Yes, I'm happy to say we do," I said, smiling at both men.

By that time, Sam had opened the front door, so we all traipsed inside. "Take a seat anywhere you want to," said he.

"Think we'll go to the kitchen," said Mr. P. "It's closer to the backyard, and after we have our juice"—for some reason, he grimaced—"we'll go outside and look around."

"What about the dogs?" I asked of Sam. "Should I bring Spike home or leave him across the street?"

"Why don't you go over there and ask your father. It might be best if Spike stayed there during the whatever the heck is going to take place tonight. Or we could just leave him inside the house."

"Good idea. Be right back," I got on my tiptoes and gave him a smack on the cheek, and then turned and left for my parents' house. Sam could serve juice to the two old men.

THIRTY-ONE

I'd neglected to remember my mother would surely be home by that time of day, and she was. When I walked into the house, instead of being barked at and greeted by only one shiny black-and-tan streak of houndhood, I was greeted by *two* of them. Only one of them, Spike, responded to my command of "Sit."

He sat like a champ. Rosebud, on the other hand, leaped and barked and wagged as if there was no tomorrow. Oh, dear. I foresaw another trip to the Pasanita Dog Obedience Club in my future. Aw, what the heck. The first time, with Spike, had been fun. Maybe Rosebud would respond well, too.

"Daisy, that dog is absolutely *precious*," my mother exclaimed as she jumped up from her chair in the living room. "What a dolly. I've begun calling her Rosie. I hope you don't mind."

"Why would I mind?" I asked, puzzled.

"Well, because you said her name is Rosebud. I didn't know if you'd want us to change it."

"She's Pa's dog, Ma. He can call her anything he wants to call her. Except late for dinner." I know, I know. It was an old joke, but it got a couple of chuckles from my parents.

"Daisy!" said Vi, coming into the living room from the dining

269

room. "Would you, Sam and Mr. Prophet like to have supper with us tonight? Roast pork. Your favorite," she said with a tease to her voice.

She was right. I loved Vi's roast pork. Unfortunately, Sam and I had other plans for the evening.

"Oh, Vi, I hate to miss one of your roast pork meals, but Harold is bringing over Chinese tonight from the Crown Chop Suey Palace. I'm sorry. You should probably join us."

"Nonsense," said Vi. "You need to have some time with your friends from time to time. But I'll save some pork for sandwiches for you and Sam and Lou tomorrow."

"Thank you," I said. "Um, how are the dogs getting along? Do you think I should take Spike home with me, or should he stay here for another night or so?"

After rubbing his chin in a judicious manner for a second or two, Pa said, "Why don't you take him home with you? Rosie's got to realize one of these days that she lives here and Spike lives across the street, so we might as well start now. She sure doesn't have Spike's manners, though."

"No. Want to take her to the Pasanita Dog Obedience Club's next session? I don't know when it will be, but I can always telephone Mrs. Hanratty and find out."

"Great idea," said Pa with real enthusiasm. "I enjoyed watching you work with Spike. Maybe I can work with Rosie, and you can help me."

"Sounds perfect," I said.

So I clipped the leash to Spike's collar and left my parents' house. Rosie—I guess that was her new name—barked a couple of times, but I was pretty sure that by the time the door closed behind Spike and me, she'd be in Pa's arms, and they'd be napping on the living room sofa in a very few minutes.

"Oh boy, Spike. I'm not sure I'm ready for tonight's exorcism."

Spike as much as told me he was ready for anything, any time. Bless the dog. He became instant best friends with Mr. DeLoera when the two were introduced. Bless Mr. D, too.

And bless Harold Kincaid, as long we're blessing people. It had just turned six o'clock when our doorbell rang. When I opened it, there Harold stood, holding a big cardboard box.

"Let me in. This is heavy."

"Here," said Sam at my back, "let me help you."

"No need for that. No room either," said Harold as he kind of staggered into the hallway and made his way to the kitchen. Mr. Prophet and Mr. DeLoera had been swapping lies in the living room, and they both got up to see what was going on, following the exotic aroma of Chinese food.

"What darling containers," I said as Harold lifted the top off the cardboard box to reveal several smaller white containers, each equipped with a wire handle, so we could pick up each container and set it on the kitchen table.

"Why not just fill our plates here and take 'em into the dining room to eat?" Suggested Sam.

I considered this a brilliant suggestion, mainly because it would save time and not dirty any serving dishes. I could clean up the plate, forks and spoons in a jiffy and stuff the leftover containers in the Frigidaire.

"Brilliant idea," said Harold, echoing my thoughts. Guess he could read my mind as well as Sam.

Boy, that was a good dinner! It probably wasn't any better than Vi's pork roast, but it was right up there in the top echelons of cookery. Everyone else enjoyed their meal too. Somehow or other, Spike managed to find himself the recipient of a few stray pieces of chicken or pork, so he was happy too.

Because we all felt some urgency about the backyard ghost, I just filled the sink with soapy water and left the dishes and flatware to soak while Sam and Harold filled the Frigidaire with leftovers in their clever containers, combining items as they deemed appropriate.

"I'm going to take Emilio out to the yard," said Mr. Prophet as we were doing our chores. He wants to sit out there and get a feel for the place at night. He said it might take some time to raise the spirit and get it to tell him where it came from and how to get it back there."

"Does Mr. DeLoera need a coat or a blanket or anything? Or do you?" I asked.

"Naw. Emilio has his *serape* and I got my own coat."

"All right. We'll join you out there in a bit," I said.

"Make it a half-hour or so," said Mr. P. "Emilio has to prepare himself."

"Sounds just like you before a séance, Daisy," said Harold.

Lifting one of his grizzled eyebrows, Mr. P said, "Exactly. The exorcist has to pray and get ready for the ordeal ahead of him."

"I'm not an exorcist," I said in a small voice.

"No, but it amounts to about the same thing," said Mr. P. "Don't fret, Miss Daisy. Emilio knows what he's doin'."

"Good," I said.

So Harold, Sam and I finished up things in the kitchen. Because we'd been told not to go outdoors for thirty minutes, I went ahead and washed up the dinner dishes. What the heck.

"Have you decided what to do with the lamp?" asked Harold as he dried a dish and handed to Sam to put away.

"We're going to leave it on the piano unless Daphne and Daniel's daughters visit. Then I'll hide it away in a closet and lock the door to that room so they can't possibly, by any means whatsoever, knock it over."

"Crumb, it's not all that delicate, is it?" asked Harold, eyebrows lifting over his slightly protuberant eyes.

"Looks like it to me," said Sam.

"I thought it was bronze. Those kids couldn't break a bronze lamp, could they?"

"They could sure break the lampshade," I said. "That's glass."

"Oh, yeah, that's right," said Harold, drying a teacup. "Might be difficult to replace it, too."

"Maybe Tiffany could replace it," said Sam, referring to a rival jewelry company in New York City. I call them rivals because Sam's parents had jewelry stores in NYC, too. "Hell, maybe my uncle could replace it."

"Does your uncle work with glass?" I asked, amazed. I swear, my Sam had depths I had yet to plumb.

"Sometimes, but let's just not break the lampshade and we won't have to find out."

"Good idea," said Harold.

"Indeed," I agreed.

We all heard the back door open, and Mr. Prophet clumped into the kitchen. "Might as well start this party. Better keep Spike inside. Emilio said it's gonna take a while, so take chairs out with you. Keep 'em a few yards away from Emilio, though. He's got a tough job ahead of him."

"Does he think he can do it?" asked Sam.

"Doesn't know yet."

"Great," I said under my breath.

Harold whacked me on the shoulder. "One *artiste* shouldn't denigrate the work of another *artiste*, Daisy."

"Is that what she is?" said Sam. "An *artiste*? Well, how about that."

"Ya got yourself an *artiste*, by crikey," said Mr. Prophet.

I waited, but he didn't add anything about this particular *artiste* not being able to cook. I appreciated him for it, because my nerves had started crawling like ants up my spine. I don't claim to have any spiritualistic abilities, but after last night I wasn't altogether sure about anything, and I wanted that poor ghost *gone*.

When we reached the back porch, Sam and Harold each lifted two chairs and carried them down the porch steps. Spike wanted to join us, but I told him he had to remain in the house, so he reluctantly obeyed. I didn't know where Yuyu was, but I hoped he was nowhere near the burial site. Or the non-burial site. Whatever it was.

Sam and Harold placed the four chairs in a semicircle several yards away from where Mr. DeLoera was. He seemed to be squatting on the bare earth in the area where Timothy O'Toole's bones had been scattered. His open burlap sack sat beside him, and he'd built a small fire. We onlookers took our seats and watched with interest.

Every now and then the old man picked something out from his burlap sack and threw it on the fire. He spoke softly, too, but I didn't understand a thing he said. Listening hard, the only thing I could tell about his words was that they were neither English nor Spanish. Tongva was my best guess.

I sent a sideways glance at Mr. Prophet, but he stared straight at Mr. DeLoera and didn't bother looking at me. Guess I could ask him about the language later, if he even knew. As I'd been unable to learn a blessed thing about the Tongva culture, I didn't know if its language was similar to any of the Apache, Comanche or whatever other tribes' languages he'd come across in his youth.

After what seemed like several hours of watching Mr. DeLoera throw things into the fire—every time he did that, we'd catch a whiff of what smelled like pine sap—he started chanting softly. Then he reached into his sack and withdrew a rattle. I couldn't tell what kind of rattle it was. I'd seen some Navajo or Hopi rattles made out of dried gourds, but couldn't see well enough to tell what his was made of. It clacked, though. And clicked.

And then, after another four or five decades had passed, darned if the fire didn't flare up, and a huge plume of smoke appeared, looming over Mr. DeLoera. I clutched Sam's coat sleeve, and he put a big hand over mine. A strange humming filled the air, along with something that sounded like a violin string being scraped with a bow that needed resin. Eerie. It sounded eerie. The fire settled down, but the smoke plume covered Mr. DeLoera. I jerked in my chair, but Sam held me down.

"Good lord, what's happening?" I whispered as softly as I could.

"Emilio's doin' his ghost-removal thing," whispered Mr. P back. "Now shut up."

Very well then. I shut up.

Strange sounds emerged from the pile of smoke. The same kind of humming chants as we'd heard at last night's séance filled the air. Then a mournful singing sound. Then, by gad, a long and pitiful "Woo" wailed from the smoke. So those rotten kids *had* been wooed at. I'd never tell Pudge. I didn't want anyone other than the people in our backyard right then to know anything at all about this evening's goings-on.

The pile of smoke remained on Mr. DeLoera for I don't know how long, but it seemed like centuries. The chanting, singing and wooing continued, as did the rattling sounds. Then, as if the yard had been invaded by a pack of wild coyotes, yipping sounds came from the smoke. I heard Spike barking in the house and wished I could go inside and comfort him, but I didn't dare move.

Suddenly a cat hissed, and Yuyu raced from underneath the smoke, heading straight for Mr. Prophet. With a pitiful yowl and his fur puffed out like a feather duster, Yuyu leaped onto Mr. Prophet's chest and clung. He let out a grunt but he was wearing his coat, so I don't think the cat's claws got through the coat to his skin. When I squinted through the dark at him, he had a pretty dramatic grimace on his face, so maybe I was wrong about the claws. I again fixed my attention on the pile of smoke. A drumming sound started, at first faint, then getting louder and louder until I thought my eardrums might burst. I clapped my hands over my ears and hoped the neighbors wouldn't call the cops.

All of a sudden, the night air was pierced by a shrill shriek, the cloud of smoke lifted into a gigantic plume and vanished, and we saw Mr. DeLoera sprawled, face-first, spread-eagle on the ground, clutching dirt in both fists.

"Oh, my lord," I whispered. "What happened?"

"Don't move," ordered Mr. Prophet, attempting to pry Yuyu's claws from his coat. "Emilio told me something like this might happen, and he said don't approach him. He'll come out of it when he's ready."

"Do you think he got rid of the ghost?"

"Don't know. Be quiet."

I decided to be quiet. Frankly, I was terrified. I'd never seen or heard anything like the undertaking Mr. DeLoera achieved for us that night. As I reached for Sam's hand, I heard Harold's nearly silent chant of "Good god. Good god. Good god," repeated I don't know how many times. He was barely perceptible in the dark of the night, but I saw him clutching the seat of his chair as if trying to prevent it from flying into the air and carrying him off.

Sam clamped his hand over mine hard. The evening's act had unnerved him too. If it hadn't, I'd have wondered about him.

So we sat. And we sat. And sat.

I don't think I was the only one of the four of us watchers who let out a huge breath of relief when we saw Mr. DeLoera begin to stir. The fire he'd built was mainly ashes by this time, but it still emitted a faint glow. By its light, we saw Mr. D push himself up from the ground, shake the dirt from his hands, draw his serape tightly around him, and begin to repack his burlap sack. Then he sat with his back to us, seated with his legs folded across each other. I don't know what he was doing, but after experiencing a few odd happenings at séances myself, I suspect he was attempting to collect his wits.

After I don't know how long, Mr. DeLoera shoved himself to his knees and then creaked to a standing position, leaning heavily on his stick. He bent and picked up his burlap sack, stood breathing in and out heavily for a minute or more—it seemed like hours—and then slowly limped toward us. We all rose, but didn't walk up to meet him.

Mr. Prophet was the first to stand and speak, which seemed proper somehow. "Emilio? How did it go?"

With a nod, Mr. DeLoera said, "*salió bien*," which sounded like good news to me.

Then he reached into his burlap sack, steadying himself in Mr. Prophet's chair and withdrew a skull. A dark-colored skull. A skull that looked as if it would fit perfectly with the jawbone Spike had brought us.

"Oh, my," I whispered.

Mr. DeLoera nodded. "He say you have rest of head?"

"Yes," Mr. Prophet said. By this time, he held Yuyu in his arms. The cat still looked scared. "It's on the back porch."

That was true. While the Lamb Funeral Home had come and taken away Mr. O'Toole's bones, they'd left the table set up, and we'd deposited the jawbone there, under a kitchen towel.

"We need it. We need to take this"—he held up the top of the skull—"and the other and take them to his home."

"Where is his home?" I asked. "Do you know what his name was?"

"He was Hahamog-na. His home was where the devil waters run."

"The devil waters?" I asked, not enlightened.

"He said a *soldado hispano* shot him when he was dancing. The dance was to force the *sacerdotes y soldados* to go away. The priest told the *soldado* to shoot Hahamog-na because he was defiant."

"The fellow whose skull we have was defiant?"

"*Sí.* Because the priests and soldiers wouldn't let him worship his gods and lead his people in the old ways. He was their......what you call it? Their chief."

"Their chief?" I muttered. And Spike had brought us his jawbone. Crumb.

"Makes sense," said Sam. "Europeans did that to everyone they encountered everywhere they went."

"Yeah," said Mr. Prophet. "But now we have to figger out where the devil waters are."

My brain slowly began to function. It had got stuck back there in the smoke and drumming and shrieking. "Wait. Maybe I know. Maybe."

"You do?" The three men gawped at me.

"Maybe. You know the big dam near the Colorado Street Bridge, right?"

"Yeah. It's about a quarter-mile from here."

"Do you remember when they were building the Devil's Gate Dam?"

"You got a *presa de la puerta del Diablo* around here?" Mr. DeLoera's stare almost pierced my own personal skull, it was so sharp.

I nodded. "Just up the road and west a little bit. At the Arroyo Seco."

"A dry riverbed?" asked Mr. Prophet, squinting at me.

"I know where it is," said Sam. "Do we need to do this now? What time is it?"

"Don't know," said Mr. DeLoera. "But it's best to do it as soon as we can. Hahamog-na has been lost from his family for many, many years."

"A couple of hundred, probably," I said, thinking about the building of the Devil's Gate Dam in 1920. I hadn't paid a whole lot of attention to civic improvements—if that's what they were—back then, as I was busy nursing a sick husband and earning a living for my family. "I think that's around the time I read in the papers about Indian artifacts being discovered as they were clearing way for the dam."

"Cripes. What'd they do with 'em?" asked Mr. Prophet.

"I have no idea," I told him. It was the truth. From what we'd discovered—or not discovered—at the Southwest Museum, they didn't seem to have ended up there. "Lordy, there may be no way we can reunite him with the remains of any family he had." I could hear the despair in my voice. "Whatever remains there were might have been washed away or buried under tons of concrete or taken home for various people to gawk at."

Mr. DeLoera made a hissing noise through his few teeth.

"Let's go inside," said Sam. "I'll get the jawbone. Maybe we can figure out what to do."

As no one seemed able to think of a better idea, I went to the table, scooped up the jawbone, keeping the kitchen towel around it, and we all traipsed inside, where a delirious Spike greeted us. I bent and scooped him up, too. "Oh, he's trembling. I think he was scared by all the noise."

"Good *perro*," said Mr. DeLoera of Spike. As he held his sack and his stick, he didn't attempt to pet the dog.

Sam, Harold and Mr. Prophet made up for Mr. D's deficit, and I held Spike as we went through to the kitchen, where we sat at the kitchen table.

After gently putting Spike down, I unfolded the kitchen towel to reveal the jawbone. Mr. DeLoera reached into his burlap sack and withdrew the top part of the skull. Except for holes where the eyes and nose had been, it was more or less intact. Mr. DeLoera seemed not to be uncomfortable picking up the jawbone and matching it to the rest of the skull. The two pieces fitted together as well as any two things that old could be expected to fit, I reckon.

"Yeesh," said Harold. "I've never seen that one before. I only saw the other bones."

We all stood back from the kitchen table and stared at the remains of a Tongva Indian chief named......well, whatever Mr. DeLoera had said his name was. Would we ever be able to get him back to where he'd been happy? I kind of doubted it, but I didn't want to say so.

Mr. Prophet wasn't as reticent as I. "Well, hell, how the devil can we get him back to his homeland if his homeland is gone, along with the remains of whatever family he used to have?"

Silence filled the kitchen. When I looked at the clock on the wall, its hands told me the time was half-past eleven. When I looked down at Spike, he told me he didn't appreciate being left alone while his humans went outside and did scary things. Didn't blame him one little bit.

THIRTY-TWO

"Can you drive me to this *arroyo seco*?" Mr. DeLoera asked after several tense seconds had passed.

"Any time you want us to," said Sam.

"I think maybe you better do it now. We take this." He wrapped the upper and lower skull back in the kitchen towel and tucked both in his burlap sack. His hands were filthy, but I didn't think it would be prudent to ask him if he wanted to wash them. "You got any *café*? No. Better. *Pulque*?"

"They got no *pulque* here, Emilio," said Mr. Prophet sadly. "But when we get home, I got me a bottle o' *tequila* we can drink."

I deemed it prudent not to ask what either of those two drinks were. I figured they were full of distilled spirits. Or maybe not. If Mr. Prophet and Mr. DeLoera knew what they were, maybe there were products made in homes all over Mexico and this part of California. What I didn't know about our native people's history could fill volumes if anybody cared to write them. So far, it didn't seem to me that anyone had.

"*Bueno*," said Mr. DeLoera. "Then you better take me and my *saco* to this place of the *Diablo* you talk about."

"Sure."

Holding up his filthy hands, Mr. DeLoera said, "May I wash?"

"You bet!" I said, glad he was interested in cleanliness. I turned on the taps at the kitchen sink, showed him the lye soap hanging out on a folded washcloth, and said, "Here you go."

And there he went. Taking off his serape and folding it over a kitchen chair, he shoved up his white sleeves and scrubbed his hands and arms until they turned red. As he washed, I got out another couple of kitchen towels so he could dry off if he ever finished washing. I noticed he seemed to be saying something very softly as he scrubbed. When I peered at his face, his eyes were shut. Maybe he was going through some ritual or other about which, as ever, I knew nothing.

Harold whispered in my ear, "I think I'm going to leave you at this point. What happened outside was fascinating and I expect a full report tomorrow, but I have to be at the studio at the crack of doom, and it's already late."

"Tomorrow's Sunday," I reminded him.

"I know, but I still have to report to the studio. Mr. Goldfish doesn't care much about Sundays, being Jewish and all."

"Ah, I see. That makes sense," I said.

Sam only laughed softly.

"Thanks a lot for dinner, Harold," I said, giving him a kiss on the cheek.

"Yeah, thanks for the food," said Sam. "It was almost better than the show."

Harold chuckled softly. "I'll just let myself out," he said, still whispering so as not to interrupt whatever Mr. DeLoera was doing. Or thinking. Or praying about.

"Bye, Harold. I'll call you tomorrow."

"If you don't, I'll call you," said he, and he left as Mr. DeLoera still stood at the sink with his eyes closed, as if he were meditating about something as the foamy bubbles grew and grew into a pile darned near as huge as the smoke cloud outside had been. Not really. But he created a big blob of bubbles.

"*Bueno,*" he said after several soapy minutes had passed. He turned on the tap and rinsed his hands. "*Gracias*," he said to me when I handed him a towel.

"You're welcome," I said. Recalling my high-school Spanish, I added, "*De nada*." Meant the same thing, but at least it wasn't in English.

"All right," said Mr. Prophet, "let's get going. You know where to, Sam?"

"Yeah. I think so," said Sam.

"Do you mind if I take Spike?" I asked everyone. "He's been left alone too much this evening, and he was scared."

"Okay by me," said Mr. Prophet.

Mr. DeLoera shrugged.

Sam said, "Keep hold of him. Don't want him falling off the bridge or anything."

"I'll put the leash on him," I said stiffly. Fall off the bridge, my eye.

So Sam drove us all to the Colorado Street Bridge, which had been built in 1912 and spanned the Arroyo Seco, which was aptly named most of the time. When we had lots of rain, the water would rage down the arroyo, but that didn't happen often. Street lights had been put up I don't know how long after the bridge was built.

People also called this bridge "Suicide Bridge" because occasionally a melancholy person would leap from it to his or her death. The city fathers were discussing erecting barricades to discourage such activities, but they were always discussing stuff, and very little of it ever got done. Or maybe I'm just repeating words I've heard from my father. I still didn't pay much attention to what the city leaders talked about, truth to tell.

Pulling the Hudson to a stop at the curb about in the middle of the bridge, Sam turned in his seat and said, "Is this okay, or do you want to get closer to the hillsides? That will require some walking in the dark through brush and so forth, although I brought a couple of flashlights in case we needed them."

"Huh," said Mr. Prophet, who opened his door and struggled to get out of the car. Mr. DeLoera struggled out of the car on his side. Both men limped up on the curb and leaned over the railing, looking left and right and straight ahead, probably wondering what would be best to do.

Spike, who sat in my lap looking alertly out the window, gave a little whine.

"What's the matter, boy? Do you need to do your duty?"

Spike only whined again.

Mr. Prophet and Mr. DeLoera conversed for a few seconds after looking around, then returned to the Hudson and hove themselves into the back seat. Mr. Prophet said, "Emilio says to go on down to the end of the bridge. Then turn around and go back the other way. He thinks what we need is on the west side of the bridge."

"It is?" I asked.

"We will see," said Mr. DeLoera, being enigmatic, blast him.

Spike whined again, but didn't piddle on my lap, so I guessed he could wait until Sam drove to the end of the bridge and back again.

Bless the dog, he did. However, once the car had stopped, Spike insisted on being let out. As I held the other end of the leash clipped onto his collar, I had to get out with him. He took off as if I wasn't even there, drat it!

"Spike!" I hollered. "What the heck are you doing?"

What he was doing was virtually dragging me off the road and down the hill.

"Sam!" I called out. "Please bring a flashlight! Spike's found something!"

"Cripes," said Sam, leaping out of the car—for so solid an object, Sam could move quickly when he had to—and raced after Spike and me, clicking on the flashlight.

The light didn't give much illumination, but I could tell Spike wasn't chasing one of the bobcats or mountain lions that frequented the arroyo. I wasn't too worried about coyotes, as they might attack dogs of Spike's size, but only when their humans weren't around. They and the big cats also preferred to work in the dark, from everything I'd read about them.

Suddenly Spike stopped dead in his tracks, and I darned near stumbled over him. "Spike, what the heck are you doing?"

"Cripes," said Sam again, playing the light around the brushy area.

All I could see were bushes, grass that had been left to grow long and weedy, and the occasional straggly tree here and there. There might have been cats in the trees, but the branches looked too spindly to hold so heavy a creature as a mountain lion. Not sure about a bobcat.

"What's going on down here," asked Mr. Prophet, puffing and limping behind us.

"Don't know," I said. "Spike just took off like a greyhound after a rabbit. Oh. Maybe he saw a rabbit."

Spike, who didn't add to the conversation in words, suddenly uttered a low growl, and the hackles on his back went stiff. Oh, dear. What did this mean? Maybe a gang of hoboes lived in the arroyo. Naw. Probably not. Spike would have merrily run up and greeted them.

Mr. DeLoera, using his stick to help him cover the rough ground and still holding his sack, walked up and stopped behind Spike. "*Cuidado*," he said, "*Callarse*. Be quiet. Stay still. There's something here."

Great. Just the words I wanted to hear. As he'd told us all to be careful and be quiet, I didn't say so.

I'm not sure how long we all stood there, Mr. Prophet with a hand on Sam's shoulder because his peg kept sinking into the ground, Mr. DeLoera staring off into the distance, past the puny illumination of the flashlight, and I struggling to keep my dog from either running forward towards whatever had upset him or backward, away from whatever had upset him.

And then—I don't expect anyone to believe this, but I don't expect anyone to believe anything else regarding our former Tongva neighbors—we heard faint drumming noises. Gradually Spike's hackles settled. His tail began to wag. Humming sounds emanated from beyond the flashlight's range. A plume of smoke drifted toward us. It didn't seem as thick as the smoke at the séance or in our backyard, and it smelled remarkably of balsam. Faint chanting noises filled the space around us.

"*Este es el lugar,*" whispered Mr. DeLoera. "This is the place."

And then Spike yanked on his leash again, and he lunged forward, still wagging happily. Then he sort of bowed, reaching out with his front paws and with his butt in the air, and he looked for all the world like a dog meeting another, friendly dog. Only there was nothing there—well, except for smoke, chanting and drumming. Spike let out a friendly yip and bounced as well as he could at the end of his leash, and darned if he didn't begin tugging on his leash, as if he was following the plume of smoke, which seemed to be headed in a southeasterly direction.

"What the hell?" murmured Mr. Prophet.

"This is the place," said Mr. DeLoera. "Follow the smoke and the dog. He's found *un amigo.*"

"What kind of friend?" asked a skeptical Sam.

"A ghostly one would be my guess," said Mr. Prophet.

"*Si. Si,*" said Mr. DeLoera. "Follow the *humo*. The smoke."

So we followed the smoke. Actually, we followed Mr. DeLoera, who followed Spike, who followed the smoke and whatever friendly Indian's dog he'd just met. I don't even believe this as I report it.

The grasses were long and the bushes were bushy, and I was exceedingly glad I'd worn sensible shoes that day. Only wish women were allowed to wear trousers like men wore because, although I wore a pair of old cotton stockings, twigs and spiky things snagged them as we followed the smoke, chanting, drumming, Mr. DeLoera and Spike. From the occasional curse word, it sounded as if the men weren't faring much better than I.

Finally, after I swear to god we'd tramped through acres of wilderness in that stupid arroyo, the smoke, Spike and Mr. DeLoera stopped. Sam still held the flashlight, which still illuminated our surroundings. Sort of. I mean, we could sure see a lot of boulders, bushes, spindly trees, long grass and weeds.

Spike headed toward a pile of rocks, almost covered over with moss and weeds. He stopped right next to it, sat, looked back at us and yipped. Another, ghostly yip answered his. Unless the second yip came from a coyote.

But no. Mr. DeLoera, praising Spike as a *perro bueno*, got down on his knees and began parting plant life at the base of the rocks. I prayed (silently) there were no rattlesnakes in there. It was winter and they'd be in their hidey-holes, but they'd probably be peeved if anyone disturbed them.

After a few minutes of that, the drumming grew louder, and the chanting merged into a song. It was like no song I'd ever heard before, but it definitely counted as a song. I think. The balsamic scent of the smoke lingered in the air, although the smoke itself had thinned to almost nothing.

Nodding, Mr. DeLoera started singing, too, in a language I didn't recognize. I suspect it was Tongva. He reached into his sack and drew out the towel-wrapped skull pieces. In his digging, he'd revealed a hole in the pile of rocks. Using great care, he made a nest of the long grass around us, laid the skull gently in the nest and placed the nest with the skull inside the hole. He had to poke at it a couple of times for it to fit but fit it did at last. Then he stuffed more grass and bushes into the hole to hide the skull. The singing and drumming faded, and the smoke disappeared entirely.

We heard two soft plops after Mr. DeLoera stopped singing and the hole was filled in. Sam played the rays of the flashlight on the ground where we'd heard the two soft sounds.

"By gawd," said Mr. Prophet, sounding almost reverent, considering it was he speaking.

"Good lord," said Sam.

Mr. DeLoera stood, using his stick to help him and smiled at the ground. "They left gifts. One for Mrs. Majesty and one for the *perro noble*. You both led us to the place of Hahamog-na's people, and we've been able to return him to his *patria*."

"We did?" I asked, astounded. "I'd kind of figured his *patria* would have been destroyed by this time, what with the bridge and the dam and everything that's been built here."

"It was enough," said Mr. DeLoera. He knelt and picked up the two so-called gifts: another small woven basket and a bone carved in an intricate pattern. "A basket for you," he said as he handed me the basket. "And a carved bone for *el perro*." He handed *that* to me, too.

I stared at the two trinkets. I wouldn't have believed in them if I weren't holding them. I figured I'd wait to give Spike his bone until we got home and it couldn't get lost here in what remained of Pasadena's wilderness.

"And now," said Mr. DeLoera, "I am tired."

"Me too," said Mr. Prophet. "And I need a drink."

"Don't talk like that in front of me, Lou. I'm a policeman, remember?"

"Hellkatoot," said the old sinner. "Pretend you didn't hear."

"Gladly," said Sam.

Oddly enough, climbing back up the hill was easier than climbing down it had been. I don't know if it's because ghostly Indian hands cleared the way or because Spike no longer yanked me along, but we made it back to the car with ease.

Sam pulled the Hudson into our drive at approximately one a.m. on Sunday. What a night! And I had to get up and sing in the morning. Oh boy.

We all piled out of the car and went into the house. There Mr. Prophet said he and Mr. DeLoera would carry on out the back door and to his cottage.

"Don't wake us up early. We're probably both gonna have bottle heads."

Mr. DeLoera only smiled.

"Not a problem," said Sam.

I pretended not to be shocked.

As for the relics received that night, I took them to the living room, along with the little woven pot I'd been given at the séance, and placed them on the mantel above the fireplace. I put Spike's bone there, too. I'd showed it to him, but he displayed little interest. He didn't care for bones unless they still had meat on them.

Sam carried Spike upstairs, and Sam and I took turns washing arroyo remnants off of ourselves. I brushed Spike until he shone, then Sam set the alarm clock for seven a.m. "I'll go to church with you and your folks," he said. "I don't think Lou and Emilio will be in any shape to go to the mission until sometime in the afternoon."

Again I pretended not to be shocked.

THIRTY-THREE

Seven o'clock Sunday morning arrived too soon, but both Sam and I rose and dressed anyway. The day was a cold one, so I wore a long-sleeved gray dress with a sash that tied below the waist and accessorized it with my black shoes, hat, handbag and coat. That was easy.

By the time I got downstairs, Sam had already brewed a pot of coffee and was looking in the Frigidaire for foodstuffs. "How about cold noodles for breakfast?" he said as I walked into the kitchen.

"Sounds good to me," I said, yawning. "Want to talk about last night?"

"Not yet. I'm not awake enough."

"Good. Neither am I."

So we ate cold noodles and some cold chicken with almonds and rice and called it breakfast. I downed two cups of coffee, and I think Sam had three. Spike had his usual broken biscuit breakfast, then went to the living room to curl up on the hearthrug.

After brushing my teeth and powdering my nose so it wouldn't shine, squinting at myself and wondering if a little white chalk might hide the dark circles under my eyes and deciding it wasn't worth the effort, I joined Sam in the living room, where he sat in his favorite chair, reading the newspaper. When he saw me, he rose and said, "Ready?"

"As I'll ever be," I said.

Sam drove Ma, Pa, Vi and me to church in the Hudson. The church was just up the street, but the day was cold, and at least Sam and I were exhausted. When I discreetly asked if my family had heard any odd noises during the night, they all said they hadn't. Guess the show had been only for us. I was glad of that.

Lucy and I did a lovely job with our duets on the second and fourth verses of "O, For a Thousand Tongues to Sing." I know we did, because Mr. Hostetter said so, and he didn't fling out compliments indiscriminately.

"Can you stay for dinner with us?" asked Vi, sounding kind of wistful. "I have leftover pork for you to take home for sandwiches, but I have a lovely chicken stew in the oven, and it will be ready when we get home."

Sam and I glanced at each other and Sam said, "That would be great. Thanks, Vi."

"Yes, thanks, Vi. We'd love it."

Sam pulled the Hudson into my parents' drive and parked it behind the Chevrolet. We all piled out and went into the house. Rosebud—well, I guess she was Rosie now—greeted us with joy and jumps and exceedingly high-pitched barks that grated on my ears. In order to shut her up, I knelt down and allowed her to wiggle all over me. She was a sweet dog, but she *really* needed to be trained. She calmed down after everyone condescended to greet her.

"Did you two have fun last evening? Daisy said Harold was going to come over and you had plans for the evening," said Ma.

"Yes, we had an enjoyable time," said Sam. "Lou decided to teach us all how to play poker."

Poker! That was the card game Sam and Mr. Prophet had been playing the night of the séance. I might have known.

"Ha. Did you lose the family fortune?" asked Pa, hanging up his hat and coat.

"Naw. We played for toothpicks," said Sam. "But Lou ended up with most of them."

"I think that's because he cheats," I said, being mean for no reason.

"Naw. He's just been playing poker for decades longer than either of us has been alive," said Sam.

"Do you want to ask Lou for dinner?" asked Vi, who had a fondness for the ancient bounty hunter.

"I think he's got other plans for today, but I'll ask him," said Sam. He walked to the kitchen and telephoned Mr. Prophet. As I watched him, I saw his grin widen and knew we'd be Lou-less for dinner that day.

"Nope. Just us," he said when he hung up the receiver.

Dinner was, as ever, delicious. I know, because both Vi and Ma had told me, that women had been fixing stews for hundreds, if not thousands, of years. Surely I could learn how to fix a chicken stew. After dinner, I helped wash up the dishes, and Vi gave us a good deal of leftover roasted pork wrapped in waxed paper, which I took home. We could have sandwiches if we ever felt hungry again on Sunday.

I aimed to ask Vi for her chicken stew recipe after I'd rested up.

Speaking of resting up, when we got home and after we greeted an ecstatic Spike, Sam said, "Lou and Emilio are probably still sleeping. I'm going to change into something comfortable and take a nap on the sofa. Unless you want to nap on the bed with me." He waggled his eyebrows suggestively.

"I'm going to change into something comfy and nap, too. We'll catch up on other things after we're both rested."

"Spoilsport," said Sam, but he laughed when he said it.

I don't know how long the two of us napped in the living room, but I felt better when I woke up around three that afternoon. Sam was already awake. He and Spike were sitting on Sam's favorite chair. Sam had his feet on the ottoman and Spike curled up on his lap, and he was again reading the newspaper.

After I yawned, I asked, "Anything newsworthy in there?"

"Afternoon, sleepyhead," he said, smiling at me. "No, not much. The Russians are having trouble with ergot again."

"With what?"

"Ergot. It's a disease that infects grains, like rye. They've had trouble with it before. Now that Russia's part of the Soviet Union, I guess I should say the Soviet Union is having trouble with ergot."

"What happens if you eat bread that's made from infected grain?"

"Hallucinations, burning sensation. Some people, according to this article, call it 'St. Anthony's Fire' because of the burning sensation."

"Can we get it here?"

"I expect so. I think we monitor our milling processes better than the Soviets do."

"I sure hope so."

We both heard the back door open. Spike leaped from Sam's lap and raced down the hall, through the butler's pantry and into the kitchen. Sam and I heard low talking noises, and we deduced Lou and Mr. DeLoera had finally risen from the dead. Or their beds.

"Want to go to them or let them come to us?" asked Sam.

"The latter will be better, probably," I said.

"Agreed."

We heard the men shuffle around in the kitchen for a bit, and then they both made their way to the living room, a happy Spike following them.

"You both look like hell," said Sam pleasantly.

"We both feel like hell," said Mr. Prophet.

"*Sí*," said Mr. DeLoera.

"Would you like a sandwich before we take you back to the mission, Mr. DeLoera?" I asked, also pleasantly.

Both his and Mr. Prophet's faces contorted as if I'd asked him if they'd like to go back to the Colorado Street Bridge and jump from it into the arroyo.

"Okay, so no food, right?" said Sam.

"Right. No food," said Mr. P.

"Are you ready to return to the mission, Emilio, or would you rather stay here for a while. Maybe until you feel a little better?"

"No. I got to go back," said Mr. DeLoera, sounding dolorous.

Aha! DeLoera? Dolorous? Oh, never mind. It just slipped out.

"All right, then. You coming, Daisy?"

"Sure," I said. "Happy to take a Sunday drive."

"Uh," said Mr. Prophet.

"Uh," said Mr. DeLoera.

So Sam drove Mr. DeLoera back to the San Gabriel Mission. We thanked him fervently for his help in exorcising our ghost, and Sam gave him a fat envelope. Mr. D looked into the envelope, opened his eyes wide, and nodded his thanks at Sam. Then he groaned, pressed the hand holding the envelope to his head and slowly turned, carrying his burlap sack and using his polished stick, and limped off toward the mission's plaza.

"Want to see him home?" Sam asked Mr. Prophet.

"Naw. He knows where he lives."

So we drove home again. Once we got there, neither Sam nor I saw Mr. Prophet again that day. Sam and I enjoyed our roasted pork sandwiches for supper.

Graveside services for the late Timothy Sean O'Toole were held at Mountain View Cemetery on Saturday, February 6, 1926, with Captain Johnny Buckingham officiating. Sam and I picked up Mrs. O'Toole and drove her to the cemetery. As she'd begun attending the Salvation Army Church not long after having met Johnny, quite a few fellow parishioners also attended, among them Chris Edwards, who supported Mrs. O'Toole when she broke down.

Flossie attended, too, and she stood with Sam and me, looking pretty but tired. Little Billy was clad in his best Sunday suit and behaved like an angel. Little Daisy was a brat. One of the church ladies took her from Flossie, walked her around the cemetery and wove between the headstones, bouncing in her arms and trying to get her to shut up. Billy frowned hideously but didn't call his sister a brat, which I considered quite noble of him under the circumstances.

Just because he figured he should, Mr. Lou Prophet attended the services with us. It wasn't easy for him to walk in the cemetery because his peg sank into the soil quite often, but he persevered.

Overall, those few weeks in January and February of 1926 weren't boring. We never again saw a bone in our backyard, and we never discovered precisely how Tim O'Toole had died. I guess some mysteries aren't meant to be solved, but at least his mother now knew where he was. That was kind of a victory.

About once every couple of weeks, since he helped our backyard ghost return to his family, Sam, Mr. P and I visited Emilio DeLoera at the San Gabriel Mission. He was always pleased to see us, and we'd chat with him about life at the mission and how it differed from the ways of his original people.

On one of our jaunts, he handed me an image he'd made out of polished wood. It was small and shiny, and he'd created a beaded string from which to hang it.

"*Esto es para ti*," he told me. "*Para el bebé.*"

"Thank you very much," I said, surprised.

"What's that about a *bebé*?" asked Mr. Prophet, staring at me.

I felt myself blush.

"Daisy?" said Sam. "Is there something you want to tell me?"

"Well, I wasn't really sure," I said, which was the absolute truth, curse it. "I mean, I thought I was, but anything might happen, you know?"

"No, no," said Mr. DeLoera. "*Tendrás un buen hijo.*" He tapped his grizzled head. "I know. I see. A fine son."

"A son?" Sam asked, his voice sounding slightly odd.

"*Si*," said Mr. DeLoera.

"Hellkatoot," muttered Mr. Prophet.

"Thank you very much, Mr. DeLoera," I said, feeling kind of stiffish. I had aimed to tell my family myself as soon as I knew for sure I was preggers. Oh, well. Sometimes it astonishes me how little control we have over our own lives.

Holding a hand to his head, Sam said, "I think I'm going to faint."

I'm pretty sure he was only joking.

LIBRARY SPIRITS

A DAISY GUMM MAJESTY MYSTERY, BOOK 19

"Wanna sit in the gazebo and read for a while?"

The question, which had come from Mr. Lou Prophet, former bounty-hunter in the Wild West and current one-legged curmudgeon who'd managed to end up in civilized Pasadena, California, surprised me.

On the other hand, it was a gorgeous day and the gazebo wouldn't be around for much longer. Our lovely Pasadena Public Library was scheduled to be replaced early in 1927, less than a year away. I'd miss it a lot. I'd all but grown up in that library.

"Sure," I said. "The new library won't have a beautiful park and pond."

"Yeah. It'll be a big, ugly building and all this open space will be gone and filled with more buildings. That's called progress."

"I wouldn't go that far," I told the cranky old man. "I think the new building is... Elegant. Dramatic. You know, impressive. It's part of a grand plan to make a civic center in Pasadena, along with the new city hall and everything."

"Huh."

"Oh, very well, I agree with you. I love this library, and I'm going to miss it like fire."

"Figgered as much."

As we approached the gazebo, which had been built near the library pond, my heart held a whole glob of conflicting emotions. I was madly in love with my husband, Sam Rotondo, thrilled beyond measure that we were expecting our first child and loved my hometown of Pasadena. What's more, I was learning how to cook better and more easily than I'd ever expected. In short, I was happy.

I was also kind of annoyed because Sam was entirely too overprotective of me in my current condition. I was also darned sad that my beloved library was going to be demolished.

Then there was a niggling anxiety about Stacy Kincaid, daughter of my most lucrative client, who had escaped a week or so earlier from the hospital ward at the Castleton Hospital. What vexed me was the notion that Stacy might not have the sense God gave a goose and flee Pasadena. I worried she might stick around and do more mischief.

In particular, because she blamed me for the death of her late felonious gentleman friend, I worried she might wish to do me harm. It would be just like her. She'd hated me almost as long as we'd known each other. Mind you, the sentiment was returned by me in full measure, but still, I never tried to harm other people. Stacy had tried to kill me two or three times.

"Pretty day," said Mr. Prophet, startling me out of my confused thoughts.

"Yes," I said, "it is. Sometimes March can be chilly, but today is perfect."

"Never gets chilly here, if you ask me," grumbled Mr. Prophet.

"If you wanted cold weather, you should have moved to Maine or Minnesota or somewhere like that. You didn't get chilly weather in Arizona or Mexico, did you? Or Georgia, your old home state?"

"Naw, but at least Arizona, Mexico, and Georgia were kinda normal. This place is... not normal."

"Bother. You're just grumpy because you're old and have a cat instead of a horse." Much to my personal amazement, Mr. Prophet had found and adopted a mutilated marmalade-colored kitten while Sam and I were on our honeymoon a few months back. He tried to deny ownership, but I found him out one evening when I walked to his cottage in the back of our house and heard him whispering sweet nothings into his ragged—extremely ragged—cat's tattered ears. He'd resented me for it ever since.

"Huh," said the old sinner again.

I began squinting as we approached the gazebo. "I think somebody's already in there. Darn."

"Well, it's a purty place. Besides, I'm sure we can fit. It's got benches all around it."

"Yeah, you're right. I guess we don't have to be alone together." My tone was sarcastic because the occasion seemed to call for it.

"Huh."

"Oh, lord, whoever's in there is asleep," I said, frustrated. Why couldn't people sleep in their own homes? Why'd they have to sleep in the library gazebo and make everybody else who wanted to sit in the gazebo feel bad for waking them up?

Not awfully charitable, was I?

Naturally, Mr. Prophet said, "Huh," once more.

Whoever occupied the gazebo was deeply asleep because s/he didn't move, even though we didn't bother to lower our voices. I'd taken a step into the lovely hexagonal structure when suddenly Mr. Prophet stopped me by means of gripping my arm with one of his gnarled hands. I gave a start of alarm and turned to glower at him, but didn't when I saw his face.

"Don't go in there. That ain't no sleeping beauty. It's a dead woman."

"What?" I squealed. Then I whirled around and saw what Mr. Prophet had seen: a pool of blood on the floor of the gazebo. The blood no longer dripped from the slashed throat of...

"Oh, my God!" I shrieked. "That's Stacy Kincaid!"

Available in Paperback and eBook from Your Favorite Bookstore or Online Retailer

ABOUT THE AUTHOR

Award-winning author Alice Duncan lives with a herd of wild dachshunds (enriched from time to time with fosterees from New Mexico Dachshund Rescue) in Roswell, New Mexico. She's not a UFO enthusiast; she's in Roswell because her mother's family settled there fifty years before the aliens crashed (and living in Roswell, NM, is cheaper than living in Pasadena, CA, unfortunately). Alice would love to hear from you at alice@aliceduncan.net

www.aliceduncan.net

facebook.com/alice.duncan.925